WHEN FRIENDSHIP
TURNED TO PASSION . . .

"Give me a chance to show you that I can change. Let me kiss you, Meg."

Meg averted her eyes. "I'm no good at kissing. I don't know how."

The well of tenderness inside David, from which only Meg could drink, expanded as he urged her softly, "We have so much to learn from each other, Meg. Shouldn't we start now?"

Silence.

"Meg, look at me." The resounding clamor of his heart overwhelmed the hammering of the rain on the roof over their heads as Meg raised her face to his. "Nothing will ever be right for either of us unless we set our feelings right. You know that, don't you? Put your arms around my neck, Meg."

David barely restrained a gasp of pleasure as her arms encircled his neck. Intent on the pink trembling lips so close to his, David closed the distance between with a soft, "I love you, Meg . . ."

Praise for Elaine Barbieri's
previous novels

WISHES ON THE WIND

Elaine Barbieri

JOVE BOOKS, NEW YORK

WISHES ON THE WIND

A Jove Book / published by arrangement with
the author

PRINTING HISTORY
Jove edition / February 1991

ISBN: 0-515-10535-X

Jove Books are published by The Berkley Publishing Group,
200 Madison Avenue, New York, New York 10016.
The name "JOVE" and the "J" logo
are trademarks belonging to Jove Publications, Inc.

PRINTED IN THE UNITED STATES OF AMERICA

10 9 8 7 6 5 4 3 2 1

Benji baby, I love you.

WISHES
ON THE
WIND

PROLOGUE

"Fire! Fire!"

The shouted warning echoed deep below the surface of the Lang mine, raising Dennis O'Connor's head toward the entrance of the gangway as thick, choking smoke spiraled toward him. Coughing, his eyes smarting, the big man retreated with stumbling steps, refusing to succumb to panic. Shouting orders to the men around him, he turned to seek the figures of his sons within the group scrambling into an intersecting tunnel where the air was still clear.

O'Connor counted—five. All of his sons were safe. But his relief was temporary as a panic-stricken voice reached his ear.

"Dennis, there's no way out! We've not a chance! We're doomed, man, doomed!"

"Close yer mouth, fool!" Turning his handsome, smoke-streaked face toward the smaller man at his side, O'Connor continued in a more guarded tone, "I'll not have ye panic any of me men, John Bannen. I'll not give up me life so easily as ye seem inclined to do. Now be quiet and give a man time to think!"

Chastised, Bannen collapsed back against the rear wall, his eyes on O'Connor as the big Irishman scanned their immediate surroundings.

Spying a pile of bracing timbers and equipment in the corner of the shaft, O'Connor raised his startling light blue eyes toward a small vent over his head. Coughing again, realizing smoke was gradually penetrating this area of the shaft as well, O'Connor turned back to the men around him.

"Pile them timbers over here! Quick, boyos! James, Kevin—get the tools! We'll barricade ourselves against the smoke and stuff our jackets into the cracks. Then we'll pray that trickle of air above our heads'll keep us alive until the fire's out!"

Frowning at the silence that followed, Dennis snapped a quick, "Step lively, lads!"

Working alongside his men as they moved the heavy timbers,

O'Connor grimaced as the first nail was pounded home. He glanced at his sons as they worked effectively with the older miners, and his heart swelled with pride at the courage they displayed despite their youth. They'd get out of this together, his sons and him, and his boys would grow to strong men who'd do both him and Mary proud. He'd see that his sons and Meg had a good life . . .

His optimistic thoughts halting, O'Connor glanced up in dismay as black smoke began barreling into the shaft. He gasped for breath, tears running from his burning eyes as the men around him dropped their tools and strained to breathe. He staggered, coughing violently as his sons, equally affected, gathered around him. Sinking to his knees in the rapidly darkening shaft, O'Connor curved his arm around the youngest of his boys, choking, furious as he realized that someone atop had been fool enough to turn on a ventilation fan, forcing the smoke back upon them.

The silent appeals in eyes so similar to his own registered sharply in his mind as his sons' faces began fading from sight. In the moment before consciousness slipped away, Dennis O'Connor realized that this mistake would be the death of them.

A fine rain fell as Meghan O'Connor stared at the freshly dug grave a few yards from her feet. Her eyes drifted to the huge mounds of earth piled beside it, and she shuddered as moisture began penetrating the shawl covering her head and shoulders. She avoided looking at the uneven rows of markers surrounding her in the hillside cemetery, and lowered her head as solemn mourners behind her responded to Father Matthew's signal and began reciting another prayer. Her lips moved with the familiar words, but no sound emerged. She swallowed with difficulty, her eyes moving to the six unadorned coffins beside the gaping hole. She struggled to recall the faces of those enclosed within, but they strangely eluded her. Her frozen mind recited the names of her brothers: James, twelve years old, two years younger than she; Kevin, sixteen; Patrick, seventeen; Daniel, nineteen; Dennis, twenty. And Dennis O'Connor, Sr. Da.

Her mind suddenly deluged by the images which had evaded her, Meghan was swept by a sorrow beyond tears. She closed her eyes and clutched her hands together more tightly, her fingers whitening with the desperation of her effort to speak the prayers still resounding around her. A hand closed supportively on her thin shoulder and she looked up at her only surviving brother.

Sean's youthful face was emotionless, but she recognized the pain that lay behind his light blue eyes. It mirrored her own. She glanced at their mother, but turned swiftly forward once more, unable to bear the dear woman's agonized distress.

A moment passed before Meghan realized the last prayerful rumble had ceased. She looked at Father Matthew as he offered once more:

"May the perpetual light shine upon them. Through the mercy of God, may they rest in peace. Amen."

Holy water mingled with rain, falling on the coffins. The drops blended, becoming indistinguishable from each other as a flurry of movement preceded the slow descent of the plain wooden boxes into the ground. Muffled sobs grew louder, the sorrowful sounds having no effect on Meghan's frozen state until the sound of her mother's low, shuddering keen reached her ears. Meghan watched her mother take a few steps forward, her grief-ravaged face white in the gloom of the overcast morning. Mary O'Connor's frail frame swayed unsteadily as she took a handful of soil from the nearest pile and dropped it into the open grave.

The falling dirt struck the coffin lids, the sound appearing to reverberate within her mother in the brief second before she sank limply to the ground. Concerned mourners scrambled to the fallen woman's side, leaving Meghan temporarily forgotten and more frightened than she had ever been in her life.

A gentle arm curved around Meghan's shoulders, and she looked up. An encouraging smile on his lips, Father Matthew whispered, "We must not question the ways of the Lord, Meghan. We must trust in His wisdom. Will you try to do that, dear?"

Anguish clearly reflected in her tear-filled eyes, Meghan did not even attempt a reply.

1869

The Pennsylvania
Coal Fields

Chapter 1

Her breathing labored, Meghan climbed the steep hillside, grateful to leave the shadow of the towering breaker behind her. She turned her back on the constant red glow of hillside furnaces, on the mountainous dumps of cinder and slag, and the great, brackish pools that grew larger each day. Her spirit lightening with each step, she realized she would soon be at her favorite spot, a small natural garden above the valley on a hill untainted by the Lang Colliery, where the sun's rays were not dimmed by the unnatural haze of coal dust below.

Meghan paused, ignoring the voice in the back of her mind reminding her that she was trespassing, that the hill she climbed was part of the Lang estate situated on top. She reasoned defiantly that the Langs had no right to keep the only beauty still remaining on the scarred landscape to themselves.

Concern crept into the silver-blue eyes unmistakably marking her Dennis O'Connor's daughter as she brushed a wisp of curly dark hair from her cheek. Always close, Sean and she had grown even closer in the two months since the deaths of their father and brothers. Sharing his pain, Meghan was aware of Sean's mounting bitterness as their lives became increasingly difficult.

She knew Sean was right. Martin Lang controlled their lives and the lives of everyone in this section of the valley, while treating the poor Irish who worked in his mines with less respect than he gave his household animals. Like so many others, her Da had been lured from his native Ireland to the Pennsylvania coal fields with promises of a new life of plenty. He soon discovered, however, that his reward for eleven-hour shifts of backbreaking labor was working conditions that often broke lesser men, and a wage that kept him bound to a mounting tab at the company store. Unions had little effect on the situation, except to encourage strikes that did more harm than good when there was always another trainload of immigrants eager for work.

7

Desperation had finally brought the dreaded Molly Maguires back to life among the Irish miners, and Meghan heaved a sad sigh at the thought. Her father had not approved of making the coal fields a battleground, or of the savage methods of the secret group. Da, and many men like him, had been ashamed to see murder and fear again become tools of an Irish organization. He said the Mollies made every Irishman less in the eyes of other men, but he hadn't dared to speak that opinion outside their home. The organization had become so powerful, and its secrecy so carefully guarded, that no one knew when a Molly was near. Da said there was a better way to escape the mines. He taught his children that if a man believed in himself, he would find his way to a better life.

Tears brimmed in Meghan's eyes. The brief, formal note of condolence Ma had received from the Lang family the day of the funeral was all she had to show for Da's belief. A week after Da and the boys were killed, a new group of immigrants replaced them, without a single step being taken to see that the same thing wouldn't happen again.

A familiar anger flushing her youthful face, Meghan raised her chin proudly. It made no difference to her what the Langs and their like thought. The O'Connors knew the worth of themselves and their own. But Sean's anger wasn't as easily satisfied. At fifteen, her brother was a bitter young man, and she worried about him. He listened too much to the men who said her father and brothers would have escaped the fire if Martin Lang had cared enough about his miners to have an emergency exit in the deep shafts. He brooded about ways to make Lang and other mine owners learn to respect the Irish in the mines. And he brooded about making Lang pay for the deaths of Da and the boys.

Climbing again, with a strength that belied her fragile appearance, Meghan remembered Father Matthew's warnings against allowing Sean's bitterness to infect her. But it was so very hard not to.

Stepping onto level ground a few minutes later, Meghan forced all dark thoughts from her mind and followed the trail that led to the spot she sought. Reaching it at last, she breathed deeply. She needed the peace of this place very badly. It was beautiful on the hill with the trees allowing just enough spring sunshine for comfort, and a great honeysuckle bush nearby scenting the air. A bed of violets edged a heavy carpet of moss beneath her feet, and Meghan dropped to her knees, silent as she allowed her mind to inhale as deeply as her lungs. Oh, if only the whole world was as beautiful as it was here. If only—

Hearing an unexpected sound, Meghan froze into stillness. Her heart leaped at the sound of footsteps and horse's hooves approaching on the nearby trail.

Panicked, Meg scrambled back out of sight into the overgrown honeysuckle bush and held her breath.

David Lang cursed softly as he stumbled again on the uneven trail and turned to cast the great black stallion trailing at the end of his lead an angry glance. He jerked the reins sharply, instantly regretting his pettish action as Fabian gave a nervous snort.

Damn! It was his own fault that Fabian had thrown him. He should have known better than to allow his thoughts to wander when the great brute hadn't been exercised for a few days and was primed to take advantage of his lack of concentration. But he'd be damned if he'd limp back to the stables in full view, with his riding clothes stained and torn from his fall. Townsend would snatch the opportunity to report to Uncle Martin that he had been right all along, that Fabian was too much to handle, and that the great stallion should be gelded or sold.

Over his dead body!

David's handsome face stiffened into familiar, obstinate lines. Sparks of gold danced with angry determination in his hazel eyes as he drew himself erect. The unconscious posture of his tall, lean frame reflected the arrogance and tenacity so much a part of his strong personality as he muttered, "No, damn it! I will not allow Fabian to be gelded!"

David darted a glance over his shoulder at the beautiful animal behind him. The great fellow would sire a stable that would one day be famous in this section of the country. His uncle had imported an Arabian mare who would produce Fabian's first foal within a few months. Uncle Martin and he had already agreed that when he came of age in a few years, and received his inheritance, he would reimburse his uncle for the total investment and the stable would be his. It was a dream he held dear, and he would not jeopardize it with a foolish moment's loss of concentration today.

Annoyed with himself and the need to take a circuitous route back to the stables so he might avoid Townsend's critical eye, David urged the big horse to a faster step with another tug at the lead.

"Step lively, you lazy brute! I'm not going to eat a cold lunch today and miss Abigail Hutton's visit because of you!" His lip twitched with vexation at the thought of losing the opportunity to further ingratiate himself with the blonde daughter of his uncle's friend. He added impatiently, "And you can stop limping. Your leg is hardly bruised."

Turning back to the winding trail, David kicked a rock out of his path, and continued walking. His disposition was becoming more foul with every step. To his discomfort, he had discovered that his expensive, custom-made riding boots were not made for extended walks, and that this trail was much longer than he had remembered. Still, it would save him some embarrassing explanations and some fast talking if he—

Fabian snorted, suddenly straining backwards, his eyes bulging with fright, and David turned toward him, taking a tighter grip on the lead. Allowing the animal a short retreat to salve his fear, he assessed the area and frowned when he came up with nothing that should have spooked the animal. Satisfied the threat existed only in Fabian's mind, David again attempted to lead the horse forward, only to have him balk more violently than before. Glaring, his temper already short, David brushed his heavy brown hair back from his forehead with an angry hand.

"Damn you, horse! I'm your only ally here. Give me any more problems and I'll let them take the knife to your tender parts after all!"

Another attempt to lead Fabian forward failed as miserably as before, and David attempted to control his impatience as the horse drew back as far as possible from a portion of the trail all but obscured by a huge honeysuckle bush. A small movement in the bush started the horse snorting anew and David shook his head with disgust.

"You won't take another step until I flush out whatever's frightening you, will you? All right, you overgrown coward."

Taking a moment to secure Fabian's lead over a low-hanging branch nearby, David leaned down and rustled the bush. Nothing emerged and David shook it harder, halting abruptly as he spied a shadowed form within the sweet-smelling mass. He reached in. His hand closed around a warm, slender arm, and with a grunt of surprise, he pulled a slight, disheveled girl out into the open.

Wildly curly hair covered with dried leaves and webs hung in the girl's eyes, partially obscuring her face, and a long, nasty scratch marked one cheek. The faded dress stained with grass and mud that covered her thin, adolescent body marked her a child from the valley, but the spirit shining from her brilliant blue eyes was as much of a shock as her insolence when she commanded, "Let go of my arm!"

David glared. "Who are you, and what are you doing here?"

"I said, let go of my arm!"

"I give the orders here! Do you realize what you did? You nearly spooked my horse into bolting!"

"Don't be blaming me if you can't control your horse!" The girl swept him with a deprecating glance that brought a flush to his cheek. "If the great beast is too much for you, you shouldn't be riding him!"

Incensed, David squinted into the girl's small, white face. It wasn't bad enough that his bloody horse had thrown him, that his rump and leg were throbbing painfully, that Fabian was limping as well as he, and that he was forced to sneak back to the stables in order to avoid a confrontation with the head groom. Now he had to suffer the insults of a dirty little snip from the patch who made no bones whatever about her thoughts on his horsemanship!

Gripping the girl's arm tighter, David growled from between clenched, perfectly shaped teeth, "I asked you a question. What are you doing here?"

"That's none of your business!"

Unable to remember ever having been more angry in all of his eighteen years, David responded, "Can't you read? This is private property. That sign at the bottom of the hill says, 'No Trespassing'!"

The girl's bright eyes momentarily wavered before she raised her chin a notch higher and glowered, "Can't YOU read?"

David dropped the girl's thin arm abruptly. Certain she was well aware of his identity and his right to be there, and just as certain that if he did not release her he would probably end up wringing her skinny little neck, David stepped back. His eyes were blazing.

"You're part of that Irish riff-raff from the patch, aren't you? I suppose your father's in his favorite *shebeen*, too drunk to keep his daughter home where she belongs, but I—"

The girl's sudden leap at him was unexpected. Staggering backwards under her clawing, pounding attack, David twisted his foot on a stone and fell down on his back. In a second the girl was atop him, her small fists pummeling his face and shoulders as she shouted, "Take that back—everything you said about my father! Take it back, I said!"

Finally succeeding in grasping the girl's flailing fists, David held her immobile, stunned by the rage in her flushed face as it loomed over his. A deft turn reversed their positions, putting him atop the girl's squirming form as he subdued her struggles with more difficulty than he cared to admit. Confused by her unexpected violence, and suddenly embarrassed that the exchange between this child and himself had come to this, he questioned roughly, "What's the matter with you? Are you crazy?"

The girl was motionless beneath him, but fury was evident in her eyes as well as her tone.

"Let me up."

"I asked you—"

"Let me up!"

Realizing he had no recourse, David released the girl's trembling hands and stood up. She scrambled to her feet, her bright eyes brimming as she raised her chin proudly.

"Don't worry, I'll leave. And you needn't worry that I'll be back. Now that you've been here, this place is soiled."

Not allowing time for response, the girl turned and ran down the path and within moments was out of sight. Perplexed, David stared after her for a few moments before reaching for Fabian's reins.

Fabian was walking docilely behind him a few minutes later, when David became conscious of the bitter taste of blood and a dull throbbing in his upper lip. Raising his hand to his mouth, David shook his head, incredulous. The little chit had bruised him!

David gave a harsh laugh and attempted to dismiss the nagging truth that he had handled the unexpected situation with the girl badly. A low snort from behind interrupted his thoughts, and David turned toward Fabian with a muttered curse. Resuming his step a moment later, David was determined to forget the girl, her welling blue eyes, and his own unspoken regrets.

Her breath still coming in short, gasping gulps after her rapid flight down the hill, Meghan glanced over her shoulder. Satisfied that she had left David Lang far behind her, she slowed her pace. A sharp sense of desolation returned as the familiar, denuded landscape of the valley closed around her. Coal dust did its work well. There was little beauty left here. Even the few patches of green edging the dirt road were covered with the fine, gritty residue.

Making a quick turn, Meghan headed toward the bank of the

nearby stream. Pausing as she reached the edge, she attempted to assess her reflection in the rippling water. Despairing at the effort, she consoled herself that perhaps it was kinder that she was spared the full effect of her humiliating appearance.

Meghan had no doubt that she looked as much the hooligan as she had behaved only a short time before. Her dress was a mess, and she could feel the sting of a scratch that stretched the full length of her cheek. The thick, unruly hair that tumbled to her shoulders was filled with the residue from her retreat into the honeysuckle bush, and she knew she would have a difficult time explaining the grass and mud stains that had resulted from her rough and tumble with the haughty David Lang. The heat of restrained tears still burning her eyes, she also knew she could not return home in this condition.

Leaning down, Meghan scooped up a handful of water and splashed it on her face. Gritting her teeth against the sting on her cheek, she scrubbed her skin and dried her face with her skirt. She then ran her fingers through the stubborn snarls of her hair in an attempt to restore a semblance of order. Soon realizing the effort was useless, Meghan felt tears of angry frustration again fill her eyes. David Lang's ridicule had not yet faded from her mind, and Meghan felt her hatred for the arrogant, privileged nephew of Mr. Martin Lang soar anew.

"Meghan . . ."

Whirling at the unexpected sound of her name, Meghan faced Father Matthew as his kindly brown eyes surveyed her disheveled appearance with concern.

"What happened, Meghan?"

Raising her chin, Meghan fought for control. Finally able to trust her voice, she responded unexpectedly, "Can you read, Father?"

Surprise reflected on his thin, clean-shaven face, Father Matthew nodded. "Yes, of course I can read, my dear."

"Will you teach me?"

Pausing only the moment it took to absorb Meghan's unexpected request, Father Matthew nodded again. "I'll be happy to, Meghan. We can start tomorrow afternoon in the rectory if you like."

"Thank you. I'll be there."

Turning without another word, Meghan started rapidly down the path toward home.

• • •

Her slender, childlike figure silhouetted in the kitchen doorway a short time later, Meghan hesitated as Aunt Fiona looked up from the well-floured breadboard at which she worked. The thickset matron's face moved into lines of concern.

"Meghan, m'dear, what happened to ye?"

"I . . . I fell."

"Are ye all right, then?"

"Yes. Is Ma still sleeping?"

"Aye, mind not to wake her. 'Tis best she sleep awhile longer. She was fair worn out after she finished up this mornin'." Aunt Fiona gave her head a worried shake. "I'm thinkin' yer mother's lookin' poorly and can do with a tonic from Dr. McGee."

"I'll speak to her about it."

Nodding, Aunt Fiona turned back to her work, and Meghan took the opportunity to escape, grateful her aunt was again engrossed in her own thoughts.

Moments later, Meghan paused at the doorway of the room Sean and she shared with her mother, the sound of her mother's deep, steady breathing temporarily soothing her fears. There was no denying Mary O'Connor's chronic illness had worsened since the funeral. Her coughing seizures had become more debilitating, and a drastic weight loss had stolen the last traces of the refinement of feature which had been her only claim to beauty. But it was the absence of hope in her mother's warm brown eyes since they had lost their house in the patch and moved in with Uncle Timothy which caused her true concern.

Meghan stepped silently into the room and carefully removed her only change of clothing from the dresser drawer. It was not that the small patch house where they had lived with Da and the boys was very much, really. Standing in the shadow of the Lang Colliery, it was one shack in a cluster of a few dozen company-owned homes on a crooked, unpaved street. No more or less than those around it, it was framed from one-inch planks and clapboard that never knew a drop of paint, and it consisted of two small rooms with one glassless window in each. The dirt floor was often wet with rain from the leaking roof, and there were holes in the side walls. The small coal stove used for cooking and heat was fed with coal gathered from rail-car spillage, and it was never warm enough during the cold months of winter. It was crowded and uncomfortable with little privacy, but it had been home.

Not so this much larger house where the presence of Mother,

Sean and herself was suffered with Uncle Timothy's poorly concealed resentment. Meghan was well aware that were it not for Father Matthew's intervention, her uncle would have stood silently by when, unable to meet the rent, they were thrown out on the street. Increasing the difficulty of their situation was the realization that the room they now shared had formerly been let to boarders, a loss of income Uncle Timothy did not take lightly.

Angry and bitter, Sean had whispered to her when Ma was out of earshot that they would pay back Uncle Timothy every penny, but she knew there was rare chance of that coming to pass with Sean's wages at the mine as low as they were.

Aunt Fiona's attempts to compensate for her husband's grudging hospitality served only to increase Sean's bitterness, but Meghan did not share her brother's contempt for the unhappy, downtrodden woman. The truth was, now that Da and the boys were gone, Ma, Sean, and she didn't fit in anywhere, much less in this quiet, childless household where they were outsiders despite the common blood her mother and Aunt Fiona shared.

The echo of her brothers' happy voices returned to haunt her, and Meghan's grief stirred anew. Da had allowed them to start work in the mine at the age of seven, as was common practice, and at twelve to go below where the pay increased. Da had wanted an education for his boys, and he knew he could get ahead of his tab at the "pluck me" company store only in that way.

Abruptly forcing her thoughts to a halt, Meghan blinked away encroaching tears. She had no time now for dreams that would never become reality when there were more crucial problems at hand.

Meghan changed her clothes and applied a quick brush to her hair. With a last look at her sleeping mother, she slipped back into the hall. In the kitchen a few moments later, she was warmed by a smile on her aunt's face that was seldom seen in her uncle's presence.

"Ah, that's better. Ye have a bit of color in yer face now. Glad I am I made ye go off for some fresh air this mornin'. Yer far too pale for a child. And between us now we can finish yer mother's chores so she'll not be pressed when she awakens." Pausing, Aunt Fiona flushed with embarrassment as she continued, "It'll not do to have yer uncle thinkin' I'm encouragin' either of ye to be slothful."

Nodding, Meghan walked quickly toward the waiting washboard. Strangely, it was not her aunt's embarrassment that remained with her as she withdrew the soaking clothes from the basin and started scrubbing, but her own—and the even sharper memory of David Lang's handsome, haughty face.

Sean O'Connor emerged from the first shift at the Lang Colliery, momentarily grateful to be lost in the crush. His face and hands blackened from hard labor, his overalls and rubber boots clotted with sweat and coal dust, and the small oil lamp affixed to his cap extinguished until the next day's shift, he attempted to replace the exhaustion on his face with a casual expression. He raised his stubborn O'Connor chin. He would not let anyone know how badly he ached inside.

Gripping his lunch pail with a numb hand, Sean maintained his steady pace. Every bone in his body hurt, but his greatest pain was not physical. Not even Meghan, dearer to him than his own life from the first moment he stood beside her cradle and took her hand in his, entirely understood his distress.

He didn't want to be like the miners walking beside him. He didn't want to believe that, at fifteen years of age, he could look forward to nothing more than these men had now.

Fully recuperated from the temporary illness that had saved his life, keeping him out of the mines the month of his father's death, Sean had again adjusted to the eleven-hour shifts underground. The close air below no longer made him sick and giddy, and he was growing stronger every day. With his bright blue eyes and handsome, Irish face, his resemblance to his father was startling, but he was not his father's match in size and never would be. He lamented that caprice of heredity as he strained to load the twenty tons of coal daily that was the lot of a miner's helper.

With a bitter smile, Sean remembered earlier days, when at the age of seven he worked alongside disabled miners and other young fellows as a breaker boy. The roar of ore being dumped at the top of the one-hundred-foot breaker, filtering its way in the grading process through crushing equipment and sliding metal screens before it met his bleeding fingers for the final sorting, had been deafening. The dust had been so thick he could hardly breathe. He recalled the mangled limbs he had seen, and the faces of young friends who lost their lives because of a moment's carelessness. He had followed the route of his brothers before him as he progressed underground from there to work as a door boy; then as a mule driver; and finally, just shortly before the accident, to the position of miner's helper. He had been elated that the best paying job he could hope to achieve underground was within reach.

But now, as a part of McCarthy's team since Da and the boys were killed, he labored with growing resentment. He split the large blocks of coal blasted from the seams, loaded the cars, helped McCarthy at whatever was needed in working at the breast, knowing that no matter how hard he worked, his meager earnings would keep his mother, sister, and himself beholden to Uncle Timothy.

Suffering his silent fury, Sean continued walking toward his uncle's house. As the man of the family, he must remain there with his sister and mother until he could support them otherwise, but he despised suffering even one more night of Uncle Timothy's begrudging aid. A familiar hatred welled inside him. Truly at fault were the Langs and the system that kept miners captives of their own debt. It was slavery of the worst kind, and facing that slavery daily was turning his heart to stone.

Sean looked up at the late afternoon sky overhead, then glanced at the nearby mountainside, scarred by crisscrossing railroad tracks that served the colliery. He remembered scouring those tracks with his brothers for coal spillage to heat their home during the freezing days of winter. He remembered the laughter and song despite their dire straits. He remembered the times they returned with their bags full, assured of a warm night's sleep. He remembered his father's pride in his sons and the dreams he cherished for them and Meghan.

Sean walked into the yard of his uncle's house and turned toward the kitchen door. That was all in the past now, and his sole consolation came from the knowledge that this night, those same railroad tracks would deliver him another memory to savor. His spirits rising at the thought, he called out as he entered the house, "Meg, where are you?"

A bright half-moon lit the night as Meghan stumbled on the rough hillside terrain. She strained to see, her only security on the uneven, unfamiliar path Sean's hand as it gripped hers firmly, pulling her onward.

Halting impatiently, Sean whispered, "Come on, now, Meg! Now's no time to be actin' the faint maid."

"But where're we going, Sean? You shake me awake in the middle of the night, tell me to be quiet and get dressed, and pull me out of the house behind you without a word of explanation. What's this all about?"

Softly Sean questioned in return, "Have you no faith in your big brother, Meg?"

"Of course I do, but—"

"Then close your mouth and follow me. I've somethin' I want to share with you."

The peculiar light in Sean's eyes gave Meghan a moment's pause, but she knew she could not disappoint his confidence in her.

A few minutes later, breathless and uncertain Meghan kneeled beside her brother, concealed at a vantage point on the hillside opposite a narrow stretch of railroad tracks leading from the coal yard. The excitement evident on his youthful face set her heart to pounding a moment before a whistle sounded, announcing a train's departure from the yard not far away. The sound echoed eerily in the stillness of the hills surrounding them, and Meghan questioned anxiously, "What's to happen, Sean? Why did you wake me to bring me here?"

Turning from his avid surveillance of the tracks, Sean slipped an arm around her quaking shoulders, mistaking the reason for her sudden shuddering.

"Are you cold, Meg? It was foolish of me not to think to tell you to bring a shawl against the bite in the air."

Suddenly angry with her brother's secretive behavior and with herself for her weak-willed response to his concern, Meghan felt her fear mounting.

"Answer me, Sean O'Connor! Why have you brought me here?"

A train whistle sounded again and Sean turned abruptly from his sister's questions to fasten his gaze on the steaming locomotive as it roared into sight. He drew her closer to his side. "Now, Meg. Watch! Just a few more minutes and it'll be—"

His whispered entreaty interrupted by a sudden explosion on the tracks below, Sean uttered a low, triumphant sound. He turned briefly toward her with barely restrained exhilaration as the engine lurched crazily from the tracks, dragging the heavily loaded cars behind with it.

With horrified fascination Meghan watched as the cars fell from the embankment with a groaning ring of crushing steel that reverberated in her mind long after the derailed cars had tumbled to a broken, lethal heap below them. Gasping, Meghan turned terrified eyes toward her brother, pained by the satisfaction reflected on his face.

"Sean, what have you done?"

"Oh, no, not I, Meg! I can't take the credit for this."

"Credit?"

Gripping her chin firmly, Sean turned her face back to the scene of the steaming wreck.

"No, don't look away, Meg. Look and enjoy the only satisfaction you'll ever get for the deaths of Da and the boys, and thank providence for givin' us both the chance to witness it."

Confused, Meghan shook her head. "What are you saying, Sean?"

"I'm tellin' you that I overheard a conversation in the shaft this morning, saying the Sons of Molly Maguire would make Master Lang pay for the deaths of Dennis O'Connor and his sons."

"Sean—"

"The Mollies've hit the bastard in the pocketbook, where he feels it most, Meg! It's a poor vengeance, but the only one we'll see, and it does my heart good to know there'll be a wailing and the gnashing of teeth in the Lang residence this night!"

"But what of the men who were on that train? Innocent men, Sean, the engineer—the others in the crew?"

"Welsh—Modocs, every one of them! Not a man of the old sod amongst them!"

"Sean!"

At a sudden rush of footsteps in the darkness close by, Meghan froze. Bursting out of the shadows beside them, three men came to a startled halt, then stared at them in silence for a few terrifying seconds before continuing their flight.

"Were those the men who set the charge on the tracks, Sean?" Meg's voice was an incredulous whisper. "I know them all—good family men, every one!"

Fear entering his gaze for the first time, Sean grasped Meghan's shoulders and gave her a hard shake.

"You never saw them men, Meg. Not a one! And you'll say nothin' about the things you witnessed here this night."

"But, Sean—"

"You'll say nothing, Meg, or it's with your life that you'll pay."

Nodding, her throat suddenly too tight for speech, Meghan did not resist as Sean drew her to her feet.

"The Mollies are the only men of courage left among us, Meg.

You'll soon realize as do I that the Brotherhood is the only place we poor Irish can turn for justice."

Not waiting for a reply, Sean gripped her hand tightly. He pulled her into motion behind him as he started back down the hill and together they faded into the night.

Chapter 2

"Damn the Molly Maguires to hell, every last one of them!"

"Martin!"

Millicent Lang's shocked exclamation went unnoticed by her husband as he stood seething with anger in the spacious foyer of his mansion. Awakened in the middle of the night by a pounding on the front door, Martin Lang had jumped out of bed, tied his dressing gown over his nightclothes, and reached the door at the same time as his groggy servant. Now as he stood glaring at the two, blue-uniformed members of the Coal and Iron Police, his short, wiry figure fairly bristled.

"I don't need you to tell me this train wreck is the work of the Mollies! The Molly Maguires have terrorized the anthracite fields for over twenty years. Even the President of the United States has avoided confronting them! The members of their damned clandestine group have been at the bottom of every unlawful incident since I assumed ownership of this mine five years ago, but they've gone too far this time!"

Affixing his eye on the massive Scottish captain who cautiously maintained his silence, Lang continued in a lower tone. "I want to know how that group of assassins found out about that unscheduled shipment long enough in advance to effect a plan. Thanks to their sabotage, traffic on the tracks will be tied up for an inestimable period. The fools! They'll be putting their own people out of work if I have to suspend shifts because of backup in the coalyard. Of course, the layoffs will be my fault, too."

Frowning as his uncle's tirade continued, David Lang shot an anxious glance toward his aunt's stricken face where she stood a few steps to his rear. Her fading blond hair unbound, a powder-blue dressing gown that accented her delicate coloring hastily thrown over nightclothes, she appeared unexpectedly fragile as her gently rounded body trembled with anxiety. Beside her, his fifteen-year-old cousin, Grace, stood silent, fear and curiosity equally mingled in her wide-eyed expression.

David stepped toward his aunt and slipped his arm around her shoulders. His whisper bore true concern as she looked up at him with a bewildered expression that bordered on tears.

"Aunt Letty, why don't you take Grace back upstairs with you and try to go back to sleep?"

"Oh, David, I couldn't!" Her pale blue eyes wide with uncertainty, Millicent glanced again at her husband's flushed face as his ranting continued. "Martin is so upset. I fear he'll go into apoplexy if I'm not here to calm him."

David suppressed the smile his aunt's response elicited, despite the gravity of the moment. The woman had raised him from childhood after his parents had been killed. She was endlessly kind and generous, and treated him as well as she did her own child. He loved her dearly, but he knew that she concerned herself with little outside of the workings of her lovely home and the education and future of the children consigned to her care. For five years she had managed to divorce the Mollies' acts of terrorism and murder from her own personal world, fearful only for her husband's "state of mind."

Realizing at the moment, as the volume of Uncle Martin's voice rose another notch behind him, that there was much to be said for her fear, David forced his most reassuring smile.

"Uncle Martin will probably stay up the rest of the night, Aunt Letty. I can give him all the help he needs right now."

Aunt Letty blinked and a weak smile touched her pale, gracefully aging face. "Do you really think so, David?"

"I'm sure of it, Aunt Letty." Taking Grace's arm, aware that his cousin was too curious for her own good, he drew her forward. "And I think it's best if you take Grace upstairs. She looks frightened."

Her momentary bewilderment apparently past, Aunt Letty nodded and took Grace's arm firmly. She ignored her daughter's protests as she ushered her up the staircase, and David found himself hoping the time would never come when the dear woman would be put to the test of truly trying circumstances. He doubted she would be able to survive.

"David."

Turning at his uncle's summons, David followed as Martin Lang gestured the uniformed police captain and him into the study. Not for the first time, David felt a flush of pride at the unspoken confidence that caused his uncle to request his presence whenever matters of importance at the colliery were discussed. He had long ago resolved to be worthy of that confidence.

Inside the elaborately paneled room, Martin Lang turned toward the big, dour-faced captain of the mine owner's private police force. Barely waiting until David closed the door behind them, he questioned the man sharply.

"All right, Captain Linden, I'm anxious to hear what you have to say that's so secret that it can't be discussed openly in the foyer of my own home. It'd better be good. I'm tired of dancing to the Mollies' tune!"

"I'm well aware that the Mollies accept only Irish Catholics within its ranks, sir. And I know you employ neither Irish nor Catholics in your household, but that doesn't mean their ears aren't within hearing."

"Not in my house, Captain!"

Dark eyes sober under unruly brows, the huge Scot shook his head. "I wouldn't be so sure, sir. The Mollies maintain such a degree of secrecy that even members of the fellows' families are uncertain of their membership."

"Hogwash!"

"Not so, sir."

"I tell you, it's hogwash! It's a pretended ignorance. They either fear for their own lives or share the guilt! How many murders have there been in the past two years alone? Henry Dunne in Pottsville was killed in broad daylight on a well-traveled road by five armed men—yet no one saw or knew anything. Dunne's mistake was in urging publicly that the draft laws be enforced, when most of the Irish want nothing to do with fighting any war but their own.

"Then this official of the Glen Carbon Coal Company was shot to death a mile from his home after having fired a trio of Irish miners. The damned bastards shot out his eyes! In Ashland there was that fire boss and the dog he took on his rounds. They disappeared the night after he had a run-in with some of the Irish under him, and neither have been seen since. And Henry Johnson, poor fellow, was bludgeoned to death by four Irishmen! Those are just a few. Murders, atrocious assaults, colliery and mine fires of suspicious origin—all directly attributable to the Molly Maguires! And now sabotage."

David took a deep breath, realizing how close his uncle had come to losing control. He agreed completely with his uncle's opinion of the Irish element in the mine fields. With few exceptions they were ignorant, lazy, and dedicated to drink.

David frowned as the girl on the hillside appeared unexpectedly before his mind's eye. It was unfortunate. For all her spirit and obvious intelligence, that sassy little chit would probably go to seed sooner or later, just like the rest of her kind. It was inevitable.

"David."

Silently cursing the small, angry face that had popped into his mind at such an inappropriate time, David replied, "Yes, Uncle."

"The papers we were looking at earlier—the superintendent's reports on men reprimanded or fired within the last few months—where are they?"

"In your bottom drawer, sir."

Taking a few steps to the massive desk that dominated the center of the room, Martin Lang retrieved the file he sought. Lowering himself into the high-backed chair behind the desk, he looked up at Captain Linden and David in turn.

"Draw chairs up to the desk and make yourselves as comfortable as you can, because I tell you now, we're not going to budge from this room until we've found a link to tonight's heinous crime."

"Mr. Lang—"

"No excuses, Linden! The Coal and Iron Police is a private police force. We mine owners pay your salary, you know!"

"I'll not argue that point, sir." Nodding, the big Scot added quietly, "But I've an appointment that might net me more than studying files at this moment."

"An appointment?"

"It's a matter to which I must swear your utmost secrecy."

"You have my word as well as my nephew's, so out with it, man!"

"We've succeeded in putting a man undercover in the Mollies organization."

Martin Lang's expression tightened. "And do you expect he will remain *alive* long enough to do us some good?"

"I do."

"Is that what you called me in here to say?"

"Yes, sir."

"Then get to your meeting. And report back to me as soon as you find anything—anything at all, do you hear?"

"I'll do that, Mr. Lang."

The door closed behind Captain Linden, and Martin Lang

shook his head and sighed. "Two good men were killed tonight. It never ends."

Finding words inadequate, David solemnly took the folder from his uncle's hand. He picked up a nearby pen as he opened the file.

"Michael O'Toole, fired on the first of the month for drunkenness on the job. Shall we start with him?"

A faint smile touched Martin Lang's lips as he looked into his nephew's young, handsome face.

"I suppose that's as good a place as any."

"Bless me, Father, for I have sinned . . ."

A familiar warmth stirring inside him as he recognized the voice of his youthful confessor, Father Matthew directed his response through the confessional screen separating them.

"How may I help you, my child? How have you sinned?"

A short pause, and then came a soft response bearing a note of shame. "I'm unable to forgive, and I have hatred in my heart."

"God understands your human failing, and He'll forgive you if you strive to overcome these weaknesses. You must pray for the strength you need. Hatred is a sickness that can consume your soul. You must put it out of your heart. You must look into the eyes of those you hate and try to substitute understanding for your darker feelings. Will you try to do that?"

"Yes, Father."

"Is there anything else, my child?"

"Father, I . . ." The girl's voice dropped lower. "I saw the train wreck a few nights ago. I know who caused it. Two men were killed, Father, but I haven't told anybody, and the men who caused it are still free."

Father Matthew inhaled sharply, but his hesitation was brief.

"The sin is theirs, not yours, my child. In confessing your sin of omission, you have relieved it from your soul and the Lord forgives your weakness."

"But the men are still free, Father."

"They aren't free, my child. They carry the yoke of their sins on their shoulders, and it's a heavy burden indeed. You must pray for them as I will, and together we'll ask God to forgive and strengthen them so they'll never sin in this way again."

"Yes, Father."

"Is that all you have to confess now?"

"Yes, Father."

Reciting the prayers of absolution a few moments later, Father

Matthew heard Meghan O'Connor's voice join his own as she spoke her Act of Contrition. He warmed to the sound.

Meghan rounded the corner of the house at a breathless pace and entered the yard. Halting abruptly, she brushed the perspiration from her forehead with the back of her arm and ran a smoothing hand over her hair. Taking a few moments for her breathing to return to normal, she then approached the kitchen. Two steps inside, and she knew all her efforts had been for naught.

"All right, miss, where've ye been when ye should've been helping yer aunt with preparation for the evenin' meal?" Uncle Timothy's hard eyes pinning her, he continued tightly. "With yer mother upstairs, lying abed like a queen, and ye out on a lark, yer aunt's been takin' up the slack, and she's had a hard day of it, too!"

Meghan lowered her gaze at the censure in her uncle's tone. Uncle Timothy's anger had become familiar to her in the two months she had lived in his home, and she was well aware that there was little that Sean, Mother, or she could do, short of leaving, to satisfy him. Glancing at his narrow, lined face, she saw his small, yellowish eyes still pinned her. His wiry brows had furrowed into a straight line over his sharp nose, and his thin, bony frame was hunched into an aggressive posture that never failed to put her in mind of an angry bantam rooster about to attack. She knew from experience that his tongue could cause as much pain as physical abuse, and that at moments like this, Aunt Fiona silently shared the distress he evoked.

The advice Father Matthew had given her in the confessional a short time earlier returned to mind, and Meg raised her head to look directly into his eyes as Aunt Fiona spoke nervously in her behalf.

"The child was gone a short time, Tim, and only left after she finished both her mother's and her own chores."

"I won't stand for yer shielding the girl's laziness, woman! She'll do her part here or find another roof to cover her head. And she'll answer me questions, too!" He turned sharply beck to Meg. "I asked ye where ye was, wastin' yer time when ye should've been here with yer mother's kin, workin'."

"I . . . I was in church—in confession."

"That so? Well, it'll do ye well to remember that idleness is a tool of the devil. Now get ye to work and help yer aunt with them potatoes! We've boarders that'll be expectin' a good meal—*payin'* boarders, too, and don't forget it!"

Turning on his heel, Uncle Timothy stomped out of the room and down the hall on wobbly legs that would have betrayed his extended stay at Murphy's Pub, even had not Meghan's nose warned her of his condition as soon as she had walked into the room. Meghan turned to her aunt's flushed face.

"I'm sorry, Aunt."

"Aye, but ye have a right to yer consolation, m'dear. Yer uncle's a hard man. Sometimes he's not very understandin'." Her round face flushing even darker at her own soft words of criticism, Aunt Fiona darted a guilty glance toward the doorway through which her husband had disappeared. "But he's a good man. He's not laid a hand to me in all our years of marriage, despite his threats. So I ask ye to be patient with him, and kind in yer thoughts."

"Yes, Aunt."

"Get yerself upstairs to check on yer mother now. She was feelin' poorly when she awoke and I sent her back to rest."

Nodding in response, Meghan left the kitchen, taking the stairs as quickly as she dared. Relief surged through her as she pushed open the door of their room and her mother inquired softly, "Meg, are ye there, m'dear?"

"Aye, it's me, Ma. Are you feeling poorly?"

"I'm just a little tired. Aunt Fiona decided I needed a bit of rest and sent me up. She's a good woman, yer aunt. We're fortunate to have her."

"And Uncle Timothy, too."

The face Meghan pulled as she spoke those words brought a rare smile to Mary O'Connor's lips.

"Oh, Meghan, ye mustn't make me laugh at such an unchari-table joke. Ye know Uncle Timothy's not a happy man."

"Yes, I know, Ma. And he doesn't want anyone else to be happy, either."

"Meg, darlin', yer not to criticize the man who's put a roof over our heads and food on our plates."

Regretting the distress she had caused as her mother's eyes filled with tears, Meg took her hand and squeezed it tightly. "I'm sorry, Ma. I'm happy I still have you and Sean, and I'm going to try to understand Uncle Timothy, just like Father Matthew said."

"Understand him, ye say?"

"Father Matthew said to look into the eyes of the people you ha— . . . dislike, and try to understand them." Meg shrugged her narrow shoulders. "I tried it a few minutes ago, but it didn't work. I guess I'll have to try a little harder."

Her wan smile returning, Mary O'Connor nodded. "I suppose we must all do that."

Mary paled unexpectedly, her smile disappearing as quickly as it had appeared, and Meghan's heart began a slow hammering. She didn't need Dr. McGee to tell her that Ma was weakening. It was all too apparent in the waxy pallor that was now constant on her face, and in the deep circles that gave her formerly bright eyes a frighteningly sunken quality. And she also knew that beneath Ma's worn cotton dress there was little more than skin covering her fragile frame.

Ma was dying.

Meghan squeezed her mother's hand, willing away the tears that had begun to gather in her eyes.

"Ye have beautiful eyes, do ye know that, Meg? They're yer father's eyes. All of ye children are handsome, like yer father." Mary continued softly, "I know me boys are beautiful angels now, and I think ye know, darlin', that I'll probably be seein' them soon."

"Ma . . ."

"I don't want to leave ye, Meg, but I've no choice, ye see. And if I've to be honest, it's not ye I worry for the most. Yer a good girl. Ye'll be a beauty someday and I know even if yer uncle makes yer days uncomfortable for a while, ye'll be taken to wife by some handsome young man in a few years. Ye'll be a good wife and mother, 'cause there's no real bitterness in ye, despite your heartache. But with Sean, it's different."

"Sean's unhappy, Ma."

"And angry. He blames God for the tragedy that befell us."

"No, he—"

"Oh, yes, he does, Meg! I've seen it in his eyes."

"No, he doesn't blame God, Ma. He says there isn't any God because if there was, He wouldn't have let Da and the boys die the way they did."

"Oh, Meg!"

"Don't cry, Ma."

"He's too bitter, Meg! I'm afraid for him, and it pains me to know that I'll soon be addin' to his despair." Tears trailed from the corners of Mary's eyes, but she brushed them away with an impatient hand. "I want ye to make me a promise, Meg. Will ye do that?"

"Yes, Ma."

"I want ye to promise me that ye'll keep true to yer brother, and help him when I'm not around to soothe his anguish. I want ye to promise me that ye'll never give up on him, Meg, no matter the path his anger takes. Because the truth is, there's no one in the world Sean loves better than ye, not even me."

"No, Ma, that's not true!"

"Aye, 'tis true. There's been somethin' special in his heart for ye since the day you were born, and we all knew it, even your Da. I'm thinking if any two of us are to remain together, 'tis best for it to be Sean and ye."

"Sean'll be all right, Ma."

"Sean will want to take care of ye, Meg, and he'll do it the best he can, I know. But the truth is, 'tis ye who'll have to take care of him. The dear boy has a lot of hate inside him."

"But he might not listen to me, Ma." The terrible secret of the night of the train wreck coming to her mind, Meg repeated, "He might not listen."

Seeing beyond her daughter's response, Mary nodded. "I know, darlin', but the important thing is that ye don't stop tryin'. Can ye promise me that, Meg?"

Dull brown eyes fused with brilliant blue in the silent seconds that followed, and Meg felt her mother's determination steel her own.

"I promise, Ma."

Mary's painful grip abruptly slackened. Her eyes closed, and fear pounded anew in Meg's chest in the long moment before Mary whispered, "I'm tired, Meg. Tell Aunt Fiona I'm sorry I can't come down to help her."

"I'll help her, Ma."

"That's a good girl, Meg. And tell Sean to come up to see me when he comes home. I'm missin' the dear boy, ye see."

"Yes, Ma."

When the steady rise and fall of her mother's chest finally revealed she was asleep, Meg drew herself to her feet. She was grateful her mother was only sleeping and she would be with them a little longer.

In the hallway, Meg pulled the door closed behind her and swallowed again. Aye, at least a *little* while longer . . .

Chapter 3

The sun shone brightly through the French windows as Millicent Lang bustled around the master bedroom of the mansion, but her mind was far from the gleaming massive furniture surrounding her, the matching satin drapes and bedcover, and the luxurious rug of which she was so proud. Martin had left for the mine a short time earlier, and she had immediately arisen to prepare for the day. She was not usually an early riser, but today she was a woman with a mission.

It had come to Letty in the middle of that horrible night of the train wreck that there really was very little she could do about the whole, terrible situation that existed in the valley. And then she had broken down and cried.

She had cried for so many things. She had cried for the deaths of those two poor men on the train, she had cried for her husband's frustration, and then she had cried for the hatred that seemed to be all around them.

She had never been certain just who or what those Molly Maguires were, except that they were terrible men. The truth was, she couldn't understand why they hated Martin and the colliery so much. After all, the men in the mines owed their livelihoods to Martin, didn't they?

It had occurred to her, though, there was something she could do. As small a thing as it was, she decided in that moment to do it.

Her plans now formulated, Letty walked quietly to the wardrobe and drew open the door to scan the vast array of day gowns within. Her pale eyes pensive, she touched a manicured finger to her cheek. It would not do to appear too elaborately dressed. Neither would it do to appear too staid. She withdrew a deep blue gown with front buttons that was particularly flattering to her generous proportions, and which she could slip into without calling for her servant's aid.

31

Giving her appearance a last check a few minutes later, she picked up her hat and bag before heading out into the hall and down the staircase in the direction of the morning room. A quick but nourishing breakfast, and she'd be on her way.

Letty smiled. Martin would be so proud of her. She really was feeling better already.

Standing at the door of Father Matthew Mulligan's rectory an hour later, Letty listened as an approaching step sounded in response to her knock. The door drew open to reveal the slight, young priest she knew to be Father Mulligan, although she had only seen him once before in passing. Obviously startled by her presence, he stared at her, speechless. True, she was a devout Protestant, but his amazement was almost comical as his small brown eyes widened and his youthful face fell slack.

Smiling, she addressed him. "How do you do, Father Mulligan? My name is Millicent Lang. We've not met before, but it occurred to me last night that you'd be the perfect person to help me with a small problem that I have."

Rallying, his young face flushing at his lapse, Father Matthew Mulligan drew the door open wide. "It's a pleasure to meet you, Mrs. Lang. Please come in. What may I do to help you?"

Accepting his invitation with a gracious nod, Letty stepped into the small, tidy quarters. "Very much, I hope."

She was still smiling as the door closed behind them.

Father Matthew looked down at Meghan's bent head, barely resisting the urge to pluck a dark stray curl out of her collar as she labored over the sheet of paper in front of her. She was such a pretty child, and so bright. He could not help but marvel at her rapid grasp of the letters he taught her. It had taken her no time at all to learn to write the alphabet, coordinate the sounds, and put the letters into words.

Looking up, Meghan met his gaze with her startling O'Connor eyes, and sadness touched the pleasure he always experienced in the girl's company. She had lost so much. Worrying him still was their conversation several days earlier in the confessional. She and Sean were so close, and he knew only too well the bitterness the boy nourished inside him. He knew Sean's faith had suffered because of the accident, and he feared for the direction in which the boy was leaning.

"How's this, Father?" Holding up her paper for his approval,

Meghan waited for his nod before adding, "If it's all right, I'd like to try to read again today."

"Meghan O'Connor, you're a greedy lass. You hardly master one skill before you're grasping for another."

Father Matthew's teasing did not elicit the response he had intended. Instead, intensely sober, Meghan nodded.

"Aye, Father. I've a lot to make up, and not much time to do it in."

Concerned by her sudden seriousness, Father Matthew became as sober as she. "There's no need for such haste, Meg. You're young and you've a quick mind. I've no doubt you'll be reading very soon."

Meg avoided his eye. "But there *is* a need for haste, Father. I've come here this past week without Uncle Timothy's approval. He's made it clear what he thinks about girls learning to read and write. He has a few more boarders now doubling up in the rooms, and Aunt Fiona's working harder than before. He'd be angry if he thought I was wasting my time here."

"Wasting your time?"

"So he says."

Silent for a moment, Meghan finally raised her clear eyes to his once more.

"Is it wrong to want to do this because of pride, Father?"

"Pride, my dear?"

"Da said it gave a man power to be able to read. He said it wasn't a power that others might see, that it was a power inside that gave a man pride and a will to go on to better things."

"Your father was right, Meg. A little pride for such reasons never did a person harm unless it went to excess."

Holding his gaze, Meg finally nodded. "Then I think we must hurry, Father, because I don't know how much longer it'll be before Uncle Timothy finds out I'm still coming here for lessons. He'll not accept it lightly."

The determination in Meghan's tone solidified a decision with which Father Matthew had been struggling. He touched a hand to her thin shoulder. "We'll do that, dear, but first I have something to discuss with you. I had a visit from Mrs. Martin Lang several days ago."

Meghan's sudden paling was unexpected and Father Matthew smiled encouragingly. "She's a very nice woman, and she's concerned about the feelings of the Irish in the valley. She thinks that she may have contributed to the hostility people in the valley seem to feel for everyone connected to the house on the hill by bringing in all her servants from Philadelphia—and all Protestants, at that. She thinks we might think she considers Irish Catholics a step beneath them, or that she doesn't trust us in her house."

Meghan's slender nostrils quivered momentarily, and Father Matthew frowned at her unreadable reaction.

"She wants to change that kind of thinking. Since she's in need of another servant, she asked if I could recommend someone who might do. She said she'll pay well and provide a uniform, too."

Father Matthew hesitated again, his eyes on Meghan's suddenly averted face.

"Is something wrong, Meghan? I thought you'd be happy to have a chance for an income. Your uncle would have less cause for complaint about financial strain if you could pay him something, and you could stop here at the rectory to continue your lessons before you go home every day." Father Matthew hesitated again. "Meghan, would you rather I recommend someone else?"

"No, Father!" Meg's eyes snapped back to his, and she shook her head emphatically. "You're right. It'll be much easier at home if I can give Uncle Timothy money on a regular basis. And . . . and I thank you, Father, for thinking of me."

But Meghan's smile was forced, and Father Matthew struggled against a growing sense of disquiet.

"You're sure, Meg?"

"Yes, I'm sure."

"All right. I'll speak to Mrs. Lang and see if I can bring you up to the house for her approval tomorrow."

"Thank you, Father."

Still uncomfortable with her reaction, Father Matthew forced a smile. "Well, now that we've settled that, we can try our reading."

Pushing her chair back from the table unexpectedly, Meghan stood up. "I think I'd better be going now, Father. Ma wasn't too well this morning, and if I get home early, I'll have some time to spend with her before I begin my evening chores."

"All right, my dear."

A peculiar discomfort lingering, Father Matthew was still staring at the door moments after Meg had slipped from sight.

• • •

Meghan cast Father Matthew a quick glance as she stood silently beside him in the formal study of the Lang mansion. The interview was not going well.

It wasn't as if she hadn't tried. In an attempt to present her best appearance prior to leaving the house that morning, she had donned the newer of her two worn dresses, and had taken extra time to tame her willful dark curls. However, it had taken no more than a brief glance in the mirror to reveal that her efforts had accomplished very little. The girl reflected in the glass was undersized for her years, and her dress, faded to an almost indistinguishable color, hung limply on a frame untouched by budding maturity. In contrast to her unimpressive stature, her mass of hair appeared wilder than ever, and her bright eyes seemed to overwhelm her small, tense face.

She had left the house after a quick word to her mother earlier that morning, and with concealed trepidation had joined Father Matthew to make the long climb to the manor on top of the hill. What a house it was! It was even larger than she thought when up close, with great white columns in the front that appeared to stretch endlessly to the second floor, and a wide white porch that curved out on either side of the entrance like two graceful arms embracing it. She had gotten only a glimpse of the well-kept grounds and the grand stable that sat a considerable distance away, but she had noted then that Sean was right. Martin Lang provided better housing for his horses than he did for the men who worked in his mines. The thought stirred bitter emotions indeed. She'd had time to see no more before Father Matthew led her up the front steps to the great oak door.

Ushered down the hallway into the darkly paneled room where they now stood, she had come face-to-face with Mrs. Lang for the first time.

Raising a limp hand to her brow, disappointment obvious in her demeanor, Mrs. Lang openly evaluated Meghan's appearance.

"I . . . I'm really uncertain if the girl will do, Father Mulligan. I had an older girl in mind, a more sturdy person who could do some of the heavier cleaning our aging Mabel can't manage any longer."

Father Matthew's fine lips stiffened. "Meghan is a strong girl, Mrs. Lang."

"But she's a child. I expected someone older."

"Meghan is fourteen years old, soon to be a young woman, and she is intelligent and hard-working."

Mrs. Lang shook her head, her expression vague. "I had thought to have someone bigger . . . stronger."

"You asked me to bring you a person who would make a reliable servant, Mrs. Lang. That I have done."

A light color flushed the matron's smooth cheeks, and Meghan fought to conceal her satisfaction at Father Matthew's sharp response. The sting of her contact with David Lang still had not faded. David Lang had made it only too clear what he thought of the people in the valley, and of herself. Holding them in less than contempt, he did not think they were worth his time of day. But there was little work in the valley for a girl her age, and she could ill afford to decline this opportunity.

Glancing again at Mrs. Lang as she started to speak, Meghan decided that her own feelings would be of little consequence at any rate. Mrs. Lang didn't like her.

"Father Mulligan, I'm sorry if I offended you. It's only that I find it difficult to believe this frail child will be up to the work expected of her."

Father Matthew's fair face colored. "And I apologize as well, Mrs. Lang. But in all good conscience, I can't leave here today without having done my best to persuade you that you're wrong. I think the most convincing argument I can make is to have Meghan speak for herself." Father Matthew looked at Meghan encouragingly. "I think Mrs. Lang has some questions to ask you. Speak up, dear, so she may have an opportunity to get to know you."

Swallowing tightly, Meghan turned to Mrs. Lang's doubtful expression.

David walked swiftly up the carpeted hallway, preoccupied with his thoughts. His informal, well-tailored riding garb of white shirtwaist, dark pants, and high riding boots showed the abuse of a hard morning's ride and his normally well-groomed hair was still ruffled from the wind. He was frowning, his dark brows furrowed over eyes glinting with frustration.

Damn that Townsend! The man was intent on seeing problems with Fabian even when there were none. His reaction to the temperamental scene Fabian had just staged was all out of proportion, and he was certain he was going to have to do some fast talking when it was reported back to Uncle Martin. But Townsend was wrong. Fabian was well worth any trouble he caused.

His thoughts interrupted by the mumble of conversation behind the closed study doors, David halted abruptly. Incredulous, he listened more closely to the voice that had caught his attention.

"No, I haven't been in service before, ma'am, but I've much experience with household duties, coming from a family of nine."

"I understand that, dear, but you must also understand your duties here would be quite different from work in a home where you're expected to do no more than can comfortably be accomplished by a girl your size."

"As Father Matthew said, I'm very strong, ma'am."

"But the heavy laundry baskets, the gardening chores . . . My dear, you're so small."

"I'm growing every day, ma'am."

Those polite responses on the other side of the door . . . David's incredulity grew. He knew that voice! It had sounded repeatedly in his mind after that disturbing hillside confrontation. His discomfort at the memory bothered him still as he took an involuntary step forward and opened the door.

"Oh, David, dear!" Turning with the genuine smile she reserved for David alone, Letty stretched her hand out toward him. "Have you finished with your ride? I didn't expect you back so soon."

"Fabian was acting badly, so I put him back in his stall."

Taking Aunt Letty's hand, David turned toward the slender priest and the girl who stood beside him. Damn, it *was* her! There was no mistaking that wildly curly hair and those accusing blue eyes.

Briefly meeting the girl's gaze, David was startled by the flash of hatred he saw there.

"David, dear, this is Father Matthew Mulligan from the valley. And this is Meghan O'Connor. I approached Father Mulligan a few days ago about hiring a dependable girl to help with some of the downstairs chores that are beyond Mabel now. However, I was just explaining to him that Meghan is a bit too young for the work I had in mind."

"I think you're making a mistake, Mrs. Lang." His thin face reflecting consternation, the priest responded directly to Aunt Letty without acknowledging the introduction, but David knew the slight was not deliberate. It was obvious the priest was upset.

Looking again at the girl as she stood silently at the priest's side, David saw she deliberately avoided his gaze. He knew what she was thinking. She was waiting for him to tell his aunt about their clash on the hillside, and he wondered at his own reluctance to mention the incident. Surely, if the girl was inclined to violence such as she had demonstrated that day—if she was unstable in some way . . .

"There's no doubt in my mind that Meghan is a very special girl, Mrs. Lang." The priest was still talking. "She'd be a welcome addition to any household, including your own. She's dependable, steadfast, and even-tempered."

The girl's mouth twitched and David withheld comment as the priest continued, "There's another reason you might feel inclined to decide in Meghan's favor." Casting the girl a glance, he continued soberly. "Meghan's father and brothers are the O'Connors who were killed in the mine fire a few months ago. It was a terrible accident, and no one's fault, but Mrs. O'Connor, Meg, and her brother, Sean, are all that's left of the family. And Mrs. O'Connor isn't well, you see."

The priest continued speaking, but David heard only the echo of his own angry remarks that day on the hillside when the girl attacked him so unexpectedly. His face flushed.

A glance at Aunt Letty revealed she was still unconvinced, and David slipped his arm around her shoulders, surprised to hear himself say, "Why don't you give the girl a chance, Aunt Letty?" At her doubtful look, he continued with a careless shrug, "She's probably stronger than she looks."

"She's so young, David."

"Father Mulligan seems to think she's the right girl, and he know her best." David squeezed her arm reassuringly. "You can snap her into shape if anyone can, Aunt Letty. Just look what you did with me."

"Oh, David!" Her smile growing, Aunt Letty shook her head. "You're such a dear. I can't imagine why you'd concern yourself with a matter as trivial as the hiring of a servant, but I do know your interest pleases me—as does most everything else you do."

Aunt Letty turned to the waiting priest. "All right. We'll take the girl for a trial period, Father Mulligan, and if she proves herself, we'll keep her on." And then to David. "Will that suit you, dear?"

"It's your decision, Aunt Letty."

"It's settled then. She may start tomorrow. She may speak to Cook about the time to report."

Unexpectedly relieved, David looked at the girl as the maid led her out of the room. Startled at the unexpected look of hot resentment she flashed back at him, he felt anger rise.

Damn it all! It served him right for speaking up for the unappreciative little snip! What had gotten into him, anyway?

"Letty, what have you done!"

Her pale eyes filling with tears as she stood opposite her husband in the study later that day, Letty faced Martin Lang's anger with acute surprise. He had arrived home from the mine a few minutes earlier. She had immediately followed him into the study, proud of herself and anxious for her husband's praise. She cast her nephew a helpless glance where he stood a few feet away.

"I thought you'd be pleased that I hired someone from the valley, Martin."

"Pleased! Letty, whatever made you think it would please me to entertain a papist in the bosom of my home?"

Letty hesitated. "We're not *entertaining* the girl, dear. We're merely employing her. She's little more than a child, and I thought it would be a healing step for us to take—showing the people below that we're not prejudiced against them, or afraid to have them in our house."

"It's not a matter of prejudice, Letty!" Shaking his head, Martin Lang closed his eyes briefly in an effort to contain his impatience. "But I don't want one of them spying in my home. They're not to be trusted, any of them!"

David interrupted, his expression wry. "Uncle Martin, this Meghan O'Connor is only a girl. I don't think she's been inducted into the Mollies yet."

Martin turned toward his nephew with a warning glance.

"I'll thank you to keep your sarcasm to yourself, David. The girl may seem harmless enough, but her father, most probably, is not."

"Her father was the O'Connor who was killed in the mine fire, along with her five brothers."

At David's response, Martin Lang's face went momentarily still. "I see. I didn't know."

"The girl needs the work, dear." Letty's expression was ardent. "Father Mulligan confided in me that the girl's mother is ill— dying. She only has one brother left, and he works in the mine. They've been forced to live with relatives, and the girl needs money to—"

"Enough! Enough, Letty." Martin shook his head, remorse

apparent on his face as he considered his wife's brimming eyes. He slid his arm around her shoulders. "I can see you meant well, and perhaps you've done well, dear. Who can tell?" Looking back at David, he continued. "Perhaps you're both right. I may have overreacted, but I do want you to remember that everyone in the valley has a sad story to tell if you'll listen to it. They're a crafty lot down there, and I don't want you to be taken in by them, or to go out of your way to try to court them, either. On the whole, they're not worth your effort."

"Martin, that's a terrible thing to say!"

"As far as the girl goes, she can remain in our employ as long as she does her job well. And, I appreciate the effort you took to try to help—but, Letty—" Pausing to press a light kiss to his wife's cheek, Martin Lang continued softly, "Next time, speak to me first, will you?"

Letty smiled tremulously. "Yes, dear."

Waiting only until the study door closed behind his wife a few minutes later, Martin turned to David with a frown.

"What do you really think of all this, David?"

Still stewing at the girl's sharp departing glance, David responded with uncharacteristic hesitation and an uncertain shrug.

"Uncle Martin, there are some times when I think it would be best if I didn't think at all."

"I'll not have a sister of mine workin' for them black-hearted Protestants! You'll not go back to that house, Meg! I'll not abide it!"

"Sean, please!" Meghan darted a worried glance at the kitchen doorway where she expected her uncle to appear at any moment. She had waited for Sean to come home from his shift at the mine, her apprehension growing at the thought of his reaction to the position she had accepted that morning.

"I thought you'd be glad that I'll be able to earn money toward our keep here. It may keep Uncle's mumbling down so Ma can have a little peace."

"You'd work for *them* just to keep Uncle Timothy quiet?"

"Father Matthew says it's a good opportunity for me. He says I'll learn a lot from working there."

"Oh, is that what he says?" Sean gave a bitter laugh. "What'll you learn? How to cheat decent, honest men out of a fair wage, and to work them like slaves until they're ready to drop and they've not a thought left in their heads except to go down to the pub and drink away their cares? Aye, that's valuable fare, all right."

Meghan felt a familiar despair. "Sean, things aren't as black as you paint them."

"Are they not, Meg?" His handsome young face a familiar mask of anguish, Sean took her slender shoulders between his hands. "Look at me. What do you see?"

Meghan's throat tightened. "I see my brother, Sean. And he's a fine-looking, decent young man, just like Ma says."

"Is that so? I'll tell you what them Langs see. They see nothin' at all! They look through me and my like as if we don't exist, because to them we don't, Meg. We're just the kind that take the coal out of their mines so they can buy their fine clothes and live in their fine houses and eat all that rich food, while some down here in the valley go about without a change of clothes and lie abed at night with their stomachs rumblin' from hunger."

"Sean—"

"And it'll be no different with you, Meg. They'll look at you and not see you, except to complain when somethin' ain't right or done on time. And I'll speak my mind, no matter Uncle Timothy's objections to the contrary. Them damned Langs've taken my father and brothers from me, but they'll not steal my right to speak my thoughts. I'll not stay silent for anyone!"

"Not even for me, Sean?" Her soft plea halting Sean's angry tirade, Meghan continued. "Please try to understand. I want to take this position for Ma. I can't do anything else to help her, and we both know she won't be lasting . . ." Unable to finish, Meg shook her head. "I'm not a child anymore. It's time I carry my own weight. You're doing all you can to provide but—"

"But it isn't enough." Sean's eyes narrowed, and he ran an anxious hand through his shaggy dark hair. "I'm the man of the family now all right, but I'm not much of a man, am I."

"You're only fifteen, Sean."

"Our Da would've found a way to keep you from bein' a servant to them Langs."

"Maybe, but Father Matthew says—"

"To hell with Father Matthew!"

"Sean!"

"I'll not listen to a word the man says! I've put the days of dreaming about 'The Almighty who watches over us all' behind me. Listenin' and believin' makes a man weak when he should be strong—makes a man sit back and wait for justice when he should be fightin' for it. I'll not waste another day of my life that way, Meg, so don't tell me what that man said to you."

"Sean, I want to go to work at the house on the hill for Ma. Will you be angry with me if I do?"

Sean hesitated, his eyes filling unexpectedly as he placed a heavy hand on her shoulder.

"Ah, Meg, how could I be angry with you when it's because of my own shortcomin's that you're to work in that place. I've let you and Ma down. I should be able to provide for you."

"Sean—"

But Sean would hear no more as he turned away. "Aye, Meg. I should be able to provide for you."

Her heart a grievous ache inside her, Meg watched as Sean stepped through the kitchen doorway without another word and slipped from sight.

Chapter 4

"All right, miss, step lively! We don't have all day to get this laundry done."

Casting the rotund Mabel Strong a glance that spoke volumes, Meghan held her tongue and picked up the laundry basket. She suppressed a grunt as her aching muscles strained at the oversized load, certain the smallest sound would bring the usual negative comment from the critical maid.

Maintaining a firm grip on her burden, she followed the woman's lumbering gait into the yard. She was glad to be out of the kitchen, where she had worked since five that morning, and to have the spring sun on her head and a cool breeze drying the perspiration on her brow.

Reaching the area where clotheslines were strung to accommodate the endless laundry generated by the Lang household, Meghan halted at last and lowered the basket to the ground.

"All right, miss. You know where the pins are by now. There's no time for dallying."

Meghan returned the older woman's gaze with deliberate silence. Mabel's normally pleasant, aging face tightened with the same resentment she and the rest of the loyal Lang staff had evidenced toward her since her employment over a month earlier. The resentment was now mutual. It grew stronger as Meghan recalled her first day at the Lang mansion.

Hannah Worth, dark hair graying, small brown eyes snapping under uneven brows, her matronly bulk wrapped in a dark uniform and an oversized, spotless white apron, had met her at the kitchen door. Referred to as "Cook" by all, the woman had taken in every aspect of Meghan's appearance in a glance—faded cotton dress and shawl, stockings with visible signs of mending, badly worn shoes, and the untamed mass of her hair. Her tone had been demeaning when she spoke.

"It's a good thing you'll be wearing a uniform while you're in

43

service here. Those clothes would never do for a house of quality. And make sure to wear your cap. The mistress don't tolerate an unkempt appearance."

Deliberately ignoring the flush her comments had raised, Cook then proceeded, "Just so's you get things straight right off, Mrs. Lang consults with me each morning about the menu and the running of the household. You'll be helping Mabel here." Cook turned momentarily to indicate the big, older woman behind her. "Mabel's been having trouble with her legs of late, and Mrs. Lang don't want her to become too uncomfortable with her work. You're to take up the slack, so that means you'll be getting your orders from Mabel most of the time. When you're done helping her, you can report to me in the kitchen. There's always something for you to do here."

Not waiting for a reply, Cook had motioned to another frowning, middle-aged woman a few steps behind. "This here's Margaret Seller. She's Mrs. Lang's maid, and she works upstairs only. She don't touch nothing down here—and you're not to touch nothing upstairs. Understand?" At Meg's nod, Cook had continued. "From time to time, when he ain't required by the Master outside, we have Johnny Law helping us here in the house. You'll meet him soon enough. Then there's Mr. Townsend, the head groom, the fellows that work in the stables, and them that work on the grounds. You're not to bother with the menfolk, you hear?"

Picking up a dark dress and a white apron from a nearby chair, she had handed Meghan the garments she now wore. "You can change in the storage room. When you're done, come back here. No dallying, hear? We start our day early and we work until everything's done the way the mistress likes it. Keep in mind, you'll work for your money in this house, miss. There'll be no dragging your feet, or out you go!"

Cook's directions had continued, but Meghan's concentration had lapsed under the staff's unfriendly stares. She realized then, as had been confirmed only too clearly in the time since, that they all considered her an outsider and she was not welcome.

Her stiff O'Connor pride had come to the fore at that point, and she decided that like it or not, they'd have to get used to her, and to blazes with them all and their opinions of the Irish!

As time passed, however, she found it more difficult than she expected to hold her tongue and accept unwarranted criticisms on a daily basis. She knew her patience was nearing an end.

Returning to the present, Meghan tuned out Mabel's abrasive

tones and took another shirt from the basket of clothes she had scrubbed so diligently for the past hour. She pinned the garment carefully to the line, marveling again at the superior quality of the fabric. She had no doubt this one shirt alone was more costly than her mother's and her own meager wardrobe combined.

Turning as Cook called from the kitchen doorway, Meghan saw her beckon to Mabel.

"No need for you to stop working, miss!"

Frowning at Mabel's sharp admonition, Meghan replied with a controlled, "Yes, ma'am."

Watching as Mabel waddled toward the kitchen in a huff, Meghan resisted as long as she could before sticking out her tongue at the woman's retreating back.

Her satisfaction minimal, Meghan returned to her work with a disturbed shake of her head. Maybe Father Matthew was wrong about her coming to understand these people, because the truth was, the more she came to know them, the more she disliked them. Pausing, Meghan amended her thoughts. Actually, she wasn't being fair. She had seen very little of the Langs since she had begun working in the house. Confined to the servants' area as she was, she had gotten only a glimpse of Mr. Lang the first day, when he appeared in the kitchen doorway and gave her a keen, penetrating glance. She saw Mrs. Lang briefly each morning when she came to the kitchen to speak to Cook, but the mistress seldom glanced in her direction. She had seen the pretty, blonde Grace Lang a few times. Each time she saw the girl she looked more perfect than the last, so well-groomed was she, and so stylishly clothed in outfits that showed not a day's wear. She couldn't quite believe that mature-looking young woman was only a year older than she.

As for the arrogant David Lang, she had only heard his laughter in the hall and gotten glimpses of him outside as he galloped by on his great stallion. Oh, but she had heard plenty about him.

Groaning inwardly as she pinned another wet shirt onto the line, she recalled the endless tittering in the kitchen about "Mr. David's fine sense of humor" and his playful teasing of Margaret when she attended Mrs. Lang. She had all but gagged at the fussing that went into making his favorite desserts at dinnertime and at the haste with which the staff responded to his summons. She had gritted her teeth against Mabel's repetitive warnings to take special care when she scrubbed Mr. David's fine lawn shirts.

Oh, she was sick to death of pampered "Mr. David" who used

his guile to twist everyone in the household around his finger, and who remained kind and generous solely when things went his way. Couldn't anyone see beyond his handsome face and false charm? Didn't anyone see the coldness in his eyes? Whatever his reason for speaking up for her the day she was hired, she had not forgotten the *true* David Lang; the nasty, abusive fellow who had clearly voiced his opinion of her and the Irish in the valley that day on the hillside.

Fidgeting in her uncomfortable uniform, Meghan scratched her arm, then ran her finger under the tight collar. The stiff fabric had rubbed her delicate skin raw on more than one occasion, and the haste with which the garment had been cut down to accommodate her small size was apparent in its ill fit. The oversize apron that bound the uncomfortable garment against her skin only added to her physical distress, as did the cap, which she had been instructed to pull well down on her forehead, so not a trace of her unmanageable hair could escape.

With sudden anger, Meghan jerked the annoying cap from her head and flung it to the ground. Her relief was immediate as the wild curls spilled free onto her shoulders and a gust of cooling air moved against her face. Standing still, Meghan luxuriated in the refreshing breeze. Her hands resting on the line, she raised her face to the sun and closed her eyes at the simple freedom of the moment.

A soothing calm gradually overcame her agitation, and an unspoken comfort swelled inside her. Oh, yes, there was a God up there in that endless expanse of blue above her. She could feel His touch warming her skin and His sweet breath bathing her face. He was telling her He was close to her, just as Father Matthew had said.

Opening her eyes, Meghan clipped the shirt to the line with fingers that moved with renewed purpose. Now, if only *He* would do something about *them* . . .

Taking a moment to tie Fabian's reins to a nearby tree, David had turned to watch Meghan O'Connor pin another garment to the clothesline as Mabel watched with a critical eye. Suffering the conflicting emotions he felt every time he thought of the girl, he had unconsciously shaken his head. For the life of him, he couldn't understand his preoccupation with her. She certainly wasn't an appealing sight in that baggy dress and apron, and with her hair stuffed into that ridiculous white cap she wore pulled down on her forehead.

Despite himself, he still felt guilty for his comments about her father when they met that first time on the hillside, and for that reason he had deliberately avoided contact with her. Even now, as annoyed as he was when he remembered how she had attacked him and pinned him to the ground, he had to admit to a reluctant admiration for the girl's spirit. He had no doubt that if the rest of the Irish in the valley had as much grit as she, they wouldn't be suffering their present lot in life. Instead, they found it much easier to bemoan their situation and take cowardly vengeance against imagined wrongs in the dark of night.

Not Meghan. She didn't complain about a full day's work. He had received that reluctant report directly from Cook on each occasion when, under one pretext or another, he had checked on her progress. Cook had praised the girl's work, despite her obvious resentment of "the outsider from the valley," and he was well aware that any praise from that woman was praise indeed.

Frowning, David had deduced from the scene in front of him a few minutes earlier, when both Mabel's and Meghan's expressions had been so revealing, that things were not going well between them. An unexpected summons from the house had sent Mabel waddling back toward the kitchen. Without realizing his intention, he had then taken a step toward the girl only to halt as, obviously believing herself unseen, she made a grimace at the maid's departing back and then stuck out her tongue.

Unable to resist a smile as Meghan resumed her work, David had taken another step toward her as, just as unexpectedly, she ripped the unbecoming cap from her head and threw it on the ground. But the anger and resentment in that gesture didn't strike David as much as when the girl then deliberately turned her face into the breeze, raised it to the sun, and closed her eyes. Touching his heart was the childish innocence of her countenance as she allowed the brilliant rays to warm her face. He saw a budding beauty there, as well as the peace that touched her features in the moment before she opened her eyes again and continued her work.

David was within a few steps of her when the girl became aware of his approach. She turned, a familiar hostility appearing in those incredibly beautiful eyes as she asked abruptly, "What are you doing here?"

David's sense of well-being faded rapidly under her gaze.

"I live here, remember?"

"Yes, I remember."

For the life of him, David couldn't understand why he so deeply regretted the wariness that sprang into her eyes. But he did, and he tried his most disarming smile.

"I had Fabian out for a ride when I saw you, and I thought I'd ask how you like working here."

The girl's eyes narrowed further. "I do my job."

"Is the work too much for you?" And then at the suspicion that leaped into the girl's expression, he added hastily, "Cook's sometimes inclined to test the new help sorely."

"As you said, I'm stronger than I look."

Gritting his teeth at the bite in her tone, David felt his smile grow stiff. Uncomfortable with their verbal fencing, he had taken another step that brought him closer to the girl when he noticed the ring of raw skin that encircled her neck just under her collar. Frowning, he unconsciously reached out to touch the abrasion. The girl drew back, and his irritation increased.

"What happened to your neck?"

"It's nothing."

"I asked you—"

The girl's eyes snapped with anger as she offered a carefully controlled response.

"This collar's too tight."

"Too tight? That uniform fits you like a sack."

Anger flickered more brightly in the girl's eyes and David groaned inwardly at his own clumsiness as she responded through tight lips, "Mrs. Lang provided this uniform. Cook said my own clothes weren't suitable."

David was determined to reverse the negative flow of their conversation. "I'm sure Cook meant that my aunt likes the staff to be harmoniously dressed. She's very particular."

"Yes, sir."

David paused, realizing the girl was doing all she could to conclude the conversation. Yet, he was somehow unwilling to allow the conversation to end on a sour note, as had all conversations with her in the past. She studied him, her gaze cautious. She didn't trust him, and he supposed he couldn't blame her. He had behaved like a spoiled child the day they first met, and some of the things he said were unforgivable. He regretted them, but not enough to give the little chit the upper hand by apologizing to her.

Impatient with his silence, the girl spoke abruptly. "I have to finish hanging these clothes or Mabel will be out here after me in a minute."

"Mabel's an extremely kind woman. I'm sure she doesn't mean to be abrasive."

"Oh, she's very fond of you, too, sir."

Her comment delivered with a sarcastic twist of her lips, the girl turned abruptly and resumed her work. Flushing at her abrupt dismissal, David felt the last of his patience slip away. Frowning, he gripped the girl's shoulder and turned her back to face him.

"I haven't finished speaking to you, and I don't like being dismissed."

Anger flared in the girl's eyes. "Take your hand off me."

David dropped his hand back to his side, cursing himself for again allowing their conversation to get out of hand. He tried once more.

"I don't expect you to believe me now, but I intended this conversation as a friendly overture. We started out poorly when we first met and I—"

"You're wasting your time, Mr. David." The girl's lips twitched at the form of address used by the servants. "I don't like you, and I never will. You have too high an opinion of yourself for my taste. I'll wash your clothes, and serve your table, and do everything that's required in my position, but I'll not pretend that you've pulled the wool over my eyes like you have the rest of the staff here. I know what you think of me and my own, and what you think of the rest of the staff, for that matter. You think yourself a step above us all, most especially the 'Pap' from the valley. You play on your charm and good looks, and wrap your aunt and everyone else around your little finger, but my eyes were opened up to you the first time we met. So, you see, if you'll leave me be, Mr. David, I'll be happy to do the same. If that's all right with you—*sir*."

The ice in her gaze freezing him, David nodded stiffly, and the girl turned back to the laundry without another word. David felt his face flush anew. He was striding back toward the tree where Fabian awaited him when he realized he had been set roughly in his place, whether he liked it or not. Vowing he wouldn't give the little Irish brat the same chance again, he snatched at Fabian's reins, pulling the stallion along behind him as he strode back toward the stables.

Minutes later he walked into the morning room, his expression determined, as Aunt Letty turned toward him with a smile.

• • •

Meghan swung the empty laundry basket onto the bench outside the kitchen door and took a deep, steadying breath. Her first step into the kitchen was met with Cook's and Mabel's intense frowns, and she raised her chin against the dropping sensation in the pit of her stomach.

They had seen it all. She was in for it, now.

"All right, miss, what did you say to Mr. David to send him walking off in a temper? Tell me the truth! I'll find out sooner or later if you don't."

Cook's angry inquiry started Meghan's heart hammering savagely, but her tone was level as she replied, "What I said to Mr. David is my business."

"Oh, the gall of her!"

Mabel's gasped interjection heightened Cook's irate flush.

"I run this kitchen, miss! Everything that goes on in it and in this house is my business, and I'll thank you not to think anything different!"

Turning at the sound of a step in the hall, Cook paused as Margaret Seller appeared in the doorway and addressed her. "Mrs. Lang would like to see you."

Her expression tight, Cook turned back to Meg. "We'll finish this when I get back, miss. In the meantime, get to them potatoes—and put your cap back on your head! You look the true hooligan you are with that wild hair streaming about your face."

Deliberately avoiding Mabel's eye, Meghan pulled her cap out of her pocket and put it on her head. Quickly stuffing her hair out of sight beneath it, she picked up a knife and began peeling the potatoes as ordered.

Meghan's mind was reeling. Now she had done it! By indulging her temper and her shrewish tongue, she had queered it for herself in this house with the pampered David Lang and the staff alike. She didn't doubt David Lang had gone directly to his aunt and filled her ear with the truth about her from the day she had trespassed on the hill to this afternoon's unwise behavior.

Breathing deeply against the emotion choking her throat, Meghan blinked back threatening tears. She had let Ma and Sean down, and Father Matthew, too. She hadn't lasted more than a month here, and the worst of it was yet to come when she faced Uncle Timothy and told him that she'd been dismissed.

Still cursing her lack of restraint, Meghan turned at the sound of a step in the doorway a few minutes later. Cook had returned, and she tensed as the woman addressed her.

"Mrs. Lang wants to see you in the study."

Nodding, glancing away before Cook could see the tears that welled in her eyes, Meghan raised her chin a notch higher. She'd not let any one of them see an O'Connor cry.

Wiping her hands on her apron, Meghan walked out of the kitchen without response. Taking a deep breath as she reached the study door, she knocked lightly.

"Come in."

Her chin high, Meghan stepped into the room, her eyes on Mrs. Lang's troubled expression as the woman approached her.

"You wanted to see me, ma'am?"

"Yes, I did."

Coming to stand directly in front of her, Mrs. Lang paused. The mistress's pale blue eyes surveyed her from the top of her head to the tips of her worn shoes.

"David was just in here to see me. He told me he was talking to you behind the house a few minutes ago." Meghan blinked and swallowed hard as Mrs. Lang shook her head. "I had no idea . . ."

Unexpectedly, Mrs. Lang raised a delicate hand to the line of irritated skin that ringed Meghan's neck. "It was extremely negligent of me to provide a uniform that would cause you physical discomfort. David was right in bringing the matter to my attention. I've already instructed Cook to give you some of Dr. Biel's salve for your neck, and I told her that I want you to change immediately into your own clothes, and that you're to be allowed to wear them until your new uniforms arrive from Philadelphia. I've also told Cook that I won't require you to wear a cap in the kitchen." Mrs. Lang looked pained. This last concession was obviously difficult for her, confirming Meg's thought that David Lang had again exerted his influence over his totally beguiled aunt for her benefit. "A simple ribbon to tie back your hair will do. I'll send one down from my room in the event you don't have one with you. And I hope you'll accept my apology for your discomfort, dear."

Meghan blinked again. "Yes, ma'am."

In the hallway, Meghan pulled the odious cap off her head and shook her hair free. Her frown darkened and her light blue eyes were pensive as she entered the kitchen to face Cook's and Mabel's scrutiny.

Cook broke the silence with a sharp, "All right, you heard what the mistress said. Get yourself changed out of those clothes and into your own." Cook pinned her with her stare. "And I hope you know who you have to thank for all of this. Mr. David is a dear boy with a kind heart and a concern for all them around him, even when it ain't returned in kind. Fie on you! If anyone was to ask me, I'd say you aren't worthy of his concern."

Responding with a brief, cold stare, Meghan turned toward the storage room, anxious to be back in her own clothes again. But Cook's words lingered, and as she slipped her worn cotton dress over her head, she wondered. What was that David Lang up to?

The same question lingered in Meghan's mind throughout her lesson with Father Matthew, prompting quizzical looks and an occasional concerned frown as her concentration faltered several times. She carefully avoided his gently probing questions as she had since starting work at the house on the hill. She didn't want him to know about the staff's resentment toward her.

Of course, there was one member of the staff who didn't feel the same, but that was of little comfort. Johnny Law had made enough of a pest of himself to incur Cook's wrath on both himself and her on more than one occasion during the month. No more than sixteen, Johnny was young and lonesome for someone his age, having been brought from Philadelphia to work at the house without a single member of his family. Miss Grace Lang was off limits to the poor servant boy, and that left only her.

It had been difficult maintaining a cheerful facade for Father Matthew when at times she had been so low. As for today, she preferred to keep the shame of her shrewish behavior with David Lang to herself. She was not proud of it.

Her lessons done, Meghan walked swiftly home, nodding to her friends Mary O'Neil and Sheila McCrea as she passed them on the street. She had no time for conversation now. Breathless, she entered the kitchen a few moments later, only to come face-to-face with her uncle's frown.

"Yer late! Yer aunt's been workin' herself into an early grave here alone in the kitchen, while yer mother's been sleepin' upstairs all day and ye've been dallying in the street."

Meghan turned worriedly toward Aunt Fiona.

"Ma wasn't down at all today?"

The brief shake of her aunt's head all she needed to turn her toward the staircase, Meg was halted abruptly by an angry grip on her shoulder.

"Oh, no, ye don't! Ye'll not go upstairs to pass another hour lazing at yer mother's bedside while yer aunt works herself into the ground!"

"Take your hand off her!"

Snapping around at the sound of Sean's voice, Meghan felt herself pale at the fury in her brother's face as he stepped into the room. Straight from his shift at the mine, he was dirty and tired, and of a mood that looked close to savage.

"I said take your hand off my sister, old man!"

Meghan felt her uncle's clutching grip lessen as he responded tightly, "Ye'll watch yer mouth or ye'll find yerself out on the street, me buckoo!"

"Take your hand off her or you'll find I'm more of a man than you think you are!"

Uncle Timothy's hand dropped from her arm as Aunt Fiona took a hesitant step forward. "Yer uncle wouldn't harm Meg, Sean. He's worried for my sake and the work I'm to do to keep up the place."

Sean's sneer twisted his face into an angry grimace. "Uncle Timothy worries for no one but himself and the tidy sum he's put away for his old age."

"Sean!" Meghan took her brother's arm with a low plea. "Let's go upstairs by Ma for a few minutes. She's not been down today at all. She must be feeling worse."

His heated flush paling, Sean glanced dismissingly toward his uncle. "Aye. This one won't bother you anymore today."

Meghan cast her brother a sidelong glance, her heart wrenching as they reached the top of the staircase and turned toward their room. Bitterness was beginning to mark his handsome face with downward lines. It hurt her that his smile was so infrequent and that the eyes that had always danced with life were now so cold. That coldness frightened her because she knew it went deep inside him.

Unable to find words to comfort him, Meghan proceeded to the door of their room, aware that Sean walked close behind her. Slowly pushing open the door, Meghan looked inside as Sean peered over her head. She emitted a low gasp of fright. Ma was so still and white. Meg dashed to her bedside, her heart pounding, just as the frail woman slowly opened her eyes.

"Oh, Ma!"

Mary O'Connor's blue-veined hand reached out to pat hers as she managed a feeble smile. "Not to worry, Meg. Me time's not come yet." Raising her gaze, Mary smiled more broadly at her son, standing protectively behind Meghan. "It does me good to see yer face, Sean." She paused. "Smile for me, boy, 'cause it warms me heart to see yer Da alive in ye when ye do."

"Aw, Ma." Sean shook his head. "I'm not of a mind to smile much these days."

"There's a reason to smile that we have each other, and that we've the love that keeps us together."

"It's not love that'll keep a roof over our heads and food in our bellies, Ma, not if Uncle Timothy has anythin' to say about it."

"He's kept us this far, and with Meg now addin' to the income, he's not likely to put us out."

Sean shook his head. "I wouldn't count on it, Ma."

"Ah, but I do, Sean, 'cause I've faith that things'll turn out right in the end."

Meghan could sense Sean stiffening behind her, and she knew he withheld further response for the sake of their Ma. Forcing a smile she didn't feel, Meg spoke into the awkward silence.

"I can't stay, Ma. Aunt's busy downstairs and I told Uncle Timothy I'd give her a hand." Meg stroked a strand of hair back from her mother's wan cheek, sick to the heart that her eyes were so sunken and dim. "If you're too tired to come down to the table tonight, I'll bring you up a plate that's fit for a queen."

"A queen I'm not and will never be." Mary smiled. "But I'm a lucky woman to have two who love me standin' by me side. Now off with ye both for a little while. I'm needing me rest."

Taking a moment to tuck the coverlet more tightly around her mother, Meghan turned to the door. Outside in the hallway, she whispered up into her brother's tense face, "You should've smiled for her, Sean. It was little enough to ask."

"It was more than I could give, Meg, for I'm thinkin' I've not a smile left in me."

"Fie on you, Sean!"

"No, the shame's not mine, Meg! It belongs to the Langs, and people like them with their need to subdue every man in the valley."

"What are you saying, Sean?"

"I'm sayin' that Lang's drivin' every man in this valley with any gumption left to hard retribution with his treachery and sneakin' ways. He's been on a roll since the train wreck with his questions, and detectives, and Coal and Iron Police comin' down on a man even if he so much as speaks up against him. But it ain't workin' out like he thought it would. The Mollies are too smart for him."

"What do you know about the Mollies?"

"I know Lang and Captain Linden of the Coal and Iron Police thought they'd put it over on the men of the old sod by sneakin' an infiltrator into the organization. But the informer was found out."

Meghan's heart went cold. "And?"

"And they found the fella dead in the woods this mornin'. His lyin' tongue had been cut out."

"Sean!" The blood drained from Meg's face. "How can you praise such a dreadful deed?"

"Because I take my satisfaction where I can, and if it takes the way of the Mollies to make the mine owners regret their treatment of the Irish in the mines and to make them respect us, so be it. But the truth is, there's precious little even in the informer's death to make up for the lives of Da and the boys."

"That was an accident, Sean! Mr. Lang—"

"Don't tell me about Mr. Lang! As far as that bastard is concerned, Da and the boys never existed! I'm tellin' you, Meg, we're too far below the man for him even to see us. But the Mollies are makin' him sit up and take notice that the Irish in this valley aren't goin' to be treated like the dirt under his feet any longer. He'll soon learn that he can't get away with the threats and cutbacks he's been makin' since the train was wrecked, and he'll find out that the reward he's offerin' won't make a single Irishman turn on his own. As for the good family men he fired today, he'll be made to pay."

"Don't get involved in any of this, Sean. It would break Ma's heart, and my own as well."

Sean's anger appeared to drain away, as he considered Meg's adamancy in silence. A sad smile touched his lips. "Would you not stand behind me whatever course I decided upon, Meg? Or would you abandon your only brother when the truth is that there'll soon only be the two of us left?"

Long suppressed tears brimmed in Meg's eyes as Sean awaited her response. Taking an abrupt step forward, she wrapped her arms around her brother's waist and hugged him tight as she whispered into the rough fabric of his coat, "You're my blood, Sean, and my brother you'll always be. No matter what."

Sean's voice was hoarse as his arms closed around her in return. "Aye, I expected no less." With those words, Sean urged her toward the stairs, and as she walked beside him, Meg was reassured. There was no real harm in Sean. There couldn't be.

"I think you're in for more trouble, Uncle Martin."

Standing beside his uncle's desk in the small mine office, David watched his uncle turn toward him. His wiry brows drew together over his sharp nose, and his small brown eyes held him fast. Not for the first time David felt the sensation of being pinned by a bird of prey.

"What suddenly makes *you* an expert on the men in the mines, David? I'm the one who's been dealing with them for five years."

"You've had one problem after another, sir."

"My mine is flourishing, isn't it?"

"Not without harsh payment."

Uncle Martin seemed to swell with rage. "I will not allow common terrorists to think they intimidate me!"

Realizing he had managed to raise his uncle's ire with the remarks he had intended simply as a warning, David glanced at the big Scotsman standing a few feet away. Captain Linden made no comment, and David knew the fellow would remain silent until he talked his way out of the corner he had backed himself into with his uncle.

It was time to try another tack.

"I'm sorry, Uncle Martin. You're right. I'm not an expert on the men working in your mine." David's short laugh lifted the planes of his handsome face and lit a familiar glow in his eyes. "As a matter of fact, not only do I have a lot to learn about the mine itself, but I'm pretty vague about the management of all the outbuildings that comprise the colliery. That's why you've had me accompany you here every day this past month, isn't it?"

"You know very well why I've taken you in to work alongside me, David." Somewhat mollified by David's apology, Martin Lang continued with a lessened frown. "I hope to familiarize you with operations here, now that you've temporarily finished with your academics. It's my hope that before you go off to college next year, you'll have a true working knowledge of the business in the event that you might be called upon to take over for me at some time."

"I appreciate your confidence in me, Uncle Martin. I really do. And it's for that reason that I feel obliged to be honest with you."

At his uncle's stiffening posture, David continued earnestly. "Uncle Martin, please consider what I'm saying. You fired several men today whom you suspect were involved in the train wreck last month, even though you have no proof."

"Arthur Bailey, Kevin Murphy, and William DeFoe are troublemakers, every one! If they're not responsible for the wreck, they're responsible for any number of problems we've previously had here. It's time to get rid of them. I've circulated their names to other mine owners, and they'll leave the coal fields soon enough when they can't find work to support their families."

"Unless they have other plans."

"I'll not quake with fear every time I make a decision here, David! With those men gone, there'll be three less agitators to think about."

Frustrated by his uncle's rising temper, David shook his head. "Stop and think a moment, sir. What happened every time you ordered similar firings?" Martin Lang's expression tightened and David continued without waiting for his response. "More trouble, right?"

"This is my colliery, and I can hire or fire anyone I want!"

"There've been rumblings of a strike of late."

"A strike! The fools haven't a chance, and they know it as well as you do. Let them go out on the street if they want. I can get another trainload of immigrant miners here in a week to take their places, men who'll be glad for the jobs and thank me for it. No bloody Paddy's going to tell me how to run my own mine!"

"These men won't give up. That agent who was found dead in the woods is proof of that."

"Bloody murderers! There's not a decent man amongst the whole race of them!"

David frowned. Meghan O'Connor's stubborn face unexpectedly appeared before his mind's eye, her small chin raised defiantly, determination oozing from every pore of her body. He saw again in her proud, youthful bearing a nobility that was out of place with the common people of the valley.

Martin Lang's low oath brought David back sharply to the present. "I'll find the persons responsible for killing that man if it's the last thing I do."

"Uncle Martin, you're as familiar as I am with the atrocities the Mollies have committed. Eighteen murders in Schuylkill County within a year's time—all men with supervisory positions in the mines, or men who spoke out against the Mollies in some way. Six collieries have been dynamited, rail cars have been overturned, our own train was blown from the tracks, and your operative was found murdered."

"Would you have me tremble with fear at the retaliation you think is planned against me?"

"I think you should prepare for it. Have Captain Linden increase the guards at the mine. Put on extra patrols down here and up on the hill."

"We have adequate protection already. I'll not let these men think they have me frightened."

"Uncle Martin—"

"The subject is closed, David. We have all the protection we need from these ragamuffin murderers. Let the bloody bastards try their damnedest. They'll not get the best of me!"

Tuning out the sound of his uncle's raving anger as it continued on, David heaved a frustrated sigh. Uncle Martin's pride was standing in the way of his common sense, but his own was not similarly affected. He had felt the hatred in the valley since he had become more heavily involved in his uncle's affairs, and he knew that even those men who did not participate actively in the work of the Molly Maguires were Mollies in spirit.

David made a small grimace. They were a despicable lot, all of them. Pausing in his thoughts, David frowned. Well, maybe not all . . .

Sean unconsciously slowed his step as Muff Lawler's drinking establishment and residence came into view. This night was to be very important to him. He need join with men of his own agitated persuasion who were determined to change things for the Irish in the valley. He need join with them for the sake of his peace of mind, so bad was the fury of his circumstances eating at his insides. The Ancient Order of Hibernians was to meet at this place tonight, and he was determined to take his place among them. As any Irishman knew, not all Hibernians were Mollies—nay, most despised their works—but *all* Mollies were Hibernians. The only difficulty there was was that no one knew for certain which ones they were.

Sean paused, remembering Da once saying that he'd heard a fellow Hibernian remark after a meeting that "indeed, ye never know if a Molly be sittin' beside ye, and ye best watch yer tongue when puttin' the organization down, or it might be taken out of yer hide." His brothers and he had been greatly confused by that statement, prompting his Da to explain.

As Da told it, the Mollies came into being on the old sod. They took their name from an old woman, Molly Maguire, a woman victimized by the landlords until she was driven to unrelentingly violent retribution. The oppressed thereabout took heart when she struck back, and when responding in kind to similar oppression, declared themselves Sons of Molly Maguire. Organizations bearing her name and dedicated to violent retribution quickly formed in the atmosphere of hunger and despair that prevailed.

Hoping to escape the tyranny and the violence, good men had taken their families to this new land of opportunity, only to find themselves similarly tyrannized, with the additional hardship of being singled out and cast to the bottom of the miners' lot because of their Irish birth. "Irish need not apply" signs began springing up everywhere, and in the only defense remaining to these hungry, sorely-afflicted men and their families, the organization soared to life again.

Molly's sons went underground in the Pennsylvania coal fields when their work became tainted with blood. Pressure from the church, government, and mine owners was so great that the secret organization finally worked its way into the Ancient Order of Hibernians, an organization of good conscience and good works in the coal fields.

Da told them that the inner core of Mollies remained firm and prospered under cover, and that the chain of organization throughout the coal fields, linked by bodymasters heading each local group, grew in strength. Da hadn't known much more than that about the workings of the organization, but Sean was determined to find out the rest.

Sean came to a full halt when a few feet from Muff Lawler's Saloon, his expression tense. He didn't want to make a mistake in the way he approached the man, for although it was never spoken aloud, it was understood that Lawler stood high in the Shenandoah Molly organization. He cautioned himself to remember not to push or he'd find himself suspect. He also knew it would be difficult to bide his time with his present feelings running so high.

Resuming his step, Sean took a deep, fortifying breath and strode over the threshold into the brightly lit saloon. Inside, he blended inconspicuously into the crowd as he acquainted himself with his surroundings.

It was a simple enough place. The front part of the first floor was the usual barroom with a counter extending across one side. Behind the counter were the usual tools of the trade—fixtures, glasses, decanters, bottles, and the like. At the one end was a door opening up into the kitchen which also looked to be a dining room of sorts, where he could see a staircase going to the upper floor. He knew Lawler lived up there with his wife and children, but the stealthy movement of several men up that staircase indicated a covert activity that afforded him far more interest than the meeting about to convene.

A thrill of anticipation warming his blood, Sean moved toward the long bar and situated himself at the end. He had not a smile for the men who turned at his unexpected appearance with obvious surprise, tensely determined as he was that this would be the night for which he had been waiting.

Chapter 5

"Away with you, Johnny!" Meghan's voice hissed in the silence of the yard as she cast a cautious glance back toward the kitchen of the Lang mansion. "You'll get me in trouble again."

"Aw, Meg . . ."

The thin, light-haired young fellow had appeared beside her clothesline a few minutes earlier, his freckled face split in a wide grin. But his present air was despondent as he jammed his bony hands into his trouser pockets, and kicked at a clump of grass.

Meg glanced back at the house again. Cook and the rest of the staff had been unusually quiet. She wasn't sure if their silence was due to the stepped-up activity of the mistress's newest cleaning campaign, or the two new uniforms which had been delivered to the kitchen earlier that morning, only a week after Mrs. Lang had talked to her in the study.

Accepting them from Cook in silence, she had immediately retired to the storage room to change. A passing glance at her reflection mirrored in the kitchen window had actually given her a measure of pleasure. The new uniforms were quite an improvement. The black fabric was softer, of a much better quality that was not as abrasive to her skin. The fit was improved to the point where she was actually comfortable during the heat of the day, despite the high neckline, and the white apron accommodated her slenderness moderately well. A heavy white ribbon, one of two that Mrs. Lang had sent to the kitchen, bound her curly black hair back neatly from her face in a becoming fashion, and she was silently grateful to finally reflect the same professional appearance as the rest of the staff. Unfortunately, judging from the silence which had ensued within the kitchen when she returned fully uniformed, the staff did not share her pleasure.

But whatever the reason for the truce that seemed to prevail between her co-workers and herself, Meg was relieved. She had come out into the yard with her second load of laundry a few minutes earlier, also grateful that Mabel had abandoned her supervision of this task a few days previous.

Then she had heard Johnny Law's voice behind her.

The young fellow still stood beside her, despite her sharp admonition a few moments earlier. His eyes were downcast, and she offered by way of explanation, "Cook nearly burned the skin off my hide with the tongue-lashing she gave me the last time she caught you hanging around here. I'm not about to make the mistake of passing the time of day with you again."

His brown eyes rising to meet hers with unexpected resentment, Johnny shrugged his thin shoulders. "It's not like I'm ducking out on my chores, Meg. I'm finished for a while and Mr. Townsend said I could busy myself with whatever I wanted until he called me again."

"But I've not finished mine! And Cook will make sure I don't if she sees you, that's for sure."

Spotting movement at the kitchen door out of the corner of her eye, Meghan whispered in a rush, "Quick, hide! Mabel's spying on me again."

Tempted to laugh as Johnny dove onto his stomach behind a nearby bush, Meghan picked a wet piece from the top of the basket with studied nonchalance. She released a relieved breath as a sideward glance revealed that Mabel had turned back into the kitchen again.

"Are you angry with me, Meg?"

Johnny peered at her from behind the bush as Meghan frowned.

"Why are you always hanging around me, Johnny Law? Surely you've friends enough among the men to find somebody to pass the time of day with. You know I'm not one of your sort. I'm suspect here because of all the trouble going on in the valley. Every one of Master Lang's employees looks on me as an outsider."

"I don't, Meg."

Johnny's brown eyes were earnest and Meghan paused in exasperation. "Well, the truth is, what you think doesn't count!" Regretting her outburst as Johnny's angular face flushed, Meghan shook her head. "Can't you find yourself another friend, John?"

"Not as pretty as you."

Johnny's face flushed even darker as she gave him a disapproving glance. "John, I'm thinking you're a bit young to have such faulty eyesight—either that, or you're trying to find my good side."

Johnny shifted uncomfortably and squinted up at her with a disturbed frown. "Aw, Meg, if you was to stop fighting with me and try some simple talk, we'd be friends by now. I'm getting tired of having you run me off every time I come near you. I've half a mind to give up on you and to go back to the stables—"

"Fine by me."

"—except I don't want to."

"And suppose I tell you I won't talk to you even if you stay?"

The extended silence that followed caused Meg to look again toward the bush as, his expression troubled, Johnny responded softly, "You wouldn't do that, would you, Meg? You know I've not a single friend here who's near my age." He made a small grimace. "That fine young lady up there in the house is curious enough to talk to me, all right, but they watch her like a hawk. Besides, she ain't as pretty as you."

"John Law, I'll not stand for your flattery!"

"Would you rather I say that you're ugly as a toad and I'll be expecting a wart on my nose if you touch me?"

A short laugh momentarily brightened Meghan's eyes. "John, you're a foolish boy!"

The pleasure her smile gave him was obvious, and Meg felt a sudden rush of shame. Had she let the people in this house turn her into a person who would refuse a smile and a kind word to someone in dire need of both? Had she forgotten that Ma always said only the poor of spirit couldn't afford to share a bit of themselves when it was needed?

"But I suppose you're not much more foolish than one of my own brothers when they were looking to pass the time of day. If you've no objection to staying out of sight behind that bush, you may talk away—and I'll respond if I've the chance without revealing myself."

Almost regretting her concession a short time later, as the persistent young fellow all but overwhelmed her with his unexpected humor, Meghan flashed him a quick, reproving glance and a short, "John, you'll get me dismissed yet."

Standing unseen a short distance away, David glared as he watched the covert conversation progressing between Meghan O'Connor and the stable boy, Johnny Law. Having come from the mine on an errand for his uncle, he had made his way toward the back entrance of the house, refusing to admit that a nagging, inexplicable concern for the little Irish termagant who had been so outspoken in her contempt for him was the reason for his circuitous route. As he watched, the girl struggled to restrain another burst of laughter, and David's annoyance soared.

Plagued by guilt at his behavior, he had reviewed his volatile encounters with the O'Connor girl over and over again in his mind. In truth, he was as confused by his own concern as he was by his failure in setting things right between them. It was now obvious, however, that he had wasted valuable time in giving the matter a second's thought, when the girl apparently had not. He felt like a fool, and he resented it badly.

The girl turned with a short quip that widened young Law's grin, and David's resentment deepened. There was no doubt the girl was brighter than most of her kind, although she did not deign to share her quick mind with him. That haughty little Irish piece was all smiles and laughter for that lanky stable boy hiding behind the hedge, while she had not a civil word for him. The thought rankled, as did the realization that his easy smile and charm, always so effective in the past, were completely impotent on this girl.

It occurred to David that the girl's response to young Law might be related to the look of adoration so obvious on the fellow's face. Law was looking at her as if the sun rose and set in the bright blue of her eyes. He had half a mind to—

Suddenly exasperated by his own trend of thought, David turned on his heel and made his way back toward the front entrance of the house. Anger marked his step. He'd not had a minute's peace of mind since that afternoon on the hill when the little snip had irritated him into behavior that was embarrassing to him even now. Well, now he was finished with it! The girl was on her own!

Stepping out of the bright sunlight into the shadows of the house's central foyer, David frowned as his eyes adjusted to the light. Well, he'd leave the arrogant little twit to her cow-eyed stable boy if that was what she wanted.

Pausing a moment longer, David drew his well-tailored, athletic frame stiffly erect. His arresting hazel eyes darkened with his next thought. It seemed the simple truth of this situation had needed to be brought home to him the hard way. That truth was, that in attempting to befriend the Irish girl from the valley, he had stooped below himself.

• • •

Fiona O'Reilly gave her orderly kitchen a last appraisal. She smoothed her graying hair against her head in a self-conscious gesture and reached behind to untie her apron. Looking toward the staircase to the second floor, she frowned. Mary had grown worse these past two weeks, and she feared her dear sister's time was fast approaching. With that thought, Fiona's nagging guilts intensified, and, unable to bear their weight a moment longer, she folded her apron, placed it on a nearby chair, and snatched up her shawl.

It was early afternoon, and Meghan would not be home for another hour or so. Neither would Tim and Sean, and, last she had looked, Mary was asleep. Fiona left the house and started down the street, her pace slowing only as the simple wooden Church of The Blessed Virgin Mary came into view. Fiona again ran a nervous hand against her hair. It was difficult to enter God's house when ashamed.

Pulling her shawl over her head, Fiona climbed the few steps to the door. Inside, she crossed herself and slipped into a pew at the rear of the church. She was kneeling in prayer when she noticed that she was not alone. A few rows in front of her, his slight form concealed in the shadows, was Father Matthew. Tears welled in her eyes, and she brushed one away as it slipped down her cheek.

Embarrassed by her weakness, Fiona did not see Father Matthew rise to his feet and walk toward her. Her head snapped up in surprise at his voice beside her.

"Are you ill, Fiona?"

The young priest's concern increased her shame, but courtesy forced her response. "Nay, Father. I'm well."

Pausing, Father Matthew silently observed the pain in her eyes before continuing in a softer tone. "If a problem of the spirit is troubling you, I'm here to help, Fiona."

Fiona shook her head, unwilling to risk her voice. When she finally spoke, her voice was laced with regrets.

"Aye, Father, 'tis a problem of the spirit which causes me pain. You see, I'm findin' it hard to understand some things."

"What things are they?"

"'Tis a matter of the new burden that's been added to me household at the death of Dennis O'Connor and his boys." Father Matthew stiffened at her words, and Fiona hastened to deny his accusing glance. "No, 'tis not a burden in the way you think, Father. Finances have always been the concern of me husband, Tim, and I've little time for them. But me sister, Mary, is lyin' ill abed the full day now, and well . . ." Fiona's eyes brimmed once more. "Aye, there's the rub."

"You resent the work you must do in caring for her?"

"Nay, Father. I love the woman dearly." Fiona's throat filled again, and she swallowed against the emotion which threatened to overwhelm her. "The truth is, I'm findin' it hard to understand why God has put her there instead of me."

Obviously startled by her statement, Father Matthew hesitated in response, allowing Fiona the opportunity to proceed with her halting words.

"You see, I've been of little true use as a woman most of me life, Father. I've been married for over thirty years to the same man, and I've failed him."

"You're too harsh on yourself, Fiona."

"Nay, I've not given me husband what he wanted most. Not a single child of the six I bore him lived past the first week, and he's a hard and bitter man because of it."

"You take unnecessary blame on your shoulders, my dear."

"Nay, 'tis true. The whole of his life me Tim's been jealous of those who have children of their own, and jealous of Dennis O'Connor and Mary most of all. Yer well aware that Tim had no true wish to take Mary and the children into our home. He sees the children he could've had, and he's found a way to relieve his feelin's by takin' things out on them. He feels little sympathy for the plight of Mary and the children 'cause there's no lessening of the love between them. If he could, he would destroy it, ye see, so they might be as miserable as he."

Shaking his head at the hopelessness in Fiona O'Reilly's eyes, Father Matthew shared her pain. "All you say is probably true, my dear, but you're at fault for none of it."

"Oh, but I am!" Nodding, unwilling to accept his words of consolation, Fiona held Father Matthew's gaze with her own.

"I failed me husband, and I'm failin' again because I've not the courage to go against him, ye see. I've not the courage to speak me mind and face his threats by tellin' him he's wrong in abusin' Sean with his anger, and in tryin' to wash the goodness from Meg's heart with his bitterness. I've only the courage to speak me mind when Tim's not present, and to try to soften the edge of Tim's spite. So ye see, I'm not a worthy person a'tall, and with every day that passes, I'm findin' it harder to understand why 'tis Mary, the good, lovin' woman that she is, who's lyin' on her bed, nearin' the end, while 'tis me that could so easily be spared here."

"Ah, Fiona . . ." Father Matthew's young face was pained. "There're so many things we can't reason through, but it's not for us to question God's way."

"But Father, I fear for the futures of Sean and Meg when Mary passes. And the time's comin' close, ye see."

"Will you keep them with you then?"

"Aye!" Her eyes lighting with uncharacteristic determination, Fiona nodded, but her quivering lips betrayed the price of that effort. "I'd follow them out on the street if it came to that."

Silent for long moments, sympathy for the poor woman's plight clearly visible in his eyes, Father Matthew took Fiona's callused hands to hold them comfortingly in his. "There's little I can do for you, my dear, except to tell you that where your courage is found lacking, your heart's kind and filled with understanding. You're a good woman, Fiona O'Reilly, and you must stop thinking poorly of yourself. And you must continue to share your goodness with the O'Connors, especially the children when Mary's gone. I'll do my best to help you, for I'm committed to them, you see. And in the meantime, we'll pray for the strength to do what we must."

Pausing, Father Matthew saw unexpressed gratitude in Fiona's eyes, and welling along with it, a light of hope that far surpassed his own. As she lowered her gaze respectfully, Father Matthew began the recitation of a heartfelt prayer.

"Oh, Mama, Beverly Hutton will think we're barbarians here on this lonely hilltop! Not only did the letter telling us of Mrs. Hutton's intended visit fail to reach us, but they've arrived when every bedroom is dismantled and in a state of disrepair! The beds are even stripped of their linens and the mattresses bare! You know how Beverly loves to ridicule. She'll tell everyone I know about this, and they'll all laugh at me."

Grace Lang fought to control the trembling of her lower lip at the calamity that had befallen the Lang household. But now facing her mother in the privacy of the master bedroom, she found her mother not in the least sympathetic. Instead, Millicent Lang's pleasant face lost its usual air of languorous tranquillity as she grasped her daughter's arm and gave it a firm shake.

"Grace, you're behaving badly! The Huttons' unexpected arrival is unfortunate, I admit. But I should think you'd know me better than to think I'd allow anyone to view my household in anything but perfect order. Now pull yourself together and go back downstairs. It's unforgivable of you to have left our guests alone just to follow me upstairs with your foolish whimpering."

Grace raised her short, pert nose, her pretty face assuming a pettish air at her mother's rebuke.

"The Huttons aren't alone downstairs, Mama. Papa and David are entertaining them, and you know Abigail and Beverly don't see anyone else at all when David's in the room."

"I suppose that's true." Pride brought a smile to Letty's lips that faded as she continued. "But that doesn't excuse your absence. Beverly is your friend, and entertaining her is your responsibility."

"But it's already three o'clock, Mama! How will Cook manage the increased number for dinner?"

"She'll manage. She always does. Now go downstairs and smile. We wouldn't want the Huttons to suspect their visit has put us at a disadvantage." Pausing, Letty looked unwavering into her daughter's face. "Is that understood?"

"Yes, Mama."

Waiting only until her daughter had slipped back out of the room, Letty raised a hand to her temple in an uncertain gesture she could not afford in her daughter's presence. Looking up as Margaret appeared in the doorway, Letty stiffened her back and spoke in a soft, urgent tone. "You're to see that all the bedrooms are set to right as quickly as possible, and I want you to tell Cook to serve tea now, so dinner may be delayed to afford her more time to accommodate our guests."

"Yes, ma'am."

Her expression tense, Letty smoothed a wayward blonde wisp from the back of her neck as Margaret disappeared from sight. Her reputation as an efficient housekeeper and faultless hostess was at stake, and she did not take the situation lightly. As difficult as some aspects of her life in Shenandoah had been in the past five years, she had never compromised her standards. This house was so beautiful and well kept that could be in the center of Philadelphia proper, instead of being isolated on a hilltop from which she could view only a devastated valley and the homes of a working class whose station was far below theirs. And as unexpected as was this visit from Harry and Sybil Hutton and their daughters, she was determined they would see both her home and herself only at their best.

In the hallway Letty turned toward the central staircase to the first floor, where her guests awaited her.

• • •

"Gather the fresh linens off the line and be quick about it, miss! The mistress wants everything in tip-top shape when she shows the Hutton family upstairs to their rooms."

Cook's instructions were issued in a brusque tone, but Meghan knew her curtness was not intentional. Pandemonium had broken loose in the servants' quarters upon the arrival of Mrs. Lang's unexpected guests, and she felt a sudden certainty that, despite the lateness of the hour, the day's work had only just begun.

Snatching up the laundry basket outside the door, she hastened toward the portion of the yard where the bed linens flapped in the afternoon breeze. Minutes later, she followed Margaret and Mabel up the rear staircase to the second floor.

It occurred to Meghan as she continued down the hallway behind the two women that this was the first time she had been allowed to set foot above the first floor of the house. Unable to deny her curiosity, she glanced around her at the lavish paintings that lined the walls, and the lush flowered runner beneath her feet. Stepping over the threshold of the bedroom into which she was directed, she could not restrain a gasp of amazement. The size of the place! The room she shared at Uncle Timothy's with Ma and Sean could fit into it four times over. There were huge windows that overlooked the rear yard, and there was a great, majestic bed—four towering posts and all! She was still marveling when a sharp voice snapped her from her bemusement.

"There's no time to waste, miss!"

Caught unawares, Meghan nodded in silent response. Her hands were working deftly at her chores a few minutes later when a smile slowly spread across her lips. Oh, she'd have plenty to tell Ma about the house on the hill tonight. She could hardly wait.

David's smile was forced. He just wasn't up to this effort today.

"You're so quiet, David. I thought you'd be happy to see me."

David looked at Abigail Hutton's petulant expression where she sat across from him in the living room. He groaned inwardly. Just a few weeks ago, he wouldn't have been able to think of anything that pleased him more than Abigail Hutton's visit, unexpected or not, or a better sight to behold than Abigail's strawberry blonde curls and flirtatious smile—not to mention the way her body filled her fashionable pink gown. A year younger than he, Abby was ripe and totally delicious in many ways, but somehow the memory of her soft, womanly proportions pressed tightly against him, and her gasping response to some of his more intimate explorations, had lost some of its potency. He wasn't opposed to getting to know her more intimately still, but he simply was not of a mind today for her inane conversation.

Glancing around the room, David was especially grateful that Grace had returned and claimed the attention of Abigail's younger sister, Beverly. For the truth was, he couldn't stand the girl's mooning gaze. Uncle Martin was discussing the state of the economy with Harry Hutton, and Mrs. Hutton appeared engrossed in their conversation. So, it appeared that left Abigail to him.

David suppressed a groan. He'd had a damned irritating day.

David glanced again at his uncle, and remorse for the angry words they had exchanged on the way home from the colliery swelled inside him. The argument was his fault. He had been more irritable than could be excused. Seeing Meghan O'Connor joking with that stable boy in the yard earlier had raised feelings he could not understand.

The truth was that he was still annoyed with himself. If he'd had the good sense to mind his own business that day in the study, Aunt Letty wouldn't have hired the girl, and he would have been spared the nagging of his conscience which had led to the mess he had made of things. One thing was certain. The girl was a thorn in his side, and he wasn't quite sure what to do about it.

Aside from that, David was uncomfortably aware that he owed his uncle an apology. It was the least he could do to relieve the weight of his uncle's many concerns, for the situation in Schuylkill County was grim and becoming worse. Prices of coal had plummeted, and it was frightening to think that the price was expected to drop even lower. The unannounced visit that morning from Franklin Gowen, Chief Counsel of the Philadelphia and Reading Railway, had caused a disagreement between Uncle Martin and himself that was based on his uncle's admiration for the man, while his own reaction to Gowen was quite the reverse. He distrusted the man's motives, and had told his uncle so in a way that had only raised his uncle's ire.

The poor situation in the coal fields was magnified ten-fold at the Lang Colliery. Uncle Martin's hard-nosed policy since the train wreck and murder of his spy had caused the unrest in the shafts to approach a danger point. Captain Linden had reported only that morning that there were rumors the Sons of Molly Maguire would soon be taking action again.

They had been fortunate that the Mollies' vengeance had not

come closer to home. It wasn't as if David feared for himself. He knew he was well able to take care of himself in any emergency, but the same could not be said for Aunt Letty or Grace.

"David . . ."

Abigail's whining snapped him from his thoughts as Aunt Letty walked back into the room. David released a silent sigh of relief that his dear aunt had arrived in time to take the pouting Abigail off his hands. Standing up, he smiled apologetically.

"If you'll excuse me, Abigail. There are some things I have to take care of upstairs." Responding to the girl's irate expression, he took her hand. "Once I'm free again for the evening, I look forward to a long conversation that will catch us up on all that's happened since I saw you last. Perhaps we can walk in the garden?"

Abigail's light flush revealed that she remembered only too well their last excursion there. She smiled widely, and David's inner groan deepened.

Acknowledging that his rapid path toward his room constituted temporary flight from the day's many irritations, David had reached the top of the staircase when sounds of unexpected activity coming from the bedrooms drew his attention. Glancing through the doorways as he passed, he saw Margaret first, hastily dressing the bed in the guestroom nearest the staircase. Mabel was working efficiently in the next. As he approached his own room, David slowed his step. Sounds of movement within indicated someone worked as industriously there as in the previous two, and process of elimination told him there was only one other person it could be.

A dark frown knitting his brow, David stepped into the doorway, his irritation soaring as his unpleasant expectations were fulfilled. Damn it all! This was the last straw! There was no escape from the little chit!

Turning to draw up the coverlet, the girl jumped at his unexpected presence and gasped, "By all that's holy, are you spying on me?"

Her question too close to the truth of his former behavior for comfort, David felt his face flame as he responded tightly, "Spying on you? This is my room!"

There was little satisfaction in the way the girl glanced around her, as if to verify his statement. When she failed to respond, he offered with a brittle smile, "Would you like to call Margaret in here to confirm my claim?"

Meghan's mouth twitched with the restraint of her reply. "I'll be finished in here in a minute. The coverlet—"

"Hang the coverlet!"

"But—"

"Out!"

The girl did not move. Certain that if the stubborn little twit didn't respond to his command soon instead of standing there, glaring at him, he'd—

Interrupting his mental railing, the girl spoke with quiet dignity. "My Ma's often said that the term 'gentleman' is loosely used these days. After having met you, Mr. David, I now know that to be true."

Turning, the girl walked past him into the hallway, and it was minutes before David realized that he was staring after her, his mouth agape.

Stepping back into the room, David grasped the handle of the door and slammed it shut with a force that rattled the hand-drawn, expensively framed map of the Pennsylvania coal fields on his wall, and caused his valued etching of William Penn to fall to the floor with a crash.

And it was at that moment he realized that Meghan O'Connor's short, departing statement was decidedly profound.

Meghan had walked several steps down the hallway when the slamming of the door behind her shattered the pregnant silence. Gritting her teeth against the anger that sound evoked, she turned into the nearest bedroom to find Margaret busy with a few, last-minute details. The older woman looked up with a frown as she approached.

"What was that noise I heard? It sounded like a door slamming."

"Yes, it did." When Margaret's frown darkened at her cryptic response, Meghan added innocently, "The window was open in one of the bedrooms. The breeze must have blown the door closed."

At Margaret's nod, Meghan picked up a new set of linens and moved on to the next bedroom, her conscience sore. Well, she hadn't lied. The window *was* open in David Lang's room, and the breeze *could* have blown the door shut.

But she knew it hadn't.

Meghan paused, frowning as she placed the clean linens on a nearby nightstand. She'd really done it this time, all right. She was uncertain why she had been unable to walk away from David Lang's arrogance without speaking up, but it was probably for the same reason that his nastiness seemed to be reserved for her alone. The truth of it was that the high-born nephew of the house and she grated on each other's nerves.

Meghan was suddenly angry. But another truth was that money did not make the man, and David Lang was a cad with no more manners than the poorest tramp traveling the rails. Not only that, he was a poor judge of people, ignorant of life's true values, and vain to boot! Neither she nor her brothers had a tenth of his schooling, but he was the one who was truly ignorant. And if the opportunity presented itself, she'd tell him so, too!

Meghan sighed. It was a hopeless predicament, for she knew that as much as she would have things different, she didn't truly regret anything she'd said to David Lang. He had deserved it.

How such a handsome face could hide such a devilish personality, was beyond her. All was lost here for her, and as Ma often said, only an act of God could save it.

David walked down the staircase toward the living room later that night, greatly subdued. He'd had the worst of days, and he was determined that it would conclude on a more pleasant note than it had begun. Accordingly, he had decided to take his uncle aside and voice his apology before the day ended. He was prepared to be cordial to Abigail and to exert the full force of his charm to compensate for his former discourteous behavior.

In order to please his aunt, he had donned her favorite suit, a dark serge that she had often remarked complemented his coloring to a fine degree, and had taken great pains with his appearance. His dark hair shining, his face smoothly shaven, his eyes reflecting his serious intent, he was prepared to be congenial to all, even the aggravating Beverly Hutton, whom he found difficult to endure. These things accomplished, he would succeed in reversing the negative flow of the day, and his conscience would be set to rest—almost.

David joined the quietly conversing group prepared to enter the dining room. It didn't take more than a few minutes to see that Abigail would be easily won over, and his tension relaxed the slightest degree. Catching his uncle's eye, he saw to his relief not the slightest sign of hostility there, and he was vastly relieved. He saw the approval in Aunt Letty's gaze, and he knew she was aware of the effort he had expended to please her. He even managed a halfhearted smile for Beverly, along with a wink for Grace.

Observing the strictest etiquette, he seated Abigail at the table, relieved to see that Beverly and Grace had seated themselves, and retired to his chair. His conversation with Abigail was progressing nicely, and he found himself warming to her coy, provocative glances. He was beginning to feel decidedly better when Aunt Letty rang her little silver bell for the first course.

David looked up as Mabel's lumbering bulk entered the room, followed by a smaller, daintier figure. He stared in disbelief. Brilliant blue eyes met his, turning glacial as Meg O'Connor set a plate of steaming soup in front of him with great care. David stiffened, his stomach knotting with a familiar irritation.

Watching as the girl followed Mabel back into the kitchen, David was at a loss with his ambivalence. He felt an abject desire to encircle that skinny white neck with his hands and squeeze for all he was worth, yet he admired the little chit's indomitable spirit.

Still engrossed in his thoughts, David mechanically spooned his soup into his mouth. His eyes bulging as the scalding liquid scorched his tongue, he swallowed convulsively, choking and gasping as the blistering fluid burned a fiery path to his stomach.

Attempting to alleviate the concern of those around him with a sickly smile as he caught his breath, David silently acknowledged he had been too optimistic a few minutes earlier. He should have realized the moment that blue-eyed little Irish witch stepped into the room that he could expect the worst.

It was growing dark as Sean made his way home along the nearly deserted street with an easy swagger reminiscent of better times. Swinging his lunch bucket, he pushed back his cap and grinned as Uncle Timothy's house came into view, his smile faltering only when he considered the thought that he was hours late coming home from his shift, and that Ma and Meg must have begun to worry at his being so delayed. But he consoled himself that he had good reason.

Sean's smile widened, his even teeth appearing even whiter against a face blackened with coal dust. Ah, yes, his heart was lighter in the knowledge that he'd begun taking control of his life at last. A low laugh escaping his throat, Sean admitted a portion of his present lightheartedness could also be called lightheadedness, resulting from the hours he's spent conversing and imbibing at Muff Lawler's place.

His eyes suddenly growing more serious, Sean nodded to himself. He'd taken a wise step when he'd first walked across Lawler's threshold almost a week earlier and revealed his commitment to become a part of the society there. Too young to be accepted by the older members, he'd been taken under the wing of some of the younger fellows, only a few years older than he, and this afternoon that contact had proved its worth.

Aye, it was just like Da said. Word got around, even if names and particulars didn't. A man just had to put himself in the place where he'd hear what was to go on, and Muff Lawler's was that place. And Lenny Dunne, his newest friend and a proud Irishman to boot, was a man on the in.

Feeling too good to take the usual precaution to dust the coal dust from his clothes before entering the house, Sean dropped his pail by the back door and stepped inside. His grin faded slightly as Aunt Fiona's small, tired eyes rose to meet his, and he felt a moment's shame for his coldness toward this woman of his own blood. Consoling himself a moment later that his aunt had done nothing to earn more from him, he returned her glance with silence.

"Yer late, Sean. Ye've missed yer supper, but it's plain to see that ye've had yer fill anyway. Aye . . ."

Sean frowned at his aunt's unwanted criticism, his resentment obvious as he lifted his chin in uncharacteristic arrogance. "Aye, I've had a few, but I'm not near the state you find your own husband in most nights. And I tell you now, I've no intention of growin' in his image—not that it's any of your concern, Aunt."

"But yer Ma's me concern, and she's been worryin', upstairs all alone in her room, waitin' for ye to come home."

"Alone, you say?" All trace of arrogance leaving his young face, Sean was suddenly alert as he took an anxious step forward. "Where's Meg? Why ain't she with Ma?"

"A young fella that works at the Lang place came down with word to yer Ma that she'd be workin' late at the house. Them Langs have some people visitin' that weren't expected, and she—"

Fiona halted abruptly at the terror flaring in Sean's eyes in the moment before he turned sharply toward the dark hillside behind him.

"What's wrong, Sean? What do ye know? What's—"

Reacting without conscious thought, Sean bolted out of the house. He crossed the boardwalk toward the street in a few long steps and broke into a run. He was breathless from his mad dash when he gradually slowed his step, squinting in the limited light in an attempt to locate the rough path that wound up the hill to the rear of the Lang residence.

"Does it seem to you that Mr. David ain't up to his usual self tonight, Mabel?"

Margaret's soft inquiry was met with Mabel's worried grunt as she arranged the bread artfully on her tray. The kitchen of the Lang residence was unaccustomedly crowded with all hands contributing to the preparation and serving of the first meal for the unexpected guests, and Meghan listened with silent disgust to the servants' concern for their darling pet.

"I've seldom seen him quiet as he is tonight." Mabel's tone confirmed her concern. "Not that he's the type to be loud or overbearing, mind, but I'd say his mind's not on the present company, that's for sure. And I'm telling you now, Miss Abigail Hutton ain't taking it kindly. Why that young miss is fit to burst." Meghan paused in her task of scooping the roasted potatoes from the pan, her eyes moving to Mabel's jowled face as the woman continued, "No, Mr. David ain't really been himself of late at all, and I don't mind telling you, I'm worried for the boy. His uncle's driving him hard at the mine, and he's not one to spare himself."

Meghan barely restrained a laugh. David Lang, selfless and giving without sparing himself? That wasn't the David Lang *she* knew! Not realizing her thoughts were so apparent, Meghan was startled as Cook turned hotly toward her.

"I'll not have you mock Mr. David in my presence, miss! He's a fine young man, who's better than most you'll ever know, and I'll thank you to keep your sassy looks and comments to yourself. You're not above being turned out on your ear, you know. It's only Mr. David who's stood up for you in the past, and you've shown him little appreciation for it. If you keep up this tack, I'll speak to Mrs. Lang myself and I'll—"

Thudding footsteps at the back door interrupted Cook's harangue, turning all eyes toward Johnny Law's white face as he stumbled in from the yard, breathless.

"Fire! There's a fire in the stables, and it's a bad one!"

"Quick, inside to the dining room with you, to the master!"

Following Cook's instructions, Johnny ran across the room and pushed open the dining room door. His unexpected appearance there was all that was needed to bring the men of the house to their feet.

"Fire, sir! In the stables!"

In a flurry of movement, the men kicked back their chairs and turned at a run. Meg heard the women's frightened squeals as they jumped to their feet and followed, but she did not realize she was racing out into the darkness behind them until she first saw flames leap against the night sky.

Easily outdistancing his uncle, David reached a scene of wild pandemonium. The stable burned in a brilliant fiery display against the black sky, the thick smoke and searing heat emanating from the blaze intense. Terrified whinnies rent the night air, punctuating a din of roaring flames, creaking beams, and anxious shouts. All around him terrified, wild-eyed horses rescued from the fire screamed their protest as stable hands and grounds guards alike attempted to restrain them. A disorganized brigade threw buckets of water at the flames, their frustrated shouts growing louder as the fire grew more intense.

Shrieking whinnies from within the blazing structure ripped at David's insides. He grasped Townsend's arm as the stocky, gray-haired man strove to bring a semblance of order to the chaotic scene.

"Townsend, how many horses are still inside?"

"Three."

"Fabian?"

"He's in the rear stall. We can't get him out."

"Can't get him out? The west side of the building isn't fully engulfed. We can get him out there."

"The roof's ready to go. I can't send my men in."

David shot a desperate look into the growing inferno. He could make it. He had to try!

With no thought to safety, David broke into a spontaneous run, his mind registering the incredible heat of the flames as he cleared the doorway. The smoke so thick that he was unable to see a few feet ahead of him, David halted just inside the door, gasping for breath as he attempted to get his bearings. The burning heat seared his lungs as a wall of smoke closed around him, and panic touched his mind in the moment before a shrill whinny sounded nearby. Staggering a few feet forward, he saw Ribbon Lady straining at her halter, her wild eyes bulging with fear, and he yanked the stall door open, managing to untie her just as a hand reached around him from behind to take the lead from his grasp. Nodding as a young stablehand led the frantic mare out of the building, David gasped for breath, coughing and swaying as the intensifying heat increased his confusion.

He heard another frenzied whinny nearby and recognized the sound. Fabian! He could hear the big fellow, but he couldn't see him.

A strong grip on his arm turned him unexpectedly, and he saw Townsend peering at him from under a water-soaked blanket, but the man's words were muffled by the crackling roar.

". . . out of here! The roof . . ."

Again Fabian's shrill cry for help, and David shook off Townsend's clutching grip and headed toward the sound. Only a few steps more and he'd find him. He couldn't give up now.

But the smoke was too thick. It blinded him, choking him, and David swayed weakly, disoriented. He couldn't breathe, couldn't stand, and he dropped to his knees. The heat . . . the flames . . .

Flat on his face as he gasped for breath, David crawled toward the agonized whinnies. He was almost there . . . almost, when the thought penetrated the muddled functioning of his mind that the whinnies had ceased.

A new, more terrifying sound filtered through David's addled consciousness—the snap of breaking timbers. David looked up, squinting as tears ran from the corners of his burning eyes. The roof seemed to flutter over his head, lifting and swaying with the power of the flames devouring it.

Choking, his lungs aflame in his chest, David stared upward, the fiery outline of the massive beam above him the last thing he saw as the heat consumed him.

Frozen with horror, Meghan stared at the blazing stables, unable to look away as the roar of the fire reached a deafening crescendo. Her mindless step had brought her to the terrifying scene shortly after David Lang, and she had called out in spontaneous protest as he had dashed into the inferno. Shocked, she had watched as Martin Lang arrived breathless a few moments later, and she had seen incredulity turn to horror as Townsend shouted over the roaring flames that David had gone inside.

Uncertain exactly what happened after that, her stunned mind registered a blur of movement as Mr. Lang attempted to follow his nephew into the flames but was forcibly restrained. Unexpectedly, a stable hand broke away from the frantic scene and ran into the flaming building. Her relief was intense when he came out a few moments later, pulling a fear-crazed mare to safety.

But David Lang did not emerge.

Townsend threw a water-soaked blanket over his head and dashed into the blazing structure. As Meghan watched, he stumbled back out a few minutes later, gasping for breath as his men dragged him to safety.

Hysterical crying behind her grew louder as the entrance to the stables ringed in flame. The snap of burning timbers jerked her gaze up to the roof as it shuddered and swayed. An echo of shrieking protest rose in her throat.

But what was that—a shadow, something moving along the ground just inside the entrance, crawling . . . ?

It was . . . !

Meghan raced toward the burning entrance, reaching it as the timbers overhead groaned a deep warning. The roof shuddered above her as she reached David's side and grasped his coat. He was unconscious, and she pulled with all her strength as the cracking of the beams grew louder.

Unexpectedly, rough hands swept her from her feet and out into the night air. She was coughing violently when she saw two other men drag David Lang's limp form into the open.

She was staring at his motionless body, shaking uncontrollably, when the blazing roof crashed to the ground, but she no longer saw the flames. Instead she turned to look at the people around her—Millicent Lang crying over her nephew's prostrate figure, her husband, stricken, beside her—Grace Lang weeping in Mr. Hutton's arms—Mrs. Hutton and her daughters clutching each other, silent, staring. Johnny Law, Mr. Townsend, the stable hands, miscellaneous guards . . . all were safe. Only David Lang was—

Suddenly David Lang was coughing, his lean body jerking with violent spasms as he sought to draw cleansing air into his tortured lungs. He was gasping, choking. He twisted momentarily toward her, and she saw tears streaming down his cheeks.

But he was alive.

Turning slowly, Meghan walked back to the house. She was strangely numb. Experiencing neither elation nor sadness, she had only one thought. The fire had not won this time—as it had with Da and the boys.

• • •

From the fringe of darkness surrounding the fire, Sean watched his sister walk back toward the house, his heart hammering wildly in his chest. He saw her look back at the stable as she reached the doorway, and fought the desire to rush from his hiding place to take her in his arms and reassure himself that she was safe and well.

Meg stepped out of sight and a low, ragged sound escaped Sean's throat. Covering his eyes, he gave full vent to his terror as he sobbed deep and long into his hands. If anything had happened to his Meg . . .

He'd not thought for a minute when he'd heard the Mollies were planning to burn the Lang mansion that there was any chance Meg would be in danger. During her month of employment, she'd never returned home later than six, and he'd known the Mollies wouldn't make their move until dark, when they could sneak past the guards with a measure of safety. His horror upon realizing Meg was in danger was worse than anything he had suffered in his life.

He had been halfway up the hill when he had first spotted the flames, and was all for running straight for the house without thought of cover before he came to the crest of the hill and realized that it wasn't the house that was afire, but the stables. Frantically searching the crowd gathered outside the stable, he had seen Meghan standing a distance from the others as all attention focused on a motionless figure lying on the ground. His relief had been overwhelming.

For the first time he was grateful for Lang's guards, grateful that the Mollies hadn't been able to slip past them to fire the house as they had planned. His Meg, his dear Meg was safe and well, and that was the only thing that was important to him. Only Meg—and seeing that the Langs pay their due.

Chapter 6

David was lost again in the choking smoke that haunted him. The heat seared him. Disoriented, he staggered blindly, each faltering step seeming to take him deeper into the fire.

Echoes of shrill, frenzied whinnies increased in volume, reverberating in his ears as an unseen fire licked at his face and hands, burning him. Almost mad from the sound, he turned to see Fabian, and his fear turned to terror. The great horse reared above him, flames leaping from his eyes and mouth, pain reflected in every sinew of his powerful body as he twisted and thrashed in agony.

But David's own pain was such that he was helpless to aid the tortured animal. Instead, gasping for breath, the pounding in his head so severe that he could not think, he struggled to remain standing.

He sank to his knees as flames began consuming the great animal beside him. The sounds of Fabian's physical torment grew louder, and David called out, but his scorched throat refused to emit the sound. The horse reared once more in the throes of an agonizing death, his powerful hooves lashing out, and David grunted in pain as he was struck to the ground.

The smoke and flames a deadly blanket above him, David managed to turn his head. Fabian lay beside him, his eyes empty sockets from which fire blazed. The smell of burning flesh caught in his nostrils, and he retched at the realization that it was his own.

The flames were devouring him, and David cried aloud as life seeped from his body slowly, excruciatingly. The echoes of Fabian's cries mingled with his own as he called for deliverance.

But no one heard him.

"David!"

The sound of his name dragged David from the edge of an endless eternity.

"David, speak to me, dear. Please."

David opened his eyes to Aunt Letty's tear-streaked face, but he could not respond.

"David, dear, please."

David closed his eyes to his aunt's plea. He could do no more. He was gone, you see. He had ceased to exist.

Meghan knew the face of mourning, and as she looked around the silent Lang kitchen, she recognized it plainly. Two days had passed since the fire, and in the Lang household she was no longer an outsider foisted upon the staff by Mrs. Lang's guilt. The fire had succeeded in burning away the ragged edge of resentment against her, and she was now treated with courtesy and respect, if not affection. She knew the staff's change of attitude would be more complete if she were to display the same guise of mourning as they, but she felt little of their despair. Instead, a familiar resentment was building inside her that she sensed she would soon find impossible to conceal.

The whispers, the catering, the low sympathetic clucks all turned her stomach. There had been no real tragedy here, and she would not pretend there had been. David Lang was alive. And he had shown himself unworthy of the life restored to him by throwing it back in God's face. He had accepted the gift as he had all the other advantages in his life, without gratitude.

Da and the boys would not have done the same.

Father Matthew's words returned to her mind with a clarity that could not be ignored, and Meghan paused in her angry thoughts. He had advised her against bitterness, telling her it would hurt her and her own more than those against whom it was directed. But her present bitterness was difficult to overcome.

Darting a glance at the silent staff around her, Meghan reached for another potato and skillfully peeled it. No, she'd not grieve for one who'd received more than he deserved, while Da and the boys had received far less.

No, she would not shed a tear.

"Are you angry with me, Meg?"

The courage to ask that question had been difficult for Sean to find. In the two days since the fire, Meghan had been unnaturally quiet, but all in Uncle Timothy's household had attributed her silence to the shock she had suffered at the Lang fire, with its reminder of Da and the boys' deaths. But it was tonight, after she spent some time in Ma's room with Aunt Fiona, that she had emerged with an accusation in her eyes.

Sean breathed deeply and steeled himself for his sister's reply.

Her eyes were still averted from his, and Sean looked around the kitchen to make certain curious ears were not within hearing distance. But it was late, two hours past supper. Aunt Fiona had retired to her room, and Uncle Timothy had not yet returned from his favorite *shebeen*. Since the other boarders seldom lingered past the meal hour, he had been certain he would find his sister alone when he followed her downstairs a few minutes earlier.

His gaze lingering on her small face as he awaited her reply, Sean felt a familiar thickness rise in his throat. She'd be a beauty someday, would be his Meg. Her features were so fine, and her eyes were shining mirrors of her bright soul. O'Connor was written as clearly across her face as it was across his own, but where he was a pleasant looking fellow, Meg's unusual beauty was growing each day. He saw that, now that the thinness of childhood was beginning to slip away. She'd always been a tiny lass, and she was still, but her daintiness was beginning to take on a different shape. It meant that she'd soon be courted by some young fellow, and the truth was that there wasn't a man good enough for Meg in this valley, where the sun was dulled by a dusty mist from the colliery that never truly settled to the ground, and where a man was bound to groveling in the earth for the whole of his life from the sheer lack of a choice to do else and survive.

Aware that Meg still had not responded to his question, Sean swallowed against the painful frustration that now directed the course of his life. His eyes still on his sister's averted face, he told himself as he had so many times before that the future Da wanted for them had died with him. The responsibility for Meg's future and his own now was his. The only trouble was that he had almost bungled it, and bungled it badly. And Meg, the other part of himself, the only good and joyful part that remained, had come close to suffering for it.

Sean bit down on his lower lip, a frown tightening his youthful brow. He'd not had the courage to speak truthfully to Meg of the fire on the hill, but he knew Aunt Fiona had finally spoken to her of his behavior that night. He also knew he needed to set the matter straight between them, and that the time had come to do it.

"Meg?"

Meg's eyes snapped up to his with a suddenness that was as startling as her whispered question.

"Did you have something to do with the fire, Sean? I want you to tell me true, for I've not the heart for the pain of not knowing."

Reaching out a tentative hand, Sean rested it on his sister's narrow shoulder as he attempted a smile.

"And I've not the heart to see you turn from me another time. Nay, I had no hand in it, but I knew of the plan."

"You knew some were to set fire to the stables in the hopes of burning innocent animals alive, or maybe catching a poor stable boy, ignorant of the affairs of the valley? Where's the justice in that?"

"It wasn't to be the stables, Meg. It was to be the house itself."

Meg's gasp tore at Sean's heart, but his bitterness would not allow him shame.

"It's no worse than what's been done to some down here. Whole families have been put out to starve when Master Lang closed a shaft through a whim, and troops called in to bring us all to our knees when we strike in protest."

"But the fire was deliberate!"

Tears welled in Meg's eyes, and Sean felt the first pang of true regret for the events of that night on the hill. Touching his sister's cheek with a gentle hand, he whispered hoarsely, "I never for a moment thought you'd be in danger, Meg. I thought you'd be safe at home when it all came about, so I had no fear for you at first. It was only afterward, when I came home and Aunt Fiona told me you were workin' late that I—" Sean paused to take his racing emotions under control, a defensive frown darkening his brow. "But you've naught to fear now. I've heard it from good sources that the organization's put the house off limits—that they've found it's not worth the risk."

Meg shook her head, her bright eyes cloudy as she looked up into his face. "Strange to hear one of my own say it's not worth the risk of one life, when he speaks of taking others."

"Meg, you've been too long at that place. You're forgettin'—"

"I'm forgetting nothing, Sean! And I want you to make me a promise. I want you to tell me you'll not let something like this happen again without giving warning. Tell me, Sean!"

"Meg—"

Her blue eyes intent, Meghan stared into his face with a gaze that seared him, and Sean felt his anger melt away. This was his Meg, after all, and he owed her something for the way he had almost failed her. The cost would be slight in granting her this request, for, in truth, it would change very little. "Aye, I promise."

With a choking sound, Meg stepped forward and wrapped her arms around his waist to hug him close. Closing his arms around her in return, Sean felt his throat tighten.

Aye, this was his Meg after all, and he sore loved her.

"Mama, David won't talk to me!" Facing her mother in the hallway outside David's room, Grace continued despairingly, "I tried and tried and talked and talked. I attempted to feed him breakfast, too, as you asked, but he wouldn't take a thing. He opened his eyes and looked at me, but I don't think he saw me at all. Oh, Mama, do you suppose he's blind?"

Letty drew her daughter into her arms, glancing over her shoulder toward the door to David's room. She had experienced similar fears many times in the past three days.

Stepping back, Letty tilted up her daughter's pretty face and saw that it was blotched and wet with tears. There was still more child than woman in this girl who usually made such a great effort to appear mature.

"Mama, what's wrong with David?"

Curling her arm around Grace's shoulder, Letty drew her along down the hall.

"Dr. Biel says David is suffering a form of shock, dear. The burns on his face are minor, although the ones on his hands are a bit more severe. It's the wounds he suffers in his mind that are the true problem."

"Mama, his eyes . . ."

"He can see, dear, but he's suffered a trauma. Right now our only fear is—" Momentarily unable to go on, Letty took a deep breath, aware that her brimming eyes were causing a resumption of her daughter's agitated state. She attempted a smile. "As you know, David hasn't eaten since that night, and we've only been able to get a little liquid past his lips. If he continues this way for much longer, Dr. Biel is worried that he might—"

"Oh, Mama!" Breaking down into sobs, Grace threw her arms around her mother, resting her pale head on the woman's shoulder. "I don't want anything to happen to David. I'd be so lonely without him."

Realizing tears streaked her own cheeks as well, Letty patted her daughter's back and whispered in a breaking voice, "Then I suppose we must do all we can to help him. And we must pray,

Grace. David is such a good boy. Surely our prayers will be answered."

Her gentle heart breaking, Letty led her daughter down the hall.

Meg climbed the rear staircase to the second floor, a deep frown marring her clear brow. There had been many changes in the Lang household since the day of the fire. She was now allowed to work on the second floor with Margaret due to the older woman's increased duties in sharing the care of David Lang.

Stepping onto the second floor, Meg took a deep breath. Sean's shared confidence the previous night had left its mark on her, and she was greatly ill at ease. The former antagonism she had felt for David Lang had turned to guilt with the realization that one of her own had been responsible for his injuries. In truth, if the household were not so preoccupied, she was certain they would easily have read the guilt on her face. Strangely, though, her guilt only made her resent the young master more.

Meghan had not entered David Lang's room nor seen him since the fire, and she was glad. Mrs. Lang had personally expressed her appreciation for Meghan's help in rescuing her nephew. She supposed this new freedom in the house was Mrs. Lang's way of showing her appreciation, but Meg was not particularly impressed with her new "honor." As far as she was concerned, the farther she stayed away from David Lang, the better.

Upon reaching his bedroom door, Meg knocked lightly. It had become her duty to deliver Mr. David's meal to Margaret, and to return an hour later to bring the tray back to the kitchen. There its untouched contents caused a new round of sniffles and worried clucks from the staff below. Were it not for Mabel's faulty legs, Meg would have been spared the chore; and she wished very desperately she had, so greatly did she despise it.

Frowning when her knock did not bring the usual response, Meg waited a moment longer and knocked again. A sluggish step sounded from beyond the door in the moment before it was drawn open to reveal Margaret's white face.

Stunned by the maid's sickly appearance, Meg was silent as Margaret whispered weakly, "I'm not feeling well, miss, as you can doubtless see. The mistress will return shortly, but I've not the strength to wait. You may tell her when she arrives that it's the old complaint—she'll understand. In the meantime, you may take my place here."

Meghan's gaze swept past the woman toward the unmoving shape on the bed, but she did not move.

"In here now, miss! I've not much strength left, and Mr. David can't be left alone."

Meghan took a few tentative steps toward the bed as the door closed behind Margaret. Still, she hesitated. It was not as if the sight of a sleeping male was unfamiliar to her. The small patch house where she'd grown up with Da and the boys had allowed little privacy. Nor was it the idea of sickness itself. Was it not she who had nursed Sean through the month-long illness which had kept him out of the shaft that fateful day the others were killed?

But, somehow, this was different.

Quietly approaching the bed, Meghan noted the elaborate comforter that covered David's still form, the lace-trimmed bed linens and pillow slips on which he lay, those that had been washed with her own hands. They were far different from the simple cotton used at home, as was the fine lawn nightshirt that covered his broad, motionless shoulders.

Laying the tray on a nearby table, Meghan looked at David's still face, and a sudden anger transfused her. He was hardly marked at all! His handsome face bore a tender, reddish look, similar to the look of skin irritated by the first of the summer sun's hot rays, but beyond that, it had not a scar. Looking at his hands, Meghan saw they were both bandaged and the flesh exposed above the wrist had showed signs of a deeper burn. Aye, there would be some pain there, but she'd seen many a man suffer similar injuries, and worse.

Studying him more closely, Meghan saw his dark, waving hair had been badly singed, and that it appeared his well-shaped brows had suffered a similar fate. She was staring at him with increasing concentration when his eyes opened suddenly, and he gave a short tortured cry.

Meghan jumped back in surprise, expecting a sharp reprimand typical of his difficult personality, but there was no recognition in David Lang's gaze. Instead, she saw a frenzy stir to life as unseen terrors were released before his mind's eye. Suddenly twisting and turning in the throes of his vivid nightmare, David called out desperately, sending tremors of fear down her spine.

As she watched, his torment grew visibly stronger, and Meghan's fears slipped away as an unexpected anguish came to life inside her.

Ashamed of her harsh judgment of him, and of the bitterness

that had allowed her to acknowledge no pain but her own, Meghan stepped closer to the bed. Taking the cloth that lay on the nightstand, she dipped it into the basin of cool water there. Without a second thought, she sat down on the side of the bed and began to bathe his anguished face.

David's eyes closed and his agitation appeared to lessen. Encouraged, Meghan dampened the cloth once more and placed it against his lips. His mouth moved lightly against it, and Meghan marveled at how different he appeared with arrogance absent from his even features. He looked as vulnerable and appealing as her own dear brothers. Like her brothers, aye, but different in a way that touched a new place inside her. However, the tenderness she felt was as true and full as if he were one of her own.

Slipping into a mode of gentle consolation which mimicked her dear mother's soft brogue, Meghan leaned down to whisper in David's ear as Ma had so often comforted her when she was ill.

"Rest tight in yer mind, and cease yer worryin'. Ye've those who love ye and bear yer care gladly. Yer sufferin', aye, but it'll come to an end if ye stir yer mind from that place of dark shadows. Look up and open yer eyes again to really see. 'Tis a bright day full of sunshine and light, and ye've been given the blessin' of life."

Her own thoughts momentarily darkening, Meghan paused, her quiet brogue slipping away as she continued softly. "Open your eyes, David Lang, and look about. You've loved ones all around you, and a life far better than many. You mustn't cast it away because of a faint heart."

David had grown still under her ministrations, and, encouraged, Meghan damped the cloth once more to run it over his face. His eyes opened again, but she remained perched on the side of his bed, her former fears allayed as she mused that perhaps Father Matthew was right. Perhaps she would come to know and understand these Langs after all, and the bitterness would disappear.

Meg was running the cloth against David's cheek when she realized that his eyes searched her face, that the peculiar ring of green that surrounded the dark pupils of his eyes had widened so that it almost excluded the soft brown rim. It was then that she saw the familiar lines of a frown crease his forehead and saw him blink.

Her heart beginning a steady hammering, Meg smiled, almost

unwilling to speak for fear her hopes would be dashed to disappointment.

"Tell me true, Mr. David. Are you really awake or are you looking at me through eyes that don't see?" David continued to stare, and she prompted softly, "Do you hear me, truly?"

David Lang's full, parched lips moved in a faint whisper, and Meg's heart pounded louder. Leaning down, she put her ear to his mouth and strained to hear as he whispered once more.

Jerking back as the grating sound registered in her mind, she stared at him in silence, only to hear him rasp more clearly than before. "It *is* you. What are you doing here?"

Uncertain that he had merely changed one haunting dream for another, David blinked again at the clear blue eyes returning his stare. But there was no response to his question, and David searched the small, heart-shaped face above his with growing confusion. He had been lost in a nightmarish world for so long. Even now as that still face stared down at him, he remembered the horror of eyes that blazed with fire, the choking thickness that filled his lungs, burning him. Shrill cries of pain, some of them his own, still echoed in his ears, and he fought their terrifying control of his senses.

Still the girl didn't speak, and David fought an escalating fear. He remembered the soft voice that penetrated his dark dreams. It was different from the others, speaking in a quiet, lilting tone that was foreign to his mind. But it soothed him as the others had not, and he sensed in it a note that went beyond understanding.

Then the voice changed, and he recognized it more clearly. With recognition came disbelief that forced him awake, and his eyes opened once more to a clear, brilliant gaze bathing him with unexpected concern. The concern he saw there comforted him, but it was the unexpected smile that forced the first words from his lips.

But there was no response.

David's mouth was parched and his head was pounding. He licked his dry lips. The girl touched the moist cloth to his mouth again, and he raised his hand to hold hers fast, only to gasp at the pain the effort caused him.

"Breathe deep. That's right. Da always said that a man was master over pain when he breathed deep and firm."

David wanted to speak. He wanted an answer to his question.

He wanted to know why this girl who so despised him now sat on the side of his bed and consoled him.

And he wanted to know why he wanted her to remain.

The girl was slipping her slender arm under his neck and was raising a glass to his lips. The cool water was as sweet as nectar to him and he grunted his protest as she allowed him only a few, short sips.

"No, you mustn't overdo. In a little while you may have some more."

Submitting to her restrictions without further protest, David allowed himself to be lowered back to his pillow. When she had settled him down, weakness began taking its toll even as he managed to rasp again, "What are you doing here?"

There was a long silence as the girl's expression became pensive. When she finally spoke, her response gave him little enlightenment, and as his eyes drifted closed her cryptic reply echoed in the shadowed chambers of his mind.

"I thought that I came to help heal you, but now I wonder if the healing might not be my own."

Father Matthew was uncomfortably warm, but he was uncertain whether the weather or the circumstance caused his discomfort as he made his way up the familiar narrow street toward the O'Reillys' front door. Surely the sun was warm on this fine afternoon, but the breeze was brisk enough to prevent overheating. He could only conclude that the urgent request he had received a short time earlier to visit with Mary O'Connor was the true source of his disquiet.

Squinting as a gust of wind raised the fine dust of the road to sting his face, Father Matthew turned briefly to the side. His vision clear, he ascended the steps to the O'Reillys' front door and knocked.

Father Matthew rubbed a hand across his troubled brow. He had come to console Mary O'Connor, but in truth, it was Meghan he was worried about. She was caught in a morass from which she had little hope of escaping and he feared her bright light would be squandered.

Checking his thoughts abruptly, Father Matthew felt a flush of shame color his cheeks. So great was his concern for the daughter, that he was giving little thought to the mother who lay in her deathbed within this house. Sparing not another moment, Father Matthew knocked again. The sound of rushing footsteps from within revealed the anxiety that awaited his arrival, and he prepared for the worst.

Fiona greeted him soberly and Father Matthew followed her upstairs. Cautiously opening the door to Mary O'Connor's room, he released a short, relieved breath, for as frail and white as was Mary, her eyes were clear and strong with determination. His smile sincere, he approached the bed and took her hand.

"Ah, Mary, you had me that worried when I received your summons. I thought you had been taken bad."

But Mary didn't return his smile. Instead, she clutched his hand and drew him down to the chair beside her bed with a surprisingly strong grip as Fiona retired quietly to the corner of the room.

"Nay, Father, me time's not come yet, but in truth, I feel it gettin' nearer." Smiling when Father Matthew declined comment on her statement, Mary squeezed his hand with what appeared to be the last of her strength as her arm then dropped limply to the bed beside her. "Aye, ye know it as well as I, and I thank ye for not denying it. But, ye see, knowin' me fate has forced the urgency of things, Father, and I would ask yer help so I might pass on with some measure of comfort."

"Mary, you know the concern I feel for Sean and Meghan is great. They're dearer to me than my own blood."

"Aye, and I know though Sean's been a thorn in yer side these long months since Dennis and the boys passed on, ye understand his bitterness, and don't fault him for his lapse of faith."

Father Matthew frowned, his anger self-directed. "I've failed the boy, Mary. I've not been able to reach him, and were it not for Meg and you, I fear he'd not give me the time of day."

Fear entered Mary's dark, sunken eyes, and her breathing quickened as her color turned gray. "But ye've not given up on the boy, Father!"

"No . . . no . . ." Taking Mary's hand again, Father Matthew was startled at its sudden chill. It was the coldness of death, and an unexpected tension gripped his stomach. "Sean's a good boy, Mary, and I'd not give up on him."

Nodding, her breathing slowing back to normal, Mary closed her eyes briefly before continuing in an earnest voice. "It's because of Sean I've called ye here, ye see, Father." Darting a glance toward her sister, she then turned her attention fully back in his direction. "Ye know of the fire at the Lang place, Father."

"Yes, I heard. I was frightened for Meg when I first saw the flames, before I realized she was at home by then."

"She was workin' late, Father. She was there, all right."

Mary's statement struck Father Matthew speechless. Meg's lessons had dropped to thrice weekly, and he had seen Meg since the fire, but she hadn't mentioned a word.

Tears filled Mary's eyes as she continued in a lower tone. "Aye, yer right to look shocked, but yer no more shocked than was Sean when he came home to find that his sister was still at that place. He knew about the fire before it could be seen from the valley, Father! Whether he had part in it or not is somethin' of which I'm unsure."

A tear slipped down Mary's cheek at that, but she wiped it away with a firm hand. "I told Meg the whole of it, Father, and it hit her hard. But she had to know the direction Sean's leanin', ye see, if she's to help him. And it was me thought that ye'd need to know, too, if ye was to guide him from that path."

Mary paused for another deep breath, her strength obviously waning. Gaunt and pale as she was, she looked suddenly closer to death than ever, and tears sprang unexpectedly into Father Matthew's eyes.

Mary smiled. "I can see the depth of yer feelin's for me children, Father, and I know, now, they're in as good hands here as I can expect them to be. But I'll ask one more thing of ye, if I may."

"Of course, Mary."

"It's a thing I've asked of Meg, too—that ye not give up on the boy, no matter how difficult he may be. But I also ask of ye, that whatever Sean chooses to do, ye try to remember that Dennis O'Connor's blood flows in his veins, and that makes his heart good, and that makes him worth all yer effort and more."

"I'll remember, Mary. And you may set your mind at rest that everything you've said to me this day has been taken into my heart."

"Aye, Father, aye. I can see it in yer eyes. I've naught to fear in leavin' what's left of me brood in yer hands."

Momentarily unable to respond, Father Matthew nodded. "I thank you for your confidence. I hope to be worthy of it. Shall we pray together now, Mary? Your Heavenly Father likes to hear your voice."

Gripping Mary's hand more tightly at her solemn nod, Father Matthew crossed himself with a fervent, silent prayer for the strength and the wisdom to help Sean. For even as Mary's weak voice joined his, he saw no way that he could reach the boy.

Meg raised the spoon to David's lips and slipped the warm broth into his mouth. He accepted it without comment, and as she dipped the spoon to the plate once more, she heard a low sound from the side of the room that turned her briefly toward Grace Lang's tight face. A moment later, Mrs. Lang ushered the girl out of the room, but Meg had no time to ponder the reason for their quick departure as she raised the spoon again to the young master's mouth.

Her eyes on Mr. David's face, she was aware that despite his brief period of consciousness earlier in the day, things had not gone well. She remembered turning around after he slipped back to sleep to realize that Mrs. Lang had entered the room and witnessed their entire halting exchange. She then became aware of her improper position, seated as she was on the side of the young master's bed. She immediately slipped her feet to the floor and began her explanations, but Mrs. Lang remained curiously silent as Meghan gathered up the tray and left the room.

There was turmoil in the household after that. Dr. Biel was summoned and dismissed with little progress noted in Mr. David's condition. The lunch tray was delivered and returned without being touched. In the kitchen where she had returned to work, it was rumored that Mr. David had rallied only to fall back into the same unnatural sleep, and she had been more disturbed than she expected by the thought.

She was summoned to the library shortly afterward and arrived to find both the master and mistress waiting for her. She was startled to see Mrs. Lang's usually smooth complexion was blotchy, her eyes red-rimmed, and Meghan's heart leaped into her throat when Mr. Lang broke the silence with unexpected sharpness.

"Is it true David was speaking to you when Mrs. Lang returned to the room early this morning?"

Meghan nodded.

"How did you communicate with him?"

Meg gave him a quizzical look. "I spoke to him."

Her response appeared to incense him. "Spoke to him! Are you aware, miss, that those most dear to David have spoken to him and gotten no response?"

Meg shook her head. "None at all?"

Turning with an aggravated shrug that displayed his lack of

patience with her answer, Martin Lang walked to the window. He stared out in silence, his turned back more explicit than words.

"Martin, please!" Her pale eyes brimming, Mrs. Lang took a few steps toward her husband before turning back to Meghan. "Mr. Lang is very upset about David's condition. He loves the boy dearly. Dr. Biel has been unable to ascertain the cause for David's relapse. To be honest, if I hadn't heard David speaking myself, Dr. Biel would have disbelieved that it happened at all. The dear boy is as severely afflicted as before, you see, turning and thrashing in bed . . ."

Unable to go on, Mrs. Lang then covered her face with her hands, and within moments Mr. Lang was at her side to comfort her.

"Letty, you owe this girl no explanation."

"Martin, you don't understand." Raising her tear-filled eyes to his, Mrs. Lang gestured in Meghan's direction. "David spoke to her, several times. And he drank from the glass when she offered it to him."

"He's slipped back, Letty."

"No, he hasn't! He just isn't responding to us the way he did to her." Mrs. Lang then turned back to Meghan. "We've called you here to ask your help, dear."

Meghan nodded, uncertain what to say.

"We'd like you to try speaking to David again."

"Letty, this is a waste of time." Mr. Lang's voice was gruff with pain. "David is—"

"David will be well, and I won't have you say otherwise!" Visibly shaking, Mrs. Lang raised her chin and turned back to Meghan. "Meghan, we—Mr. Lang and I—would like you to try to talk to David again, if you would. Would you do that for us, dear?"

Meghan nodded again, tears welling in her own eyes at the sight of Mrs. Lang's distress. It occurred to her that a ma was a ma, no matter the accent with which it was pronounced, and she felt the poor woman's pain.

She had then followed Mr. and Mrs. Lang as they climbed the central staircase toward his room. At the door to Mr. David's room, she paused, seeing him lying as still as before, and fear pounded unexpectedly in her chest.

Urged silently by Mrs. Lang, she approached the bed. David's thrashing begin anew, and her throat tightened hurtfully. She knew if she had been given the same opportunity with her brothers, she would not have stood by as their pain went unassuaged, and she was suddenly grateful to be afforded the chance that had been denied her with the boys.

Without a thought to the propriety of her actions, Meg perched herself on the side of the bed and stroked David's head as she would one of her own. Her heart was in her voice as she searched his tortured expression.

"So, the devils are back to haunt you. You must drive them away for good, do you hear? They've no place here. Come on, look up and speak to me. You've not the time to waste reliving pain when it could be better spent getting well." Her voice dropping then, so it could be heard by no one but him, Meg whispered earnestly, " 'Tis a time for healing, David, mine as well as your own. Don't disappoint me now. I'm counting on you to bring the two of us through."

One of her curls had strayed to tickle David Lang's cheek as she leaned over him, and an annoyed shadow flicked across his face.

"Aye, it's like you to find a way to complain even when you're silent. There's little change in your manner, sick or well, awake or asleep."

Unexpectedly, David Lang stirred. Fighting to focus his eyes, he rasped in response, "You're angry . . . black Irish temper . . ."

Low gasps from behind turned Meghan to Mr. and Mrs. Lang where they stood a short distance behind her. She returned their startled glances with a short nod.

"Aye, he's all right. You needn't fear. But I'm thinking it's a strange game of cat and mouse he's playing."

"I'm thirsty."

The hoarse statement drew Meg's attention back to the bed where she met the young master's unsteady gaze. Taking the glass from the nearby stand, she supported his head carefully and held it to his lips. He sipped cautiously, and Meg saw that the green in his hazel eyes had expanded again, and she frowned with concern.

"Are you in pain, Mr. David?"

Struggling to hold her gaze, he croaked, "You said not to worry, but you left. Then it all went bad again."

A strange pain tightened inside her, and Meg whispered softly in return, "Then I'll have to stay this time, won't I?"

A hint of a smile touched David's lips in the moment before he closed his eyes, and it was only after she'd turned back to the two behind her that she realized the foolishness of the promise she'd made him. This was not her Da or one of the boys, and no amount of deceiving herself could change it.

Silently acknowledging that reality, she slipped from the side of the bed only to have David's eyes snap open, accompanied by a rasping protest.

Mrs. Lang stepped forward, her expression alarmed. "No, stay. He wants you here."

Concerned, Meghan did not see Martin Lang's mouth tighten as she resumed her seat. She released a small sigh of relief as David's agitation calmed with her whisper, "Not to worry. I'm here to stay as long as you need me."

And there she had remained.

It was hours later now, and the supper tray had been delivered into her hands. The family had drifted out of the room, and then back in again; however, she had not realized Grace Lang was present until the girl made that first sound.

David's eyes were drooping, but she was not about to allow him to slip away again without having consumed a bit more of the nourishing broth. She held the spoon against his lips.

"Just a little more."

"No."

Putting down the plate, Meg slipped to her feet, only to see David's heavy eyelids lift again.

"Where're you going?"

Meg looked at the clock on the wall before responding. "It'll soon be time for me to leave."

"You said you'd stay."

"My Ma will be waiting for me."

David's voice weakened. "You said you'd stay."

The need in his voice tightened her throat, prohibiting response, but Meg would not allow the loss of control. Leaning over the bed, she whispered, "I'll be back in the morning, and in the meantime you'll not be alone. The mistress will be here with you."

A sound behind her turned Meg to Mrs. Lang as she approached the bed, forcing a smile. "David, dear, you have been neglecting me badly, you know."

"Aunt Letty . . ."

At the sound of her name on her beloved nephew's lips, Letty Lang burst into tears. Within moments, Meg was gruffly brushed aside as Martin Lang took his wife into his arms. David Lang's halting words of reassurance to his sobbing aunt brought a bittersweet smile to Meghan's lips. It was strange, that in their weakness, some forced others to be strong.

The faltering conversation at bedside continued as Meg picked up the tray and turned toward the door. But the relief she experienced as she pulled the door closed behind her and started down the hall was temporary. For she belatedly realized that the scene at bedside was deceiving. All had not really ended well. It had only begun.

Chapter 7

"Grace, stop that foolish crying right now!"

Grace's red-rimmed eyes rose to meet her mother's with surprise at the unexpected reprimand. The small defensive rise of her chin touched Letty's soft heart, and, taking a moment to close the door of the morning room so they would not be overheard, Letty drew her daughter into the comforting circle of her arms. Grace's fair, carefully coiffed head dropped to her mother's shoulder, and Letty despaired at the soft, hiccuping sob that escaped her.

"Grace, dear, this is all so unnecessary. David is recuperating from a terrible experience, and we must allow him to find his way."

"But it's been almost a month, Mama!" Drawing back, Grace wiped the tears from her cheeks with a delicate hand. "He never let me help him or feed him, and every time I went into his room to spend time with him, he told me he was tired. He's on his feet now, and nothing has changed. He doesn't talk to me at all anymore, except for 'good morning' or some silly such thing."

"He *is* tired, dear. Dr. Biel said physical injuries aside, David's suffered a terrible mental trauma."

"He spends time with Meghan O'Connor, and she's an Irish from the valley—a Catholic!"

"Grace, the kinship David may be feeling with this girl is something entirely different from the relationship you and he share. They've both suffered, dear, Meghan in the terrible loss of her father and brothers, and David in the pain of his burns and in the terror of being trapped in the fire. I think that suffering has become a common bond. But whatever it is, I'm sure it will fade. Meghan O'Connor's a nice girl, but she's simple and uneducated. David and she truly have nothing in common. When he recovers he'll see that."

"And will he have time for me again, Mama?"

"I'm sure he will. Be patient, dear, and try to be generous with the girl. She's done us a great service, and I shudder to think what might have happened if she hadn't been able to get through to David. I shall always be grateful to her for that."

Stepping back, Letty surveyed her daughter's pale countenance. Grace's words were more revealing than she realized, and Letty felt a familiar despair. Dear David stirred such strong emotions in everyone who came into contact with him. She had always thought that to be a blessing, but now she wasn't so sure.

"Damn!"

Gritting his teeth, David again attempted to button his shirt. It was the simplest chore, but so far beyond him at times.

He gave his room a sweeping glance in an attempt to divert his mind from his present, irritating disability. His gaze skipped past the dark, massive furniture, the same which had greeted him when he had moved in with his aunt and uncle as a child after the death of his parents, past the masculine bed covering and drapes and fixed on the window. He frowned at his view of the burned remains of the stables, and a chill moved down his spine. A sweat broke out on his forehead, and he fought the trembling that began to shake him.

Oh, no, he'd not succumb to that nightmare again!

With a deep breath, David diverted his gaze to the new structure, not yet completed, that stood a short distance beyond the charred debris. He had listened to the sounds of that construction day after day as he lay abed fighting his nightmares, and it gave him hope. It had seemed an eternity before he was allowed to walk downstairs and inspect it more closely, and he remembered the triumph of that day. Somehow, it had taken all of his strength to accomplish that feat, and he knew it was not simply a weakness of the body that had held him back.

He had gotten the strength he needed from an unexpected source. Even now David could not quite comprehend how a few soft words with the lilting influence of a brogue, and a glance from bright blue eyes that looked farther and deeper inside him than any had before, had succeeded in restoring his courage. He supposed he never would.

The thought giving him a moment's pause, David stared at the stables under construction a few moments longer. Beginning to become impatient, he flexed his stiff hands and prepared himself again for the ordeal of buttoning his shirt. He was well now, and impatience was his most difficult test. He almost regretted having come upstairs to change his shirt. He indulged a moment's sulky regret in the thought that he would have been better off wearing it stained with tea from his clumsiness at lunch, rather than having put himself in the position of enduring this frustration for the second time today.

David flexed his finger again and inspected the healing scars. Strange, he didn't even remember how these burns had come about, but he supposed it wasn't important. Dr. Biel said exercise would eventually eliminate the stiffness, and that the scarring would fade. He shrugged. He wasn't concerned about the way his hands looked—only how they felt and functioned.

Glancing up, David frowned at the reflection that stared back at him from the dresser mirror. He supposed he would have felt differently had he suffered more severe burns on his face, but he'd never been overly vain, even if Meg had accused him of that particular vice during one of their many conversations while he was healing.

David gave a short laugh. Leave it to Meg to say exactly what she thought. She was such a feisty little chit.

But as things stood, the superficial burns on his face had healed so well that hardly a trace of his ordeal remained. A light trimming of his hair had removed the singed edges, and he looked well, if he could discount the visible weight loss that sharpened the planes of his face.

He stared at his reflection a little longer. What did Meg see that had caused her to study him so intently during the weeks when she had spent most of her time nursing him back to total reality? He had awakened many times to see those incredible eyes fixed on his face, but he'd been unable to read the look in them. He'd asked her what she was thinking on those occasions, only to have her respond with cryptic responses about healing that were typical of the convoluted manner of Irish speech and thought.

Well, he knew what he saw when he saw Meg. He saw a thin, quick-minded, outspoken girl who was prettier than he had thought that first day on the hillside. It was hard to believe she was fourteen, so undersized was she for her age, but she had only to speak, and a maturity far beyond her size and years poured out. He knew there was a wisdom in her words that was instinctive, and which she, herself, didn't realize she possessed. He also knew that somewhere along the line the animosity between them had disappeared and they had become friends. He valued that friendship dearly.

Damn!

While lost in his thoughts, David's fingers had strayed to the buttons on his shirt, but he was achieving as little success as before in performing the routine task. Clamping his teeth tightly together, he muttered under his breath.

"Damn it all, I'm as helpless as a baby!"

"And as impatient as a babe, too."

David didn't bother to turn toward the voice that sounded from the open doorway behind him. It could be no one else. Instead, he waited for the approach of the familiar step without response. Meg's perceptiveness sometimes annoyed him. It stripped him of his pride and left his emotions naked. He was not always comfortable at being so exposed.

"Stubbornness and pride have a way of shortening a man's patience. Another pair of hands—that's the ticket."

Jerking up his head, David met Meghan's gaze as she offered him her small, chapped hands. "These two have a few seconds to spare if they're needed."

"I can button my own shirt."

There was a moment's silence.

"Aye, you can, and you will."

Turning, Meghan disappeared back through the doorway just as quickly as she had appeared. David heard her light step move down the hallway, and he frowned at his own short-tempered display. But he'd button his own shirt. It was time he stood on his own feet and acted like a man again.

That determination fueling his efforts, David concentrated on the elusive pearl buttons that evaded his fumbling grasp. An interminable few minutes later, he released a tense breath, knowing the satisfaction of success as he slid the last one through the tiny handstitched buttonhole. Taking only a few moments longer to push his dangling shirt tails into his trousers, he gave himself a last fleeting glance in the mirror before turning toward the hallway.

Standing in the bedroom doorway a few steps down the hall, he waited for Meghan to become aware of his presence as he used the time to assess her misleadingly frail stature. The reason Aunt Letty had been deceived into thinking Meg was too young for the position crossed his mind. Her slenderness and size made her appear no more than a child, and that wildly curly dark hair that even now was slipping the bonds of the ribbon tied so securely around it, seemed only to emphasize her petite proportions. But he remembered the strength in those thin limbs as she had supported his shoulders while feeding him during the past month, and he remembered her unspoken determination. He supposed he'd never forget them.

Appearing to suddenly sense his presence, Meg turned to look at him, her gaze taking in his frown. She shrugged. "Sometimes my hands are so willing that they forget others might want to use their own. It does my heart good to see you managed well without me."

"Does it?" Walking into his cousin's chamber, David surveyed it critically. As usual, Grace's room was cluttered with foolish, nonsensical treasures that no one dared touch. Dear Grace. So grown up on the outside, and on the inside such a child. The opposite side of the coin from the girl who now attempted to bring a semblance of order to the confusion.

"Aye. Ma was always after me to quit doing things for James when he was small. She said he'd never learn if I didn't let him struggle a bit with his skills. She said he'd never grow up to be a man if he—"

Her expression going suddenly blank, Meg was silent for a few short moments before she averted her face and resumed her work. David took the few steps to her side, his deliberate taunt calculated to distract her from the unhappy memory he had unintentionally provoked.

"Are you likening me to a baby, Meghan O'Connor?"

The eyes Meg raised to his were devoid of their former shadows.

"No, you're too big for a babe."

Her response pleased him, but David wasn't about to let her escape easily.

"You're not."

"Is that so?" A smile touched Meg's lips. "Well, I'm thinking I was big enough to handle you."

"I was injured and unable to protest."

Meghan was suddenly very serious. "Aye, you were that."

David was startled by the hot rush of feelings that accompanied the realization that Meg was equating him with her lost brothers again. Well, he wasn't her brother, and he didn't want her likening him to them in her mind.

"But I'm not injured anymore. And you're not my nursemaid."

David held Meghan's bright eyes with deliberation as he continued in a softer tone, "But you are my friend."

Meghan's surprise was marked by a stunned moment's silence. Then she frowned. "Ah, Mr. David, we're not friends."

David instinctively avoided a reply, responding instead with, "Come on, I have something to show you."

"But I've not finished my work here."

"Here?" David turned to give the room another disapproving glance. "There isn't much you can do here. Grace won't let you touch anything."

"Aye, but I can dust around things and straighten up if she's not around to protest. That's why Margaret sent me up here when the mistress closed the morning room door behind the two of them."

David could not suppress his amused laugh. "If Grace only knew how you all work around her to get your way. I can only hope the deviousness of the staff is never turned against me. I wouldn't stand a chance."

"It never would be. They all love you, down to the very last one. Every one of them in the kitchen was fair to expiring with sadness when you were ill."

David sensed a tinge of mockery in her tone, and suddenly impatient with the direction their conversation was taking, he grasped Meghan's arm. "Come on. I've waited long enough. I have something to show you."

"But I'm not finished!"

"Look around you. Do you really think Grace or anyone else will see a difference in here when you're done?"

"No, but—"

"No buts." David tried to propel her toward the doorway, but Meghan's expression turned mutinous as she stood her ground. "Shall I tell Aunt Letty that I'm in need of help and you say you don't have time for me?"

Meg's lips separated with surprise. "You wouldn't!"

"You think not?"

Meghan's lips dropped open a notch farther, and David could not resist a smile. "Let's not put me to the test, Meg. You know I'm a spoiled sort and liable to do anything to get my way."

"Aye, I've seen that."

David's smile fell and his eyes narrowed. "If you think you're going to make me angry enough to forget the whole thing, you're wrong. Come on."

Determinedly, David pulled her along beside him. He was all

but dragging her down the staircase when Meghan's soft protest slowed his step.

"Let go of my arm, please." David looked at her suspiciously, and she continued with a slight rise of her chin. "You're having your way as usual, but I'm not your prisoner, you know."

Tempted to smile, David released Meghan's arm. There were some who'd protest the pride in those bright eyes, but not he—not anymore.

They reached the foot of the staircase and David started toward the door, assured that Meg would keep pace beside him.

The pungent odors of horse manure and freshly cut board mingled with the lingering smell of smoke and charred wood still seeping from the burned remains of the old stables as Meghan followed David's lead toward the new building underway. Birds twittered musically in the shrubbery nearby, and the heat of the summer sun was warm on her shoulders, relaxing her. She breathed deeply, grateful to have escaped the confines of the house even briefly.

She cast David a concerned glance. He was frowning, the freedom of the warm outdoors making no impression on the sudden severity of his expression, but Meghan understood. She knew the courage it had taken for David to approach this spot for the first time—to come close enough to see and touch the burned ruin where he had almost met his end. She knew that shadows still lingered in his mind, waiting to spring into life each time he passed the remains of Fabian's funeral pyre, and that he kept them at bay with pure courage and determination. She knew because she had suffered the assault of similar shadows where Da and the boys' faces lingered, and she had exorcised them in much the same way. She had exorcised them before she had come to know David Lang well, but it had only been since the stable fire that she had finally put them to rest.

David had done that for her. He had turned to her in his pain, and his need had healed her. In her gratitude, Meghan wanted the same for him.

Struggling to match David's rapid step, Meg found herself annoyed, nevertheless, at his high-handed treatment. Characteristically, he had chosen to ignore the repercussions that would undoubtedly follow this impulsive behavior, and she knew that Mrs. Lang would not be pleased with her excursion into this portion of the yard. The mistress was a generous woman, but she had many pressures put upon her that Meghan had not understood before coming to the Lang household. The greatest of them came from Mr. Lang, who had disapproved of Meghan's employment from the beginning. He resented the part she had taken in the care of Mr. David even more, and she knew that were it up to that hard man, her employment at the Lang mansion would meet an abrupt end.

Mr. David's expression was lightening with the remains of the old stable behind them. He turned to Townsend as the fellow appeared at the entrance of the new stables. She had seen the man only once since the fire, and his surprise at seeing her now with Mr. David was obvious.

"I wasn't expecting you back so soon, Mr. David. Your mount's not ready yet, but it'll take only a few minutes to get her saddled."

"That'll be fine. I wanted to show Meg something in the meantime. Come on, Meg."

Not waiting for her response, David walked into the stable, and Meg followed, inwardly groaning at the curious glances of the men present. They'd not let go of this one easily, and she was certain she'd hear of this jaunt again. But she had little time to consider the gossip Mr. David was provoking when he stopped in front of a well-kept stall, his smile proud.

"Well, what do you think?"

An obviously pregnant mare raised her muzzle to David with a soft snort of welcome, and David's smile widened as he rubbed it affectionately.

"This is Loma Linda. She was born on a beautiful little hill in Spain—that's where she got her name. She's carrying Fabian's foal." David's smile dimmed only slightly as he continued. "She was one of the first to be rescued from the fire, so there should be no problem when her time comes in a few more months."

"She's a beautiful animal to my eye, but I'm sorry to say I'm not much of a judge, knowing as little as I do about horses."

"She's an Arabian—a thoroughbred. She belongs to me, as did Fabian. Uncle Martin advanced money from my trust so I could start my own stable. If everything goes well, Fabian's bloodline will survive and flourish. I hope so, because there aren't many horses like him."

"Aye." Meghan grimaced, unseen. "I remember."

David turned sharply. The critical note in her response did not escape him and his eyes narrowed as they searched her face.

"You're thinking about the first time we met, when Fabian threw me. Well, that was my fault. I wasn't at my best and I got what I had coming that day."

"Oh, did you, now?"

David did not respond, and Meg regretted her obvious reference to the harshness of their first exchange in the uncomfortable silence that followed.

"Your horse is ready, Mr. Lang. It's waiting for you outside."

David nodded to the groom before turning to follow the fellow outside. Meghan walked behind them, cursing her sharp tongue. Outside the door, David stepped away to speak a few words to Townsend, and Johnny Law stepped unexpectedly into sight. Her friendly, "Hello, John," was met with a hostile turn of his lips.

"Oh, so you're still speaking to us common folk now that you have a friend in high places."

"A friend in high places? Is it Mr. David you're speaking of?"

John's expression tightened. "Who else?"

Meg's short laugh momentarily startled the surliness from Johnny's face. "John Law, you are a fool if you mistake a servant for a friend."

"Oh, am I? Is it a servant or a friend the master's nephew takes to the stables to show off his prize mare? You always drove me away with the excuse you had your work to do and feared for your position. But I suppose you needn't fear when you're away from your work with Mr. David because he'll speak up for you."

Meghan stiffened at his tone. "And what business is it of yours what I do, may I ask?"

"It's my concern because . . . because . . ." Stammering to a halt, John pulled his cap off his head and ran an anxious hand through his straw-colored hair, unconsciously standing it up in damp spikes on his perspired head. Meg watched his agitated display with surprise, startled as Johnny continued hotly, "Because you led me on into thinking you was my friend until you found better game."

"I led you on—I found better game—!" Meg's words were an incredulous hiss, and she darted a quick glance around her before turning back to the flushed stable boy with slitted eyes and an angry tightening of her lips. "Not only are you a fool, but you've a poor memory to boot, John Law! It was you that hung around, always talking to me and trying to get me to laugh when I should have been working! And if I was fool enough to speak to you in return, I can see that it was a mistake indeed. If I ever thought you to be a friend, I was wrong, and I regret the time I wasted with you!"

There was a moment's silence before Johnny's expression turned sheepish. "Aw, Meg . . . It's just that I ain't had nobody to talk to of late and—"

"I'll listen to no more!" The fine, straight line of her nose raised haughtily, Meghan turned away from Johnny's penitent expression, only to have the misery in his tone touch a chord inside her as his voice dropped a notch lower.

"I'm sorry, Meg."

Turning slowly back to him, Meg saw Johnny's flush, unconsciously noting that the freckles on the bridge of his broad short nose stood out darkly in contrast, and she regretted her lapse of patience. John was, after all, still lonesome in this place, and she had given him little time of late. She was being less than kind, and Ma would be ashamed of her.

Hesitating only a moment longer, Meg slipped her hand onto Johnny's arm as she attempted to catch his downcast gaze.

"We've both said things that shouldn't be spoken between two friends, Johnny Law, and I have my regrets, too, for speaking them."

John's small brown eyes were bright with hope as they jumped to meet hers. "And when Mr. David's well and not in need of your attention anymore, you'll find the time to talk to me again?"

What was it Ma always said—"boys will be boys"? She was discovering more and more each day the wisdom of her Ma's words. And if ever there was a plea for compassion, she was hearing one now. How could she turn it down?

"Sure and I don't see why I shouldn't."

"Meg!"

David's clipped summons turned her to his tight expression as he advanced toward them. Visibly irritated, he glared at the thin stable boy.

"Don't you have anything to do, Law? It seems to me some of the stalls need cleaning. If you can't find enough work to keep you busy there, you can always report to the kitchen. Uncle Martin doesn't countenance an idle staff."

Meghan gasped at David's unfair attack, only to have him cast her a warning glance.

"Keep out of this, Meg."

"But—"

"I said, keep out of this."

Before Meg could react, John had turned on his heel and disappeared around the side of the building. The sparks of gold floating in the green of David's eyes were hotly animated as she returned his stare, and Meg knew what that meant. But she was too angry to heed their portent as he took the reins of the gelding the groom held waiting.

David mounted, and without warning, leaned down and lifted her up onto the saddle in front of him.

"What're you doing?" Struggling in his grasp, Meg gasped with disbelief. "Are you mad? Put me down!"

"Did you forget what I said to you that day on the hillside? I give the orders here. Now sit still or you'll fall. Here we go!"

Closing his arms tightly around Meg, David spurred his horse into motion, and Meg clutched the saddle in front of her with fright as the big animal took off at a gallop.

"Do ye not know what that means, man? How can ye be so blind?"

Without interrupting his step in the informal line of miners making their way home at the finish of the day shift, Lenny Dunne probed Sean's puzzled expression. A hot flush of exasperation colored his thin, freckled face beneath the layer of coal dust blackening it, and he grunted as he savagely kicked a small rock out of his path. Squinting up at the late afternoon sun, he paid little attention to the dust he had raised on the dry road, the inquisitive glances of the men around him, or the annoyed look of a miner a few feet away as the rock bounced sharply off his boot.

Sean kept a cautious silence. Lenny's temper was well known. Some said it burned as bright as the shaggy red hair that stuck awkwardly from the sides of his miner's cap, and Sean was not of a mood to test it this day. The early summer sun felt warm and good after hours below in the damp shaft, and he wanted to do no more than let it heat his bones for a little while in silence. But Lenny was in a rage at the rumor that had reached his ears only a short time before the shift ended, and he knew he'd not have that luxury.

The empty lunch pail Lenny carried swung between them as Lenny raised his hand toward Sean's face with an emphatic gesture. Suddenly seeming to realize that he was calling attention to himself, Lenny lowered his voice guardedly.

"Our man in the state legislature knows well enough what a law allowin' the railroads to own mines would do, and that's why he sent the word back here. Do ye not know what monopoly means, boyo? It means power! 'Cause there's power in unity, ye know, and it's power Mr. Franklin Benjamin Gowen's seekin'—power to use against all of us poor Irish who dare opposin' him. It riles the fellow that poor, ignorant men like us will go up against him, and he's out to break us. He's a lawyer—Chief Counsel to the President of The Road. He'll get his way. Ye'll see. But I'm thinkin' if he does, there'll be the devil to pay with the Sons of Molly Maguire takin' their satisfaction whatever way they can."

His friend's fury was obvious, but Sean was having difficulty following him. His mind was on Meg. She'd been working longer hours at the house on the hill in the past month, and he didn't like it. They were paying her well, and that was the hardest thing for him to fight. They were paying her too well for him to do much more than make a few bitter comments, or to curse the bloody priest who put her there in the first place.

Whatever the reason for his lack of concentration today, he could see Lenny was fast losing patience.

"Are ye listenin', boyo?"

"Aye, I'm listenin'." Sean nodded his head and squinted up into the taller fellow's face once more. "But my brain's as fair worn out as the rest of me today. Nothin' much is gettin' through."

Lenny's face drew into a familiar frown. "Yer mind's somewhere else, and that's the truth of it. And I'm thinkin' I know where it is."

"Do you, now?"

"Aye. It don't sit right with ye that yer sister's workin' for them bloody Protestants on the hill."

A hot flush colored Sean's face. "My sister's *my* business."

"Is she, now? Seems to me yer wanderin' mind cleared up real fast at the mention of her."

"I said my sister's *my* business, and if you know what's good for you, you'll not speak of her again to me."

"Aha! So there's some hot blood in yer veins today after all, O'Connor. Well, ye'd be better off savin' it for them that mean to do ye wrong than to waste it on a man who's tryin' to bring ye along a bit."

Glancing toward the fork in the road where Lenny and he were soon to part, Sean looked back at his friend with a shrug that was all the apology he could manage.

"You're right, Lenny Dunne. And I'm thinkin' it's time that I take my foul disposition home and soak it in a bucket of cold water before it does me more harm than good."

"Aha, right again, me boyo!" His mirth momentary, Lenny was sober once more as he raised his hand in a short salute and stepped onto the turn-off toward the patch. "And should that cold water put ye in mind of sharin' an hour with a friend, ye might come to yer favorite *shebeen* tonight, 'cause I've the feelin' there'll be more on the minds of many than whilin' away the hours. And ye've much to learn."

"All right. Perhaps I'll see you then."

His step more purposeful, Sean turned toward home, dismissing Lenny for problems closer to his heart. Meg would probably be home by now. If they kept her working late on the hill again, there'd be the devil to pay. Aye, he'd make sure of that.

Were she not so angry, Meghan suspected she would almost be enjoying the ride.

From the back of the powerful gelding on which she had been riding for the past half hour, the landscape appeared far different than it did when traveling afoot on the dust of the trail. Oh, she was frightened, to be sure. She'd never ridden on horseback before—not like this, with nothing to hold onto except the smooth leather of the saddle and the strong arm that held her firmly upright. But the fear that had first kept her clutching David Lang's arm, despite her anger, had relaxed as David had slowed his mount's gait to a steady, non-threatening step.

In truth, the hills and valley below were something to see from this vantage point. Meg revised that thought. It wasn't as if the valley was a pretty sight, all but stripped of vegetation as it was, and dull and dingy with the coal dust that cloaked everything for miles around. But it gave a person food for thought that the hand of man could make such sweeping changes on the world God had made. She supposed it was impressive—all those miles and miles of train track criss-crossing themselves, and the towering collieries built over the mines below. Even the cinder dumps and great heaps of slag took on another appearance when viewed at a distance. It was easy for a person to separate himself from it all up here, on the back of a powerful animal, riding free and unfettered, and Meghan realized the reason was very simple.

From a distance, a man could see all except the misery below him.

That thought tempering the anger that had kept her silent for the duration of their ride, Meg turned to look up at David's sober face.

"So, your temper's finally cooled."

Meghan's frown returned at his remark, and she looked away.

David rode only a few feet more before finally drawing his mount to a halt. Dismounting, he knotted the reins in a nearby bush and then turned to lower her to the ground. He took the few steps to a shaded spot under a tree and sat down. Meghan followed him for lack of else to do.

David broke the silence with an unexpected question as she sat also. "Are you still angry with me, Meg?"

Silent for a moment, Meghan studied David's face. His expression was sober, devoid of the irritation that had marked his exchange with John Law earlier. She noticed that the green rings that surrounded the black pupils of his eyes had expanded again, almost eliminating the outer circle of brown, but the bright, angry flecks of color were almost stilled, and she puzzled at the unpredictability of this fellow's nature.

"You didn't answer me, Meg. Are you still angry?"

"The heat of my anger's cooled, but not the feelings that prompted it. I don't take lightly to your high-handed manner, and I'm thinking I should tell you that I'll not suffer such treatment again. But mostly, Mr. David, I'm confused into wondering which one of the two faces you've shown me is the true David Lang."

David's annoyance returned.

"My name's David, Meg, and I'd like you to address me that way."

Meghan's fine dark brows knit in a delicate line.

"That would be unwise. The mistress wouldn't think well of it, and neither would the master, not to speak of others in the house."

"I don't care what anybody thinks. If I can call you Meg, then you can call me David."

"You call Margaret by her given name, and the same goes for Mabel and all the others, but I've not heard them addressing you as 'David.' "

"It's not the same with you and me, and you know it."

"Oh, is it not? Then what would the difference be? I'm a servant in your house, just like them."

Unexpectedly, David took her hands into his, and Meghan winced at the harsh feel of the tortured skin.

"My hands aren't very pleasant to see or touch, are they, Meg?"

"They have harsh scars, indeed, but they'll heal."

"That's right, they'll heal, and I rarely give them a moment's thought, except for their stiffness and the clumsiness they cause when I try to perform delicate tasks. But if it wasn't for you, my scars would have been far deeper."

"I did nothing at all but a few menial tasks."

"That's not true, and you know it."

"No, I don't. You had the best of care with Dr. Biel, and you had loved ones all around you to nurse you through your despair."

"I had ceased to exist until I heard your voice, Meg."

Meg saw the shadows return to David's eyes as he spoke, and a tremor moved down her spine at the pain that stirred to life there.

"I was breathing—I could hear and see, but I had ceased to exist. You brought me back, Meg."

"You answered my voice because it was foreign to you, and because it stirred angry memories. You didn't want me near. The first thing you said to me was 'What are you doing here?' "

"Because I was surprised."

"You were angry."

"Like *you* are now?"

Finally giving in to her annoyance, Meghan nodded. "Yes, and I suppose my anger will simmer inside me until I tell you the whole of what I think—and that is, not only were you high-handed in your treatment of me earlier, you were also unkind and harsh with John Law. You acted the part of the man everyone in the valley says you are."

"Do you think I care what they say about me in the valley? But I do care what *you* say, because we're friends."

"We're not friends, Mr. David."

"David."

"No, I'll not play your foolish games!" Meg's irritation swelled. "You say you don't care what anyone in the valley says about you. Well, you see, that means you don't care about what I say, either, because I'm one of them."

"You're *not* one of them, and you know it. You don't belong down there, Meg. You're too bright, too quick. You have too much life in you to have it smothered by the ignorance and prejudice of those people."

Meg's lips tightened. "Aye, there's much of that down in the valley—but there's a fair share of ignorance and prejudice up here, too." Meghan gave a hard laugh. "But we're just wasting our breaths, you know, going 'round and 'round like this, because nothing we say will make much difference."

"What do you mean?"

"Surely you know how fast I'll be out of the house when word gets around about this little jaunt we've taken."

"No one would dare fire you!"

"Not so. Your uncle's been looking for the excuse, and you've given it to him today. Taking me riding was a foolish thing to do, but I don't suppose you gave a second thought to the consequences, since you've doubtless escaped paying the price of unwise actions in the past."

"Have I, Meg?" David held his scarred hands up for her to view again. "What would you call this?"

Impatience twisted Meghan's features into a sneer.

"Oh, you are a foolish fellow! You put so much stock in physical pain because you know so little of despair. I'll tell you what true pain is, David Lang! True pain is being without hope! Every man in the valley can tell you how that cuts into a man's vitals more sharply than a knife."

"You're making excuses for the lazy drunkards below, and I've no patience for it, Meg. Their type would prefer to rant and rave about the inequality of things, but aren't willing to work to correct it. No, instead they've elected some men into the state legislature that have no other purpose in mind but to further the Irish cause at the expense of all others by bribing or coercing other officials into their way of thinking. They don't have the sense to consider the overall picture when things don't go their way. They'd rather settle their grievances with a cowardly shot in the dark, or a fiery torch!"

"And you speak of *our* ignorance! Despite what you choose to think, the work of the Molly Maguires isn't accepted by most Irish in the valley. Most men of good conscience despise their deeds and condemn it as well, as does the Church. Most know that the Mollies' terrible acts do no more than increase hatred. But that doesn't mean that most don't agree that the cause is just, even though the methods are poor."

"The miners' lot isn't as bad as they'd have people believe."

"Oh, is that so? Do you know what it is to go to bed at night with your stomach growling from hunger, and to know your children are as hungry as you? Do you know what it is to see your children go without proper shoes and clothing, not to mention schooling? And worst of all, do you know what it is to live without hope that things will ever change?"

"The men in the mines make a fair wage."

"So much the fool you for believing what you say. And even if it were true, what of the 'pluck me' stores that take a man's wage from him faster than he can earn it, where a man's boots sell for $2.75 but are $4.50 on the book, and where eggs sell for 20¢ elsewhere, and 30¢ there? And what of the unspoken rule that says if a man protests his lot, he's laid off, or his credit is stopped. Do you know what it's like to realize that no matter how many hours you spend below the ground, or how hard you work your pick, you've not a chance of changing the order of things?"

"The miners don't have to deal at the company store if they don't want to."

"And where else would they deal, being paid monthly as they are, and with no cash to deal elsewhere in the time between? But all this talk of wage is naught but a sham, when the truth is that a 'bobtail check' telling them the amount of their current debt is all most men see at the end of the month."

"You exaggerate."

"Oh, do I, now? What of my brother, Sean? Fifteen years old, and bound to the company store for—"

"If he was stupid enough to run up a tab, he got what he deserved!"

"Stupid, you say? Nay, you're the one who's too stupid to see what's going on around you! Sean was as fortunate as many others before him. He received an inheritance, you see. Whether he likes it or not, he's taken on the legacy of my father's debts, with little chance of him ever paying them off in full, for they'll last a lifetime."

"It's plain to see that you're just repeating the trash you've heard others speak and not using your own head to think."

"And it's plain to see that I've fooled myself of late into believing you're not the man I first thought you to be!" Meg drew herself to her feet and turned away, only to have David's heavy hand on her shoulder turn her back to face him before she'd gone a few steps.

"Where do you think you're going?"

"Back to the house. I've no doubt I'll be told to collect my things and leave when I get there, and I'm thinking it's for the best."

"Meg—"

"Please take your hand off me."

David's hand dropped to his side, only to spring back to her shoulder as she attempted to turn away again. "This has gone far enough, Meg." Frowning darkly, David shook his head. "I don't know how this all went wrong. I wanted to take you to the stable to show you Loma Linda because I thought you'd be interested. And I wanted to take you for a ride because . . ."

Meghan waited in silence as David paused. The silence lengthened until she completed his statement for him.

"Because your harsh words to poor John Law didn't satisfy your anger at me for the comments I made in the stable, and you wanted to impress both of us with your authority."

"You make me out a true villain, Meg."

"Does it hurt to see yourself through another's eyes?"

David sighed. "I don't want you to be angry with me."

"Aye, now we truly have something in common. There're a lot of things I want that are beyond me, too."

"And so you want to see me suffer in the same way."

Halting, Meghan considered David's low comment. "No, I've no desire to see you unhappy, Mr. David."

"David."

"No, *Mr.* David. I know my place, even if you choose not to see it."

"If you don't want to see me unhappy, why are you arguing with me?"

"Because I've much to be upset about! You said terrible, harsh things about the people of my blood just now, and you've not bothered to try to understand any of the things I've said in return. I'm thinking that the problem between us lies there, and it's not something that'll easily be overcome."

"I was angry, Meg. I didn't mean everything I said."

"Oh, with the excuse of anger, all's to be forgiven? I must remember that for the future."

Irritation flared in David's eyes as he took a step closer. "It seems you Irish think you've the only causes for grievance in the world." Holding his hands up in front of Meg's face, he demanded, "What of these? Some say the fire in the stable was deliberately set, and that the Irish are responsible."

Meghan's face paled, but her voice was firm and clear when she spoke again. "And some say your uncle's negligence was to blame for the deaths of my Da and the boys."

David's eyes bore into hers, and Meghan no longer felt the warm summer sun on her back or heard the trill of the birds for the chill which overwhelmed her.

The silence between them lengthened before David unexpectedly scooped her from her feet and deposited her back on his horse. Mounting behind her, he spurred the gelding into motion.

Stumbling on a rut in the narrow dirt road, John Law caught himself with a curse and continued his steady pace. He looked around him and saw that his presence stirred little curiosity in the nearly empty streets of late afternoon, accustomed as the people were to seeing him run errands for the staff on the hill. But today he was on an errand of his own.

John frowned, acknowledging to himself that he had been nasty and unfair to Meg when he said those things outside the stable earlier in the day. But he had been angry. Things had been going well between them until the fire, and from that time on, Meg had seemed to push him aside. She hadn't spared him a word or a smile, and she had looked through him as if he wasn't even there the few times he saw her away from Mr. David's bedside. When he saw the two of them walking toward the stable, he had suffered a fit of jealousy that had torn painfully at his insides, and angry words were the result.

But it seemed he wasn't the only one who was fit to burst with jealousy.

David Lang's angry face replaced Meg's in his mind's eye. The master's privileged nephew wasn't about to share Meg with a fellow so far beneath him, and he knew what that kind of interest held in store, even if Meg didn't. The trouble was, she'd never listen to him. But there was one person she *would* believe.

The building he sought came into view in the distance and John's stomach knotted. A few minutes later he stood before the door. Wiping his sweaty palms on his pants, John took a deep breath, and knocked. A few seconds passed before the door opened to reveal the man he sought. John swallowed nervously as the thin, pale-faced priest spoke.

"May I help you?"

"Yes." Johnny attempted a smile. "I'd like to talk to you for a few minutes, Father."

"Come in then."

The door opened wider and John stepped inside.

Secluded in a section of heavy brush that bordered the hillside trail behind the Lang mansion, David waited. He swatted again at annoying insects that buzzed around his uncovered head and raised his arm to wipe his perspired brow. Several hours had passed since he had brought Meg home from their unscheduled ride in the hills, and he'd had a difficult afternoon at best. If he were to judge from the length of time he'd been standing there, he would be tempted to think things were not going to get much better.

Meg had been right. He had no sooner pulled up to the stable and lifted her to the ground after their silent ride home than he was given the message that Aunt Letty wanted to see him. He was grateful that Meg hadn't overheard, because he knew she would have guessed the reason for his aunt's summons.

Waiting only until Meg disappeared around the back of the house, he had started toward the front door, his heart taking up a slow pounding, his regrets soaring. Damn, what had gotten into him? His sole intention in taking Meg out to the stables that morning had been to show her Loma Linda. He wasn't truly certain of the reason, except that he had discovered a bond of the spirit with this girl from the valley during his recuperation. He had also discovered he valued that bond. During his recuperation, she had forced him to dig down deep inside himself for a courage he was certain he would not have found without her, and he wanted to show her she had succeeded—that he was looking to the future and was going on.

But things hadn't worked out as he intended. Meg's remarks about Fabian had annoyed him, and her reminder of his behavior on the hill that first day had pushed his irritation up another notch. That annoyance was nothing to compare with the explosion of ire inside him, however, when he turned around to find Meg wasting her time talking to that stable boy, her hand on his arm.

Everything had fallen apart after that, and the defense he had seen rising in Meg's eyes for that fellow had been the last straw.

The last straw—that was exactly what Aunt Letty had said a report of his behavior that afternoon would be if it was reported to Uncle Martin. Now in hindsight, he supposed he agreed. Uncle Martin would have been furious, and he supposed, for Meg's sake, he should be grateful that Aunt Letty had instructed the staff that word of the incident was not to be repeated. He realized now that he had put Meg's future in the household in jeopardy to salve his own senseless anger, and for that he could not forgive himself.

Meg had been right. He had acted foolishly, unforgivably. Now, at the end of the day, he was waiting for Meg to make her way back down the hill toward the valley so he could tell her so.

A reluctant smile flickered across David's lips with the realization that in all probability, Meg would not make things easy for him. She was such a stubborn girl. He supposed he'd been drawn to her from the moment of their first meeting because she was the only person who had ever challenged him and forced him to take a good look at himself. He wasn't always pleased with what he saw, but he couldn't hold her to account for that. They had never spared the truth from each other, and he supposed that was the reason exchanges between them were often so volatile. Yet, the honesty between them was one of the things he valued most in their unlikely friendship. It was too rare to lose.

He wanted the best for Meg—far more than she could expect to attain, considering her common lot in life. For if there was one thing he knew, Meg was no common girl.

The sound of Meg's familiar step caused David to draw back farther into the bush. He waited until she drew abreast of him before stepping out, and he cursed himself as she jumped with a start and gasped, "What're you doing here?"

Suddenly at a loss for words as Meghan's eyes pinned him, David shrugged. "I suppose I didn't want you to go home today before setting things straight."

Meghan did not respond, and David managed a sheepish smile. "Would it make you feel better to hear me say you were right, that I acted like a spoiled child this afternoon?"

Still no response.

"And that I regret my 'high-handed' manner?"

Silence.

"Meg . . ." David placed his hand on her shoulder. She didn't flinch from his touch, and he was encouraged. "I'm not proud of the way I acted this afternoon."

Silence.

"Come on, Meg. Talk to me. We've never had trouble talking, or arguing either, for that matter. And even if we don't agree on some things, I'd still like to consider you my friend."

"Friend?" Meghan broke her silence with the single word, its inflection tearing at his insides. "I think you've no idea what the word truly means, Mr. David, so accustomed are you to giving orders and getting your way."

David stared silently into the translucent blue eyes holding his. They did not spare him the criticism he deserved, and he knew it was their integrity, and something else he could not name, which made him want to see approval registered just as clearly there.

"I think you're right, Meg. For all the advantages that have been shown me, and for all my considerable education, there are many things I don't know. I'm hoping you can teach me those things, because I've come to value the openness between us."

"I'm not a teacher, Mr. David."

"Yes, you are, Meg."

Meg's fine lips twitched. "You're making sport of me."

"No, I'm trying to be honest. I'd like you to teach me what it means to be your friend."

Silence again.

"Meg?"

"I don't know if that's possible. There's too much in the way."

"You never let things get in the way before, Meg. We had nothing but hard feelings between us, but you tended my wounds and helped heal the scars that no one else could see."

"But that was different, because you helped heal mine, too."

Startled by her reply, David paused, allowing Meghan opportunity to continue. "I had more than a fair amount of bitterness inside me after the deaths of my Da and the boys, but I had only to see your pain to know, just as Father Matthew said, that on the inside we're all the same—some better and some worse than others, but always with good mixed with the bad. You opened your eyes and looked at me without seeing. You were tortured, and I saw your heart in your eyes. I saw need there, too, and my heart went out to you. When it did, the bitterness started seeping away."

David reached deep for the courage to ask the next question. "Did I make the bitterness return today, Meg? Did I spoil it all?"

Meg hesitated, frowning as she finally spoke. "I'm thinking you came very close."

David gave a short, relieved laugh. "So, all's not lost. You haven't written me off. We're still friends."

"Friends? We've not reached that level of understanding, and I doubt we ever will."

"Meg . . ." Wondering at the torment that had started inside him at those words from this sober young girl, David shook his head. "Won't you even try?"

David saw his own torment reflected in Meg's eyes. He saw the conflict in her mind as she considered his earnestness, and he saw her hesitation in the moment before she answered solemnly, "Aye, I'll try."

"I want you to call me David."

"No, that's not possible!"

"At least when we're alone, Meg. I won't have that foolish formality between us."

Another silence.

"Please, Meg."

"All right—David."

A peculiar elation surged inside him at Meghan's use of his given name, leaving David at a loss for a response. Meg took the opportunity to continue. "I must be getting home now. My Ma's waiting for my return, and it won't do to keep her. So, I'll say goodnight—David."

Realizing he still hadn't responded as Meghan turned out of sight on the path, David also realized Meg's soft pronunciation of his given name was echoing in his ears, and he was savoring it—the sweetest sound he'd ever heard.

"Ye need not fear, m'dear. I'm not so sure how many more days yer Ma's left in her, but she'll make it through this night."

Dr. McGee's raspy whisper achieved the volume of a shout in the soundless room, and Meghan looked quickly toward her mother's bed a few feet away.

"Not to worry. The dear woman's into a deep sleep. She's had a hard day of it just laborin' to breathe, and she'll not hear a word I say to ye now."

Giving Meghan's shoulder a comforting pat, Dr. McGee looked up at Sean, standing slightly behind Meg. "As for ye, Sean, I'm thinkin' I should take this time in the presence of ye both to say ye can't expect much more of yer mother's brave heart than to last through the summer, she's that weary of fightin'."

Dr. McGee saw the tremor that quaked the girl at his words, and he shook his head with regret, his eyes turning to Father Matthew where the man kneeled on the opposite side of Mary's bed. Although the young priest was deep in his prayers, he knew the fellow had heard every word he said.

"Is there nothin' you can do for her, doctor?"

Dr. McGee attempted a smile in response to Sean's halting question. "Ah, Sean, ye see here a mortal man who with the best of intentions cannot do more than ease the way when God calls one of us home. And I'm thinkin' Mary's beginnin' to hear His voice. I'm sorry, me boy."

"Aye, everyone's sorry." Sean's bitter retort turned Meg toward him. His expression was stiff as he then squeezed her shoulder in an attempt at comfort. "So it looks like it's to be just the two of us soon, Meg, and we've to set our minds to it. But we both knew that, didn't we?"

Able to do no more than nod, so tight had her throat become at his words, Meg saw Dr. McGee had chosen to ignore Sean's sharp response and was back at Ma's bedside for a last check before leaving.

Allowing Sean to lead her from the room behind Dr. McGee a few minutes later, Meg leaned against her brother's side, comforted as his strong young arm tightened around her shoulders. She had come home only a short time before this most recent attack of Ma's sent her flying for Dr. McGee. Gasping breathlessness had turned Ma's gaunt face so gray as to appear void of life by the time she returned with the doctor, were it not for the agony reflected there. It was that appearance of imminent death that had caused Aunt Fiona to summon Father Matthew as well.

The arrival of Dr. McGee and Father Matthew had been almost simultaneous, and it was more frightening still to see how helpless these two men were in attempting to fight the inevitable. Meghan had never been more aware than during the last hour that Ma's life was in the hands of a far greater power than they, and she had never felt more vulnerable. She knew Sean's most recent display of bitterness was a reflection of that same realization, and her sense of impotence grew.

Silent at her side as she listened to Dr. McGee's instructions, Sean waited only until the front door closed behind the doctor before uttering a savage oath.

"Sean, Dr. McGee's done his best!"

"Aye, they've all done their best, haven't they?" His light eyes glacial, Sean faced Meghan's soft reprimand with increasing bitterness. "Every last one of them has done his best. Uncle Timothy's done his best by us, and resented every minute we've spent in this house. Aunt Fiona's done her best, and not had the courage to open her mouth to a husband that treats her no better than a servant, and treats us like a burden he can't escape, despite our bond of blood. Father Matthew's done his best by puttin' you in the hands of them Langs and by prayin' to a God that's deaf to all our pleas, if, indeed, He's up there a'tall."

"Sean, you're sad and angry and frustrated because Ma's slipping away from us, but the truth is, there's nothing anybody can do. Ma knows that, too, and she'll not be too sad to go. She told me so. She told me she's looking forward to seeing Da and the boys again, and she—"

"I'll hear no more of that rot, Meg!"

Her words coming to an astonished halt at Sean's outburst, Meg gasped as Sean grasped her by the shoulders and gave her a hard shake.

"Has all the fight gone out of you since you began working in that viper's nest on the hill?" Pausing only a moment to take in Meghan's startled expression, Sean continued heatedly, "Do you not remember all the things Da told us?"

"I remember, Sean, but Da didn't mean we should stop short of realizing what's right or wrong."

"Right or wrong?" Sean's sudden, bitter laughter sent chills racing down Meghan's spine. "Ah, sometimes I forget how innocent you are, Meg." Suddenly quieting, Sean stroked his callused palm against his sister's smooth cheek. "And sometimes I forget for all the closeness that's between us, that it's not your place to take the necessary steps in this affair, but mine."

"What are you saying, 'necessary steps'? All that's necessary for us now is to see that Ma passes in peace. It's what we owe to her. Ma only wants you to be happy and live a good life when she's gone."

"Aye, that I'll do, or know the reason why. And I'll see that you do, too, Meg. Don't you worry. We'll be out of this house one day soon, you'll see, and I'll make a place for the both of us when Ma's gone. No matter what anybody thinks or says, there's more in Dennis O'Connor's son, Sean, than anybody knows or sees."

"Anybody but me, Sean. I know exactly what's inside you, 'cause it's inside me, too. And I know you want the best for me, just like I want the best for you. That's why I'm saying I want you to remember the other things Da said—how a man has to pull himself up without anybody else helping or suffering for it; that a man must look at his own face in the mirror each day, and if he can't meet his deeds in the eye, it's all been for naught."

"I'll not shy from facing what I see, Meg. And I'll not regret doin' what must be done."

An unexpected step from behind turned both Sean and Meg to Father Matthew's stern expression as he spoke into the sudden stillness of the hallway.

"And what might that be, Sean?"

Anger tinted Sean's face as he sneered, "If I was to confide in anyone, you'd be the last one, Father."

"Sean, you shouldn't say such things to Father Matthew!"

"Shouldn't I?" Appearing to relent in the face of the unexpected tears that brightened his sister's eyes, Sean shrugged. "Well, if you say so. I'm not going to argue with you, Meg, for it's not my wish to add to your burden of this night. And since I can say no more with any honesty without makin' matters worse, I'll take my leave to go to a place where there's more sympathetic company."

Glancing at Father Matthew as he grasped the doorknob and prepared to leave, Sean turned back to his sister once more. "It's my thought that you'll hear little good of me while I'm gone, but I've only to look in your eyes to see that it'll make little difference to you. 'Cause you know as well as I that it's soon to be you and me against them all. Isn't that right, Meg?"

The import of Sean's question registered deep inside her as Meg returned the intense stare of brilliant eyes so similar to her own. And she responded with a whispered, "Aye, that's so."

Sean's eyes narrowed as he walked the familiar, moonlit street on the way home. His step was uncertain, but his mind was steady and racing at the feverish pace of fury. He clenched his fist, wincing at the pain, and gave a satisfied snort. He'd taught Kevin Mulrooney what it cost to make unwise comments about one of his kin!

Grunting as he stumbled on an unseen rut in the road, Sean cast a glance toward the house on the hill, lit brightly as it was each night with complete lack of regard for the cost. A low oath escaped his lips. Damn all them up there to hell!

His mind returned to the noisy saloon where he had spent the past few hours after leaving Meg and Father Matthew in the hallway. He dismissed the angry dispute that had raged about Franklin Benjamin Gowen and suspicions of monopoly. For all their talk, none of the men there could influence the outcome of Gowen's endeavors, and as far as he was concerned, most of the talk was wasted effort. But he had gone to the *shebeen* with thoughts of learning, and learn he had. If he was not wrong, the Mollies would gear up their efforts should Gowen be successful, and he was anxious to see the result. However, he presently had things of a more important nature to consider this night.

Kevin Mulrooney's drunken leer again coming to the fore, Sean growled low in his throat. Could what Mulrooney had said be true? Had he really seen Meg out riding with David Lang, comfortably sharing the bastard's saddle as if she wanted all the world to see her there?

No, it couldn't have been *his* Meg. His Meg wouldn't let David Lang bring her so low as to have some saying she was going against her own. And Mulrooney wouldn't repeat that tale again, at the risk of losing more of the few teeth he had left in his mouth.

Sean came to an abrupt decision. He would not question Meg about the story, not with Ma being so bad, and with Meg torn up inside as she was. He'd not allow the loose tongue of a fool to cause her more grief, but that didn't mean he'd forget. He'd watch and wait, and if the time came when he found the nephew of the proud Martin Lang trying to take advantage of his Meg, he'd handle it.

Raising his chin determinedly, Sean gave a short, decisive nod. And if he had to take care of David Lang, he'd not use his naked fist, either. There were better ways.

Chapter 8

" 'The Molly Maguires is a society rendered infamous by its treachery and deeds of blood—the terror of every neighborhood in which it exists . . . the disgrace of Irishmen . . . the scandal of the Catholic Church . . .' "

Father Matthew faced his sober parishioners across the altar rail at Sunday mass, his youthful face austere, his small eyes gleaming with the ardor of his words.

"So stated Bishop Wood of Philadelphia in the September issue of the *Catholic Standard* only a few weeks ago, and every decent Catholic here in Shenandoah should loudly affirm his words! The war between the states is now over, but here, in the coal fields, an endless war still rages. It rages in the patches, on the streets of towns all around us, a thousand feet beneath the earth's surface, on country roads, and on speeding trains. It is vicious and merciless, and its violence harms assailant and victim alike, because it is a violence that erodes the soul. Only we can make a difference. We must decry the existence of all secret societies. We must speak up with courage against those who would commit crimes against the decency of man. We must remain steadfast and protest the outrage we see around us, not turn our backs and allow the criminals to go free! Each and every one of us here shares the guilt of the Mollies if we do not stand against them. We must deny the label 'informer,' when we merely act as witness against the atrocities of this villainous group. And we must remember that thugs, murderers, arsonists, and assassins are not honest Irishmen—are not one of our own—despite their claim!"

Pausing to take a deep breath, Father Matthew surveyed the faces of those filling the pews of his small church. Familiar faces all, they betrayed no emotion at his zealous speech; but young and old, he allowed not a one to escape his scrutiny.

"We all know what happened only this week in Pottsville. Two men were shot in broad daylight on a crowded street—the

127

supervisor of Wilson's Colliery and his assistant. They were shot in the presence of many, yet there was not one good man among the witnesses who would testify as to what he had seen. We know the reason for this silence, as well as we know that the assassination was in return for the deceased Mr. Blaine's firing of two Irish miners for drunkenness after they had been repeatedly warned not to report to work under the influence of drink. Mr. Blaine leaves behind him a wife and three children, and his assistant leaves a wife and four more little ones without a father. Some would say that is justice. But not I! And in good conscience, neither can any one of you!"

Father Matthew paused again, to continue in softer appeal.

"We all bear our portion of guilt in this heinous affair, and in the many previously committed, for allowing the cloak of anonymity to remain over the faces of these murderers. Search your souls, my dear people, each and every one of you, and see if you can hide from the truth. I can abide this horror no longer. With this last criminal act, the Molly Maguires have forced me to commit myself to the dissolution of their organization, and it is to that cause that I pledge myself before you today. No longer will my battles against these monstrous men be halfhearted with the thought that members may be represented here, in our very midst today—a part of my own flock. No more will I rely solely on prayer when God has given me the strength and determination to take steps of my own. No longer will I bear the weight of these atrocious acts in my heart without urging each and every one of you to stand up and join me in my cause to bring honor back to the name of our countrymen.

"I call on you now, my good people, all those of you who wish to save your souls from putrefying with these Irishmen who befoul the name they bear with their murderous deeds. I call on you to speak up against them and oust them from amongst you. I ask you to do this from this day onward, as shall I."

Silence met the conclusion of Father Matthew's fervent sermon, and he paused to survey his congregation a moment longer. As he turned back to the altar, he bent his head in silent prayer—not for himself, but for the souls of those who had heard his words and now condemned him.

"Well, he did it!"

David's reaction to Uncle Martin's triumphant statement was reserved sobriety as he glanced toward the sheet of paper his uncle held in his hand. Two months had passed since the fire, and it was well into autumn. David was fully recuperated from his injuries and had regained his manual dexterity, but things had not been going well between his uncle and himself since returning to work at the office early in the month. Instead, an unacknowledged barrier seemed to keep them from the easy communication of the past, and David was at a loss to identify it. It had been a long, difficult morning, and David had the feeling things would not get much better as he scanned the letter his uncle held out for him to read.

"This announcement says Franklin Benjamin Gowen is no longer Chief Counsel to the President of The Road. He's now President! And at the age of thirty-two! I tell you, David, the man's brilliant! Gowen managed his father's Shamokin Furnace Colliery when he was only twenty years old, you know. Then he studied for the bar and became district attorney in Schuylkill County when he was twenty-six. That's when he first became concerned with backing down the Mollies and vowed not to stop until he had them on the run. And as you well know, he's the man we can thank for bringing the state militia in to save us from those rioting union bastards who would've seen our work smashed into the dust last year. He'll be the salvation of these coal fields, you'll see."

"Do you really think so, Uncle Martin?"

"I wouldn't have said it if I didn't believe it, David!"

An expression of exasperation crossed Martin Lang's face as he gave his nephew a hard glance, and David winced inwardly at his uncle's obvious annoyance.

"I'm sorry, Uncle Martin, but you know I don't share your enthusiasm for Mr. Gowen."

"It seems we've not had many thoughts in common of late, David, and I don't mind telling you, your attitude is beginning to give me cause for alarm."

David stiffened, concerned at his uncle's tone. "Are you looking for a 'yes' man, Uncle Martin, because if you are, I'll be happy to oblige. But I thought you brought me into the office with you to learn and to share my opinions with you. That's what I've tried to do."

"Really, David? Are you sharing *your* opinions with me? Or are you repeating the thoughts of someone else who seems to be influencing you far more deeply than I since you were injured?"

David's face flamed a deed red. "You do me an injustice, Uncle

Martin. I wasn't idle during my recuperation, and I didn't sit listening to sad stories of the miners' daily trials as you seem to think." Refusing to enter Meg's name into the conversation as his uncle obviously desired, David continued. "I've been reading books from your own library on the history of the fields, and I've taken great care to keep abreast of everything written in the newspapers about the other collieries, as well as the articles written about your friend, Mr. Gowen. I have a question to ask you. How do you expect Mr. Gowen will accomplish this salvation to which you refer?"

"Whatever way he can, according to the law."

"Shall I tell you how I expect he'll accomplish it?"

"I'll not listen to your subversive ideas, David!"

"Subversive! Uncle, at least hear me out! When you recited Gowen's list of achievements, you failed to list his failures as well. And one of those failures was the mine he bought along with a partner at Mt. Lafee, near Cass Township. Gowen claimed bankruptcy after two years. He publicly attributed his failure to his own lack of judgment, but it's reported he told intimates that the pressure of rising unionism was forcing independent mine operators to the wall, and that unless incipient labor organizations were crushed, they would soon rule the coal trade. He said that unionism could be defeated only by close cooperation of all mine owners, and that a strong and ruthless hand was needed to rule the steadily weakening independent collieries, that the only solution may be merger or absorption."

"Is there something wrong with his beliefs? I happen to agree with them."

"But you're not President of the Philadelphia and Reading Railroad, and not rumored to be supporting a bill permitting railroads to own mines."

"What are you trying to say, David?"

"Monopoly, Uncle Martin! Mr. Franklin Benjamin Gowen is taking his first step toward monopolizing the coal fields, and with his presidency of The Road, probably prices as well."

"What would be so wrong with that? All the mine owners would benefit from higher prices."

"Do you really want one man, no matter who he is, to have complete control over your future, Uncle Martin?"

Silence.

His uncle's small eyes, hard and unflinching, remained fastened on David's flushed face. David felt their scrutiny down to his toes, but he refused to retreat under their intensity.

"You learned all this reading the books in my library, David, and the newspapers delivered to my home?"

"Yes, Uncle."

"It's strange that I didn't draw the same conclusions from them."

"I think your admiration for Mr. Gowen may have influenced your views."

"As your distrust of him may have influenced yours?"

A reluctant smile tugged at David's lips. "Perhaps. I suppose we'll have to wait and see, won't we?"

"Perhaps."

The harshness in his face slowly relaxing, Uncle Martin hesitated only a moment longer before closing the distance between them in a few short steps and placing his hand on David's shoulder.

"I think I owe you an apology, David. The truth is, I missed you sorely in this office while you were recuperating from your injuries, and was looking forward to the time when you'd be back working with me. But when you were finally well enough to return, I sensed a change in you that I couldn't quite define. It bothered me because of the difficult nature of your injuries, and because you seemed to withdraw from us all during your recuperation."

"I didn't withdraw from you."

"Yes, you did, David. But I can't fault you for that. You had a terrible experience, and you needed to find strength to overcome it in any way you could. But you're like a son to me, and while I understood, I resented the loss of intimacy between us which seemed to prevail. I'm afraid I allowed that resentment to carry over into our relationship here during the past month. I apologize for that."

"No apology is necessary, Uncle Martin."

"Oh, yes, it was necessary, and now that it's said, I think we can start over again on more steady footing." His bushy gray brows meeting in an unexpected frown, Uncle Martin dropped his hand back to his side. "But I caution you, that doesn't mean I agree with your assessment of Mr. Gowen, his principles, or his intentions. However, 'forewarned is forearmed,' and you may be sure I'll examine issues more carefully in the future because of our discussion."

"Thank you, Uncle."

"Thank *you*, David, for bringing everything out into the open at last. I suppose I needed to know that the only change in you is a new maturity and perceptiveness I didn't recognize at first. I'm glad to be so reassured of your loyalty, for I think darker times may be coming with the stepped up activity of the Mollies during the past month, and with the continued investigations Captain Linden is conducting into the stable fire and the murder of our agent a few months ago."

Walking back to his desk, Uncle Martin slowly lowered his wiry frame into his chair. Glancing up unexpectedly as he did, he added soberly, "I've come to depend on you, David, and I'm pleased to see you've the courage to speak up, even when sorely pressed by a tired, anxious man who should've known you wouldn't desert him and the values he taught you. And now, if you'll get the monthly production figures from Mr. Clark, we can begin our review."

"Of course."

Pulling the office door closed behind him David paused to allow the exchange between his uncle and himself to register fully in his mind. Uncle Martin had not been entirely candid, and neither had he. As if by tacit agreement, they had both carefully avoided the main issue that appeared to be on Uncle Martin's mind. That issue was Meghan O'Connor.

David felt a familiar discomfort arise inside him. Uncle Martin didn't like Meg or her ilk. He hadn't wanted her in the house when Aunt Letty first hired her, and he seemed to resent her even more since the fire. It made little difference to his uncle that Meg had proved her dependability and her worth. She was Irish and a Catholic, and he neither trusted nor wanted her in close proximity to himself or his family on a daily basis.

And neither did he want Meg to be his nephew's valued friend.

The trouble was, Uncle Martin had never taken the time to get to know Meg. He hadn't experienced her sensitivity, witnessed her intelligence, hadn't laughed at her quick wit, suffered the barbs of her sharp but fair criticisms, or felt the incredible, healing warmth and caring of which she was capable. Uncle Martin had not experienced any of these amazing facets of Meg's personality and he never would, because he wouldn't let himself.

David's frown darkened. He hadn't realized that the friendship that had blossomed into a true exchange of thoughts and affection between Meg and himself during the past month was so obvious.

Nor had he realized that their friendship would appear a threat in his uncle's eyes.

David turned down the hallway toward the accountant's office, and with each step he took the realization became clearer that, for love of his uncle, he would have to tread carefully. For the truth was, he could never turn his back on Meg. Without him, she would be left to stagnate in the mire of her birth, and she was worthy of more.

Much, much more.

If she lived to be old and withered, Meg knew she'd never forget the sound of approaching death.

A tear squeezing from her brimming eyes, Meg clutched her mother's hand tighter still, her own chest aching as her mother's tortured breathing echoed in her ears. Her dear Ma's skin was so gray as to appear almost black, so hard was she straining to draw breath into her lungs, and the brown eyes always filled with compassion and love were now wild and rolling.

Looking to the far side of the bed where Father Matthew administered last rites with a shaking hand, and where Aunt Fiona stood a few steps back, sobbing softly, Meg bowed her head to rest it against her mother's bony arm. But she could not complete her fervent prayer for the shuddering of her mother's emaciated frame.

"Ah, Ma . . . Ma . . ." Tears flowing freely, Meg spoke softly into her mother's unhearing ear. "Don't struggle so to hold on. You told me yourself that Da's waiting for you on the other side, so let your breath slip away. You've given us all your best, every last one of your brood, and Sean and I'll not let you down. We'll be all you want of us, he and I, you'll see. And we'll—"

Meg's heartfelt speech halted as she felt the sudden shock of her mother's direct gaze.

Still struggling for breath, Ma gasped haltingly, "Meg, I wanted to speak to ye. Listen . . . listen . . ."

"I'm listening, Ma."

"Take care of yer brother. His heart's gone cold. He needs ye."

"Aye, Ma, I will."

"Be true to yerself. Listen to the voice inside ye."

"Aye, Ma."

"I love ye."

"Aye."

"Tell me darlin' boy . . . tell him—"

Ma's breathing suddenly lost its strain. Seeming to focus on a point beyond Meg, her eyes took on a glow and a smile touched her blue lips. Unable to speak for the sobs that choked her throat, Meg heard her Ma's final rasp.

"Aye, me love . . . me darlin'. We've been apart too long . . ."

Resting her cheek against her mother's cool hand, Meg closed her eyes against the harsh reality of the last hour. Father Matthew had left the silent room a few minutes earlier to make necessary arrangements, with a promise to return straightway, and Aunt Fiona had gone back to the kitchen and the chores that never ceased. Meg knew the grieving woman had purposely left her so she might have some time alone with her Ma before they came to take her away, but Meg was too numb to feel either gratitude or regret.

Stirring at the sound of racing footsteps outside the bedroom door, Meg raised her head as Sean burst into the room. He came to an abrupt halt at the sight of his mother's lifeless form. His young face still blackened with coal dust, his lunch pail dangling from his hand, he approached the bed in jerking steps, his bright, O'Connor eyes filled and glittering. Trembling, he stood at the bedside as Meg rose to her feet. His voice quavered with pain.

"Aw, Meg, she's gone, and I didn't even have a chance to say goodbye."

Tears welled in Meg's throat at her brother's torment, and she reached out to take his hand.

"Ma spoke about you before she died."

"Aye." Tears flowing freely down Sean's cheeks left white streaks in the dusty mask as his gaze met Meg's with unexpected hatred. "They wouldn't send the message down to me, Meg—the bastards in charge of the shift! They waited until the whistle blew and I was makin' my way out with the rest of the men before tellin' me my Ma was dyin'. It's because of them that I wasn't here when Ma . . ."

"Sean." His name a soft plea on her lips, Meg looked into his tear-stained face. "Ma knew you loved her."

"But I wanted to say the words, Meg! For all the times I let them go unsaid, I wanted to say, 'I love you, Ma.' Now I'll never have the chance. I'll not forgive them for that."

"Sean, please . . ."

"I swear on my life, Meg. I'll make them pay."

"Ma wouldn't want that, Sean."

"Aye, I know what our Ma wanted!" Drawing back from her, Sean turned to stare at their mother's still face.

"It was her time, Sean."

"The devil it was!"

"Sean!"

"Her time was stolen from her, just like it was stolen from Da and the boys, but I'm not goin' to sit back and let them Langs and the others steal away what's left of our lives! I'll fight back, Meg, while there's a breath in my body, I'll fight."

Suddenly dropping to his knees beside the bed, Sean grasped their mother's hand, and Meg fought to control her tears as he whispered a low, fervent oath.

"They'll not do to me and Meg like they did to the rest, Ma. I promise you that. And I'll make them pay for takin' your last moments from me. I swear on my life."

Watching as her brother's broad shoulders shook with sobs, Meg covered the distance between them and threw her arms around him. And laying her cheek against his dark hair, she cried.

Dawn had begun painting the night sky with light when David awoke again with a start. He glanced at the clock on the wall, moaning low in his throat as he ran his hand over his face in a gesture of fatigue. He had awakened countless times through the long, desperate night, and he knew that this time he was awake to stay.

Throwing back the woven coverlet on his bed, David drew himself to his feet. A chill passed over his frame at the unexpected bite in the air, but it helped to clear his mind, muddled with confusing thoughts since Meg had left him to run home at an urgent summons the previous afternoon. He'd never felt so helpless.

Several times the previous evening he had been tempted to ride down into the valley and make certain all was well with Meg. He hadn't questioned his anxiety for her welfare, knowing Meg's concern for him when he had been in need had defied convention as well. He didn't deceive himself for a moment that she needed him now as much as he had needed her. She was too strong. But that didn't stop him from worrying.

In the end, he had bowed to common sense and the realization that his appearance at Meg's door would only cause her discomfort. And so, he waited.

Glancing at the clock again, he walked to the washstand and splashed cold water on his face. Drying himself thoroughly, he dressed in a casual shirt and trousers, carelessly leaving his shirt open at the neck, so anxious had he suddenly become to reach the kitchen to meet Meg's anticipated appearance there within the hour. Taking a quick brush to his hair, he slipped into his stockings and shoes, and walked to the door.

His appearance in the kitchen brought a smile to Cook's face.

"Mr. David! You're up early today." Touching a self-conscious hand to the few strands of gray lying against her creased neck, she blinked almost comically. "It's been a long time since you paid the kitchen an early-morning visit. Margaret hasn't come down yet, and Mabel's a bit late in rising, too. I don't have a full breakfast prepared as yet, but I have rolls in the oven and your favorite blackberry jam in the pantry. It'll only take me a minute to make tea."

Realizing his appearance would cause unwanted speculation if he didn't come up with a plausible excuse for being there, David forced his smile wider.

"The smell of your sweet rolls drew me right out of bed, Cook. After that I just followed my nose, and here I am. I was a little out of sorts at dinner last night, but my appetite's returned." Staying her with his hand as Cook jumped to his service, David continued. "No, keep to your chores. I can put the kettle on myself. I've no desire to have you wait on me so early in the day."

Cook's obvious surprise went unnoted as David took the kettle off the stove and began filling it with fresh water. His back turned, she could not see the anxious glance he raked across the backyard in the direction of the trail from the valley below. Uttering a silent curse, David refixed the smile on his face and walked toward the stove. The sound of a step in the hall turned him toward Grace as she appeared unexpectedly in the doorway.

"So here you are, David! I thought I heard you prowling around your room this morning, but when I knocked on your door you were gone. You were acting so strange last night that I thought you might be sick." David attempted to conceal his annoyance at his cousin's appearance, but Grace's pale blue eyes were too quick. Her small mouth drooped. "Are you angry with me? You're always angry with me lately, David. Either angry or just plain ignoring me."

Uncle Martin's statement of the previous day returned to David's mind, and he realized that his uncle was not the only member of the household who believed he had withdrawn from them. Contrite, David smiled with true sincerity.

"I'm not angry, Grace, just out of sorts. Come on in. I've put the kettle on and Cook's going to get some blackberry jam for the sweet rolls. Do you remember how you used to love getting up early and sneaking into the kitchen to eat Cook's sweet rolls with me before you grew up to be such a proper young lady?"

Her drooping lips taking an upward curve at David's reference to her budding maturity, Grace responded by walking toward David with a ladylike step. Touched by his cousin's almost childlike desire to impress him, David slid an arm around her shoulders as she drew near and pressed a light kiss against her cheek.

"If I've made you uncomfortable in any way, Grace, I'm sorry. You're a dear girl, and I wouldn't have any other for a cousin over you. And you do get prettier every day, you know."

Grace was blushing furiously now, and guilty at his unintentional neglect of her, David gave her a quick hug.

"Oh, David, I've been so worried about you, you know. We all have. You've been so strange since the fire that we thought something was wrong with you. We—" Her small hand slipping up to cover her lips as her eyes opened wide, Grace shook her head furiously. "Oh, I didn't mean we thought something might *really* be wrong with you. I meant—"

"That's all right, Grace. I know."

Her reference to the fire renewing his frown, David glanced back toward the window in time to see someone emerge from the trail. His heart began a rapid thumping in the moment before he realized it wasn't Meg at all.

Breathless from his rapid climb up the hillside path, Johnny Law hesitated as he drew close to the kitchen door. His freckled face stiffened as he looked inside. What was *he* doing in the kitchen?

Bobbing his head with the courtesy demanded of his servile position, Johnny otherwise ignored the young master and the young mistress as he entered the house. He saw Grace Lang's gaze move between her cousin and him in open confusion. The obvious animosity between the young master and himself surprised her, but it didn't surprise Johnny, for he knew David Lang had a long memory and a jealous heart.

Johnny addressed Cook directly. "Meg ain't coming to work

today. Her Ma died yesterday. There's to be a wake today and a funeral tomorrow. She—"

David Lang interrupted sharply. "Who told you Mrs. O'Connor died?"

Johnny eyed David Lang's belligerent expression with a knowing gaze. He'd never understand how Meg could believe this haughty fellow just wanted to be her friend.

"I asked you a question, Law."

"Meg told me."

Young Lang's expression tightened, but John stood his ground. There was no rule that said he couldn't go down to the valley on his own time, and that's what he had done. Lang couldn't get him in trouble for it.

David Lang took an unexpected step forward, grasping him by the shoulder, and Johnny's spontaneous protest was simultaneous with Grace Lang's frightened gasp. Turning sharply toward his cousin, David Lang ordered, "Stay here, Grace. I'll be back in a minute."

Almost jerked from his feet as Lang pulled him out into the yard, Johnny remained silent as Lang turned to assure himself they were out of sight of the kitchen. Johnny did not blink when Lang looked back at him, glaring.

"I thought I told you to stay away from Meg."

"I used my own free time to check on a friend. There ain't no harm in that."

"A friend . . ." Lang's lips twisted in a sneer. "You spoke to Meg herself? How is she? What did she say?"

John responded unwillingly. "She's all right. She said to tell the mistress she won't be coming to work for a few days."

"A few days?"

"She's got that much time coming, ain't she?" Johnny's anger assumed a defensive note. "It ain't every day somebody's ma dies!"

"I ask the questions here, and if you want to keep your job, you'd better remember that! Now get back to your work. I don't want to see you hanging around the kitchen unless you're called, understand?"

"Yes, I understand." Johnny nodded stiffly. "I understand, all right."

Lang walked back into the kitchen, and Johnny controlled an almost overpowering urge to spit in the fellow's footsteps.

Johnny's fair face flushed hotly, and his frustration soared.

Damn that faint-hearted priest! He thought everything would be all right after he talked to him about Meg a while back, but it looked like the priest was just as scared of the Langs as everybody else, because nothing had changed. Well, if the priest wouldn't do anything about what Lang had planned for Meg, then he would.

Johnny stared at the doorway through which Lang had disappeared, the determination inside him growing.

The weather had turned sharply cooler, but Meg knew her shuddering had little to do with the temperature of the day as she stood at Sean's side in the familiar graveyard. She clutched her shawl tighter, and looked up as Sean slid his arm around her shoulders. Sean's face was tight with sorrow and Meg's heart squeezed with pain. The past few days had been the most difficult of her young life.

The simple wooden coffin was lowered into the ground, and Meg watched with a peculiar fascination as it finally came to rest. Father Matthew led another prayer, but she did not join in the response recited by the mourners around her. Instead, she allowed herself to indulge in the brief fantasy that had given her courage during the terrible days since Ma had left them.

Ah, yes, Ma was with Da and the boys now. In her mind she could see them as they welcomed Ma back among them. She could see Da's handsome face and his laughing eyes as he hugged Ma against his chest. She could see Ma's frailness lost in his arms as she protested his enthusiasm with a radiant smile. She could see the boys standing around them—Kevin, Patrick, Daniel, Dennis, and, aye, young James—all waiting their turn to tell Ma they had missed her. Meghan felt the warmth of their reunion in her heart, and her eyes filled for the joy of it.

But her joy was short-lived as the voices around her suddenly stilled, and her eyes were drawn again to Father Matthew's solemn face.

"Meg . . ."

Meg turned her head at the sound of Sean's voice. She knew the time had come, and gathering her courage, she walked with him to the edge of the open grave. Picking up some of the cool, black dirt piled nearby, she watched as Sean did the same. Trembling, she tossed it down onto the coffin.

Folded into her brother's arms, she did not raise her head again until she heard Father Matthew's voice beside her.

"Meg, dear, it's all over now."

Drawing back from Sean's arms, Meg was about to respond when Sean spoke in a tone threaded with menace. "You're wrong again, Father."

"This attitude will do you little good, Sean. Your mother would not have wanted to add to your bitterness, and she would not have wanted you to entertain thoughts of revenge."

"Don't speak to me of my Ma." Sean's voice was a low hiss. "Not now—not ever!" Sean took Meg firmly by the hand. His eyes softened slightly as she looked up at him with a shadow of reproach in her eyes. "No, don't preach to me now, Meg. I've a right to my sorrow, and whatever comes from it. I've earned it with the sweat of my brow and the pain in my heart, and if you dispute my feelings, leave it for another time."

Not waiting for her reply, Sean turned back to Father Matthew. "There's nothin' more you can do for the O'Connors now, Father, so I'm thinkin' you should go back to your church where you belong. Meg'll be all right. I'll take care of her. I'm sworn to that for the rest of my days, although there's no burden in the thought. We don't need you any more."

"Sean!" Unwilling to allow her brother to continue, Meg looked at Father Matthew with a plea for understanding. "We thank you, Father, for helping us as you did." Her eyes moving over his face, Meg found words slipping away, only to regain her voice again as she attempted a smile. "But we'll be all right, Sean and me."

Suddenly glancing around her to see the other mourners had drifted away, and that even Aunt Fiona and Uncle Timothy were making their way back home, Meg took a deep breath. "I thank you for your concern, and I suppose I'll be resuming my reading lessons again now that Ma . . ."

Biting her lips against the words she could not speak, Meg stepped away from her brother and hugged Father Matthew briefly. "Goodbye, Father."

Father Matthew turned toward his church, and Sean followed the priest with his gaze for long moments before looking back at Meg with a frown. "I suppose Ma would be happy to know you gain comfort from that fellow, but for myself, I've no use for the man."

"Sean, please." Her eyes holding his, Meg continued softly. "As you said, now's not the time to argue. It's a time for doing what must be done while the pain heals."

"Aye, Meg." Gentleness returning to his demeanor, Sean again took her hand. "It's just you and me, now. And while Ma's fresh in her grave nearby, I swear that you'll never be alone while there's still a breath in my body. I'll do my best for you, always, and never desert you."

"Aye, Sean. My pledge is the same, and I give it willingly."

Meg's heart lifted as Sean gripped her hand and drew her onto the path without looking back.

Still standing beside the gnarled oak in the corner of the cemetery where he had been for the past hour, David watched as the last of the silent mourners began dispersing. The morning sun had drifted behind a cloud, adding an even more somber note to the scene as Mary O'Connor's coffin was lowered into the ground. He did not think he would ever forget the way Meg's slender body quaked as she stepped to the edge of the grave to follow the barbaric ritual of dropping the first handful of soil onto the coffin.

Sean O'Connor had then drawn Meg into a comforting embrace. He had recognized the fellow immediately, for more reasons than made him comfortable.

David had made it his business to familiarize himself with Meg's remaining relatives, if only from a distance, after she came to work at the house. Meg and her brother resembled each other in many ways. Sean had the same curly black hair as Meg, even if his did not appear to have the same glorious sheen, and his eyes were similar in size and color. The same dramatic length of dark lashes that lined his sister's eyes lined his as well, but it was there that their similarity ended. For where there was a warmth and life in Meg's eyes that touched his heart, there was a look in her brother's eyes that turned him cold.

David knew of Sean O'Connor for another reason as well, for it had been reported by informers on his shift that the young O'Connor would one day spell more trouble than the Lang Colliery would deem worthwhile. Had Uncle Martin not been a fairer man, he knew the boy would not have lasted long on the job after the death of his father, despite the fact that he worked harder than most of the fellows his age, for he seemed to resent the work more than most, too. O'Connor was more vocal than his uncle appreciated in his complaints against his "bobtail" check at the end of each month, and his grumbling was beginning to spread. Sean O'Connor and he had not yet met face to face, but he had low expectations of the moment that was fast approaching.

His gaze fixed on Meg and her brother as they approached the exit gate nearby, David dismissed thoughts of the inquisitive glances he had received as the mourners filed past him onto the street. He was grateful the priest had taken another route out of the yard, because, for some unknown reason, he was not up to facing the man. But he would have remained where he was in any case, for he was unwilling to let this day pass without Meg's awareness that he was part of it with her.

Aware of the exact moment Meg and her brother noticed him, David felt his heart leap at the spontaneous smile that flickered across her lips. Noting, also, that her brother's face turned cold, he waited until they drew abreast of him before stepping forward to speak.

"Meg, I couldn't let the day pass without coming to tell your brother and you how sorry I am—"

"We're not interested in your sympathy, Mr. Lang." Meg flashed her brother a look of silent despair as he continued purposefully. "My sister will be back to do your laundry in a few days, if that's your worry. You can pass that message to all them up there on the hill."

David took firm hold on his patience. "I was concerned about Meg's state of mind, and I wanted to know if there was anything I could do for her."

"Meg's state of mind is my concern, not yours, Mr. Lang, and there's not a thing you can do for her except to stay away from places where you're not wanted."

"Sean!"

Sean gave his sister a warning glance. "Aye, Meg, I said what I meant, and I'll say it again. I've had the shadow of the Langs and their like hangin' over me all my life, but I'll not have it make this day any darker than it is already."

"Meg . . ."

Meg turned to David as he spoke her name. Freeing his sister's hand, Sean stepped forward. "I'll say it one more time. Go back where you belong, Mr. Lang. You're not wanted down here with us common folk, not today, most of all. And if you don't go, I'll send you packing."

"Sean, please!" Turning to David with a pleading glance, Meg continued softly. "Please go, David. Sean's not himself."

"Aye, I'm myself! It's this one here who's pretendin' to be other than he is, and I'll not have him use this day to play more of his charade."

David's patience began to wane. There were a few simple

things he had come to say—that he cared and suffered Meg's pain with her—that he would be there if she needed him. He tried once more.

"Meg, I just—"

Moving between them as Sean took a threatening step forward, Meg gasped softly, "Please go, David. You may tell the mistress, if you please, that I'll be mourning my Ma for a few more days, and I'll then return to work."

"I'm sorry, Meg."

"I know."

"I'll warn you one more time—"

Not allowing Sean to finish his threat, David turned on his heel and walked swiftly down the path. He did not look back to see Meg restraining her brother with low whispered pleas.

Still fighting to control his anger as he mounted the horse secured nearby, David was certain of only one thing. Sean O'Connor was headed for trouble. He had to get Meg away from her brother before he dragged her down with him.

Aunt Letty's fair brow creased in worried lines, and she heaved a soft sigh. David had returned highly agitated from an excursion into the valley only a few minutes before, and had immediately sought her out. She did not have to ask him where he had gone. News from the town below them was very prompt in arriving at the Lang manor, despite their isolation on this quiet hillside. She knew that Meg O'Connor's mother had been buried that morning. She had been totally unprepared, however, when David took her arm and urged her into the privacy of the morning room to make his startling request.

Take Meghan O'Connor into the house to live with them? Impossible!

"It's not impossible, Aunt Letty."

"Oh, my dear boy, I fear it is!"

"It isn't. And it's necessary, if we want to save Meg."

"Save her? From what, David? Her own people?"

"Yes, from them! She's better than they are, Aunt Letty. She's bright and quick, and her mind cries out for more than she'll learn among those ignorant devils."

"Meg is a dear girl, David. I've grown quite fond of her myself in the time since she's been here, and she's proved me wrong for believing that she wasn't up to the chores expected of her, for she's done her share and more. I understand how you feel about her. She didn't spare herself while caring for you during your recuperation, and I know there's a special bond between you because of it. I also share in your sympathy for her circumstances, for the pain she must be suffering at her mother's death, but it isn't as if she's alone in the world, you know. She has a brother, and an aunt and uncle—"

"She'd be better off without them! Her uncle's a penny-pinching drunkard, and her aunt's an ignorant, browbeaten woman who won't stand up to him. As for her brother, he's headed for trouble, and he'll only make her life a misery if she stays with him."

"But to take her out of the valley and into this house as part of the permanent staff, to keep her isolated from them . . . it would never work out! She's a loyal girl. She won't desert them, especially not now."

"I'll speak to her, Aunt Letty. I'll make her see it's the best thing for her."

"David—" Her gentle heart in her eyes as she looked at the handsome young man who was almost a son to her, Letty hesitated a moment longer before continuing. "Even if I agreed to take the girl in and give her a place with the other servants—"

"A room of her own, aunt. She's younger than they are, and she'll need some space to herself."

"David—" Shaking her head, Aunt Letty continued. "Even if I agreed, and she agreed, what about your uncle? You know how he feels."

"Meg's not like the rest of them in the valley."

"You won't be able to convince your uncle of that, you know."

"If I have your backing, I will." His direct gaze reflecting his determination, David watched her closely. "Aunt Letty . . ."

"This is important to you, isn't it, David?"

"Very important."

"I knew it was." With another short sigh, Letty shook her head. "You know I can't refuse you anything, dear, so I'll promise you my cooperation."

"Thank you, Aunt Letty."

"Wait, David, there's something else I want to say first." Her expression still troubled, Letty continued softly. "I think this is a mistake. Meg belongs with her people, and I think she'll be happier with them, but if she agrees to come and live here as part of our permanent staff, I'll take the matter up with your uncle."

David's smile fell to a frown at his aunt's unexpected amendment. "How can I bring this up to Meg if you haven't discussed it with Uncle Martin? It would be unfair to her if he objected."

"You know I'd never ask you to do anything unfair."

"But if Uncle Martin—"

"I wouldn't worry about it, David. You see, just as I've never been able to refuse you anything, your dear uncle has never been able to refuse me."

Unexpectedly flushing to the roots of her hair, Letty suddenly averted her eyes, embarrassed. She did not see David's smile widen, or the affection in his expression as his gaze lingered on her a moment longer.

"I'll talk to Meg about it as soon as she comes back to work."

Chapter 9

"The girl's been neglecting her position on the hill long enough! It's time she get back to work!"

Timothy O'Reilly's slurred words rang in the silence of the kitchen. Expecting Meg to return momentarily, Fiona cast a nervous glance toward the outside door. The child nowhere in sight, she turned back to her husband and took a nervous breath. Tim's complexion was mottled and his stance uncertain, and she knew he had drank heavily before coming home to harangue once more. Shaken by his agitation, she responded weakly in return.

"Me sister was put to her final rest only yesterday, Tim. Meg's attendin' a mass for her poor soul, but she finished her chores before she left."

"Attendin' mass—hah! She's playin' a waitin' game, hopin' she'll stay away from her position up there on the hill long enough to make them Langs tire and hire another. Then she'll be free to laze away her days like before. But I'll not stand for it, I tell ye! I'll not spend the rest of me days waitin' for the debts of those two surly brats to be paid!"

"Yer not wantin' for cash, Tim. The boarders give us a fair income."

"I'll not have ye tell me what I'm wantin' for! Ye never knew where I went wantin' in the past, and ye don't know now, so close yer blasted mouth before I shut it with the back of me hand!"

Lowering her head, Fiona turned back to the stove, only to be spun back to face her husband by his rough hand.

"Yer right to cower, old woman! Ye've been naught but a burden to me from the day we wed, and now ye've brought yer relatives on me like a plague. So I'll tell ye now. The girl goes back to work tomorrow, or she's out of me house, and if the boy speaks a word of sass about it, he's out on the street, too!"

Turning with an uncertain step, Timothy walked to the doorway and proceeded into the hall. His foot on the first step of the staircase, he shouted in a voice that grew more slurred by the moment. "Tell the girl when she returns, old woman! It's back to work tomorrow or she's out of me house. And her brother, too!"

Counting her husband's heavy treads as he walked up the steps, Fiona waited for the slam of the bedroom door before releasing a shaken breath.

Covering her face with her apron in sad desperation, Fiona breathed deeply and wiped the tears from her wrinkled cheeks. No, she'd not let the child return to find her crying. She'd not lay the burden of her tears on those frail shoulders that carried the weight of cares beyond her years. And she'd not let Tim throw the child out. Nay, she'd die before she'd let that happen.

The church was silent and growing dark in the fading light of late afternoon. Having shed his vestments at the conclusion of mass, Father Matthew hung them neatly on the rack in the sacristy and walked quietly back into the church.

Few had attended the mass he said for the soul of Mary O'Connor this day, but he had seen the face he sought in the quiet church as he turned for the final blessing. He needed to speak to Meg, and he was relieved to see she was still busy at prayer in the otherwise empty pews.

The ache in his heart growing as he viewed the sorrow on Meg's small face, Father Matthew took a moment to come to grips with his many anxieties for her. Lingering in the back of his mind was his conversation with John Law, which he had originally dismissed as youthful jealousy. But he had heard of David Lang's unexpected appearance in the graveyard.

Meg looked up unexpectedly and he attempted a smile. She stood as he came near, but he waved her to a seat and sat beside her.

"I'm pleased to see you here, Meg. It's my thought that your Ma is smilin' now as she looks down upon you."

"I've been talking to her, Father Matthew."

"Have you, now?"

"Aye, and I could almost hear her voice responding, so sweet was it when you prayed for her."

Father Matthew swallowed against the thickening in his throat. "I'm glad my prayers give you consolation, Meg."

"They do. I only wish Sean could find a similar comfort."

Hesitating in response, Father Matthew took Meg's hand into his own. He smiled at its daintiness, at the long slender fingers that gripped his hand in return. "Ah, Meg, I fear for Sean as well as you do. When I close my eyes, I see the face of your dear Ma as she asked me to look after his soul, and I know I'm failing her. But there's little I can do except to pray, with him resenting me so."

"Sean doesn't believe in prayer anymore, Father." Meg's voice dropped to a pained whisper. "He doesn't believe in God."

A tear slid from the corner of Meg's eye and Father Matthew felt her despair. He wiped the silver path from her cheek with his palm, and unable to resist, brushed back a few unruly curls from her face. It was pure and unblemished, just like Meg.

"Our Father is a merciful God, Meg. He sees the bitterness in Sean's heart, but He knows the pain from which it stems. And He understands. We must give Sean time to heal, for pressing him will only aggravate the pain of his wounds. They're very deep, Meg, as are yours. But he bears other burdens as well—the weight of a man's responsibility before he's truly a man, and a bitterness that would be too heavy a load for any man to carry. We can only pray Sean's anger will eventually fade."

"Aye, Father."

"As for yourself, you must pursue your studies even harder. It's the only path to independence in this hard place."

"Aye, Father."

John Law's face returning persistently to mind, Father Matthew continued purposefully. "And I remind you not to forget your promise to me, Meg, to come to me with your problems, should any arise. Your Ma asked that I look after you, and it's my wish to fulfill the pledge I made the dear woman."

Meg's hesitation was momentary. "I know, and I thank you, Father." She stood up and Father Matthew drew himself to his feet, feeling the loss deeply as she slid her hand from his. "But I must go home now. Aunt Fiona will be preparing the evening meal, and another pair of hands will speed her work."

"And will you be resuming your work at the Langs again?" Taking his opportunity, Father Matthew questioned intently. "Are you still comfortable there, Meg? Does anyone mistreat you or press you beyond your duties?"

"No, Father, they're kind enough."

"And the young David Lang—he's rumored to be an arrogant one."

"David's my friend, Father, and he's not what people say."

"David—your friend?" A sudden agitation rising inside him,

Father Matthew nodded. "But you must remember that friendship doesn't mean the same to all, and that David Lang, with his wealth and advantages, is as different from us poor Irish in the valley as a man can be."

"No, Father, he's the same—inside, he's the same."

Father Matthew paused in response. "Ah, Meg. I hope you're right."

Turning away, Meg walked swiftly to the church door, the tap of her quick step echoing against the wooden floor. Within a moment she had slipped from sight, and Father Matthew suffered an acute sense of loss as the door closed behind her.

Sean did not truly have the heart for Lawler's this afternoon, but he knew he was bound to stay. He looked at the familiar surroundings of the saloon, the tables filling the center of the small room, and the long bar that curved against the side wall where some stood conversing. He glanced at the faces of the men around him, and he was struck by the thought that although his own life had seen heartbreaking change in the last few days, nothing here had changed a bit.

The room was fairly crowded despite the early hour, and he knew the first shift at the mine had seen its spillage here, for it was from that place that he'd come direct as well as they. It'd been his first thought upon emerging into daylight at the conclusion of his shift, to return home to give Meg any consolation she might be needing. He had been uncomfortable all through the working day, knowing she spent those same hours at home at risk of being exposed to their uncle's drunken ravings. He had questioned the wisdom of advising her to remain away from work awhile longer, and it was then that he decided to urge Meg back to work on the morrow so she would be spared their uncle's savage words.

But despite his worry, he had declined to go straight home. He had other matters to attend to first. Glancing around the room once more, standing with his lean frame propped against the rear wall, the same half-filled glass in his hand he'd held since his arrival, Sean again eyed the men at the bar. Lenny's bright red head stood out amongst them, and it was for that reason that he had come this way rather than going home as he truly wished. For Lenny was about getting information, and he knew should he be present and nearby, Lenny would share all he knew.

A sudden burst of laughter all but drowned out the sound of Tom Donnigan's squeaking fiddle as he rendered yet another Irish ditty to unhearing ears, and Sean gave a low snort. Lenny's face was flushed with triumph at the center of that laughing group, and he knew his friend had been successful once more.

After all, who could suspect the motives of Lenny Dunne? Everyone knew his story, that he and his family had believed the promises of the recruiters and come from County Donegal with high hopes fifteen years ago. There had been six of them then, his Ma, Da, his grandma, two sisters, and himself. But instead of the better life they had been promised, his Da found "Irish Need Not Apply" signs more plentiful than jobs. Spat upon by most mine owners, his Da also found himself at the bottom of the hiring scale, with the English, Welsh, Italians, and other miscellaneous nationalities getting the better positions available.

They had spent their first winter in a patch house in Pottsville, waking up at five o'clock in the freezing cold, the convenience ten yards down a snow-covered path where they'd walked in shoes that were nothing more than eight-inch strips of thin leather pockmarked with holes. There'd been no soap for washing, even if the oily, icy water drawn from the pump had held any appeal, and breakfast was no more than lukewarm gruel without milk or sugar.

There had been no way out, what with short wages and empty stomachs, and summer had been no better there, with the one-room patch house turned into an oven where six sweaty bodies bumped into each other, trying to keep out of each other's way. Lenny's Grandma had not lasted through the first year, and his sisters had both died of consumption within the next five. His Ma's spirit had broken then, and she died shortly afterward. For a long time after it was just Lenny's Da and himself, but the mine got Michael Dunne in the end. It was weeks before his body was brought up from the cave-in that buried him.

Lenny moved to Shenandoah shortly after that, hatred deeply engrained. He had sworn to change the face of things for the Irish in the mines, whatever it took to do it. Revenge had become the driving force in his life.

Sean gave a hard laugh. Just like himself.

As if reading his thoughts, Lenny glanced toward him before slapping Pat Casey's broad back, and sauntering away from the bar with a pleased smile. Sean didn't have to wait long before Lenny was standing beside him.

"Well, Sean, me boyo, I'm thinkin' matters here in Shenandoah are beginnin' to come to the attention of a few important men."

Sean's dark brows rose and Lenny nodded knowingly. "Aye, very important men." Lenny's smile flashed unexpectedly. "Word is out that orders are coming from the very top now. The King."

Startled, Sean shook his head. "You can't be meanin' Black Jack himself?"

"None other."

Sean released a slow, whistling breath. So Jack Kehoe, undeclared King of the Mollies, was taking a personal hand in the ordering of the men. That meant word of the town's doings had traveled out of Shenandoah to Girardville where Black Jack abided, a fair distance down the line. And although no one knew anything about the Mollies, to hear them tell it, Sean knew Kehoe was reputed to be the man who directed local Molly bodymasters throughout the coal region.

A shiver passing down his spine, Sean remembered the one time he'd seen the big Irishman. Black Jack had gotten off the train and was walking down Main Street as big as life. A giant of a man the fellow was, standing at least two inches over the mark of six feet, with a broad expanse of shoulder and chest that stood him out in a crowd. His hair was jet-black and curly, his jaw firm, and his teeth white and even as he'd grimaced unconsciously in their direction. He had never forgotten those piercing blue eyes that cut to a man's soul, and he remembered Da's soft oath at the sight of the man.

Sean gave a low laugh.

"I see ye know the full significance of this, me dear Sean—that we've drawn the attention of a great man to our troubles here, and that we've but to show him we stand behind him to keep his interest keen."

Pausing in response, Sean raised his clear eyes to Lenny's flushed face. His expression sincere, he spoke in a tone calculated not to be overheard by those nearby.

"The truth of it all, Lenny, is that I envy you more each day."

Lenny's light brows rose in surprise. "Ye envy me, ye say?"

"Aye, for you're of an age to become a part of it all now, while it matters most, while I must spend my time waitin' for the necessary years to pass."

Unexpectedly sober, Lenny returned his stare. "We've all done our share of waitin', Sean. But I give ye me promise now. Ye may count on me to be with ye when yer waitin's over, for I saw the anger and the courage in ye from the start. I'll not let the power of it be wasted."

Unable to speak for the emotion Lenny's promise raised inside him, Sean nodded. He knew the fellow was as good as his word. It gave him heart.

Raising his glass, Sean offered softly, "Here's to the day I can be counted on to make the difference." Tossing down the contents within, Sean turned to place his empty glass on the nearby table. "I'll be gettin' home now. There's some things I must take care of while I'm still of a peaceable frame of mind. And I'll say goodbye, and thank you."

Out the door moments later, Sean turned in the direction of home, satisfaction keen within him.

Chapter 10

Shuddering as the cool breeze lifted her hair from her neck, Meg attempted to ignore the chill as she dipped her hands into the wash tub once more. A day had passed since Ma was put into the ground, and she was back to work on the hill, much to the apparent surprise of all. She knew she'd never forget the silence of the three women in the kitchen when she walked through the doorway. She had seen a tear in Cook's eye, and in Margaret's and Mabel's as well, and she knew their sympathy was sincere.

John Law appeared at the door a short time later, and in full view of all spoke his regrets again. She had felt a soaring of affection for the fellow and touched his hand—his face had flushed. She had regretted her actions momentarily then, although she knew John was pleased by her response.

Shortly after her arrival, she was called to the morning room where Mrs. Lang expressed similar sympathy. The mistress's pale eyes were glazed with emotion, which had surprised her as she hadn't thought the woman would be touched so deeply.

Things had drifted rapidly back to the norm after that, with taking up her chores in the usual way, although she sensed a new consideration behind the requests made of her. But through it all, she had not reacted much one way or another to the kindnesses shown her. She was numb in a way she had never been before.

As for David, she had not seen him at all since her return. Cook had taken care to mention that he left for the colliery early that morning with Mr. Lang because of an emergency that had come up during the last shift. The dead weight in her heart had increased, and she had almost been relieved when the laundry was collected and she went out to the wash tubs in the yard. She had needed some time to herself.

Now, still scrubbing the spotless linens, Meg wondered how many more times she'd wash clothes that showed no trace of soil, and linens that were far whiter than those on her own bed at home.

In answer to her own silent question, she knew it was easy to demand things that were fresh when hands other than your own did the work and there was nothing else to occupy your day but such simple details.

Recalling Aunt Fiona's perspired brow and callused hands that were never still, she saw the image of Mrs. Lang's gracefully aging face and well-tended hands, and she frowned at the fine material she scrubbed so diligently. For the first time in many months, a sense of futility at the inequity of life soared within her.

Still puzzling over her thoughts a few moments later, Meg paused, a sixth sense turning her around to meet pale eyes that studied her with unspoken resentment. Grace Lang's appearance behind her was unexpected, and Meg remained silent under the girl's scrutiny, studying her in return.

"Mama thought you'd be in mourning for another few days. She didn't expect you to return to work so soon."

Meg averted her eyes as the young mistress spoke, uncertain how to respond. She could not tell this privileged child that with apology ripe in his voice and with unspoken shame in his bright O'Connor eyes, her dear brother had advised her to return to work so she'd be safe from her uncle's drunken rages while he wasn't there to protect her. She could not tell this pampered heiress to the Lang fortune that the relief on Aunt Fiona's face had been far more revealing than words when she had agreed to her brother's suggestion. She could not speak aloud the words that, with Ma gone, Sean and she were drifting, belonging nowhere, and meaning no more to strangers and kin alike than an accumulated debt without hope of payment in full. She could not tell this girl who had never known a deprived day in her life any of this. She would never understand.

Instead she offered simply, because it was true, "My Ma wouldn't want me to grieve."

The tears that filled Grace Lang's eyes at her response startled her. She had seen naught but coldness in those pale eyes when they touched her in the past, although they had glowed at David's most casual word. She was at a loss for a response when the young mistress sniffed and spoke in an uncertain voice that bore no resemblance to her usual, self-possessed tone.

"I . . . I'm sorry that your mother passed away, and for all the trouble you've had. It must be very hard . . . I mean, I don't know what I'd do if Mama . . ." Once more the tears welled threateningly, and the young mistress swallowed with visible difficulty. "When you first came, I didn't like you because you were different from all of us. You're Irish, and you're a Catholic, and Papa . . ."

Pausing, Grace took another deep breath and tried once more. "I just wanted to tell you that if you come to live here, I won't care. David's right. You're not like the rest of them. You don't hate us or mean us any harm, and you gave David back to us when there wasn't anyone else here who could bring him around."

Halting abruptly as her mother called her from the front of the house, Grace turned with a frown. "I have to go now. Mama's looking for me, and she wouldn't like it if she knew I was back here loitering with the servants."

Turning away without another word, Grace raced around the house in a circuitous route obviously conceived to conceal the direction from which she came.

Still standing motionless where Grace Lang left her, Meg slowly shook her head, bewildered. She recognized an apology and an expression of sympathy in the girl's muddled words, but as for the rest, what had she been talking about?

Another cool breeze touched Meg's perspired face, and shivering once more, she dipped her arms back in the tub and resumed her scrubbing. She hadn't taken offense at Grace Lang's departing words because she knew none was intended. Her only thought was that she supposed some people became confused when they had nothing to do but amuse themselves all day. She supposed it sometimes addled the brain.

She sighed. The poor girl.

His eyes eerily bright in his coal-blackened face, Sean faced Jim Langly's unyielding expression. The ticket boss stood four inches taller than he, and carried thirty more pounds of muscle on his frame, but Sean saw none of those threatening elements as he faced the man across the coal buggy he had filled to brimming.

"Bastard! You've shorted me again, and you've done it to me for the last time."

His lined face unrevealing, Langly shook his head. "I've done nothing of the kind. I've given you a fair estimate, and I won't change my mark."

"Fair! The meanin' of the word is lost on the likes of you!"

The coal yard seemed unusually silent as Langly darted a look at the men standing nearby. The others held themselves aloof, avoiding trouble. Their silence appeared to fortify Langly as he spoke again. "I've been doing this work for twenty years, and I know my job."

"Twenty years of bein' a company man and stealin' from the Irish who break their backs in the mines! Twenty years of paddin' your employer's pockets with money that's due honest men!"

"There's not a better ticket boss in the field than myself, O'Connor! Your father knew that. It's a fact you'd better accept if you want to continue working here. And while you're at it, you'd better remember that you're no better than the other miners' helpers. You'll suffer the likes of me to use my experience to estimate the amount of silt and waste in the coal you load, and like it or not, you'll be paid only for the amount of tonnage that I record on the ticket. That's the way it's always been, and that's the way it's going to stay."

"I'd have no complaint if your figures didn't lean so heavily toward the Langs' side of the ledger! A thief, that's what you are, stealin' the livelihood of good men, and food from the mouths of their babes!"

Langly's lean face flushed in his obvious struggle to maintain his control. "I'll have no man call me a thief, no matter the losses he's recently suffered. So I tell you to shut your mouth now, or suffer the consequences."

"Aye, and now come the threats!" Turning a sharp glance around him, Sean gave a harsh laugh. "Do you hear that, boys? We work the day long until our shoulders ache and our arms are about to fall from their sockets, only to have our tickets grow lighter each day. And this fella here tells me he's the most honest ticket boss in the fields!" Sean's harsh laughter again punctuated his bitter dialogue. "And more's the pity, it may be true, so poor and damnable is our situation here!"

"I'm warning you, O'Connor. I haven't reported your grumblings before, but you're agitating trouble now that'll fall on your own head if you're not wise."

"Aye, warn me, and warn me again, for I've a need to be reminded that I must suffer injustice or be banned from the fields if I speak my mind like a free man."

His anger aroused, Langly paused a long moment before replying in a warning growl. "If you have a brain in your head you'll listen to what I say now, O'Connor, and remember it. You've pushed me as far as you will. It's only my respect for your hardworking father and his boys that's kept me from reporting your grumbling complaints before. And what I have to say about it is this. From this day on you'll do your work and take the ticket I give you without complaint, or you'll be out on your ear. And remember, there'll be another man in your spot before the dust settles around you. So think over what you'll toss away because of a need to blame others for the hardships of life that can't be controlled. And remember you have a sister who depends on you to—"

"Leave my sister out of this, you filthy dog! The whole of your rotten hide's not worth a hair from her head! I'll not suffer her name on your lips!"

His agitation becoming more apparent, Langly replied in a tight undertone. "All you say may be so, but the truth is, your future and hers are in my hands, so I wouldn't say much more if I were you." Sean did not immediately respond, and Langly pressed his advantage. "Accept your lot, O'Connor, and be thankful I haven't decided to make this day your last."

Sean became silent. His young face twitched with fury in the moment before he turned with a snap. Sparing not a glance for the men around him, Sean strode back the way he had come, his gaze riveted on the entrance to the deep hole in the ground where the only future he knew awaited him.

Sean walked rapidly. Langly didn't fool him! Praising Da and the boys, and pretending to have shown him privilege because of their deaths, was nothing more than an attempt to make him soft. But the bastard was right in some of the things he said. Aye, he had allowed his hot O'Connor blood to make him play the fool this day, and he'd not do it again. An open fight favored the opposite side too heavily for there to be any hope of victory. He'd be far wiser to store in his mind each and every injustice practiced upon him and his own, for the day would come when he'd join the only men of courage remaining in this black place. With them, he'd *force* the changes that would make life bearable for the Irish in the mines, and he'd pay back Lang, and all them like him, for every day of suffering endured.

Sean's back stiffened with determination. Aye, he had vowed revenge and his life was set on that course, no matter where it took him.

Meg stared at David incredulously. The sun shining into the leafy bower beside the hillside trail wove a lacy pattern that danced merrily against her delicate features. Still staring, she raised a chapped hand to her brow and unconsciously pushed back her windblown curls.

David moved impatiently as the silence between them stretched thin. A short time earlier, he had come home from a difficult day at the colliery, his disposition reflecting the hours spent with Uncle Martin investigating a problem in the newest shaft. Unable to comprehend how his uncle tolerated the agitation of the ignorant miners and their petty grievances, he had lost his patience with the situation in less than an hour, although he had been obliged to remain until the dispute was settled. As a result, he'd arrived home with Uncle Martin an hour later than usual, only to have Aunt Letty draw him aside to tell him Meg had returned to work that morning.

Silently cursing each and every stone-faced Irishman in the mines, he had rushed to the kitchen to find Meg had left for home a few minutes earlier.

Even now he could not quite believe the sense of loss he had experienced in the moment before he had dashed from the kitchen without a word and started down the trail after her. But his agitation had ceased the moment Meg turned at the sound of his step, a smile lifting the lines of sadness from her face.

He had taken her into his arms then, holding her childish slenderness against him for long silent moments, and she had embraced him in return. There had been no strangeness between them as he had muttered inadequate words of sympathy against her hair and as she nodded in reply. The exchange had been the first spontaneous acknowledgement of the bond between them, and he had been touched as never before by her trust in him despite their differences.

But the warmth and joy of the moment gradually changed as he began speaking his earnest plans for her.

Finally breaking the extended silence, Meg managed an astounded, "You're out of your mind!"

"No, Meg. I'm not."

"How can you imagine I'd agree to such a thing?"

"Don't say that, Meg. Don't say anything until you've had a chance to think over what I'm offering you."

"Offering me? What're you offering me? A chance to abandon my brother and those of my own blood by living in your house and spending my days in the company of the servants there?"

"I'm offering you a chance at the better things of life, that you'll never have down in the valley. I'm offering you a room of your own for which no payment will be asked. Aunt Letty said there would be no problem with that. And there will be more once you're here and I can reason with Uncle Martin."

"I want nothing from anyone that I've not earned with the sweat of my brow. I'm not yet a charity case, and I'll not be treated like one!"

"Is that what you think, Meg? That I'm offering you charity?" David shook his head. "I'm not offering you charity any more than we offer Cook, Margaret, or Mabel charity because they live in the house while they work here."

"I've no need for a roof over my head. I have a home of my own—with my own."

"Your own!" David's sneer brought a flush to Meg's face as he continued with ill-concealed deprecation. "You and I both know you're nothing at all like the rest of them in the valley. You're bright, and you have an inquisitive mind that's wasted down there. There's so much you can learn here. You'd have use of the library and all the books the tutor left behind when Grace and I finished our curriculum with him. If you have any trouble with your studies, I can help you."

"I don't need your books or your help in reading them. Father Matthew'll take care of teaching me everything I need to know."

David gave a low snort.

"Watch what you say, David, before you go too far."

"I've said nothing but the truth. You've nothing to keep you down there now that your mother's gone. There's so much more for you up here."

Meg shook her head, still incredulous. "So this is what Miss Grace meant when she talked to me today. Aye, and it's a measure of the worth people see in me that they think I'd leap at a chance to turn against my own blood." Meg's mouth tightened. "You say you know me. How can you know me and believe for a moment that I'd desert my brother now, when there's just the two of us left from the dear family I loved with all my heart? Would I be the person you truly think I am if I did such a thing just for the comfort of a room of my own and the privilege of reading a few books?"

"Meg, it's more than that. I don't want to worry about you down there, with that rabble."

"Rabble, you say? Good people, for the most part, turned to a bitter way of life by thoughts like those you've been spouting from your well of ignorance!"

"*My* ignorance!"

"Aye, *yours!*"

"Meg, wait." Taking Meg's arm despite her objection, David held it firmly against her flight, frowning at its thinness. "There's hardly anything to you. You're skin and bone."

"I eat well enough, and I'm strong as an ox. I've proven that."

"Meg, don't be angry." David frowned at her proud, flushed face. "I didn't mean to insult you. I just want more for you than you can ever hope to attain in the valley. You don't need any of them anymore, and I don't want you to go back. Stay here, with us. You won't regret it, I promise you."

Meg was silent for long moments, her light eyes moving over his face with a palpable touch. A slow sinking began inside him as her expression turned to one of open sadness.

"Ah, David, this whole thing is beyond me. It's beyond my understanding that you could think for a moment I'd abandon Sean, the last of my own blood that I can yet see and touch, the only one left who shares my beautiful memories. And it's beyond me how you can hold such a poor opinion of him and the others who've made me what I am, and still have any regard for me at all."

Her eyes filling, Meg drew her arm from his grasp. "And it's beyond me, David, how feeling like you do, that I can still think of you as a friend."

His own throat too full to speak, David watched as Meg turned and walked slowly down the path, leaving him unable to speak a word of response.

And it was then he realized that understanding it all was beyond him, too.

Drawing farther back into the bush a short distance away, John Law flattened himself against the rough terrain of the hillside, grateful for the covering of leaves that aided his concealment. Holding his breath, he listened for the sound of David Lang's heavy step as it turned slowly and started back up the hillside. Feeling safe when the sound became distant, Johnny raised his head and stared after David Lang as he turned out of sight on the trail.

Johnny seethed with anger. Yes, he'd heard it all, and Lang didn't fool him for a minute.

Glancing back down the rough path in the direction Meg had taken, Johnny felt the fury inside him increase. There was no conscience in a spoiled arrogant swine who'd tempt a sweet young thing like Meg with a life of plenty when she'd had nothing but want, just to get his way. And there was no heart, either, in one who'd try turning a girl against her own kin.

So the young master said he'd help Meg with her learning. Oh, he'd do that, all right! He was so good at wrapping the others in the house around his finger that once Meg was within his reach, there'd be not a one who'd go against him, whatever *else* he chose to teach her.

Drawing himself slowly to his feet, Johnny brushed the leaves and dirt from his clothes, realizing the condition of them was such that no one would suspect anything of the new stains. Darting a quick glance back up the hill, he saw his way clear and started back.

A smile gradually growing, Johnny remembered the look on David Lang's face when Meg put him in his place with a few soft words and sent him packing. He was so proud of her. Meg O'Connor was no easy young miss.

His smile faded as he reached the crest of the hill, and Johnny squinted into the setting sun of late afternoon. But if he had learned one thing about David Lang in the time spent working there, it was that Lang was a determined type who would not give up once he set his mind on something. And he feared this time the fellow had his mind and heart set on Meg.

Johnny's lips tightened as he cautiously made his way toward the stables. Well, the same could be said for him. Once he set his mind to something, he did not relent. And he had made up his mind that David Lang would not have his way with Meg O'Connor.

A familiar screeching whistle pierced the grunting sounds of his labor, signaling the end of the shift, and Sean dropped his tools. Arriving on the surface a short time later, he made his way into the light of day with a stiff expression and a tight, rapid stride. He was not fit company for the men filtering out of the mine behind him with Langly's harsh threats still reverberating in his mind, and he knew it.

His frustration growing, Sean continued down the path, his gaze suddenly shifting toward the fellow who stepped off the side of the path to walk at his side. Sean did not need to ask his name. He was John Law, who worked at the Lang mansion. He had come to the house that first night when Ma died, and Meg said he was a friend. But the fellow worked on the hill and was not one of their own, so Sean was suspicious.

Looking guardedly at Law, Sean was startled to see a frustrated anger not unlike his own in the fellow's eyes. He paused to consider it, and as he did, he found himself listening as the fellow started to talk.

Parting from Law as his uncle's house came into sight, Sean reviewed their conversation in his mind, knowing that he had no choice. He must find out the truth.

"I demand an answer, Letty. Is it true?"

The silent bedroom had never seemed so still as it did when her dear husband faced Letty with his tense question. She assessed his angry expression in silence. There had been no signs of agitation in Martin's demeanor when he and David arrived home from the mine earlier. Having spent an hour or more working in the library before supper, he had been highly conversant at the dinner table, and she had enjoyed his good humor as a respite from the agitation she knew David strove to hide after speaking with Meghan O'Connor.

She still had not forgotten the look on David's face when he returned from his talk with Meghan O'Connor. Simple words could not express the anxiety and the confused disappointment so obvious in his expression when he walked back into the house, and she had not found it necessary to inquire as to the girl's response to his proposal.

Letty had known from the first that the girl would refuse, for she prided herself that she understood the workings of the girl's mind far better than most. The reason was simple. Meghan O'Connor was instilled with the same strong sense of family as she, and with both her parents gone, the girl had become caretaker for all that remained of the O'Connor clan. The child would never desert those of her family remaining, no matter the inducement David offered.

How David could have overlooked that facet of the girl's character was a mystery to her. Or perhaps he had not overlooked it. Perhaps it was simply that David wanted so much to believe he could save the girl from her circumstances, that he had convinced himself he could.

In any case, it was over now, but Grace's visit with her father in his study after supper seemed to have stirred problems anew. She knew now that it had been a mistake allowing Grace to know what was going on. Grace was not as mature as she would have some think, and she wondered if more difficulty would result from her dear daughter's loose tongue.

Letty sighed again, facing her husband's anger with a pained frown.

"Letty, I asked you a question. Is it true that David offered the O'Connor girl residence in this house?"

"Yes, it's true." Taking a step forward, her pale blue nightgown making a whispering sound as she touched his rigid arm, Letty attempted a smile. "But you needn't concern yourself. The girl refused."

Silent agitation worked on her husband's face, and Letty steeled herself against the anger soon to erupt. She had not long to wait.

"It seems the girl has more sense than my own nephew! At least *she* realizes it would be an impossible situation. How could he have dared to offer that girl a place in the servants' quarters of this house, Letty? He knows how I feel about the Irish. They're not to be trusted!"

"Martin, she's only a girl—a child."

"It seems I've heard that response before. What's happened to the boy? I thought he and I had settled some things between us, but it appears I was wrong. He's still as confused as he was after that damned fire, and I'll never forgive those damned Mollies for what they've done to him."

"Martin, David's fine! He has an affection for the girl, that's all."

"Affection! What of his affection for this family and all it stands for? Has he cast it aside in favor of a girl who's destined to go to seed just like the rest of them down in the valley?"

"So you see, you and David do think alike after all."

"What are you talking about?"

"David said the same thing to me—that the girl will go to seed just like the rest of them in the valley if she remains there. He doesn't want to see it happen. He wants to help her."

"They're beyond help, the whole damned lot of them! And the sooner David realizes it, the better!"

"Martin, the girl's gone through so much. David feels sorry for her."

"Better he should feel sorry for us and the situation those Irish bastards have gotten us into with their insufferable arrogance!"

"David probably identifies with the girl, Martin. He went

through a similar tragedy with his parents dying and his being left orphaned."

"He wasn't orphaned, Letty! Not really. We took him in, and from that first day, I've thought of him as my own son."

"As have I. And I suppose that point touches him, too, because I understand the girl and her brother aren't truly wanted at their uncle's house."

Martin's face remained unyielding.

"She's not wanted here, either, and I will not allow you to think you've softened me toward the girl. I didn't want her here from the first, and if I didn't feel it would affect David adversely in his confused state, I'd dismiss her tomorrow."

"Martin!"

"I mean it, Letty!"

Letty was struck by the intensity of her husband's frustration, and she rubbed his arm in gentle consolation.

"The girl refused David's offer. It's all over."

"Is it, Letty? David's not the kind to let go of something when he's set his mind to it. I'm going to talk to him tomorrow."

"That would be a mistake, Martin."

"The boy should not have talked to the girl without obtaining permission for his foolish scheme first."

"He had permission. Mine."

"Yours!"

"I knew the girl would refuse, Martin. She won't leave her kind."

"Were you really that sure? You took a chance, Letty, and I don't mind telling you, I'm not pleased with this whole affair."

"Nor am I, but for a different reason, I fear."

"And your reason is?"

"I don't like seeing David so unhappy."

"David again! It seems of late we've all been tripping over ourselves trying to make David happy to little avail. I'm starting to think the girl's bewitched him!"

Observing the look in her husband's eye, Letty shook her head, almost amused. "Martin, the girl's a child!"

"But she'll not remain a child much longer. Mark my words. We're in for trouble if this thing goes much farther."

"It's all over, Martin."

Martin shook his head, a trace of weariness entering his expression for the first time as he squinted into his wife's face. "I have a feeling this whole affair is far from over, Letty."

"It's over for the day, at least, dear. Now, come to bed." Smiling up at him, Letty allowed her pale blue eyes to caress her husband's tired face. "It's been a difficult day for all of us. You're so tense. Would you like me to rub your back?"

Silence.

"Martin?"

Martin Lang surveyed his wife's innocent expression with a gradual arching of his wiry gray brows.

"A backrub? What's this? Are you trying to win me over?"

"Yes, I am, dear."

Silence again.

Realizing she had been successful in startling her husband from the track of his anger, Letty's smile warmed. She inched closer to him and cupped his cheek with her smooth hand.

"I want to please you and make you happy again. Will you let me do that?" Able to feel the tension draining from her husband's limbs, Letty stood on tiptoe and pressed her lips lightly to his. "I do love you very much, Martin."

Martin shook his head, his gradual smile wry.

"I'm on to your wiles, you know. You want to distract me from my anger so I'll have time to think over everything you've said when I'm in a different frame of mind."

"That's right, dear."

"Letty! At least have the grace to deny it!"

"What would be the purpose in that, Martin? You could always see right through me."

"I suppose that's true, and I suppose that's the reason I love you—because I do see right through you to your loving heart." Trailing his fingertips against her smooth cheek, Martin whispered, "Letty, though some may underestimate you, I never have and never will."

"And will you allow this situation with David more time so he may come to terms with things in his own way?"

"Letty, dear, do I have any choice?"

Taking a step backwards, Martin removed his jacket and waistcoat in silence, turning to look down at his wife once more. "But the truth is, you'd have your way in any case. You know I can refuse you nothing."

"I know that, dear."

"Aside from one thing. I won't have the girl living in my house."

"Yes, dear."

A short laugh escaped Martin's lips at his wife's prompt and unqualified acquiescence. "Ah, Letty, you're good for my morale. You continue to prove to me what an intelligent, farsighted young man I was in my youth to have realized that behind that pretty face and considerable dowry was a woman who was worth a fortune more. You're my most valuable asset, dear. With you at my side, I'm the wealthiest man I know."

Pausing at the glitter of tears that filled Letty's eyes, Martin drew her close, and Letty slid her arms around him.

Responding to her husband's familiar touch, Letty closed her eyes, seeking to ignore the voice in the back of her mind that badgered relentlessly. For it whispered that no matter her desire to believe otherwise, everything Martin said about David and the girl was true.

And it agreed that this whole affair was far from over.

Chapter 11

"Don't press me, David!"

Turning with an agitated scowl, Meg looked up at David where he walked beside her, only to see his scowl in return. He had been waiting for her on the hillside trail at the end of the day's work, and their conversation was a repetition of the previous day's. She had little patience for it.

"Wait, Meg." Grasping her arm, David drew her to a halt.

Meg's exasperation increased. "Leave go of me. I can't be late getting home tonight."

"Why? What's a minute more or less between reasonable people? Or is that the point, Meg? Your uncle isn't reasonable. From what I've heard, he's been spending more and more time at his favorite *shebeen* of late and he—"

"Stop! I've heard enough, and I'll not abide that word on your lips, David Lang!" Meghan made a visible effort to control her anger. "I remember the first time you spoke of a *shebeen* to me. You said the word with contempt, and accused my Da of spending too much time there to keep me down in the valley where I belonged. And now you're trying to convince me of just the opposite!"

"I didn't know you then, Meg. I've apologized for that day in as many ways as I can, and now I'm trying to show you how wrong I was. You *don't* belong down there with those people."

"Those people? More's the joke in that one. I'm one of 'those people' more than you can believe."

"You're not."

Meg's small face pulled into an aggravated frown. "David, it seems I can say nothing that'll convince you that it's so, so I'll ask you a question instead. What did you see the first day we met, when you pulled me out of that bush and shook me so hard I could barely think?"

David hesitated before replying. "I was in a foul humor that day because I had been thrown."

"But it didn't affect your eyesight. What did you see?"

"I saw a ragged little urchin from the village who had caused Fabian to balk again. Her clothes were covered with dirt and webs, her hair was hanging in her face, and she had a long scratch on her cheek."

"What did you think of her?"

"I thought she was a nasty little piece, and arrogant to boot, the way she shouted back at me."

"And what do you see now?"

"I see a girl with curly dark hair and clear eyes who's neatly dressed and who's far too worthwhile to spend the rest of her life with people that are less than she is."

"Ah, David." Meg shook her head. "And I suppose you think I'm really the second of those two girls, and not the first at all."

"That's right."

"But I'm not, you see."

"What are you trying to say, Meg?"

"I'm trying to say, I'm still the girl you saw that first day. That person's inside me, feeling the same strength of feelings about her people in the valley, and ready to fight to protect them. I've not changed at all."

"Yes, you have."

"Nay, I've not. That other person you see is the person you want me to be, but the truth is, the real person that I am could never be happy living in a solitary room on the hill away from those she loves. You want to believe I'm the person you see in front of you now, with a clean, neat uniform fitting me well, with my hair tied back neatly."

"It's not how you *look*, Meg."

"Aye, it is, because it misleads you. If I've changed on the outside, it's because I know I must in order to get along with the others."

"That's not so. I know you, and you didn't do all you did for me because you were obliged in order to 'get along.' "

"Aye, that's true. I did what I did because I wanted to. Because it was needed, but that same girl on the hillside that first day would have done the same. It was inside her as well as this person you want to believe is me, but you'll not let yourself see it."

"Meg . . ."

"What I'm trying to say is that I'm no different now from that

Irish ragamuffin you saw on the hill, David. And I'm no different now from most others down in the valley who you say are less than me. And even if you'd have me forget it, I won't."

"I don't expect you to see where you're different, Meg, but I see it. And I won't let you waste your life living among people who'll only drag you down."

A familiar anger started to boil inside her, and Meg shook her head in refutation. "Take care, David. Your ignorance is beginning to rub me raw again."

"Rub you raw? How else can I make you see that there's a totally different life ahead of you if you'll just—"

"Just forget who I am? And what will you give me that will take the place of my conscience, pray tell?"

"Meg, you don't owe anything to them down there."

"Not my brother, either, you say?"

"Your brother's making his own way, and he hasn't set a happy course for himself, if I'm to believe what I hear."

Meg's eyes widened. "You've been spying on my brother!"

"There's been no need to spy. He's been agitating openly."

"Agitating, you say? And you don't think there might be good cause for his complaints?"

"No, I don't! I know what goes on in those mines. I've been there every day for months."

"So, you know what it means to be an Irishman in the mines, do you?" Meghan's face flushed with anger. "You traded your fine English name for an Irish one so you could see how it feels to be pushed to the bottom of the list while the English, Welsh, Poles, Dutch, German, Italian, and every other nationality are given preference over you. And you've swung a pick and dug coal, have you? You've traded the light of day for long hours underground where the dampness gets into your bones and there's not a breath of fresh air to breathe. You've loaded cars and strained to push them into the gangway, all the time knowing that though your muscles ache and your back's near broke, you'll not see half the weight in the car reflected on your pay ticket."

"The Irish have earned that treatment in the mines because of their history as troublemakers."

"If there's been trouble from the Irish, it's because they've been treated unfairly."

Choosing to ignore her, David continued. "As for the method of payment, that's the lot of contract miners. We can't pay for the refuse that goes along with the coal."

"And it seems you can't pay in full for the coal that goes along with the refuse!"

"Your brother's been crying on your shoulder. You shouldn't listen to him."

"Unhand me!" Jerking her arm free, Meg glared up at him. "I've heard enough this day, and if I had any doubts as to the differences between us, you've made them fully clear."

"Meg, wait." David halted her with his soft plea. "You're condemning my uncle's practices on the word of those who resent everything in the mines, including the payment, because they resent the work. But the truth is that it's a fair system, and it's the only one that's reasonable."

"So you say my Da and the boys were shirkers, for they had their share of complaints."

"They were all biased, Meg."

"And you're not?"

"From my position of observance, I can see the whole picture, while they couldn't."

"Aye, I suppose you're right. Their hands were too blistered and their backs too sore to stand above it all and look down on those still laboring like rats in their holes." David's face stiffened at her barb, and Meg nodded. "Aye, they saw things differently, all right."

"Those who stay in the mines stay there because they want to or can't do anything else! Nobody makes them come to work each day. If they had a lick of sense, they'd use their spare time to educate themselves and their families, instead of wasting it leaning against a bar in their favorite—"

"*Shebeen*? Aye, *shebeen*. That's what you were going to say, isn't it? Well, perhaps you're right again and there's all that opportunity down there going to waste while life passes the poor, ignorant fools by. And so you see, I'm more like them than you think, with me letting this golden opportunity you're offering go by as well."

"Meg, I didn't mean—"

"Leave me be, David! You've said enough."

Grasping her arm again, David shook his head. "I've said it all wrong, but I haven't said enough if I haven't convinced you to—"

"I said to let me *be*!"

Again jerking her arm free, Meg started down the trail, clenching her teeth as she heard David's step behind her.

"Meg, damn it! Meg!"

Running from the sound of his voice, Meg allowed her anger to deafen her to his plea. She had reached a leveling of the path when David caught her arm once more.

"Meg, I'm sorry."

"No, you're not. Leave go of my arm."

"Meg, I—"

"You heard what she said! Leave go of her arm!"

Her head turning toward the familiar voice, Meg felt the blood drain from her face as Sean stepped out from under a nearby tree, his face livid under the layer of coal dust darkening his fair skin. David slowly released her arm as Sean walked closer, and Meg sensed more than saw the squaring of his frame as he prepared to meet Sean head on.

Stepping into the breach between them, Meg attempted hasty reassurance. "Sean, not to worry. David was but walking me to the bottom of the trail. There're some things he'd have me do at the house first thing tomorrow and he—"

"Lies do poorly on your lips, Meg. Don't waste your time expendin' them, 'cause the truth is, I know what this fella's about."

"Do you? I doubt it." Returning menace for menace, David held Sean's stare. "Meg's been offered a chance to come to live at the house as part of the permanent staff."

"Ah, great's the honor in that!"

"Your sarcasm suits you." Ignoring Sean's growing anger, David continued tightly. "If you really care for your sister, you'll urge her to accept. It's an opportunity for her to better herself."

"What with? The likes of you?" Sean gave a short laugh. "No, thanks. My sister don't need you or a place in your house."

"What can you offer her instead? Precious little."

"Aye, precious little to compare with what you're offerin' her!" Sean closed the distance between them in a few quick steps, his breathing rapid in his escalating fury. "Nothin' more than the pride and decency you're hopin' to take from her with your scheme."

The gold flecks in David's eyes flashed warning of his lapsing control as he growled tightly, "My 'scheme'? Filthy thoughts from a filthy mind."

"Not as filthy as yours! And I tell you now, you'll leave my sister alone, or you'll not live to know regret!"

"Sean!"

David's reply held a note of contempt. "He doesn't frighten me, Meg."

"Are you too stupid, then, to know reasonable fear? So, let me make myself more clear. My sister's life's her own, and if you try to make it otherwise, you'll pay the price!"

Meg's low gasp turned Sean toward his sister as he grasped her arm. "Aye, I meant what I said, Meg."

Turning back to David, Sean continued. "And don't think I fear you or your money. There's ways to bring a man to equal terms."

"Four men to one—or a shot in the dark? Those are the methods you people use to settle your differences, aren't they?"

"Aye, and they serve us well."

"Sean!" Turning back to David, Meg shook her head. "I'm sorry. He doesn't mean it. He—"

"That's enough!" Sean's face was livid. "I meant every word!"

Her glance at David a silent plea, Meg turned back to her brother. "All right, Sean. Please, let's go now. I want to go home."

"Aye, we'll go." Looking up at David, a new light touching the anger in his eyes, Sean stated flatly, "You may tell them up on the hill that my sister will not return to your house."

"Sean!"

"You heard me, Meg!"

Intensely aware of David's silence, Meg would not chance another glance at his white face as she slipped her hand into Sean's. Her heart hammered in the few moments it took for Sean to grasp it tightly and to draw her with him onto the trail.

The confrontation abruptly concluded, they continued on down the trail, and it was only when they reached the bottom that Sean halted to look into his sister's pinched face.

"You should've told me what he was proposin', Meg. It's my duty to care for you."

"It was an honest offer, Sean. It came from Mrs. Lang herself, and it was meant well."

"Not with the devil himself chasin' you to make you comply!"

"David wouldn't hurt me, Sean."

His gaze suddenly and unexpectedly tender, Sean raised a gentle hand to her cheek.

"Ah, Meg, sometimes I forget you're an innocent babe who believes the best of all. And sometimes I hate myself for havin' to make you see the world as it truly stands. But Ma left you in my care, and I'll not let them Langs have their way with you. You're not goin' back there, ever."

"But Uncle Timothy—"

"You're not goin' back."

Nodding, Meg grasped Sean's hand and turned to step onto the road. Refusing to move, Sean waited until she looked up inquiringly before speaking again in a softer tone.

"Did you hear me, Meg?"

"Aye, I heard you."

Pausing only a moment longer, they started home.

"She's goin' back to work in the house on the hill, I tell ye!"

"And I thought all the bastards lived atop the hill!" Sean stared at his uncle with visible hatred. He had arrived home a few minutes earlier with Meg, knowing in his heart what his uncle's reaction would be to the termination of Meg's employment at the Langs', and he hated the drunken sot all the more for proving him right.

Sean took a threatening step toward his uncle where he swayed in the kitchen doorway, but Meg stepped between them with a low plea. "Sean, please. Come upstairs with me and let's talk a bit. We must think things through."

"Aye, ye've to think things through, all right! But before ye go, I'll say it again and make meself clear. The girl's to go back to work on the morrow or yer both out of this house!"

Sean advanced another menacing step as Uncle Timothy turned away, finally yielding to Meg's whispered, "No, Sean, let him go. He's two sheets to the wind and not to be reasoned with."

Sean's response came from the bottom of his heart. "I'll kill that man one day."

Observing from the sidelines, Aunt Fiona silently left the room, and Meg continued earnestly. "Sean, we've naught to gain with such talk. And the truth is that Uncle Timothy's right. With most of your wage going to the tab Da left behind, he's been supporting us with his own money. It's only my wage that's free and clear."

"The debt is mine."

"No, it's shared equally between us. Ma would want it that way. You've naught to fear about my employment at the Langs'. I'll not be pressed to join permanent service, and when my learning is improved a bit more, Father Matthew will find me other employment."

"Aye." Sean sneered. "Just like he did before."

Taking a step closer, Meg looked up into his face and Sean felt the power of her heartfelt plea deep inside him. "I've not suffered for my employment on the hill, Sean. And I give you my word that should I be pressed beyond my limits in any way, I'll speak to you first so we may set it right."

Meg rubbed his arm in a way she had done since childhood when imploring him, and Sean felt the hard core of his anger soften as she spoke again. "Sean, please. Father Matthew—"

"Aye, Father Matthew!" His anger reviving at the priest's name, Sean shook off his sister's hand. "All right, go back to work for them Langs if that's what you wish, but, mind, don't deceive me. For if you do, and I discover it, Lang will be the loser."

Not able to bear the distress in Meg's eyes, Sean turned toward the door, only to pause at her uncertain, "Where're you going, Sean? You've not eaten dinner."

"My stomach's full with aggravation, Meg. I'll not need food this night." Then, at her look of growing agitation, "Don't worry yourself. I'm all right."

Out on the street moments later, Sean knew he was not all right. He had given in to Uncle Timothy this time, but he'd not give up his Meg. He'd watch and wait, and when the time came, he'd do what he must do.

The chill of early morning sank into his bones as David waited on the wooded trail where he last saw Meg the day before. The thought of spending the day at the colliery with his uncle without speaking to Meg first, or without knowing if she had returned to work at all, had gotten him out of bed at dawn and posted him in his present position to await her arrival.

A shiver passing down his spine, David adjusted the collar of his jacket against his neck, his mind drifting to the day before and his confrontation with Sean O'Connor. There was no doubt the fellow was a bad one, and he wondered again how Meg could see no wrong in the young brute. But he supposed the bond of blood was stronger than even Meg's good sense. He was grateful that the short encounter between O'Connor and himself hadn't ended in violence, for he knew Meg would not have forgiven him easily had they come to blows.

David darted another glance down the trail. Meg wouldn't allow her brother to dictate the course of her life, would she? The fellow was only a year or so older than she, and inadequate as a guardian, considering his violent bent. In the early hours of the previous night he had been certain Meg had merely appeased her brother because of the situation's potential volatility. Then he recalled Meg's eyes as she looked up at her brother. The commitment he saw there had caused his insecurity to grow.

David's stomach tightened. He had learned something else about himself as he lay abed and sleepless the previous night, and the knowledge exacerbated his discomfort. The truth was that he was *envious* of the bond between Sean O'Connor and Meg. The realization that O'Connor was not worthy of Meg's affection or her loyalty only increased his resentment.

David jammed his hands in his pockets and stared moodily at the tips of his highly polished boots. A fine layer of dust from the trail dulled their shine, but he was blind to all but the familiar face so clear before his mind's eye.

His head snapping up at a sound on the trail below him, David could hear the hammering of his heart as Meg stepped into view. His relief knowing no bounds, he stepped forward eagerly, only to be halted by Meg's frigid gaze.

Suddenly at a loss for words, David managed an uncomfortable smile. "I wanted to talk to you before you started work today, so I came here to wait."

Meg remained silent and David's smile dropped away, leaving him with nothing but words that came from his heart. "I wasn't sure if you'd come today, Meg, but I couldn't spend the whole day at the colliery wondering. I'm sorry I behaved so poorly yesterday. I know now that I did no more than aggravate a situation that I should have handled far differently."

Still no response.

"Are you still angry with me, Meg?"

Holding her silence a moment longer, Meg finally spoke in tones devoid of warmth. "I suppose you might say that."

David frowned. "I've already apologized. I can't do more than that."

Meg's sober expression increased his disquiet, and David took a deep steadying breath. "You've come to give your notice and collect your wage, then."

"I've returned to work."

Relief rang inside him, and David smiled, only to have his relief cut short as Meghan continued. "But I've a condition to my continued employment, strange as that may seem, and it's only now that I've come to realize the difficulty of speaking of it."

The look of a child, but so much more. That thought was foremost in David's mind as he said, "We've never had difficulty in saying what we think to each other, Meg. This situation's no different."

"Ah, but it is." Discomfort flickered across Meg's stiff expression. "You see, I've made my brother a promise. I told him I'd let him know if you pressed me to trade the valley for a room on the hill again. He'd suffer my return here in no other way, and I'll not break my word to him. So, you see, it's up to you whether I remain."

A deep sadness moved through David in the silence that followed. When he finally spoke, his voice held an unexpected rasp. "So you're going to cast your future aside for the sake of loyalty to something that's already lost, and you're—"

Halting in midsentence as Meg turned abruptly back in the direction from which she had come, David stepped forward and gripped her arm.

"All right, Meg."

The simple words of concession echoing within his mind, David waited until Meg turned back to face him before continuing. "There's no point in driving you away with my persistence. I've nothing to gain there. You have my word that I'll do as you say. You can forget my grand plan for your enrichment if you'll promise me something in return."

Meg's clear eyes clouded. "If I can."

"You're asking me to forget everything we discussed in the past few days, and I want you to do the same. I want you to forget all the foolish things I said that came between us, and the anger as well. I know it won't be easy, but keeping to the bargain you ask of me will be difficult as well." And then with a small smile, "Especially since I'm a spoiled sort who's always had his way."

"Aye, there's truth in that."

A flicker of a smile took the sting from Meg's familiar words, and David continued sincerely. "I want us to be friends again, Meg."

Tears welled unexpectedly in Meg's eyes, and David felt a thickness in his own throat as she fought for a voice. "Ah, David, but it's such a difficult friendship. Is it worth the wear?"

Hesitating briefly, David responded, "You know the answer to that as well as I."

Closing the last few steps between them, David slipped his arm around Meg's narrow shoulders. He clasped her against his side without chancing another word as he drew her along with him up the trail. He felt her trembling, and it was with the strictest control that he forced his step to remain steady and his voice to remain even as he began speaking of small incidentals calculated to reduce the discomfort of the moment.

Relieved as Meg's control returned, David looked down into her face as they reached the crest of the hill, only to be struck with the thought of the woman this girl would someday become.

A wealth of emotions stirred within him and he realized then he could fool himself no longer. He would not have let Meg go—at any cost.

Silent and unseen at the window of the morning room, Letty watched the area of woods through which the trail from the valley wound. As David and Meghan O'Connor emerged into the yard and she saw the girl step away from the arm David rested companionably around her shoulders. All appeared well between them, and her relief was bittersweet.

There was no doubt in her mind that David had been drawn to the child the first moment he saw her standing beside Father Mulligan in the study those long months ago, and that the girl struck a chord that rang deep within him. But she had not foreseen the problems that would result from this affinity he felt for her. The present companionship and equality of exchange she saw between them now increased her concern.

David saw something very special in Meghan O'Connor, and if she could not see those qualities as clearly as he, unlike Martin, Letty did not repudiate their existence. But she did worry and fear for the future of the commitment David evidenced for the girl.

Continuing to watch them, Letty saw David and the girl approach the house. She knew they would soon separate, Meghan to attend to her duties in the kitchen, and David to work with his uncle, where his bright future lay. In Letty's mind, that physical separation clearly marked the gulf between them.

Letty turned from the window. Dear David—she so wanted him to be happy. There was no doubt he was happier at this moment than he had been for days, for she had seen the relief on his handsome face when he looked at the girl. But the present was fleeting, and there was an unforeseeable future toward which they all inexorably moved.

What would that future hold for Meghan O'Connor and her own dear David? She worried for them and for all the people who loved and hated them. And she wished so desperately that she knew the answer.

1870

Chapter 12

The hot afternoon sun splintered the lazy mist of coal dust shrouding the valley, touching the abused autumn-colored landscape with muted shafts of gold. Shattering the deceiving tranquillity of the scene, the colliery whistle shrieked the conclusion of the day shift, and the first trickle of miners emerged from the shafts below. The ragged string of workers gradually broadened and grew in length, the expressions of the men betraying no sign of the year of disturbance recently passed or the agitation still playing underneath the surface tedium of daily routine.

Watching from his office window, Martin Lang's hawklike features tightened with distaste as he surveyed the weary line. They didn't fool him!

Martin walked to his desk, grateful that David had departed a short time earlier, leaving him alone with his thoughts. Lowering his wiry frame into his chair, Martin looked down at Captain Linden's report. It had been a troubled year in many ways, and he needed time to digest these latest revelations as his mind drifted back to the sequence of events which had led to this distressing point in time.

As much as Martin hated to admit it, David had been correct in his evaluation of Franklin Gowen and the impact his elevation to presidency of the Philadelphia and Reading Railroad would have on the coal fields. Gowen's initial move as president had been to persuade the state legislature to pass a bill permitting railroads to own mines, and the second was to change the name of the company to the Philadelphia and Reading Coal and Iron Company. From then on, only a fool would not have been able to guess the direction in which this powerful and determined young man would move.

Floating a rumored loan of twenty-five million dollars, Gowen began purchasing land in Schuylkill and Northumberland counties. With the help of strikes and financial difficulties, he convinced many individual operators to sell, and, although he was unsuccessful in adding the Lang Colliery to his long list of acquisitions, there was no longer any doubt in Martin's mind that Gowen had absolute control of the anthracite fields in mind.

It was not long before another of Gowen's intentions then became clear. Divide and destroy the unions and bring the Irish in the coal fields to heel.

Frowning, Martin rubbed a weary hand across his brow. He had no affection for the Irish in the mines. Every last one of them shared the guilt of the Mollies' crimes. It was from within their ranks that the current incarnation of the Mollies had been spawned, and their silence was collusion that allowed the heinous deeds of their murderous countrymen safety from the law.

The Irish were a troublesome lot who needed to be reminded of their place, but, somehow, he could not find it within himself to justify Gowen's underhanded, totally ruthless tactics in handling them. Innuendo, malicious slander, and job discrimination became his tools as he used the power of his position to create dissension within their ranks and confuse them with vacillating policies, sometimes favoring newly arrived Irishmen over long-established miners, and then reversing the procedure without notice. Using informants in the pits, breakers, stables, engine houses, and at outside workings, he heard each whisper of incipient unionism, and would often throw miners off balance by promoting a troublemaker instead of firing him, only to fire the next organizer and have him blacklisted everywhere within the coal fields while his family starved.

The situation among the private operators remaining was approaching chaos, as those of Lang's group were faced with heightened Molly activity and uncertainty as to Gowen's next move. Himself the recipient of one of Gowen's open scoldings for allowing the operation of a "pluck me" store in his patch, Martin was well aware that Gowen had banned such practice in his own holdings. Gowen also refused the posting of the hated "No Irish Need Apply" signs used in some areas of the fields, but he was not above lending a hand to anti-Catholicism whenever he could if he thought it would raise more dissension in the fields.

However, Gowen's totally despicable trick a year earlier was the move that finally forced Martin to see Gowen for the man he truly was. Blatantly using a disaster in which more than one hundred Welsh miners were killed to his advantage, Gowen started a rumor that the anti-Welsh Molly Maguires started the blaze. The reaction was a heightening of tensions in the coal fields, and the outrage of the silent, unidentifiable Molly organization sparked a new round of incidents at the mines that had not yet abated.

Releasing a disturbed sigh, Martin Lang shook his head. No, he had no use for such tactics. It was not his objective to control his miners and overcome the Mollies by lowering himself to their level.

His mind slipping to more personal matters, Martin experienced a similar frustration. It had been a difficult year on his home front as well. David's handsome young image appeared before him as Martin recalled the spring season of the previous year, before the fire. Everything had seemed so clear then. David had finished his curriculum, excelling in every way, and Martin had then decided to hold his nephew's advanced education in abeyance for a year, deeming it more important to introduce his nephew to the workings of the colliery during that period so he might better understand the areas in which he should concentrate his studies. As it turned out, that was his first and most vital mistake, for in doing so, he had allowed David to remain on the scene to become involved with that damned O'Connor girl.

A whispered oath escaping his lips, Martin drew himself to his feet and walked to the window once more, his eyes moving unseeingly to the hills beyond. He had been correct when he disagreed with Letty as to the threat the O'Connor girl presented. It had been only too obvious to him when he saw her before leaving for the office that very morning, that in the space of one short year, the girl had left the physical appearance of childhood behind her. She was still small and slender, but womanhood had made its mark on Meghan O'Connor's formerly childish form, and he knew the changes nature had wrought were not be lost on his young nephew.

Returning to his desk, Martin shuffled the papers there with an impatient hand before finding the letter he sought. He read it again and looked up to stare thoughtfully into space as he considered its contents. Unless he was gravely mistaken, the next few years would bring about great changes in the coal fields. His future and the future of those he loved were at stake. David placed highly on that list of loved ones, and he could not afford to make another mistake.

An expression of pained exasperation passed over Lang's narrow, lined face. He had handled the situation with David and

Meghan O'Connor poorly during the past year. He had depended on David's intelligence to bring about an understanding of the dangers of his allegiance to the young Irish girl. In doing so, he had neglected to take into account David's youth and susceptibility. Fool that he was, he had somehow forgotten how it felt to be young and idealistic and to be certain he could read more than others in the eyes of a particular girl. He had forgotten how a girl's smile could thrill, and how the promise of more could send the blood racing.

Damn it all! Now David would be the loser if he did not act quickly and wisely. Glancing down at the letter in his hand, Martin finally conceded that he must take the necessary steps, however difficult they proved to be.

A brief glance around her as she reached the top of the staircase assured Meg that she was alone. Hastening down the silent hallway of the Lang mansion, she paused before Grace Lang's bedroom and surveyed the area one more time before opening the door and slipping inside.

Releasing a tense breath, she turned and assessed the chaos, uncertain exactly where to start. How this particular chore had fallen to her in recent months was not entirely clear in her mind, but it was now an accepted part of a thrice-weekly ritual that she should employ stealth to sneak into Grace Lang's room when the girl was otherwise engaged in order to clean it without her knowledge.

Ah, she wished she could hear Ma's reaction to that one! She had no doubt her Ma's beloved laughter would ring out loud and clear even while she shook her head with disapproval. But it really wasn't funny, and she knew Ma would have been the first to agree.

A spoiled daughter of loving, indulgent parents—that was Grace Lang, and she feared the young woman would suffer for it. Not that Miss Grace was lacking in any way from outward appearances, for she was lovely to look at, to be sure. Meg had never seen such lustrous blond hair, or such clear pale skin, and there had been a wealth of change in Miss Grace's womanly proportions in the past year. Always a beautiful young girl, Grace Lang was now a beautiful young woman. But, strangely, Meg did not envy her in the least, for on the inside the young mistress was still a child.

However, it was not her place to criticize her employers' daughter. For that reason she cooperated with the conspiracy that now placed her in this room, and she knew she would perform the task as long as it was requested of her.

Leaning over the nearby bed, Meg scooped up three lacy frocks tossed there in a careless heap and walked to the wardrobe to hang them. The vast array of dresses displayed as she opened the door no longer impressed her, as accustomed as she had become to the excesses of the household, but she knew the average young woman in the valley would not own that many gowns during the whole of her lifetime. That thought somehow saddening, Meg completed her chore and began scrambling for the shoes thrown helter-skelter around the room. Aye, and so many children in the valley went barefooted.

Meg caught her reflection in the mirror as she stood frowning, but she knew she could not truly fault the conditions of her employment in this household. The new, well-fitted uniform she wore this day was evidence of the mistress's concern for her appearance. She had received new uniforms three times in the past year to accommodate her growth, and since the rest of the staff received a supply of uniforms only once a year, she had been embarrassed at the mistress's need for such unusual expense on her behalf.

Meg studied her reflection briefly. Aye, her height had seen the addition of at least two inches—maybe three—and her body was no longer straight as a stick. She had reached her fifteenth year in May, and physical changes had seemed to come suddenly upon her shortly thereafter. Small breasts bloomed as her rib cage stretched with her height, and her hips developed a gentle curve that now gave her the appearance of a young woman. But she had not needed the physical reassurance of maturity to know she was an adult, for she knew that the responsibility her Ma left her, however well she cherished it, had matured her long before her womanhood became obvious to the eye.

Aye, that responsibility was Sean, her dear brother. The passage of a year had wrought little change in him on the inside, with the bitterness that still gnawed at his peace of mind, but the outside had changed immeasurably. At sixteen Sean was now manly and broad, with their Da's same handsome face, even if his smile was not as bright or as frequent. He had not grown to their Da's full height, but he touched the mark of ten inches past five feet, and with considerable brawn added to his frame, he was beautiful to behold. And, on the rare occasions when he so chose, Sean was such a charmer. The girls were all agog about him, most especially Sheila McCrea, her closest friend, although she discouraged Sheila's interest in Sean. She did not want to see her friend suffer the heartache that would come in loving him.

Her hands moving quickly at their task, Meg allowed a difficult reality to surface in her mind. Aside from his deep and sincere feelings for her, Sean had little love inside him. He took pride in her achievements and her steadily advancing ability with reading and ciphers, although he avoided any conversation about Father Matthew, but the reality that her life was still involved with the family on the hill gave him little peace. His frustrations mounted daily, for his victories were pitifully few. He was still bent on revenge and the forcing of change, and nothing she said seemed to influence him to think otherwise.

For that reason she had been less than honest with Sean about her friendship with David Lang. She knew he would never understand, because she didn't quite understand it herself. David had been true to the promise he made her the day after that terrible confrontation between Sean and himself, and she did her best to be true to hers. His proposal for her to become part of the live-in staff at the house was never mentioned again, and she had attempted to erase his prejudice against the Irish in the valley from her mind. They began afresh, and although the honesty between them occasionally erupted in anger, strangely enough, the result was to forge their friendship stronger than before.

David's smiling image appeared in her mind, and Meg could not help but smile in return. The past year had seen physical change in them all, but having reached the age of nineteen, David was now a man. He had always had the height of a man, but where he was so slender before, he had begun filling out well. His handsome face, though still youthful, had the mark of a new maturity, and his unusual hazel eyes, so changeable with his moods, had become more fascinating still. And when he looked at her in his special way, with the disturbing affection that glowed so brightly there, she often felt her heart race.

Despite the misgivings always present when she thought of this strange friendship between herself and the wealthy, indulged David Lang, Meg refused to think of the day when her friend would come to see the hopelessness in their continued friendship, and the future just around the corner where they'd have no place in each other's lives. The thought was too painful to bear.

Tripping unexpectedly over another small slipper peeking out from under the massive bed, Meg released an exasperated breath.

Her mind thus forcibly drawn from its meandering, she attacked the task at hand.

Pausing unobserved outside his cousin's room, David peered through the crack of the doorway. Satisfied that it was indeed Meg moving industriously inside, he pushed the door open wider, but she was too deep in thought to notice him. Pensive, David watched Meg's efficient movements as she bustled around the room with an exasperated frown, gathering shoes strewn hither and yon by his careless cousin.

Watching her in silence, David felt a familiar discomfort grow inside him. He was intensely aware that although Meg bore Grace no malice, she had little patience for his cousin's pampered lifestyle. Her reaction disturbed him because he realized Meg probably had little patience for some of his vices that were reflective of a pampered youth, and he realized as well that it was only Meg's prejudices that could come between them.

That thought had become a bedeviling spot of uneasiness inside him of late. He supposed the reason was because he saw little in Meg of which he didn't approve or with which he wasn't willing to compromise. Nothing had happened during the past year to cause his feelings to change in that regard, and he knew nothing ever would.

Still watching Meg's deft movements, David recalled his disturbing conversation with his uncle that morning after receiving the Coal and Iron Police weekly report. He had been grateful for the errand that brought him home early because he needed time to think. Sean O'Connor had been mentioned frequently in weekly reports over the past year, and the general consensus regarding O'Connor since the turn of the year was that although he was less outspoken than he had been, his attitude had not changed.

He hadn't mentioned the reports to Meg because it would have served no constructive purpose between them, but the summary Uncle Martin received that morning was especially damning. It contained Captain Linden's belief that the next time trouble came, O'Connor would be in the middle of it.

However, suspicion was one thing and proof was another, and Uncle Martin knew he could not afford an open confrontation with any of these men now, when the coal fields were in such a state of flux. Realizing the inevitable was merely being forestalled, David had needed the reassurance of seeing Meg on the hill, away from the trouble brewing below. He was desperate to keep her from involvement in her brother's schemes, and for that reason he had decided only a few minutes earlier to broach another plan with Meg.

His train of thought interrupted as Meg paused in her work, smiling unexpectedly at her thoughts, David felt the responsive warmth Meg's smile always evoked. His outrageous comment as he stepped into the room was deliberate.

"You're smiling, Meg, so you must be thinking of me."

Meg's head snapped up in his direction, and the glorious blue of her eyes met his for a heart-stopping moment that made David catch his breath. When had Meg become such a beauty?

"Vanity and arrogance—it's my thought they'll be with you till the day you die, David Lang."

His laughter rumbling despite the sharpness of her annoyed response, David swept the room with his gaze. "Probably so, but you forgave me those faults long ago, Meg."

"Did I, now?"

"If you didn't, you should and you will."

Straightening up, Meg rested her hands on her hips. "So you've begun counting me one of the kitchen group that fawns over your every word and sighs at your smile."

"No, never, I swear!" David's smile broadened. "The only thing I'm sure of, is that I can get a rise out of you anytime I challenge you, and that doing it gives me more pleasure than almost anything I know."

"That you should find pleasure in such an unremarkable thing speaks poorly for your entertainment at hand." But Meg smiled reluctantly as she spoke, and David's spirits lightened.

"I knew you couldn't stay angry with me." He turned to appraise the room once more. "Cook says your chores will be done for the day once you're finished here."

"Aye, but that may take another hour at my present rate of progress."

David would not relent. "It's too beautiful a day for that. Come on, give it up. Grace will have this place back to disorder the minute she returns and she'll never notice a thing you've done."

"Would you have me shirk my duties?"

"That argument won't work, Meg. You're wasting precious time. You know there's nothing much more you can do here. You can leave early today, so take advantage of the opportunity."

Meg's light-eyed gaze moved disturbingly over his face, and

David felt their touch down to his toes as she narrowed her eyes suspiciously.

"Seems you're very anxious to be rid of me."

"I'm anxious to get you out of the house. I haven't had time to talk with you in days."

"We spoke just this morning!"

"Meg . . ."

Turning to give the room a last glance, Meg shook her head. "You're right, you know. I can do little more without disturbing Miss Grace's 'order of things,' and I've no doubt it'll be back to the way it was within five minutes of her return, more's the pity."

"Meg . . ."

"All right."

Meg started for the hall, and David fell in behind her. His gaze slipped to the pleasant sway of her trim little hips, and he suddenly realized that the rise of feelings within him had very little to do with friendship.

Father Matthew swallowed tightly, his hands shaking as he unfolded the slip of paper he had found under his door. He looked at it once more. The printing was barely legible, but the message became clear the moment he saw the crudely drawn coffin that gave the missive its name. He reread the message in his hand:

"Lay off preaching against Molly's noble sons, or suffer at the hands of those ye despise."

Breathing deeply, Father Matthew walked to the basin and filled it with water. Lowering his head, he splashed the cool liquid on his face, the spotting of his tunic far from his mind as he fought his growing agitation. This was not the first notice he had received and he had heard what happened to other priests who ignored the Mollies' threats. He had continued preaching against the Mollies in his weekly sermons as he prayed each night for the courage to continue. The courage had come slowly, despite the brave facade he maintained.

Father Matthew stepped back from the sink, reached for the cloth lying beside it, and carefully dried his face. Running his fingers through his straight brown hair, he blinked as a new realization dawned upon his troubled mind. It had been almost a year since the Mollies' last threat. The second warning could mean only one thing. They feared his sermons were beginning to succeed in turning the tide of opinion against them.

His breathing restored to normal, his quaking stilled, Father

Matthew picked up the note and folded it carefully. He clasped it in his hand as he turned and made his way out of the rectory to the sanctuary of his church.

Standing at the altar rail, he looked up at the cross, at the image of a God made man, at One who had suffered far worse than he for the sake of love. Dropping to his knees, he clasped his hands in prayer, the note that had shaken him so severely only minutes before pressed tightly between his palms. And he prayed a prayer of thanksgiving for the courage that had almost deserted him.

The echo of the colliery whistle still reverberating on the still autumn air, Sean O'Connor walked amid the stream of men that emerged from the day shift of the mine. He glanced briefly around him and took a deep, deliberate breath. As heavy with coal dust as was the air, it was fresh and clean in comparison to the foul stuff he breathed down below. But he was aware of the deceit in that thinking. It was the same deceit that was practiced in saying that he and those walking beside him were free men when they were not. For free men were not left without choice in their lives, chained to a vicious circle of hunger, need, debt, and an all-powerful system that held them helpless to escape it. And they were not free men when the law leaned so heavily on the side of the oppressor as to brand the oppressed criminals if they sought to fight their circumstances.

Sean's youthful face tightened. Aye, but the Mollies would not allow injustice to perpetuate. His agreement with the thinking of the Molly Maguires had sparked many discussions with Meg during the past year, and he had finally learned to avoid the subject. Nothing could change the convictions that were burned so deeply inside him, and he had no desire to cause Meg any more grief.

Taking a familiar turn in the path, Sean continued on his way home. Home. His mind jarring at thought of the word, Sean could not restrain a sneer. Such did he call the place where he lay his head at night and took his meals, but he remembered a time when the word had meant far more. He remembered a time when it had meant love and laughter and caring, instead of tension, bitterness, and hatred that was a festering wound inside him.

The past year, since Uncle Timothy and he had had the shouting match that had sent Meghan back to the house on the hill, had seen little change in his "beloved" uncle. The man still drank himself into near oblivion each night before coming home to harangue his wife and then stagger to bed. As for himself, he still had not rescued Meg from this home where they weren't wanted, or the house on the hill where she was in greater danger still.

Briefly closing his eyes, Sean felt the failure of it all down to his bones, and he was momentarily overwhelmed by despair. But success in another aspect of his life was close at hand, and it raised his hopes for the future. Despite his youth, he was fairly certain the time was close at hand. He had been accepted into the Ancient Order of Hibernians a few weeks earlier, and with membership in that group an important step had been taken toward his goal. He would soon be with the Mollies in body as he was in spirit, and he'd begin the work of liberation and revenge.

Slowing his pace, Sean turned a glance at the men who walked the familiar path beside him. Few of them were true friends, most believing him too hostile. Lenny had been absent from work today, and he knew the reason was a secret meeting in Pottsville with a man whose name he dared not speak. He knew the Sons of Molly Maguire were planning something big for those Protestant scum who'd placed the signs "Irish Need Not Apply" on employment offices at mines north of Shenandoah. He knew that Molly's rumored grip on the fields was not rumor at all, and that when she demanded justice, her sons were brought in from distant towns so they could not be identified. As Lenny said, "A favor for a favor."

His step slowing at the sight of a young woman standing beside the path a few feet away, Sean squinted into the sun as he sought to identify the girl's shadowed features. But that bright blond hair could belong to no other, and Sean felt a jolt of satisfaction at the realization that Sheila McCrea was waiting for him. His smile flashing teeth that were a white slash against his blackened face, Sean stepped off the path at her side, allowing the others to pass him by. His hand moved to her waist, but Sheila shook her head in warning.

"Take care not to seem too familiar, Sean." Sheila's pleasure at his nearness was obvious, her worshipful gaze familiar, despite her words of caution. "My Da's been watchin' me close of late, and I'd not want him thinkin' anythin' improper was goin' on."

"Would you keep the truth from the dear man then, Sheila?"

"Sean, please!"

"It seems you would." Giving the flushed young woman a brief wink, Sean saw her catch her breath as her gaze dropped to his lips.

Suddenly grateful for Sheila's appearance and the respite it gave him from darker thoughts, Sean smiled more broadly. His association with Lenny Dunne and a trip to Pottsville with the worldly fellow at the turn of the year had introduced him to the pleasures of the flesh. He had discovered a part of his nature of which he had been ignorant, and he had indulged that part of himself whenever possible since that time. However, it had not been his plan to seduce his sister's friend.

Straining to remember, Sean found the first night Sheila and he were together was still unclear in his mind. He remembered the education Lenny afforded him had made him conscious of Sheila in a new way during the times when his sister and she were together. He supposed Sheila had not missed his appreciation of her comely face and womanly figure, although he had been no more friendly than usual. He had caught her admiring glances as well, and although he'd been flattered, he had not approached the girl because of his sister.

It was an accidental meeting that finally did the trick—a night when he'd had too much to drink and been making his way home just when Sheila was returning from visiting with Meg. Less in control of this new side of his nature than usual, his desire for the girl had overcome his weakened inhibitions, and things had moved quickly from there. He had not found it difficult to persuade Sheila to come for a walk with him and she had shown little resistance to his advances.

However, the words of love she had whispered in his ear had stirred his conscience until it ached past ignoring, and when they had been together since that time, it was because she, not he, came seeking him out.

Sheila was a dear girl. He knew she had not been with a man before him and she was more loving than he deserved. He owed her for that, but Sean was well aware that the affair between them was unevenly balanced from the start. Sheila's feelings for him were far deeper than his could ever be for her, and he was only too aware that the emotions she stirred in him originated in a far baser part of his anatomy than his heart. But it was no reflection on Sheila's worth that his heart was closed to her, for the bitterness inside him was such that except for the spot kept warm and alive by his dear Meg, his heart had gone cold and dead.

However, the physical part of him, full of youth and vigor, continued to respond to Sheila. He could only conclude from the look on her face that she was satisfied with a limited part of him, for he'd never lied and said he loved her. As he looked down at her even now, that same remorseless part of him responded with growing warmth to the sweet flesh he had come to know so well.

Consoling himself that he gave Sheila no more or less than she asked, Sean stared at her full lips until the blood rushed to her cheeks. She became more flustered and Sean teased, "And to what do I owe the honor of seein' you here today, Sheila, my dear?"

Her face flushing darker still, Sheila bowed her head. "I . . . I've not seen you in a week. I was wonderin' if you was angry with me, or if you'd found another girl to while away your time with."

Sheila's eyes darted up to his at the conclusion of her halting speech and Sean saw her intense discomfort. Pity welled within him for the girl's plight. How difficult it must be to feel so strongly about a person when the feeling was not returned full measure. But while he could not offer her what he did not feel, Sean knew he could offer her honesty instead.

His teasing smile falling away, Sean spoke softly. "I've not found another, nor have I been lookin'. You know me well, Sheila, and you know what's inside me. And if you're satisfied with what you know, it'll do for me."

Tears glittered in Sheila's gaze. "Aye, it'll do."

Sean's heart began a familiar pounding. "Do you want to meet me tonight, then? After supper? It's still warm enough in the mill."

"Aye, the mill then."

Turning without another word, Sheila walked back toward the patch. Waiting only until she slipped out of sight, Sean continued home, anticipating the night to come.

The sky above them was a clear blue undulled by the haze of coal dust which covered the valley, the air warmed by the late afternoon sun as David and Meg walked together. The anxiety that had driven David home an hour earlier was quickly dissipating as his gaze followed Meg's progress through the waist-high weeds she called flowers.

The cleaning of Grace's room behind her, Meg had resisted him again when he asked her to walk with him so they might talk, but he had expected as much. That was Meg. He had all but dragged her to this particular area on the opposite side of the hill where others seldom ventured, but from the moment they reached this small clearing, everything changed.

Tiny purplish-blue, star-shaped blossoms on long, scrawny stems they were, but she was thrilled by them. She already had a fistful, and he was beginning to think she wouldn't be satisfied until she picked the field clean. But while he was annoyed at being ignored, he was glad it was he who had put that sparkle in her eye. He cherished her delight, and he could not help being amused by the paradox that was Meghan O'Connor. One moment as mature as a woman, the next moment as simple as a child, he found every facet of her complex personality true enchantment.

Standing as he was now, waiting for Meg's enthusiasm for the peculiar wildflowers to wane, he felt a familiar discomfort swell within him. Was that young woman whose slim, curving figure was silhouetted against the late afternoon sky really Meg? It seemed she had blossomed before his eyes after reaching her fifteenth year in spring. The occasion had gone unmarked by celebration, at Meg's request, and she had promptly refused the fine gold chain he attempted to give her, telling him it would be cause for bloodshed should Sean come across it in her things. He had been angry and disappointed. For some reason he'd gotten particular pleasure in imagining it sparkling around her slender neck and knowing it had come from him.

It had occurred to him that he was getting overly possessive of the girl, and he had searched his soul painfully then, only to find himself more confused than before. Meg was, after all, a servant in his house—a free agent who owed him and the family nothing more than a full day's work for her wage, but it hadn't taken him long to admit that the relationship between them was not that simple.

And she had grown so lovely. Where the top of her head had not reached past his mid-chest before, it was now even with his shoulder, and the additional inches had worked delicious changes on her slender frame as well. Her shoulders were as narrow and delicate as they ever were, and her arms as slender and quick at their tasks, but the length of her had stretched from hip to small, round breasts in gentle curves and a swaying bottom that was discernible even in the somber black uniform she wore.

Turning unexpectedly toward him, Meg laughed and waved the wild bouquet at him, but David did not return her smile. She turned back to her chore, but her image was still clear before his mind's eye. An ache started deep inside him at the sculptured planes of her cheek where there was only childish softness before, at unruly dark hair that was now an incredible halo of gleaming curls for the maturing beauty of her face. That same ache made him suddenly restless, and he found himself becoming angry at the time she wasted on flowers when he needed to talk to her about important things—very important things.

Striding forward, suddenly unwilling to waste another moment, David took her hand. "You have enough of those weeds now, Meg. Come on, I want to talk to you about something."

"Just a few more, David. Aunt Fiona won't be able to believe that I've found these starbursts here."

"I said you have enough."

Not waiting for her reply, David pulled her behind him, almost dragging her as he strode toward a log that formed a natural seat nearby.

"Let go of my hand, David!"

Ignoring her, David maintained his relentless grip until he reached the log. Turning toward her at last, he ordered gruffly, "Sit down."

"I take your orders in the house, David, but I'll not play the servant out here. If you've a mind to give commands, go back to the kitchen. There's those in there who'll bow and scrape for the pure love of it."

David went still inside. "But not you, Meg. You've no love of taking orders."

"No, I've not."

"What *do* you love, Meg?" His throat unexpectedly tight as the unplanned question escaped his lips, David felt his heart begin a slow pounding. Looking down into the translucent blue of her eyes, he was as intensely aware of the glacial silver in their depths that signaled her rising temper as he was of his own quickening of emotion. Raising a hand to her cheek, he brushed back a dark tendril, sliding his hand into her silky curls to hold her fast. "*Who* do you love, Meg? Do you love me?"

David's abrupt question surprised himself as much as it did Meg. Meg remained silent, her color draining, and the ache inside him expanded to encompass the whole of his heart.

"Do you love me at all, Meg?"

Meg's continued silence cut him deeply, and his gaze dropped to her still lips with the thought that his dear Meg, who often said more than she should, could not bring herself to respond. He feared he knew why.

Slipping his arms around her, David pulled her close. He closed his eyes and breathed in the scent of her—his Meg. Somewhere deep inside him he had known from the first that she belonged in his arms. It had merely been a matter of waiting to hold Meg, the woman, not Meg, the child. And this budding woman who was Meg felt so good and right pressed tight against him.

Meg remained rigid in his arms, and David drew back to look down into her white face. Speaking words that came from the heart, words he did not need to contemplate but simply breathed into the truth of the moment, he whispered, "I asked you if you love me because I love *you*, Meg. But you've always known I love you, haven't you?" Meg maintained her silence as David continued. "It's your fault, you know. You worked your way into my heart, and you're there to stay, so don't be angry. I just want you to love me back. Even if it's only a little bit for now."

David felt the nudge of panic at Meg's continued silence. Lowering his head, he brushed her parted lips lightly with his own, and joy touched the throbbing ache within him. He brushed her mouth again with his, and again, until his arms tightened spontaneously and his mouth claimed hers fully.

Meg . . . Meg . . . Her name went round and round in his brain as his mouth sank deeply into hers. He had wanted this for so long. He wanted Meg to truly belong to him so he could care for her, protect her, and now he wanted . . .

He wanted. But what did Meg want?

His breathing ragged, David drew back and looked down into Meg's sober face. "Say something, Meg. You're not angry with me, are you? Talk to me."

The shaky whisper that finally emerged from Meg's lips stunned him.

"You've spoiled it all, David."

"Spoiled it?"

"Let me go."

"Meg . . ."

"Don't you see what you've done?" Meg stared up at him, anger and pain mingled in her gaze. "We were friends!"

"That hasn't changed, Meg."

"Oh, yes it has! Friends want nothing from each other but what's best for both. But it isn't that way anymore. You want more from me now. More than I can give!"

"That isn't true, Meg. I still want what's best for you. I always have."

"Then let me go."

"Why?"

"Because you've proved me wrong and Sean right, that's why! All the times I talked to him about you, I told him you just wanted to be my friend."

"Things change, Meg, just like people change." David's voice held a plea for understanding. "You're not the little girl you were, but I still want what's best for you, only in a different way."

"You do? Will it be best for me when tongues are wagging? Will it be best when people laugh behind my back and declare me a fool for believing the glib tongue of a fellow like you?"

"I've never been glib with you." David held her fast, refusing to let her go. "Meg, you don't understand. I didn't bring you up here today with any thought in my mind except to tell you Uncle Martin talked to me this morning. He received responses from a few colleges about me."

"Let me go, David."

"Meg, don't you know what that means?" David was growing impatient. "That means that I'll be going away from here soon—probably for years!"

Meghan's gaze flickered briefly before she raised her chin. "You knew the day would come, and so did I."

"But I didn't know the thought of leaving you would wound me so deeply. I don't want to leave you, Meg!" Tears welled in Meg's eyes at his words, and David felt his own throat thicken. "But it doesn't have to be that way, Meg. I have a plan."

"A plan?"

"I saw a letter from the University of Pennsylvania in Uncle Martin's mail today. It's located in Philadelphia. I could talk Uncle Martin into making arrangements for me to go there, and it wouldn't be at all difficult for me to arrange a position for you in the Hutton household. Then you could be close by and we could see each other every day. There are so many wonderful things in Philadelphia—a whole world you've never seen. I want to show you all of it. We could—"

"Let go of me, David!" Her face flushing with color, Meg jerked at his clutching grip.

"Meg, I love you and I don't want to be separated from you. I want to take you with me when I go. Why does that make you angry?"

Meg's lips trembled. She shook her head, her gleaming sun-kissed curls dancing wildly on her shoulders as a tortured hiss escaped her. "You've not changed a bit, have you? You still want to get me out of the valley, and if you couldn't talk me into living in your grand house, you hope to lure me away from my own with talk of places and things I've never seen. You've cast aside all I've tried to make you understand about the valley and the people in it as if I never spoke the words. And you've cast aside the promise you made to me a year ago just as easily."

"No I haven't, Meg. I remember that promise, and I haven't broken it by telling you that I don't want to be separated from you."

"I'll not listen to another word!" Her eyes suddenly wild, Meg shook her head. "Sean has *my* promise that I'll tell him if you press me to leave the valley again, and unlike you, I put value on my given word."

"Meg . . ."

"My employment here has come to an end."

David stared at Meg for a moment's incredulous silence. "An end? Does all I've said to you this afternoon boil down to that in your mind—a matter of employment?" Stiffening under the frigidity of her gaze, David drew back. "Could you do that, Meg? Could you walk away from me without regret, knowing you'd never see me again? Could you forget everything we—"

"Stop! Stop speaking those words, for they'll do you no good! You still want to change me from the person I am with sweet words, David. You talk of love, but you've no idea what the word means. Oh, you think yourself to be sincere, I've no doubt, but your grand plan betrays you, because once more you're trying to separate me from the person I truly am. You'd have me abandon my only living kin on your whim, to live in a strange house amongst strangers while I wait for you to come and spend a few hours to brighten my dreary days. And as unhappy as that would make me, I've no doubt you'd be fully content knowing you've finally severed the bond of blood between Sean and me that you so despise."

"Meg . . ."

"You neither see nor care that to sever that bond of blood would be to bleed me dry."

Torn by the pain of her words, David reached out to Meg. "You're wrong. I don't mean to hurt you or change you."

Meg shook off his hand. "No, David. It's not a matter of what's meant. It's a matter of what's become so clear. You've never tried to understand the person inside me, so wrong do you believe me to be in claiming allegiance to those of my own. So all's lost between us with what you've now said, for even our friendship has gone astray."

"Meg, please."

"I'll give my notice tomorrow."

"No!"

"It'd not be by choice, for I'll have my brother to face." Meg held his gaze with brimming eyes. "In the end, it's up to you again, David."

"To me?"

"If you'll leave me be, treat me no different from the other servants from now on, I can stay."

Almost disbelieving his ears, David withdrew a step farther. He had told Meg he loved her—bared his heart to her because he trusted her, only to have her turn against him. Still unwilling to accept that thought, David pressed her one more time.

"You're telling me you want no part of me from now on—that everything's off between us, or you'll leave the hill and never come back?"

"Aye."

Incredulity froze David's face. His pain a breathing, palpable part of him, David finally gave a short laugh. "And the strangest part of all of this is that I was convinced you really cared for me."

Her small face pinched, Meg replied in a rasping whisper. "And care for you I do, but I've promises to keep to those I love."

"And you don't love me."

Meg's fine lips twitched, but she firmed their line with her reply. "You should not have thought to come between my brother and me, David."

"I didn't think to have you make a choice."

"Did you not?"

Suddenly realizing that was exactly what he had done, David briefly closed his eyes without response.

Meg nodded a soft, "Aye."

Meg turned away, only to have David's voice halt her briefly with his whisper. "This is wrong, Meg. You're making a mistake."

"Aye, and if I am, the mistake is my own."

Standing where she had left him, David was still long minutes after Meg had disappeared from sight.

The sun of late afternoon was hot against his skin, but it failed to warm him. Looking down at his feet, he saw abandoned there the wildflowers Meg had gathered with such care. He stooped down and picked up a discarded stalk, realizing he shared its fate, and he wondered how it had suddenly come about that the girl who had given him back his life and so much more, had so coldly turned against him.

Familiar aromas filled the kitchen as Aunt Fiona moved deftly between table and stove. Suppertime neared and she raised the lid of an oversized pot to stir her fragrant stew again, accepting with a sigh that this was her lot, to spend her life wearing a groove in the hard kitchen floor as she catered to the wants of those who spared her no more than a few short words each day.

Aye, it was painful to know that her boarders had better things to do between meals than to talk to a work-worn old woman who had little joy left in her, that her husband treated her less kindly than he would a servant, and that her own nephew despised her.

But then there was Meg.

Her tired eyes brightening momentarily at the thought of her dear niece, Fiona replaced the lid on the pot to turn to the breadboard once more. Raising her gaze upward toward one visible only in her mind's eye, Fiona spoke silently to the woman she was certain now abided peacefully in the heaven she had so diligently earned.

Ah, Mary O'Connor, it was a great gift, indeed, when ye brought yer dear girl to me house and left her in me care. For she's a treasure and all a woman could ask to fill the last, lonely days of her life. I thank ye, Mary. From the bottom of me heart, I thank ye.

Resuming her chores, Fiona wiped a tear from her eye and pounded the dough before her with a practiced hand. She was making sweet rolls because Meg had a weakness for them, and because with all the growing the girl had been doing in the past year, she had not an ounce of spare flesh on her. A smile touching her lips for the first time that afternoon, Fiona nodded. But the truth was, she would not change a hair on the girl's head, so much did she love her. And the wonder of it was that the girl loved her in return.

Not a woman accustomed to inspiring love, Fiona swallowed tightly and gave an impatient grunt as she acknowledged that sentimentality did not set well on the rounded shoulders of a homely, ignorant, middle-aged woman who had little but failure to show for her life.

A flash of pure hatred momentarily overwhelming her, Fiona

remembered the night before and her husband's abusive words to her dear Meg, but the passion of the moment soon passed. If she hated her husband, she need hate herself for failing to stand up to the man, and she could ill afford to dwell on the failures of her life any longer. They caused her too much pain.

The sound of a step outside the door turned Fiona toward it with expectation, for it was the best hour of the day when Meg returned home. They then talked and worked together in a leisurely way that gave them both pleasure. She was grateful that Meg saw in her the last ties to the Ma she loved so well, and she hoped the girl's feelings never changed.

Her thoughts interrupted as Meg walked into the room, Fiona felt the joy of expectation drain from her mind at the sight of Meg's white face. The girl attempted to brush past her with a brief word of greeting, but Fiona's hand on her arm brought her niece to a sharp halt, allowing her to see red-rimmed eyes that had recently shed tears.

"Meg, m'darlin', will ye tell yer aunt what's wrong?"

"It's nothing, Aunt. Just a few somber thoughts I've not been able to drive away."

But Meg could not meet her eyes, and the pain of again being excluded allowed Fiona's hand to drop back to her side. Taking advantage of her opportunity, Meg continued rapidly through the kitchen, turning with a belated thought as she reached the hallway door.

"You'll not say a word of this to Sean when he comes home, will you, Aunt? It's but a passing thing and I'll be right as rain again in a few minutes."

"Nay, I'll not speak of it. Ye've a right to a bit of privacy if ye desire. But, Meg . . ." Hesitating briefly, Fiona concluded in a softer tone. "Ye'll tell me if yer ever in need, won't ye, m'dear? For ye know I'd never let ye go wanting."

Regretting her words as Meg's eyes brimmed once more, Fiona saw Meg nod before she turned out of sight.

The thoughts within Fiona churned. She'd allow no one to hurt dear Meg. Aye, coward that she'd been all her life, she'd not fail the child.

The sound of her aunt's gentle words echoing in her ears, Meg made her way up the staircase at a pace just short of a run. Across the second floor landing in a few quick steps, she pushed open the door of her room and closed it swiftly behind her, tears brimming once more.

The worn surface of the door hard against her back, she closed her eyes for a few short moments as she strove to gain control of her ragged emotions. Her anguished whisper rasped on the silence of the empty room.

"Oh, Ma . . . Ma, I need you now to advise me, I'm that miserable and confused."

But there was no response and no respite from the image of David's face when she'd told him he'd spoiled it all between them.

Even now, Meg could not quite believe the words David had uttered, his handsome face so sincere, his eyes so open and anxious. Love her? How could he love her in the way that had made him take her into his arms and kiss her with a tenderness that had touched her soul? Did he not see the vast gulf that lay between them? Did he not see that no matter the affection they shared for each other, no matter the strength of the bond between them, it all would fall away when exposed to the hatred and prejudice of those around them? And did he not know that even if all that did not exist, the bond of blood was stronger than any other—that when it came to a choice between Sean and him, she had no choice at all?

But the answer to those questions was simple. David did not acknowledge the impediments between them because, in all of his life, he'd never been denied.

A tear slipped down Meg's cheek as the painful truth registered in her mind. She hadn't wanted to deny David love. Raising her trembling hand to her lips, Meg remembered the touch of his mouth against hers. Oh, the wonder of it . . . A flower far more beautiful than those of the fields had unfurled inside her with his kiss, its petals a bright warm gold that filled her heart with its glow. Its fragrance had spread through her, tingling down arms that longed to encircle David's neck, to fingertips that longed to stroke his cheek and smooth his dark hair. The feelings he had evoked were unexpected, and yet it was clear to her now that David and she had been leading that way from the first.

But it was all over now. All she had said was true. David loved the person he wanted her to be, a girl who was separate from the valley, a girl who would cast aside everything and everyone who'd made her what she was for him. Meghan knew with a deep certainty she could never be that girl. With a misery unlike any she'd ever known, Meg also accepted that in acknowledging that

David and she were more than friends, they had taken a step too far.

A low sob escaping her lips, Meg closed her eyes, her sense of loss intense. She would stay on at the manor, for Sean would be too quick to miss the cause if she left. She would strike the look of hurt in David's eyes from her mind, and force the sound of pain in his voice from her heart. She'd forget the closeness they had shared and all it had added to her life when so much else had been stripped away.

And she'd forget that David and she were more than friends, because that was the way it had to be.

Chapter 13

The mild air of afternoon had cooled with the setting sun, returning the bite of autumn to the twilight hour. The narrow dirt road just beyond town was silent and still, but inside the abandoned mill a few yards off the deserted stretch, the rasp of labored breathing broke the stillness and the sounds of passion grew more intense.

Sheila was oblivious of all but the bliss of Sean's lips against her flesh and wonder of his weight upon her. She gasped as Sean gripped her firm buttocks and raised her to him, biting her lips against the sting as he thrust his engorged organ inside her. But her heart swelled with love.

Ah, Sean . . . Sean . . . Sheila's heart sang. She had loved him all her life, from the day she had followed him as a child, dogging his steps on the tracks when he went to gather spillage from the rail cars for the family stove. That day was still clear in her mind. A year younger than he at five, she was desperate from the cold that settled in the house with her Da and brothers working their shift and her Ma stricken and helpless with the flu. A small, empty sack in her hands, she stumbled on the tracks, panicking at the roar of an approaching train. Screaming with fear, she was unable to move and would have been crushed beneath the racing iron wheels had not Sean dragged her from their path.

She did not thank Sean when he stood her on her feet and angrily shook her, nor did she thank him when he filled her empty sack as well as his own and dragged her back to the patch, scolding her every step of the way. Ah, but she had loved him, and she loved him still.

The change that came over Sean after the deaths of his Da and brothers frightened her, and she saw him become harder still after they put his Ma under the ground. Meg warned her then not to set her hopes on him, that it would bring her pain to believe he could love her, but she did not bother to tell Meg she was wrong. For the truth was, even now, after she let Sean have his way with her so many times as to have lost count in recent months, and after admitting to herself that Sean still did not love her, she had no regrets.

She was not the fool some thought her to be about Sean O'Connor. She saw the direction hatred was leading him, and she knew that hatred left no room in his heart for her. But she knew something else, as well. She knew for the few minutes she lay in his arms, Sean put his hatred behind him. She knew she gave him pleasure in a way no other woman did, and because she loved him, that knowledge was enough.

The rhythm of Sean's lovemaking grew more intense, and Sheila clutched him close, savoring the warm part of him that gave her life. She felt him swell inside her and her love swelled in return. She heard the ardor in his voice as he whispered into her ear, and her passion soared anew. She felt his body shudder, his ecstatic cry of release harsh as it echoed in the silent mill, and her intense ecstasy was bittersweet with the knowledge that he would soon release her as well.

Replete, Sean's muscular frame lay heavily upon her and Sheila knew that if she had her choice, she would not have this moment end. Aware that he was already stirring, and that in a minute he would be anxious to be on his way, she wrapped her arms around Sean's back and drew him closer, her palms smoothing the strong muscles there. She suffered anew the knowledge that for Sean these moments when he and she were together were but a diversion from the ghosts that haunted him, while for her they were the reason for life.

Sean stirred and Sheila whispered, "No, Sean, please. Just a few minutes longer."

Her plea halted Sean as he started to withdraw, and Sheila was alarmed at the frown that touched his brow when he looked down into her face. Aye, this new Sean, recently having become a man, was not the same boy of six who had won her loyalty forever, for there had been love and joy in that boy, and in the man there was none. And she knew that Sean would not be with her now had she not sacrificed her pride and gone to him. But she had come to terms with that thought when she decided, long ago, that it would be far better to lose her pride than to lose Sean.

"We can't stay, Sheila. It's gettin' late and your Ma will be wonderin' why you're so delayed in returning from your visit with Meg."

Aye, those visits that never were, and the loving in their stead as she and Sean lay hidden in the old mill . . . But she was not ashamed, for she'd do anything to keep him, and to save him if she could.

In a moment Sean was separate from her, and her warm, damp flesh that had been covered by his only moments before chilled in the cool air. Shivering, Sheila drew herself to her feet and reached for her clothing, aware that Sean was already drawing on his trousers and would soon be ready to leave. She thought again, as she adjusted her undergarments, that the tragedy which all but destroyed the O'Connor clan had all but destroyed Sean as well, so dead was his heart.

"Sheila . . ."

Raising her head at Sean's whisper, Sheila strained to see his face in the semi-darkness illuminated only by the light of the lamp burning low beside them. Her heart raced at the shadow of love she thought she saw reflected in his eyes for a brief moment as he reached toward her and smoothed her fair hair back from her cheek. He said no more, and she took a step forward, encouraging him.

"Aye, Sean?"

"Are you happy . . . truly happy? Or do you suffer for these meetin's in the dark and on the sneak while you know your Ma and Da are trustin' you?"

Her throat filling with the guilt that had blighted her days since she first gave in and gave all to Sean, Sheila raised her eyes to his. Frustration knotted inside her because she could not clearly see his face and read the meaning there as she responded. "And if my guilt turned all this bad, what would you do then, Sean?"

Hesitating, Sean lifted a soft curl from her shoulder. Cradling it a moment in his hand, he then crushed it in a tight fist, releasing it a second later with a whisper that bore no trace of the fleeting emotion.

"I'd leave you be, Sheila, for in truth, if you lost the joy of the moment here, there'd be little else for you at all."

The candor of Sean's words was a knife that cut deep. Sheila responded a moment later with a question of her own.

"What of you, Sean? Are you happy—here and now—when we're together?"

"Aye. I couldn't ask for more."

Sheila forced a smile with her whisper, "Then it's enough for me, too."

Slipping her arms around him, she hugged Sean desperately close, her own words echoing in her heart. It would be enough, and she'd be patient for that which would follow—if there'd be time for more.

The exuberant music of the gavotte filled the brightly-lit manor, punctuated by shouts of laughter and the shuffle of dancing feet. Letty surveyed the scene with a hostess's critical eye. The hardwood floor of the reception room had been cleared for the celebration of Martin's and her twenty-fifth wedding anniversary, and young men and women, all beautifully dressed for the party, followed the dance pattern with flashing color and gaiety. Standing around the energetic group in an appreciative circle, her elder guests watched with smiles, sipping wine imported for the occasion and engaging in pleasant conversation.

Glancing toward the buffet tables lining the far wall, Letty surveyed the magnificent culinary display she knew would tempt even the most particular palate and she inwardly swelled with pride at the splendor of the affair she had so meticulously orchestrated. Martin had not wished to spare any expense for the festivities, despite the uncertain state of affairs in the region, going so far as to insist she extend an invitation to overnight guests from the surrounding area.

An emotional mist glittering in her pale eyes, Letty knew this was Martin's way of telling the world in general, and her in particular, that he loved her and was proud of all they had accomplished together. It was a sentiment they shared, and for that reason she had complied with her husband's wishes. She was certain the occasion would be the talk of the region when all was over and done.

Her gaze moved assessingly around the room, and Letty adjusted the neckline of her fragile blue silk gown, grateful the autumn weather was pleasant enough so she might wear the delicate garment with true comfort. The exquisite length of perfectly matched pearls Martin had given her were warm against her neck, and she silently admitted that had the night been frigid as winter, she would have borne the chill just for the pleasure of displaying dear Martin's gift to its greatest advantage.

Her hand unconsciously remaining at her shoulder, Letty suppressed a surprised gasp as she glanced toward the corner of the room. Grace was deep in conversation with young Travis Whitehead. Resplendent in creamy beige silk, her gleaming hair piled atop her head in a style that added a becoming maturity to her appearance, her daughter was obviously a vision Travis could not ignore. And Grace, dear girl that she was, was flirting outrageously!

Uncertain whether to applaud her daughter's recent emergence as a coquette, or whether to make haste to her side to distract young Whitehead before he expired from rapt and breathless appreciation, Letty hesitated a moment longer, only to hear Martin's amused whisper in her ear.

"Don't look so worried, Letty. The girl's having the time of her life."

"Do you really think so, dear?" Turning to her husband's pleased expression as she spoke, Letty could not help but silently remark how very handsome he looked in the crisp black and white of his formal attire. But she had always known her husband was a very attractive man.

"Yes, I think we should be grateful Grace has finally awakened to the pleasantries of her sex. I confess, Letty. I was beginning to become concerned she'd never grow up."

"Martin!"

Laughing aloud, Martin squeezed his wife's arm gently, and Letty was about to respond further to his audacious remark when his expression abruptly changed. Following the direction of his gaze, Letty saw David standing alone beside the punch bowl, a cup in his hand. Almost princely in his evening dress, he wore the same dark expression that had chased both Abigail Hutton and her persistent sister, Beverly, from his side, as well as every other young woman who had attempted polite conversation with him that evening.

Martin's tone became touched with annoyance. "Now if only your nephew would allow some of the gaiety of the occasion to touch him, I'd be content."

"Oh, Martin, do you suppose he'll ever be the same happy, confident young man he used to be?"

Letty belatedly realized the imprudence of her spontaneous remark as her husband turned to her with a frown. "You mean by that, of course, the young man he was before he met up with that O'Connor girl."

"Martin, please!" Casting a glance around her to see if the vehemence of her husband's response had been noted by any of their guests, Letty drew him a cautious few steps toward the nearest corner. "Surely you don't blame Meghan O'Connor for David's despondency of late."

"Oh, don't I? The entire staff's gossiping about the rift between the little Irish witch and him these past three weeks, and he's not been fit to live with."

"Martin!"

"She's bewitched him, I tell you! And if you don't believe me, look at your handsome nephew now!"

Turning, Letty looked again toward the corner where David stood, only to see his expression tighten as Meghan O'Connor crossed the room with her tray.

Turning back to her husband, Letty felt the heat of tears warm her eyes. "He does look so unhappy."

His anger suddenly dropping away, Martin mumbled an epithet and then whispered, "Letty, dear, I'm sorry."

His expression penitent, Martin pressed a firm, unexpected kiss against her lips, and blinking, Letty felt a flush rise to her cheeks as she glanced self-consciously around her. She was relieved to see Martin's good humor return with a chuckle.

"You still blush more beautifully than any woman I know, my dear, but I think our guests will forgive the indiscretion of my public display. I apologize again for allowing my foul humor to dampen your spirits even temporarily. And Letty," leaning closer, Martin whispered encouragingly, "don't worry about David. I promise you, it'll all be settled soon. Now smile for me, please. You're very lovely when you smile, you know."

"Oh, Martin."

Her cheeks flushing more hotly than before, Letty allowed her husband to draw her firmly against his side while she stole a last, worried glance toward her dear David, and so very distressingly shared his pain.

His eyes following Meg as she moved smoothly around the room unobtrusively gathering discarded glasses and dishes, David felt frustration soar anew. Damn it all! How could she be so cold to him?

His fingers stiff around the cup he had clutched for the past half hour, David raised it to his lips and forced himself to take a sip of punch. His stomach revolted against the sickeningly sweet taste, and the thought registered somewhere in the back of his mind that he had never liked punch, so why had he poured himself a cup in the first place? And then he remembered that it was something to occupy his hands while his mind was occupied with Meg. In the time since he had poured it, he had neither raised the cup to his lips nor taken his eyes off Meg. He knew he was acting like a fool, but somehow that realization had little effect on the ache deep inside him.

He missed Meg. Three weeks had passed since she put an end to all association between them, and he had not had a decent moment since.

Still following Meg with his gaze, David attempted to compare her to the other young women present. But there *was* no comparison. He had to concede that at first glance Meg appeared nothing more than a slight, dainty shadow in contrast to the elaborately dressed and coiffed female guests. In her dark uniform and with her stubborn curls confined as they were in a tight bun at the back of her neck, much of her individuality of appearance was stripped away. That was only true, however, until she looked up and her delicacy of feature and those incredible eyes became visible.

Oh, Meg . . .

How had he let this happen between them? The passage of three weeks, and his review of the harsh words they exchanged, had not lessened his despair or sense of loss in the slightest degree. With a darkening frown, David acknowledged that nothing appeared to have changed on Meg's part, either, for she had not spared him a glance or a word in the time since.

As for himself, his intense soul-searching had netted him only one thing; the realization that no matter the estrangement between them, Meg was still a part of him. He no longer felt whole without her, and despite everything that had happened, he could no more bear to abandon her to her circumstances than he could willingly sever a limb from his own body.

But a new facet had been added to the fervor of his feelings for Meg. The remembered warmth of her slenderness against him, the taste of her mouth, and the desire to feel her yield her love completely to him had added a new dimension to his torment. Recalling his haughty disdain for the disheveled, ignorant young girl he had pulled out of a bush on the hillside that first day, David found himself bitterly amused that the situation should suddenly be so distinctly reversed—that the disheveled young girl should have proved *him* a fool many times in underestimating her, and that it should be she, not he, who now held him helpless in those small, deceivingly strong hands.

Turning unexpectedly, Meg glanced up. Her gaze tangled briefly with his, and the shock of the contact unleashed a new raft of painful emotions to torment him.

To his mind returned a silent plea. *Meg, tell me how I can reach you.*

Utilizing all the strength of will within her, Meg broke contact with David's intense stare and reached blindly for a glass abandoned nearby. The plea she had seen in his eyes echoed within her heart as her fingers closed around it, and it was one of the most difficult things she had ever done to place the glass on her tray beside the others and turn away. Carefully sidestepping a laughing couple, she walked directly to the kitchen and released a painfully tight breath as the door closed behind her.

"So there you are! Quickly now, take these canapes out to the table. The mistress will be annoyed if the tray is allowed to empty any further."

Temporarily unable to face David's trailing gaze, Meg ignored Cook's instructions and walked toward the staggering pile of dishes awaiting washing near the sink. She began unloading her tray.

"Leave the tray there and do what I say!" Impatient, Cook addressed her more sharply than before as she nodded toward Johnny Law where he stood temporarily employed in kitchen duty, his hands immersed in dishwater up to the elbows. "Johnny will take care of that."

Meg turned, shaking her head. "I . . . I think I should help Johnny now. We're running short of dishes. Margaret can take the tray outside."

Her busy fingers stopping still, Cook assessed Meg's colorless face. "You're feeling poorly, is that it? Tell me the truth, for it won't do to send you outside if you are."

"No . . . no, I'm fine." Not wishing to cause any further speculation, Meg attempted a smile, grateful as Margaret stepped into the breach with a knowing glance.

"Give me the tray." And then to Cook, "The girl's right. Johnny ain't working fast enough to keep up, and I'd rather be outside than in this hot kitchen, anyway."

"All right."

Turning back to the sink, Meg met Johnny's assessing gaze as she reached for the nearby cloth. Johnny had been cautious about the terms of his friendship with her during the past year, and she could not blame him. But the warmth in his eyes had not waned and she knew if he had his choice it would have been otherwise between them.

However, Meg's thoughts did not linger with Johnny Law. David's anguish, obvious when she had looked up and caught his gaze, cut her too deeply to allow it to escape her mind for long.

It had been a terrible three weeks since that day on the hill. She missed David terribly—their talks, their arguments, the knowledge that they valued each other in a way they valued no other. As brief as was the time she had spent in David's embrace, she was unable to forget the startling feelings he stirred inside her, the desire to feel his arms around her, and to feel his mouth play against hers in that loving way.

Love? Was that the name for this misery inside her that would not be assuaged? She had done the right thing—the only thing she could do, hadn't she?

The misery she saw in David's eyes would fade. David would forget her when a suitable young woman caught his fancy and he decided that the girl from the valley whom he had thought he loved was not meant for him at all. And she would be relieved of this ache inside her then—wouldn't she?

That last thought suddenly too difficult for her tortured mind to accept, Meg felt her throat choke tightly and her eyes warm to tears.

"Meg . . ."

Looking up, Meg met the sympathy in Johnny Law's brown eyes. She turned her head, only to feel his arm slide companionably along her shoulder as he continued in a whisper. "He's not worth it, Meg. Buck up. He'll be off to school soon, and things'll smooth out for you then."

That thought giving her little consolation, Meg nodded and attempted a smile, realizing belatedly that she had inadvertently encouraged Johnny as his arm tightened around her and he continued. "When he's gone and you've a chance to set things straight, we can—"

"Get away from her, Law!"

David's unexpected command brought a sudden stillness to the busy kitchen as he advanced threateningly into the room. The color drained from Johnny's face as David walked closer, his expression livid, his hands balled into tight fists. A glance around her revealed David had the attention of the entire staff as he snarled, "You heard what I said."

Johnny's arm dropped back to his side, and Meg responded, "Johnny was just trying to—"

"I know what he was trying!"

David held her gaze with a look that tore at her heart. Unable to bear more, Meg turned away. She did not look back until the sound of David's retreating step indicated he had left as unexpectedly as he had appeared, leaving a silent kitchen behind him.

"All right, back to work all of you."

Cook's sharp command broke the tense silence the moment before Miss Letty walked into the kitchen, her expression strained. "I saw David. Is everything all right in here?"

Cook looked briefly at Meg before responding, "Yes, ma'am, everything's all right."

Hesitating only a moment, the mistress walked out of the kitchen as quickly as she had entered.

Silent as she turned back to the dishes, Meg swallowed against the memory of David's anguished expression. The only thing that emerged through her distress was the premonition that she had not seen the last of this affair.

Shaking off Abigail Hutton's hand with a gruff word as he made his way past guests gathered in conversational groups, David turned toward the front doorway. Caring little for the curious glances his stiff step evoked, he strode outside into the darkness of the yard. His fury had been such at the sight of Law's arm around Meg's shoulders that he knew he need remove himself from the house immediately, before he made a scene he would regret.

Halting in the shadow of a nearby tree, David took a deep, steadying breath. Damn that little bastard, John Law! Wretch that he was, the fellow obviously thought the time was ripe to take advantage of the present state of affairs between Meg and himself.

The memory of John Law's arm around Meg's shoulder, his head lowered as he whispered into her ear, returned with sudden clarity and fury rose anew. Law would never touch Meg again! Meg was his.

That determination suddenly clear within his mind, David turned and walked back toward the house. He needed to wait until the affair progressing within was over and the last guest departed within a day or so. It wouldn't be long.

• • •

"Meg, dear, have you forgotten how to smile?"

Father Matthew's unexpected question raised Meg's head from the figures on the paper in front of her. Her attempt at a responsive smile further dropped his spirits as he sat across from her at the table in the rectory kitchen.

"I'm sorry, Father. I've been pensive of late and haven't thought about the effect on others." And then with another valiant attempt, "But I've not forgotten how to smile—truly."

But Meg's efforts were pathetically inadequate, and conflicting emotions churned inside Father Matthew. Dear Meg. She was becoming a beautiful young woman, and her new maturity rang a warning bell in his mind even as he reached to cover her work-roughened hand with his.

"You've something troubling you, that's plain to see. Oh, you've done a good job of disguising the way you feel, but the truth is, your smile's not true, and your eyes aren't happy. And you've been avoiding the confessional, too. So I ask you now to tell me if you're disturbed in a way that I might be of help. Your Ma would have wanted that, you know."

Withdrawing her hand from his, Meg lowered her gaze, looking back up at him unexpectedly with an intensity that disturbed him as much as her fervent question.

"How do you know if you've done the right thing, Father, when you're causing someone pain no matter what you do?"

Father Matthew paused, feeling the need for caution in his response. "Pain is sometimes a necessary part of maturing, but you must make yourself more clear if I'm to help you."

"I . . . it's David Lang, Father." Her lovely face flushing, Meg continued haltingly. "I've put an end to our friendship because he'd have me choose between Sean and him."

Managing to restrain a violent lurch of feelings, Father Matthew responded evenly. "The fellow must understand that ties of blood come before all."

"I've tried to tell him that, Father, but he says Sean is heading for difficulties, and that he'll draw me into them with him."

"I'll not let that happen, Meg."

Meg avoided his eyes again. "David wanted me to leave the valley."

"What?"

"He said he'd get me a position in Philadelphia if he goes to school there."

"Impossible!" Incensed, Father Matthew stood up and turned

away in an attempt to conceal the heat of his reaction. Beautiful, innocent Meg. She didn't even realize what the fellow was asking of her!

"Aye, I told him the same. And I told him that was the end of it—our friendship—because I promised Sean I wouldn't let him pressure me into leaving the valley."

Cursing himself for placing Meg in the position where she'd be exposed to David Lang's lecherous intentions, Father Matthew nodded stiffly. "Your brother is a wise young man—far wiser than I gave him credit for, and you were right to keep your word to him."

"But David's unhappy, Father. He's angry and he's suffering."

"If the devil was to tempt you and you refused him, would you concern yourself if he rightfully suffered disappointment?"

"David's not the devil, Father!"

"Is he not?" Suddenly realizing he was trembling with rage, Father Matthew took a deep breath and paused a moment more before returning to the table where Meg now stood, her expression concerned.

"Ah, Meg, my dear, don't you see? You're a beautiful woman now, and David Lang's not missed that beauty. He doesn't want you being drawn into Sean's difficulties, he says. He doesn't want to leave you, he says. He wants to take you with him to Philadelphia, he says. But does the fellow say he cares a whit for your reputation, for the name you would carry for the rest of your days if you were to follow him?"

"He didn't mean it *that* way, Father!" Her smooth cheeks reddening, Meg shook her head vehemently. "David loves me. He wouldn't hurt me."

"He said that, did he?"

Meg nodded slowly, and Father Matthew's rage exploded. "The Son of Satan that he is, after all!"

"Father!"

"Profanity is a sin to which I occasionally fall, Meg, but I don't regret it, for there's no better name for the fellow than that!"

"You're wrong, Father. David cares about me. We've been so close—almost like one person sometimes."

Father Matthew paused, his agitation intense. "Did he kiss you, Meg?" His unexpected question surprised her, and Meg took a step backwards, but Father Matthew would not relent. "I asked you a question, Meg."

His heart twisting in his chest, Father Matthew saw the courage it took for Meg to raise her chin and respond.

"Aye, he did."

"And did he take you in his arms—did he try to—"

"No, Father! He let me go when I told him that he had put an end to it between us."

But there were tears in Meg's eyes where there hadn't been before, and Father Matthew suffered her pain as well as his own. His reaction instinctive, he took Meg into his arms and held her comfortingly close against him.

"Ah, Meg . . . Meg . . . You don't want to believe poorly of David Lang, I can see. He's convinced you that he's good and wants only the best for you, but you're too innocent to realize what the fellow has in mind."

"No, Father, David didn't—"

"Shhh, Meg." Father Matthew knew he could not allow Meg to believe David Lang to be better than he was. He continued cautiously. "I'll not argue the matter with you, for you've not the experience to see the fellow's intentions. Instead, I ask you to believe me when I say that I know the weaknesses of men's natures far more intimately than you do, and that I'm in a better position to judge David Lang's actions than you are. So certain am I of the matter, Meg, that if I wasn't sure it'd cause even greater difficulty, I'd tell you to leave your position on the hill immediately."

"I can't do that, Father! Uncle Timothy would have a fit, and Sean would think—"

"I know what he'd think. And I'd not blame him for the violence of his reaction."

"Father, please believe me—"

"I believe you, Meg." The glorious blue innocence of Meg's gaze was a personal torment that tore at his heart, and Father Matthew continued softly. "I believe you think you told me the truth, but it's also my belief that you've been misled. And since it's I who placed you in the Lang household, I hold myself responsible."

"You needn't worry, Father. David and I no longer even speak. And he's soon to leave for school, to be gone for . . . years."

"The sooner the better, Meg."

Meg's gaze dropped from his. "Aye, Father."

"You did the right thing, Meg. You've nothing to regret, and if David Lang is suffering, it's well deserved."

"Aye, Father."

"Look at me, Meg."

Father Matthew steeled himself against the assault of Meg's gaze as it slowly rose to meet his. "I know what's best for you, and you must trust me to advise you. It's what your Ma wanted."

"Aye, Father."

"Gather up your things and go now, Meg. We'll not accomplish any more today. You may finish your lessons at home and I'll go over them with you the next time we meet. But remember what I said, for your future depends on it. You've nothing to regret, and you mustn't allow David Lang to make you feel you have. Do you understand, Meg?"

Meg hesitated again, torturing him with the trust in her clear eyes. He held his breath as she finally whispered in response, "I'll try."

"I can ask no more."

Still as a statue, Father Matthew watched as the rectory door closed behind Meg.

His conversation with Uncle Martin concluded, David walked to the study door with an even, purposeful stride that belied his inner agitation. He stepped into the hall and closed the door behind him. He had not looked back as his uncle's anger was not pleasant to behold after their lengthy and vehement exchange.

It was just past noon and the last overnight party guest had departed. The anniversary celebration was officially over and, unable to live with the chaos inside him any longer, David had spared no time in seeking out his uncle. Uncle Martin had been stunned by his request and he supposed, had he been in his uncle's place, he would have been stunned as well, but he was past consideration of propriety. What he needed was satisfaction, and if he could get it no other way, he was not above using his position to get what he wanted.

He had no regrets.

An hour later, Townsend strode out of the tack room, leaving Johnny in astonished silence.

Looking down at the bridle in his hand, Johnny unconsciously smoothed the fine leather with a callused thumb before abruptly throwing it against the wall with all his strength. Snatching up his cap, he walked toward the door, fury making his intentions suddenly very clear.

• • •

"No, Johnny, it can't be true!"

"It's true, all right."

Standing by the clothesline in the Lang backyard, Meg stared at Johnny's pale face. Incredulous, she was unconscious of the chill breeze that whipped her hair and molded her uniform against the slender line of her body as gray rain clouds closed rapidly overhead. The partially stripped branches of trees waved wildly in the wind, stirring brightly colored leaves into whirlwinds at their base, but Meg was oblivious of the impending storm and the freshly gathered laundry that lay in a basket at her feet as her mind reeled with shock.

"But you've been with the Langs for four years. How could they fire you without notice?"

"It ain't hard to figure out who's behind it! David Lang's had it in for me from the first time he saw me talking to you. You saw the way he looked at me when he walked into the kitchen during the party." Johnny's fair brow darkened. "He was fit to kill."

"David didn't do it! He wouldn't have you dismissed just because you were talking to me."

"Oh, wouldn't he? He's jealous, Meg! He saw my arm around you, and it wasn't hard to see how I feel about you."

"Johnny, I—"

"It's not your fault, Meg." Johnny's narrow freckled face lost some of its rage. "And to tell the truth, I wouldn't give a damn about leaving here at all, since Townsend says he's arranging to set me up with a position in Philadelphia. Philadelphia's my real home, after all. But the truth is, I don't want to leave you with the sneaky bastard. He's after you, Meg! And he's determined to get you. And I'm thinking he's not given much thought to what's best for you, except to where it suits his purpose. I knew what he had in mind from the first, but I figured I was here to watch him, and if things started getting hard for you, I'd go to the priest again."

"To the priest? Again?"

Johnny's face flushed. "Yeah, again. But now there's nobody left to watch out for you here."

"You shouldn't have gone to Father Matthew. I can watch out for myself, but even if I couldn't, you're wrong. David's angry, but he wouldn't have had his uncle fire you. He wouldn't!"

"He's not what you think he is, Meg, but I don't have time to argue with you about it. Townsend said the letter he's preparing for me will be ready in an hour, and he told me I'm to be off on the five o'clock train."

"Today?"

Johnny nodded and tears sprung into Meg's eyes. "It's a mistake, that's what it is."

"It's no mistake, but I've one last thing to say before I start gathering my things." Taking Meg's shoulders firmly between his hands, Johnny spoke urgently, his young face intense.

"Listen to me, Meg. I'll be sending you my address when I reach Philadelphia, and if you ever need me, I want you to tell me and I'll come."

"Johnny—"

Meg's throat was too choked with emotion to continue, and Johnny shook her lightly. "Promise me?"

Meg nodded.

"Don't trust him, Meg." Johnny's voice broke, twisting the knot in Meg's stomach as his eyes became suddenly bright. His Adam's apple worked furiously and, suddenly awkward, he dropped his hands from her shoulders. "I wish—" Halting abruptly, Johnny gave a small shrug. "But fellas like me don't get what they wish, do they?"

With a short salute, Johnny turned and walked toward the stable. His step quickened until he broke into a run the last few feet before turning out of sight, but Meg was insensible to his hasty flight. Her mind reeled with shock. She was still standing where Johnny left her when the first raindrop struck her face. There was a second and a third before she finally picked up the laundry basket and started for the kitchen, the turmoil inside her growing.

Oblivious of the heavy raindrops beginning to pelt the dusty ground in a rapidly increasing tattoo, Meg ducked out of the Lang kitchen and ran around the side of the house. Clutching her shawl around her, she shivered and drew back under the eaves of the massive roof to wait. Unseen amongst the last flowers of fall cultivated there, she heard Johnny's angry accusations and Father Matthew's warnings echo in her mind, and her confusion grew. This man who Johnny, Father Matthew, and Sean cautioned her against could not be the true David Lang.

She knew the true David Lang. He was the fellow who had shared his thoughts with her without holding back, the fellow who had opened his heart to her and let her see inside. And what she had seen was good, even if his viewpoint was distorted from his position atop the hill. For all his stubborn prejudice and demanding nature, David treated her with the courtesy and respect of an equal, and she knew he truly cared about her. That was the reason for all the trouble between them, wasn't it—the caring that had no true place between them, and the bond that had gone a step too far?

Another shiver passing down her spine, Meg pushed a wild strand of hair back from her face, her gaze moving once more to the path David most commonly used when riding back to the stable. The oversized drops of rain were still falling in a haphazard pattern, but the threatening downpour had not yet started.

Approaching hoofbeats interrupted her thoughts as David rode into sight, holding Max at a steady trot. He was frowning, his expression forbidding, his hazel eyes appearing focused on a thought in his mind that left him impervious to the weather's threat as she stepped into clear view and started walking toward him. His expression flickered when he saw her, then tightened as he spurred his mount and headed in her direction.

The wind whipped Meg's hair, flaying her with its long, defiant strands as David drew up alongside her, but she gave little thought to her appearance as she stood rigidly still, waiting for Max to come to a complete halt. Her gaze intent on David's face so she might not misread his response, she asked bluntly, "Is it true? Did you have Johnny dismissed?"

David's expression flickered again, his face suddenly growing darker than the rain clouds above him. Leaning down, he scooped her up onto the saddle in front of him without warning as Meg gasped in protest. Breathless from the sudden surge into motion as David spurred his horse to a gallop, she could do no more than clutch his arm as they rode off into the quickening rain without another word spoken between them.

The threatening storm was about to break around them, but David refused to heed the warning of the wind that flailed the heavy drops against his face or the blackly ominous clouds preparing to open their deluge upon them. Spurring Max to a faster pace, he pulled Meg back against his chest to shield her from the abusive elements, opening his coat to enclose her against the warmth of his body. Meg did not resist but pressed her cheek against his chest as she turned from the stinging rain. Her protests had ceased after the first few minutes of their ride, when she realized they were useless. She had not said a word since, allowing David's thoughts to run havoc.

His anger increasing, David remembered the jolt of exhilaration that pierced him when he first saw Meg waiting for him as he came over the crest of the hill. His joy turned to apprehension the moment he saw her face, but apprehension turned to silent rage when she spoke her first words to him in three weeks.

Is it true? Did you have Johnny dismissed?

Hot jealousy again assailing him, David tightened his arms around her. Meg had been temptingly close and her eyes had been too accusing for a simple response. Yielding to impulse, he had snatched her up in his arms and carried her off, but he didn't regret his actions. It was worth any cost to have her close to him again and to know they would finally talk, away from the pressures that had come between them.

Thunder rumbled again, the downpour thickening, and David heard Meg's low gasp as they were whipped by the icy drops. He felt her shudder in his arms, and he scanned the wooded area of the hill more closely. It'd been a long time, but he remembered an old hunter's shack. It had to be nearby.

Spotting a sagging roof in the distance, David pressed Max onward as the downpour began in earnest.

Drawing up beside the shanty a few minutes later, David dismounted and snatched Meg down into his arms. Striding forward, he kicked the drooping door open and proceeded inside, pausing as his eyes grew accustomed to the darkness.

"Put me down."

David lowered her to her feet and tossed his hat to a nearby chair as he squinted into the darkness. The single-room hut was a shambles of rotting furniture, spider webs, and matted leaves, but spying the object he sought, he snatched the lantern from a peg on the wall and gave it a shake. Gratified to hear the swish of oil, he struck a match to the wick.

Holding the lamp high, David looked at Meg. She was standing where he had set her. Her damp hair contoured the delicate shape of her head and raindrops glittered with the glow of jewels on her slender brows, eyelashes, and cheeks. The fine line of her lips was tight, except for an occasional quiver of movement, and her glorious eyes were fast on his face as she maintained her silence. And she was so beautiful to him that he ached for the love of her.

David placed the lantern on a nearby stool as Meg asked again,

"Did you do it, David? Did you have Johnny dismissed? I must know."

"Why must you know, Meg?" Jealousy surged anew as David closed the distance between them and grasped her shoulders. "What difference does it make?" He stroked the damp tendrils back from her face, frowning. "Your hair's wet and you're shaking. That's the most important thing to deal with right now."

Withdrawing a spotless handkerchief from his inner pocket, David wiped the glittering drops from her forehead and cheeks. Silent through his patient ministrations, Meg waited until he blotted the excess moisture from her hair and removed his damp coat to drape it around her shoulders before she repeated once more, "Did you do it, David?"

Exploding into fury at her persistence, David responded with a resounding, "Yes! Does it satisfy you to be able to call me a villain for having the fellow sent packing?"

"Why, David?"

Meg's face was pale, her expression incredulous, and David felt the pain reflected there.

"He couldn't keep his hands off you, Meg! Did you really think I'd stand by and watch him paw you? Did you expect me to go off to school and leave you behind knowing that miserable fellow was trying to take my place?"

"You shouldn't have done it."

"Shouldn't I, Meg? Has it really been so easy for you to cast me aside these past three weeks and resume your life as if we'd never come to know each other? It wasn't for me. Do you know what it's like to be cut off from someone who's become a part of you, only to see another person taking your place before your eyes?"

"Johnny had no part in what happened between us, David. It's plain for me to see that you're still the privileged young man who's never been refused, who hopes to have his way at the expense of anyone who stands in his path. And I'm still the girl from the valley he hopes to change to suit him."

"I don't want to change you, Meg." The words came from his heart, emerging in a hoarse whisper. "I want you as you are."

"Do you, David?" Meg's eyes filled, but she blinked the moisture away. "Well, even if you do, the truth is, it's not meant to be."

"Why, Meg?"

"If I must tell you why again, then there's no hope you'll ever understand me."

David paused at her response, his expression intense. "Then will you try to understand *me*, Meg? For the truth is, I never intended this rift between us. I only wanted to keep you close to me, but somehow everything went wrong." Pausing, his voice slipping a pained notch lower, David whispered. "Don't you love me at all, Meg? Even a little?"

David's heart hammered as Meg's eyes searched his, as he saw his own pain reflected there.

"You asked me that question before, David, and I answered you as best I could. I care for you, but your kind of love confuses me. It would take obligations and the feelings of others and toss them aside as if they have no meaning, just for selfish pleasure."

"Is that how you see me, Meg, as selfish?" Meg's words stung. "Was it selfish of me to want you to have more than you can expect in the valley? Is it right to throw good after bad—to waste your own life for someone who's intent on ruining his own?"

"You're meaning Sean again. Aye, that's the crux of the conflict between us, isn't it!" Anger flared again in her eyes as Meg attempted to break free of David's crushing grip. "Let me be, David! Give up to it! It's not meant to be between us."

"It is, Meg, if you'll just—"

"But I won't, David! And if I was willing to give up who and what I am, I'd not be the person you see here and say you love, don't you see?" Tears bright in her eyes, Meg held his gaze for long moments before continuing in a softer voice. "But if it'll make your pain any less to know I suffer, too, I'll admit it. I've not been at ease with my feelings these past three weeks. I've missed the closeness we shared, and it pained me to think you'd soon be leaving with this discord between us. And it hurts me to see what you did to Johnny, for it was of no use at all. Didn't you know he could never take your place in my heart?"

At Meg's unexpected words, David's heart began pounding. He had no response as she continued. "Johnny's a friend, but there's not the bond between us that you and I share. There could never be. Didn't you know that all along?"

David swallowed tightly, the ache inside him swelling. "How could I know that, Meg? Have you ever said there's more than friendship between us?"

"If you must hear the words, I'll say them, then. Aye, there's more between us than friendship. More than there should be, for you've touched a spot deep inside me that won't let go."

"I can't let go of it, either, Meg." Seeing the fight had gone out of her, David drew Meg closer, his gaze holding hers. "And if my love for you is selfish in your eyes, I suppose there's nothing I can do but try to change the image you see. I'll need time to work on it, Meg. You know I'm not good at compromise."

"Aye, I know that well."

The desolation in Meg's response dissolved the last vestige of David's pride.

"Meg . . . Meg . . ." His lips touched her brow, her temple, her cheek. He brushed her mouth with his whisper. "Don't you know I'll do anything to make things right between us again? The only thing I can't do is change things back the way they were. It's too late, Meg. My friendship has changed to love."

Meg frowned with her whispered response. "I don't know anything about the kind of love between a man and a woman, David. I wouldn't be good at it."

"Yes, you would. Love comes naturally to you. But even if it didn't, I can teach you. And you can teach me the things I don't know—like how to compromise, and how to see beyond the surface for the truth. You can teach me how to change."

Meg remained silent and David felt a nudge of panic. "Let me kiss you, Meg."

Meg averted her eyes and shook her head. "I'm no good at kissing. I don't know how."

The well of tenderness inside David, from which only Meg could drink, expanded as he urged her softly. "We have so much to learn from each other, Meg. Shouldn't we start now?"

Silence.

"Meg, look at me." The resounding clamor of his heart overwhelmed the crashing booms of thunder and the hammering of rain on the roof over their heads as Meg raised her face to his. "Nothing will ever be right for either of us unless we set our feelings right. You know that, don't you? Put your arms around my neck, Meg."

Suffering a silent agony in the few moments before Meg slid her hands up to his shoulders, David barely restrained a gasp of pleasure as her arms encircled his neck. Intent on the pink trembling lips so close to his, David closed the distance between with a soft, "I love you, Meg."

Joy erupted inside David at the first taste of her—his dear, loving Meg. She felt so right in his arms, her lips so sweet, even as her inexperience prompted his grating whisper.

"Open your mouth for me, Meg."

Meg's lips parted under his and David indulged himself, drawing from her deeply. The fragrance of her skin was perfume that sent his mind reeling, the warmth of her innocent response a sweet torment of his aching need as he clutched her closer still.

Oh, Meg . . . Meg . . . A loving litany of her name resounded in his mind. He wanted to show Meg how much he loved her. He wanted to prove to her that he could give her more than she had ever dreamed. He needed to make her see that it was meant to be this way between them from the first. He wanted—

The echo of his own thoughts snapped David back to reality with sudden clarity.

He wanted . . . *He* needed . . .

But *Meg* wanted to be sure he wasn't the man others thought him to be, the man she could never love. *Meg* wanted to understand the feelings just coming to life inside her. *Meg* needed to know he meant everything he said before she allowed her feelings full rein.

Realizing that to lose Meg's confidence now would be to lose her forever, David forced himself to relinquish her. Trembling, his control precarious, David maintained the short distance between them that cost so dearly, aware of the true sacrifice of love for the first time as he whispered, "If the rain doesn't stop soon, we'll have to take our chances getting wet, because . . ."

Her eyes great shining mirrors of emotion, her breathing as clipped as his own, Meg responded simply, "Aye."

Loving her more at that moment than ever before, David curved his arm around Meg's shoulders and drew her toward the door, where they watched the rain and lingered.

Chapter 14

"By the staff of St. Patrick, I'll get the bastards for this!"

Trembling with rage, Lenny Dunne turned sharply, knocking his shovel to the floor of the shaft with a savage kick. Glancing around him, he saw his angry display had gone unnoticed by the miners working a few yards away, and he raised his cap to run a grimy hand through his hair. Replacing it squarely on his head, he addressed Sean in a harsh whisper.

"Ye realize if what ye've said is true, if Lang is cuttin' the crews of each shift back by ten men, there'll be a weepin' and a wailin' in the patch with them that'll go hungry because of it!"

"Aye, I know, all right."

His blood boiling, Sean nodded, swinging his pick at a block of slate in an attempt to disguise the intense conversation progressing between him and his friend. He knew very well what it would be like in the patch when the day was done tomorrow and each shift went to collect its wage, only to have some discover that their livelihood was being snatched from them.

And without cause, too.

Cursing the confusion in his tickets which had caused him to leave the shaft temporarily and go to the office to straighten it out, Sean remembered the conversation he overheard as he had approached the door. As fate would have it, the clerk in the outside office had stepped away, and he was certain he'd not forget the sound of Mr. Martin Lang's voice in the next room as he spoke to Captain Linden of the Coal and Iron Police.

"No, Captain, I have a better idea than that. I agree that we must get the troublemakers out of the shafts, or put some fear into them at least, but it'll only cause more trouble if we go down the list you've compiled and lay them off as you suggest. We'd hit the Molly Maguires hard by firing some of the more obvious of their number down there, but we'd only be touching the tip of the iceberg, leaving the rest of them whom we haven't identified to raise havoc with retribution."

"So what will you do, sir?" Captain Linden's rough, gravelly voice had hesitated before continuing. "The sooner we get those fellows out, the better."

"You know which ones have done the most inciting below?"

"That I do."

"Put marks by those names, and I'll have Whittmore make another list of the least productive men on each shift. We'll make a general announcement that we're cutting back because of production problems and we'll fire five Mollies and five of our worst producers from each shift."

There was a brief hesitation before Captain Linden spoke with obvious reservations. "That means you'll be firing fifteen innocent men, Mr. Lang."

"Maybe so, but we'll have them wondering if we're really on to them, or if the Mollies that were fired just had bad luck with the draw. In any case, any Mollies that are left will do some heavy thinking before they incite openly again."

"And what of the fifteen innocent men who are to be fired?"

"They're not my primary concern, Captain! They'll be on the list because they aren't working as hard as the others, so I won't be losing much. I can replace them with efficient laborers whenever I want."

Captain Linden started speaking again at that point, but at the sound of the clerk's returning step, Sean was forced to hide behind a partition to wait until a more appropriate moment to show himself. His stomach had been in knots ever since.

He had returned below, his mind reeling with anger. He hadn't given much thought to those whom Linden suspected of being Mollies, for the men on that list knew the dangers when they embraced the organization, but the fate of the innocent men tore at him. They'd be men like his Da, working hard to support their families with the odds against them all the way.

"They'll be puttin' the slips in the pay envelopes tomorrow, ye say?"

Lenny's harsh whisper interrupted Sean's dark thoughts, jerking his eyes back to his friend's flushed face. "Aye, tomorrow."

Picking up his shovel, Lenny gave a low laugh. "So that makes us a day up on the filthy swine, don't it? Well, I'll take the information to the right people, Sean, me boyo, and we'll see what we can work up in response." Hesitating a moment, the lamp's flickering glow reflecting in his narrowed eyes with an almost demonic gleam, Lenny added, "And while I'm about it, I'll put in a good word for ye, Sean. Ye've a keen mind and a stout heart, and ye've a dedication to takin' back the honor the bastards have stolen from the good Irishmen in these fields any way ye can. It's plain to see that yer age is no detriment, there. And since I'm thinkin' me name will be amongst those who'll be on that list tomorrow, I'm also thinkin' we'll be able to do with another good man down here. So spend the night thinkin' about where ye want to go and where ye think ye'll be in the next few years, and if yer thoughts put you in the same mind with them of us who count themselves amongst Molly's sons, let me know. Is it agreed?"

The sudden pounding of his heart forced a flush to Sean's face with his short nod. His abrupt rush of color appeared to be all the response Lenny needed to see, as his short laugh sounded once more.

"So, it seems the bad luck of some might make good luck for others, don't it, me boyo? Well, I'll be askin' for yer response as soon as the layoff starts." Looking up at the sound of a step behind them, Lenny gave a short sniff. "And here comes that weasel, Gregg. Show him the strength of yer back or the damned informer will be reportin' ye. We'll not want that, 'cause we'll be needin' ye down here when all's said and done."

Looking up, Sean saw the informer positioned himself nearby, and he turned to spit his contempt onto the ground. Aye, he'd show them all the strength of his back down here, and when the time came, he'd show them much more. Then Lang and all them like him would know they couldn't hold good Irishmen down forever.

The afternoon sun filtered through the partially denuded branches but Meg was unconscious of its warmth as David held her in a passionate embrace. Two weeks had passed since that day in the hunter's cabin. David had arrived home without the realization of the staff a short time earlier and unexpectedly snatched her from her work in the yard of the Lang manor. He had drawn her out of sight behind the trees and into his arms, and he had not released her since.

David's mouth moved against her closed eyelids, her brow, trailed her cheek. A tremor of emotion shook Meg and his hand tightened in her hair, as he ground his mouth into hers.

Lost in the wonder of the emotions he aroused within her, Meg closed her eyes, allowing the wild colors careening in her mind to assume control. She had not known it could be like this in David's arms, that he could transport them to a place where only they abided and the world was held at bay. She had not realized that she would come alive as never before when his mouth touched hers, that his hungry caresses could stir a hunger in her as well, and that she could ache inside with the need to give him the succor he sought.

Her lips separating under his, Meg allowed David access to her mouth, and the violent shudder that wracked him resounded deep within her. He was devouring her, swallowing her slenderness in his arms, attempting to absorb her as a physical part of him, and she melded to him, torn by the mutual need building inside them and the instinctive knowledge that she gave him anguish with joy, and torment in her loving response.

Tearing his mouth from hers with a rasping oath, David trailed biting kisses against her jaw and throat. A passionate nip stung her neck, but Meg's soft protest was lost in another wild swell of emotion as he kissed the wounded spot with new fervor. David's sweeping caresses slid to her rib cage to capture a small breast and cup it warmly through the stiff material of her uniform, and the ache inside Meg grew. But there was no sense of violation in his touch as he fondled her lovingly. It felt right and good, even as a confusing, pleasured torment beset her.

Her mind was reeling. David was trembling as well as he held her breathlessly close, and she ached with the loving agony of being in his arms. She knew he needed her in a way he had never needed anyone else—and the knowledge was at once heady and intimidating as it ignited a new round of emotions within her.

Unexpectedly, David separated himself from her, holding her at arms' length. A short protest escaped her lips and he shook his head, the tribulation visible on his handsome face becoming more intense.

"No, Meg, please—" His broad chest heaved against his finely tailored jacket and agitated specks of gold stirred in his eyes as he raked her with his gaze. "Don't do this to me." At her obvious confusion, he continued hoarsely. "Don't make it harder for me. It's taking every bit of strength I have to stop right now. It's going too fast. You know that, don't you? I don't want you hating me later. I want you to understand the way you feel and to be as certain as I am that it's right between us. I want you to trust me."

"I trust you, David."

David's eyes closed briefly at her reply. "I know, but the problem is that I don't know if I can trust myself." Suddenly drawing her back into his arms, David crushed her close against him, his cheek against her hair. "Meg, I made an excuse to Uncle Martin and slipped home to see you because I couldn't concentrate on my work for thoughts of you. But I promised myself that I wouldn't make the same mistakes again, and I'm trying."

The warmth of his arms allowing her the consolation her aching spirit sought, Meg closed her eyes. Yes, she knew he was trying. They had been together many times since that stormy day two weeks ago, in meetings both planned and unplanned. They had taken turns talking and listening. David had told her that he had instructed Townsend to arrange a job for Johnny Law in Philadelphia, and her conscience was partially appeased to know Johnny had not made up that story to spare her additional concern.

Their attempts to learn from each other had seen little progress, however, except for the loving that grew more potent every day. Although she had fought acknowledging it, the basis for the unidentifiable force that had drawn David and her together was now totally clear to her. She knew that David had been correct. Loving came naturally to her—especially when it came to loving him.

The colliery whistle in the valley below them sounded the end of the day shift, returning reality with a harsh slap as it forced to Meg's mind a vision of miners emerging from the shafts. She heard their ragged coughs, saw their blackened faces, and watched their lagging steps—and she saw the colliery office from which the Langs viewed it all with little sympathy for the plight of the men below them.

A sudden sadness overwhelming her, Meghan acknowledged her fear that where David's heart might easily touch hers, there was still a breach between them that might never be spanned.

"Meg—"

Aware that she had stiffened in David's arms, Meg suddenly drew back. "I have to get back to the kitchen, David."

"Not yet."

"Aye, David, now."

"Are you angry with me?" Puzzled by her sudden withdrawal as she shook her head in reply, David pressed further. "Then what's wrong?"

"Cook will be looking for me."

David's face tightened, and Meg knew he saw through her

excuse. She raised her hand to touch his cheek in a conciliatory departing gesture as she turned to go. Cupping her hand with his, David pressed her palm to his lips. The heat of his kiss scorched her skin, and, unable to speak past the sudden thickness in her throat, Meg withdrew her hand and turned back to the house.

"And so, you see, Fiona, I've been worrying about Meghan. It's not like her to miss her lessons the way she has these past two weeks, even though her excuses seem valid."

Her lined face pale, Fiona turned to the stove. Father Matthew had arrived at her house a few minutes earlier. She had been surprised and apprehensive when she saw him at the door, for it was the middle of the afternoon and a visit from him at an hour when Meg and Sean were both absent seemed cause for alarm. Her intuition had not misled her.

Blinking rapidly, Fiona picked up a cloth and gripped the handle of the kettle, using the time to absorb Father Matthew's statement as he sat at the table behind her. Meg had missed her lessons with Father Matthew these past two weeks? How could that be true? She had been coming home at the same late hour thrice a week, just like before, with no explanation for the time. Of course, she'd not asked Meg for an explanation, believing the girl to be with the priest as was her usual custom, but now—

Fiona avoided Father Matthew's gaze as she turned and reached for the teapot. She poured the steaming water and watched the dried tea leaves swirl, feeling the young priest's eyes on her all the while as a slow heat began creeping up from the faded collar of her dress. She knew the moment his gaze became more intense and her discomfort increased.

"Is something wrong, Fiona?"

"No, nothin's wrong."

Clumsy with nervousness, Fiona turned abruptly. Hitting the cup she had set for herself with her elbow, she knocked it crashing to the floor. So distracted was she that she gave not a thought to the china, which was her best and which her miserly husband would refuse to allow her to replace, as she dropped to her swollen knees to pick up the pieces. A hand on her shoulder turned her to look up at Father Matthew.

"Fiona, please. I didn't come here to upset you. I'll do that."

Seated across the table from the priest a few minutes later, Fiona raised her tea to her lips, aware that her hand was shaking.

Father Matthew was speaking to her, but she heard not a word, so disturbed and bemused was she.

Dear Meg . . . dear Meg . . . What should she do? If the child wasn't where she *should* be, she was where she *shouldn't* be—it was that simple. But when it concerned a girl as honest and straightforward as Meg, it wasn't simple at all. If she had been working late at the house on the hill, she would've said so, and it was difficult to believe the girl had been on errands she forgot to mention six times during the last two weeks. So where *had* she been? Fiona's heart began pounding anew. Aye, where?

To her despair, Fiona believed she knew.

"Fiona?"

Fiona's head jerked up at Father Matthew's soft pronunciation of her name, and an instinctive response poured from her lips. "The child's been workin' long hours on the hill. They're doin' some special cleanin' up there. Cleanin'—always cleanin'."

"Fiona . . ."

Guilt flushed through her at the untruths she had spoken, but Fiona strove to maintain an unblinking facade as she responded, "Aye, Father?"

"You're preoccupied and nervous. Does your unrest have to do with Meg?"

"Nay, Father. Not with Meg! The girl's the light of me life, all I hold dear in the world. If I be upset, it's with the state of affairs in this house, here, with me husband comin' home each night in worse condition than the last, and with the boarders bein' more demandin' and himself sayin' I'm not workin' hard enough to please 'em. It's with me worry for the boy, Sean, who's away from the house more often than not without givin' explanation when asked, and the realization that I know where he's headin' although I can't see a way to stop him. And it's with the thought that the weak woman that I am, I'm not fit to guide these children onto the right path when the time might come that they need guidin'."

Father Matthew's intense brown eyes softened with compassion, and Fiona's guilt intensified. Aye, lies, all of it, every word she'd spoke. Them worries was always with her, but it was fear for Meg that now shook her. But betray her to the priest when the child sought to keep her privacy? Never!

"I've no answers for you, Fiona." The concern in Father Matthew's tone added to Fiona's guilt, but she strove to concentrate on his words, if only to escape her rioting thoughts as he continued. "But when the spirit is troubled, a child of God turns to the Father." Purposefully draining his cup, Father Matthew smiled and drew himself to his feet. "When Meghan returns, tell her I was askin' for her, and if she's not had time to come for her lessons this afternoon, tell her to stop by on Saturday. I'll give her some work to do at home. Will you do that?"

"Aye, Father."

Again placing his hand on her shoulder, Father Matthew smiled. "Some of us have a difficult lot in life, but we must remember, if our Father allots it so, it's because He feels we're hardy enough to bear it. You're stronger than you give yourself credit for, Fiona, so smile, and remember, God loves you."

"Aye, Father."

Standing in the hall a few minutes later, Fiona watched as the front door closed behind Father Matthew. At the sound of the click, she released a tense breath and allowed a reply to his last statement to surface in her mind.

Aye, God loves me. But on this earth, only two've shown they care at all. One was gone to the heaven she had earned, and the other was slipping away from her. And she feared the reason why.

What should she do? Uncertainty mingled with consternation and suspicion and Fiona felt the rise of an inevitable despair. But her despair was not for Meg, but for herself. With an abrupt clarity, Fiona knew the course she would take. The weak, despicable woman that she was, she would do as she had always done when faced with a dilemma.

She would wait and see—and she would do nothing at all.

"You're not done for the day yet, my girl! There's potatoes to peel for supper, and there's vegetables to prepare, and when you're done with that you're to set the table with the mistress's good china."

Cook's verbal attack was unrelenting. Meg had left David in the woods behind the house a short time earlier, slipped around the chicken coops to pick up the eggs she had gathered, and returned to the kitchen, but her patience with the old woman's foul disposition was fast deteriorating. Her dark glance did not go unnoticed as Cook responded with an intensifying of her attack.

"Don't go giving me none of your black looks, miss! You're not privileged in this kitchen, as much as you might think you are, and I won't have my authority questioned!"

Aware that to deny Cook's accusations would only stir her

wrath anew, Meg walked to the corner and reached for the potatoes.

"You'll *wash* the potatoes first, girl! I'll not have grime in with the food I cook when it's served to the mistress."

Maintaining her silence, Meg scrubbed the potatoes in a bucket nearby with careful control. Picking up a cloth, she dried the potatoes carefully. She had never been fully accepted by Cook or the others in the same way as the rest of the household staff, but the truce that existed between them all in the past year had recently come to an end.

Uncertain as to the cause, Meg was visited with a vision of Johnny Law's freckled face. She remembered the open animosity toward her the day Johnny was dismissed, and the silence in the kitchen when a letter from Johnny arrived for her with the family mail earlier that morning. She had opened the letter, aware that all eyes were upon her, and the obvious labor of Johnny's precise, awkward printing had brought a lump to her throat. She had read with relief that Johnny was settling in well in his new position, but sadness touched her anew when he repeated his warning against David. For that reason she had not mentioned the correspondence to David.

"Daydreaming again, miss!"

Cook's jowled face was tight with resentment as Meg looked up from her chore, and Meg's patience came to an end.

"I'm doing my job, Cook. You've no need for complaint."

"Don't I, now?" A hot color unrelated to the heat of the stove before which she stood shone on Cook's face as she took a threatening step. "I've cause for complaint against your sassy tone and your lagging step of late, and I'm telling you now, I'll stand for neither. You'll do your work like the rest of us here or out you'll go!"

A low grunt of approval sounded from the opposite corner where Mabel rested her legs, and Meg realized she had been the topic of discussion between them. Mutually accusing gazes accosted her and Meg was struck with a sudden realization. For all the care David and she had taken, the staff had found them out!

Her heart beginning a new pounding, Meg averted her face, certain her guilt was visible for all to see. They knew the deceit David and she had practiced on everyone these past two weeks. Somehow they knew she was meeting David when she was supposed to be at her lessons with Father Matthew and that despite her protests, David stole home to be with her whenever he could. And they knew that David and she were no longer just friends.

Her pride returning, Meg raised her chin. But if it was true that David and she weren't merely friends any longer, they were not lovers, either, and she did not deserve the condemnation she saw in Cook's eyes. That thought firm in her mind, Meg maintained her silence, her hands working efficiently. But neither her silence nor her attention to her duties appeared to be enough for Cook in her agitation.

"Sulking won't do here, miss!"

"I'm not sulking."

"And I won't have you sass me!"

Snapping her lips tightly closed, Meg continued her work, determined to withstand Cook's unwarranted criticism, for her problems were such that she needed no more to add to them.

"I'll not keep you in my kitchen if your attitude doesn't change, I'm warning you. My word's law in this room, and if I say you go, you g—"

"That's enough!"

The unexpected intervention of David's voice turned the staff toward the doorway where he stood, his expression livid. Chagrined, Cook took a step backwards, her gaze slipping accusingly toward Meg.

"The girl hasn't been doing her work these last weeks, Mr. David, and it's my duty to keep her straight."

"That's not true!"

Meg's spontaneous denial was met with David's flat response. "You don't have to give me any explanations, Meg, and you don't have to submit to this harassment. Go home for the day. There's nothing to be gained by your staying any longer with Cook in her present state of mind."

"The girl hasn't finished her work!" Firmly standing her ground, Cook continued. "The mistress depends on me to see to running this kitchen and I—"

"Don't press me any further, Cook!" Turning toward the woman, his tall figure rigid with anger, David continued more softly. "It's only because of my respect for you and the contribution you've made to this household over the years that I haven't said more. But I'm telling you now, I won't stand for your haranguing Meg. I want you to remember, when you abuse her, you abuse me. Is that understood?"

"If the mistress knew—"

"If my aunt knew you picked on Meg out of petty spite, she'd be more annoyed than I! So if you value a comfortable old age, Cook, mind your words. They can destroy you!"

Turning away from the old woman, David instructed with indisputable authority. "Go home, Meg. Now."

Turning on his heel, David left the room. The silence that followed his departure heavier than she could bear, Meg snatched up her shawl, and within minutes she was on her way down the hill.

Not taking her eyes from the doorway through which Mr. David and the interloper, Meghan O'Connor, had disappeared, Cook muttered a low oath under her breath. It was true! The girl had bewitched him!

Turning back to the stove, ignoring Mabel's open-mouthed stare, Cook took another deep breath, her old heart breaking. She had loved the dear boy like a son from the first day he came to live with the Langs, him with his winning ways and constant smile, but he hadn't been the same from the first day that O'Connor girl entered the house.

Fighting tears, Cook remembered the whisperings that plagued her about some of them Irish below. They had a way about them, that bunch, a cunning that came from dabbling in the black arts, and she had no doubt the O'Connor girl had that witchcraft bred into her soul. Them with their Pope and holy mass, and with their hearts as black as the coal they dug, they could charm the birds out of the trees when they'd a mind to! Poor young Mr. David had fallen victim to one of the very worst of them when he'd been too ill to fight, and now the little witch had turned Mr. David against her.

Cook brushed her tears away with the back of her hand. If the master knew what all of them in the kitchen knew, he'd be fit to kill, he would. Townsend had seen them! The disgrace of it—the two of them secretly meeting in that old shack on the other side of the mountain! And Mr. David, vulnerable as he was to the girl's smile and the wiggle of her meager frame, was becoming more smitten with her each day. That Meghan O'Connor would soon have him where she wanted him, and she would be the ruination of the dear young man. She'd drag him down to the level of them drunken sloths below and the smile would fade from his handsome face forever.

"Cook, is something wrong?"

Cook turned at the unexpected sound of the mistress's voice. Her throat closed tighter still at the concern in the dear woman's expression. The mistress had always been kind and considerate of them in the kitchen. She owed the mistress loyalty in return. And she owed her the truth.

Swallowing with visible difficulty, Cook did not respond, but turned to the corner where Mabel still sat, her legs propped up on the stool in front of her. "I've some things to say to the mistress, if you please, Mabel. Be sure to close the door behind you when you leave."

Waiting only until Mabel slipped out of sight and the door swung shut behind her, Cook turned to Miss Letty's expectant expression.

His coal-blackened face stiff, Sean stared down at the letter in his hand with disbelief. He had arrived home from the mine a few minutes earlier, his body aching and his mind in a turmoil of agitation at his secret knowledge of the layoffs to come and with acceptance into the Mollies appearing unexpectedly imminent.

Unlike most days, he had been grateful to walk into Aunt Fiona's kitchen with the thought that after some washing up, he'd soon be upstairs in his room, alone with his thoughts until Meg came home. He needed some time to think and to plan the future which appeared to be fast approaching. He needed time to allow the realization to sink into his mind that he'd soon be freed from impotence, that he'd soon be in a position to affect his future and the futures of all those like him in the anthracite fields who suffered the domination and prejudice of the wealthy few. Anticipation had set his heart to racing until Aunt Fiona held out the letter that arrived for him in the mail that morning.

Sean glanced around the deserted hallway, grateful that he had had the foresight to step out of his aunt's view before opening the envelope addressed in painstakingly laborious printing. The Philadelphia postmark had caused a tremor of premonition to course down his spine, and as he read the contents of the brief note, incredulity numbed his mind. But his mind was no longer numb. It was filled with rage.

Lies, all of it! Meg would not break her promise to him!

Crushing the letter in his fist, Sean was about to cast it aside when the first niggle of uncertainty touched his mind. He remembered the times Meg defended David Lang, insisting he was her friend, and that uncertainty became a tight knot of doubt inside him. His confidence shaken, Sean suddenly realized that whatever his feelings, he was bound by responsibility to ascertain the truth of the bitter words John Law had written.

Jamming the wrinkled sheet deep into his pocket, Sean turned toward the staircase, determined. He would do what he must, wherever it took him.

Breathless from her rapid descent down the hillside path, Meg pulled her shawl tight around her shoulders and stepped onto the dusty road. Glancing toward the colliery a short distance away, she saw the final stragglers from the first shift making their way home. Their lagging steps returned the harsh reality that despite the beauty that had come about between David and her in the past two weeks, nothing had really changed. The world outside the circle of David's arms was still the same bitter place where she and her own were condemned to an unchanging pattern of life that saw no hope of improvement. She knew that if she had come down that hill a few minutes earlier, she would have seen Sean in the midst of that dirty, exhausted, hopeless column of men. And she knew just as clearly that she could not abandon her brother to his fate, for the truth of it was, she was his only hope of escaping it.

"Miss O'Connor—"

Meghan turned at the sound of her name to face the big, dour-faced man who addressed her. Her heart leaped. The hulking figure was well over the mark of six feet, and his breadth of shoulder and muscle identified him as clearly as the dreaded blue uniform he wore. Unwilling to reveal her trepidation at being approached by Captain Linden of the Coal and Iron Police, Meghan raised her chin and responded in a level voice.

"Aye, Captain, that's my name, as you well know. What is it you want with me?"

A hint of a smile touched the big Scotsman's lips, revealing, as he spoke, a glimpse of the devoted family man he was rumored to be when away from the brutality of the coal fields. "You're a wee girl, all right, but your father's in your clear eyes and handsome features, and it pleases me to see him again. Dennis O'Connor was a good man."

Her throat choking at the policeman's unexpected sentiment, Meg nodded, unable to respond, and Captain Linden took a tentative step forward. All trace of a smile dropped away as he spoke again.

"I've come to speak to you today because it concerns me that for all your brother resembles your father as well, there's little of Dennis O'Connor inside him. The truth of it is, your brother is headed for trouble, Miss, as I think you must know. He's taken the wrong path, and he's straying farther each day."

Meg shook her head, tension knotting her hands. "I don't know what you're talking about."

"Aye, you do. You know as well as I where his sympathies lie, but I won't press the matter, other than to say he's soon to reach the point of no return. Out of respect for the honest, hardworking man your father was, and because I know your brother's feelings for you are strong, I'm asking you to appeal to him before it's too late."

"Sean hasn't done anything wrong."

"Not yet."

"Then you have no right—"

"Aye, no right at all, except that of a man of good will." His shaggy brows knitting over eyes that softened unexpectedly, Captain Linden continued quietly. "I didn't come to upset you, but to warn you, Miss, for it's all I can do for the last of Dennis O'Connor's brood. I wish it could be more."

The unexpected softness disappearing as unexpectedly as it appeared, Captain Linden straightened his massive shoulders. "You'll do well to think of what I say and remember that it was said with good intentions." He raised his hand to the brim of his cap in a short salute. "I wish you a good-day, young miss."

Captain Linden was several feet away before total realization of his words took effect. Her step wooden, Meg headed home and entered Aunt Fiona's kitchen a few minutes later, too distracted to notice her aunt's anxiety.

Meg's short, "Where's Sean?" deepened her aunt's frown.

"He washed up and out he went."

"Where did he go, Aunt?"

"The boy tells me nothin', Meg, but it's me thought he went to his favorite *shebeen*, for that Lenny Dunne was waitin' for him outside the door."

"Lenny Dunne."

"Aye, and he's a bad one, that fellow."

Her aunt's statement a pronouncement she suddenly could not bear, Meg turned toward the hallway. She was running toward her room when the first tears fell.

• • •

Her pale eyes bright with tears, Letty paused at the study door to take a deep breath. Martin had arrived home a short time earlier. She could hear him moving within, and she briefly closed her eyes as she made a silent admission that weighed heavily on her heart. With the most benevolent intentions, she had wrought a terrible turmoil in her household, and now it threatened the future of the young man she loved as a son.

In an uncharacteristic swell of anger, Letty clenched her small fists and silently cursed the day she had gone down to the valley to see the priest. And then she cursed Meghan O'Connor, whom she had so often blessed for restoring David to them when he was almost lost. But the girl had gone a step too far in casting her shadow in the beautiful future David had in store for him. Making an effort to control her trembling, Letty raised her chin with determination. She had been a buffer between David and Martin in the past, but she would serve in that position no longer.

Her back stiffening with resolve, Letty raised her hand and knocked lightly on the paneled door as she called softly, "Martin? It's Letty."

"Come in, dear."

Martin stood as she entered the room, his congenial expression fading at the sight of his wife's pale face. "What's wrong, Letty?"

Letty took another strengthening breath as she approached him. "That acceptance you received in the mail yesterday, Martin— I've changed my mind. You see, you were right all along, and I was wrong." Her facade suddenly crumbling with a sob, Letty moved into her husband's arms with a whispered, "Oh, Martin, I hope it's not too late."

An ominous silence hung over the Lang study as David stared at his uncle, darkly incredulous. His expression stiff, he finally replied, "I have no intention of going along with these ridiculous plans. I don't know how you thought I'd consider them for a moment!"

"I don't see how you have any choice in the matter, David."

Pausing again in response, David looked at his uncle. Martin Lang's wiry frame was stiff, his thin face hard, and his gaze intense. Aunt Letty stood a few steps to his rear, her face void of the usual concern in evidence whenever his uncle and he were at odds. He was suddenly aware that his staunchest ally had turned against him, and he would be receiving no aid from Aunt Letty in this dispute. Somehow that realization brought the gravity of the situation more clearly to fore, and David prepared himself for battle.

Uncle Martin's small eyes sparked with controlled anger. "You're behaving childishly, David. I should think you'd be honored to be accepted at Oxford! You've been availed of a rare opportunity for a superior education at the same college your father attended. The advantages of this exposure are endless. The travel involved will be as broadening as the formal education you will receive. You'll thank me when you finally realize how wide the world is beyond this isolated section of Pennsylvania."

"You speak as if I've never been out of reach of these mines, and you know that's not true, Uncle! You know I traveled extensively with my mother and father."

"That was many years ago."

"Not that many years! But even if that were true, I spent the major portion of the last few years on my own at school in Philadelphia. I'm not lacking in experience of any kind, I assure you, and I've already made up my mind to complete my education at the University of Pennsylvania."

"You should have talked to me before making any plans."

"I thought I had! You never mentioned an intention to apply for my acceptance at Oxford. If you had, I would have told you that you were wasting your time!"

Uncle Martin stiffened at David's increasingly belligerent attitude. "I refuse to discuss the matter further. I'm making arrangements for you to leave for London in two weeks."

"Two weeks!" David fell back a step, regaining his composure. "I won't go. I'll make my own arrangements to attend the University of Pennsylvania."

"David, my dear boy." The anger, so apparent in his eyes only moments before, faded as Martin took a conciliatory step toward him. "This discussion is really pointless, you know. You forget, I control your estate and all the funds connected with it until you're twenty-five. Your father stipulated those terms in his will, and there's nothing you can do to overturn them. He did that because he trusted my judgment, and I can only hope you'll trust my judgment in this matter as well."

"Trust your judgment—when you're seeking to change the course of my life?" David shook his head. "I know what's best for me, whether you want to see things my way or not. You can't force me to attend school in England. I won't go."

"It's because of that O'Connor girl, isn't it?" Martin Lang was suddenly livid. Ignoring his wife's soft protest, he glared. "You've been meeting her in that hunter's hut for two weeks now. Haven't you had your fill of her yet?"

"It's not like that!" David paused, meeting his uncle's glower directly. "I love her."

David was hardly conscious of his aunt's gasp, as his uncle reacted sharply. "Love? You don't know the meaning of the word!"

David's responsive laugh was devoid of mirth. "Strangely enough, Meg told me the same thing, but I proved to her that she was wrong. She loves me, too, Uncle Martin."

"What else did you expect her to say, you fool! She's bewitched you! She's had you wound around her little finger since the fire, and now she intends taking advantage of the opportunity you're affording her to get out of the valley. But she'll never get out of the valley, because she'll take it with her wherever she goes, with her ignorant Irish ways! She'll hold you back from the brilliant future you have in store, and she'll drag you down with her. Don't you see that, David?"

"No, I don't!"

Martin stared in grim silence at his nephew's resolute expression. "Then I have no recourse but to withhold any further advance from your estate until you come to your senses."

David barely controlled his fury. "I don't need the damned money! I'm not totally without recourse. I have contacts in Philadelphia. I'll get a job there, and I'll take Meg with me."

Aunt Letty began sobbing softly, and Martin glanced at her before frowning more darkly into David's obstinate expression. "What kind of a position would that be, David? Will you clerk in an office somewhere for a meager salary, or do physical labor in the streets? Or will you have the girl support you on the meager pittance she could earn?"

David took a furious step forward, and Martin gave a hard laugh. "Face reality, David! The picture I've drawn for you is harsh, but it's realistic! How far do you think you can go—what do you think you can do without money or education at your age? You're condemning yourself to a life of mediocrity for the sake of your infatuation with a common—"

"Don't say it, Uncle." David's voice was deep with warning. "Because if you speak those words, they'll remain forever between us."

"Oh, is that so? Well, you can't escape the truth, no matter how hard you try, and the truth is that your immediate future lies in England."

"It doesn't!"

"If you really love the O'Connor girl as you say you do, your feelings will bear a separation of a few years."

"A few years? Do you think I'll spend years separated from Meg just for the sake of money?"

"My dear boy." Martin shook his head with the sadness of hard-won maturity. "Only those who have never been without it decry the value of money." He took a weary breath. "In any case, I realize you've been taken by surprise with my decision. You need some time to think things over."

"I don't need—"

"I don't want to talk anymore, David." Martin turned and slipped his arm around Letty's shoulder. "Your aunt's upset, although she agrees with the validity of my judgment in this matter. We'll talk about this again tomorrow."

The sight of his aunt's tear-ravaged face caused David a moment's regret, but his rage was too absolute to entertain it for long. Turning on his heel, he pulled open the door and stepped into the hall, leaving his aunt and uncle staring at his departing back.

Meg cast Aunt Fiona a furtive glance. Suppertime had passed and evening deepened. The lamps in the other ground floor rooms had been snuffed for the night, and her aunt and she were busy with the last of the kitchen cleanup. The sound of harsh coughing came from one of the upstairs rooms, but it was too common a sound to be given much thought as they worked in an unnatural silence devoid of the normal camaraderie of their chores. She supposed her aunt sensed her tension and was reacting accordingly, but although aware of the discomfort she caused the dear woman, Meg was incapable of putting her anxiety aside. It had been a difficult day.

Captain Linden's warning still rang in her ears, and Meg was helpless against its assault. Sean's unusual silence after returning for supper had been difficult. He had met her cautious inquiries as to his whereabouts with muttered evasion, and she received no respite from her fears when he left again after supper, his destination undeclared. Her thoughts in a turmoil, she had watched his progress down the street from the window, her anxiety increasing as Lenny Dunne stepped out from a doorway to join him.

Something was definitely wrong. Sean's eyes were cold when they touched hers across the supper table, and that coldness chilled her heart. Captain Linden's warning took on an even deeper significance then, although she knew instinctively that she needed to choose a better time to broach the subject of the captain's conversation with her.

With a sigh, Meg acknowledged to herself that she needed to employ caution, and whatever leverage she could find, if she was to influence Sean's thinking. Sheila McCrea came to mind, and Meg paused in her thoughts. The state of affairs between Sheila and Sean was no secret from her. As much as she disapproved of the relationship between them, in which she feared Sheila would be the ultimate loser, she was not above enlisting aid from her love-stricken friend.

Intruding into her anxiety for Sean and adding to her tension was the manner of her own departure from the Lang kitchen that afternoon. She would pay for David's defense of her, one way or another, and she did not enjoy the thought of waiting for that particular blade to fall.

Dear David . . . His image appeared clearly in Meg's mind as she struggled with an oversized pot. Tall and handsome, he exuded intelligence, confidence, and an inborn air of privilege that was totally foreign to those of her common birth. It was only when he looked at her in that certain way, his gaze renewing the indefinable bond between them, that the impediments were stripped away and their spirits touched. She loved him then. His strong arms seemed meant to hold her, and his mouth seemed made to love hers. The fulfillment his powerful body offered her grew increasingly difficult to resist, and the yearning he inspired had taken deep root inside her.

Meg slipped the bulky pot under the sideboard and gave the kitchen a last, sweeping glance. Looking back, she caught her aunt's unusual scrutiny, and her disquiet increased.

"Is something wrong, Aunt?"

Aunt Fiona dropped her gaze back to the empty dishpan in a way that allowed her no respite from her unrest, even as the older woman replied, "Nay, 'tis nothing."

Pausing only a moment longer, Meg picked up the sack of garbage in the corner. "I'll dispense with this and be back shortly. I'm off to see Sheila for a little while."

Aunt Fiona glanced up, her wrinkled brow furrowing. "Ye be careful, Meg. I'd not have ye hurt."

Her aunt's concern giving her a moment's pause, Meg pressed an impulsive kiss against her lined cheek. "Not to worry, Aunt. I can take good enough care of myself."

Uncertain whether she saw a tear glint in her aunt's tired eyes before the woman turned back to her work with a short, "Aye," Meg snatched up the lantern beside the door and walked out into the yard. Making her way through the shadows by rote, Meg dumped the garbage. She turned back toward the house, only to be suddenly snatched from her feet as a hand clamped over her mouth. Her lantern hit the ground as she was dragged deeper into the shadows, struggling violently.

Panicking, her small fists flailing, Meg heard a familiar voice whisper in her ear, "Meg, it's me."

Her struggles ceased, and as the hand fell away from her mouth, she gasped, "David! What are you doing here?"

Meg's startled gaze held his, and David was momentarily distracted by the beauty of the shadowed face turned up to his. Her eyes were great silver saucers in the moonlight, clear as ice and mesmerizing, her hair a curly halo that reflected the pale light with a shimmering gleam, and her small features were so finely cut and perfect that he could almost believe she was a figment of his need instead of flesh blood.

"David?"

But she was his Meg . . . *his* . . . and he would not let her go at any cost. Cupping her face with his palms, David held her motionless as he took her mouth with a desperate hunger. Crushing her tight against him, he kissed her again and again, his hands moving sensuously against her back, one hand tightening in her hair to hold her mouth fast against his while the other cupped her small buttocks to press her against him.

Forcing himself to withdraw from her, David rasped, "Meg, you have to come away with me—now."

Meg shook her head, her tone incredulous. "What are you saying?"

"I'm saying my uncle knows all about us. He's made arrangements for me to further my studies in England so he can separate us."

"England!"

Meg's face drained and David felt her shock. Gripping her tighter, he whispered, "I won't leave you behind, Meg. I don't need my uncle or his money. I can get a position in Philadelphia and we can do well without him."

"I can't go to Philadelphia with you, David!"

"Meg, didn't you hear what I said? I can't stay in my uncle's house and continue to see you, and I can't go to England and leave you behind, either. I have no choice but to go off on my own, and I want you to come with me."

His gaze on Meg's white face, David watched the play of tormented emotions as the silence between them stretched. She swallowed with obvious difficulty, her eyes holding his as she finally whispered hoarsely, "Oh, David, what will become of us?"

Fiercely protective emotions rose inside him, as David responded, "You'll come away with me, and we'll look to our future together. We'll be fine, Meg. We can—"

"I've told you over and again, but you never listened! I can't leave here with you, David! I can't!"

"Because of your brother, is that it?"

Meg was suddenly angry. "Aye, because of my brother, and because of myself, and because of so many other things that you'll never understand because you're a fellow who puts himself above all. In truth, that's where the *true* barrier between us lies."

Furious at her rejection, David gripped her shoulders and gave her a hard shake. "So it was all lies, then, the bond between us, the love. It was all one-sided, with me playing the fool, believing you."

"No—that's not true!" Meg's small face twitched. "I love you, David. Aye, you've coaxed that love to life. I ache inside to think you could be leaving, to think that despite the way our hearts have touched, I could lose you. But our private world is crumbling around us, and I can't be like you! There's a part of me I can't cast aside for selfish purposes as easily as you're able to do. There's a part of me that's locked here in the valley, bound to see things through to the end for so many reasons. Deserting that part of myself would only bring us both despair." Meg swallowed again, her voice breaking. "But never doubt that I love you, David . . . please, for I truly do."

Life returning to his limbs with Meg's anguished admission, David gave a tight laugh. "And I love you too much to give you up, no matter what you say or how you plead."

Sorrow flooded Meghan's expression at his response. "Aye, David, and with those words you show too clearly the difference between us. You're still the spoiled young man who's never been denied. Deep in your heart you believe your happiness should come before all—that it's your obligation to secure it for yourself at any expense." Tears brimmed as Meg reached up a hand to stroke the tense line of his cheek with a gentleness that tore at his heart. "Ah, but for me there are other priorities."

"Other priorities!" David's hand trapped Meg's, holding it against his cheek as he shook his head. "What priorities could possibly come before the love we feel for each other?"

"Life and death." And then at David's frown, "But you've never felt the threat of either, have you, and you've no understanding of the torment of wondering—"

"Excuses! That's all you're offering me, Meg, when I'm offering you my love."

Meghan stiffened in his arms and abruptly slipped her hand out from under his. His cheek felt cold and desolate without the warmth of her palm, and he sensed Meg's mental withdrawal as she withdrew herself from him physically as well.

"Aye, and so your main concern remains with yourself and your feelings when you should be considering the torment of those you profess to love." Pausing, Meg whispered, "Go home, David."

"Meg—"

"Go home." Extricating herself from his grasp, Meg turned and ran toward the house before David could react to her flight. Cursing as she slipped into the kitchen and out of sight, certain he would never understand her, David turned back into the darkness.

His haste apparent, Sean walked down the darkened street. His mind working in riotous circles, he recalled the meeting just past in the private room behind Lawler's saloon. He remembered Muff Lawler's sharp eyes upon him as Lenny sang his praises, and he still felt the sting of the fellow's intense scrutiny. But he had weathered it all, and if he was to take Lenny's word as truth, he'd be a Molly before the month was out.

Tripping over a rut in the road, Sean cursed under his breath and turned the corner. Uncle Timothy's house loomed in the distance, lamplight glowing in the kitchen and upstairs rooms, and he cursed again, for there was little satisfaction inside him at the step just accomplished, distracted as was his mind with the letter he had received a few hours earlier. There'd been no time to face Meg for the truth, but he was determined to root it out now. In his heart he could not believe she would betray her word to him. Deceit was not in Meg's makeup, and she—

His step coming to an abrupt halt, Sean strained his eyes into the shadows beside the house. That tall figure just slipping out of sight, that posture and step—arrogant, for all its stealth. Glancing up to the window of the room he shared with his sister, Sean saw darkness flicker into light, and rage suffused him.

Breaking into a run, he closed the distance between himself and the house and turned into the backyard. Dashing through the kitchen past his aunt without a word, he took the steps two at a time toward the second floor.

Heavy footsteps in the hallway turned Meg toward the bedroom door the moment before it burst open to slap back against the wall. Striding to her side, his face twisted with rage, Sean grasped her arms. His fingers bit into her soft flesh as he gave her a hard shake.

"That was David Lang I saw sneaking out of the yard just now, wasn't it?"

"Sean . . ."

"Answer me!"

"No. I . . . I don't know what you're talking about."

Sean's eyes went cold the moment the lie escaped Meg's lips. Silence stretched thin between them before Sean's contemptuous reply knifed deep into her heart.

"You lie poorly, Meg, because the truth is, you've not had much practice. But if Lang had his way, you'd perfect the art, I've no doubt. Aye, he's taken the first step, proving what I must do."

Releasing her unexpectedly, Sean started toward the door, only to be halted by Meg's low plea.

"Sean, please forgive me."

His body rigid, Sean turned back to face her as Meg continued, her voice laced with pain. "Aye, I lied to you, and the shame of it burns inside me. But you've naught to fear now. I sent David away tonight."

"Aye, you sent him away! And how many nights were there when you didn't, all the time ignoring your promise to me?"

Her heart in her voice, Meg whispered, "With Ma as my witness, I'll tell you everything if you'll just listen."

"What can you tell me that will take away the pain of your lies?"

His coldness lashing her, Meg responded simply, "Only the truth."

Silence followed. Taking his silence for assent, Meg sat down on the bed and drew Sean down to sit beside her. Her gaze forged to his, she spoke in a hushed voice that did not cease until the whole story was told.

Her breathing ragged, Meg did not realize that her face was wet with tears until Sean raised a callused hand to brush them from her cheeks. He questioned softly, "You believed David Lang when he said he loved you?" When she did not respond, he nodded. "Aye, it's clear that you did."

Abruptly on his feet, his eyes cold once more, Sean turned toward the door. Meg grasped his arm.

"No, Sean! There's no point to any of this. David will soon be off to school in England."

Sean shook his head. "Nay, he'll be going nowhere."

His intention was clear and Meg gasped, "Do you hear yourself, Sean? You're speaking of taking a life! You're speaking of losing your soul!"

Sean's gaze became startlingly frigid. "Aye, my soul . . ."

Desperate, Meg rasped, "You may turn away thoughts of your soul, Sean, but I cannot! Will this be your gift to me—the guilt of knowing my brother lost his hope of salvation because of me?"

"Meg . . ."

Suddenly shaken with sobs beyond her control, Meg turned away, only to feel Sean's arms slip around her. Silent for a moment, he whispered, "Meg, stop cryin', please."

Separating himself from her as her tears drew to a halt, Sean spoke solemnly.

"All right, Meg, but if we're to put this behind us, we've some promises to make to each other, for I can live with it no other way." Sean's expression hardened. "If you'd have me walk away from servin' David Lang the justice due him, then you must walk away from him as well. You'll not go back to that house again. You'll forget David Lang's lies, and forget him as well. Can you promise me that?"

Meg's whispered "Aye" was torn from her heart.

"All right." Sean breathed deeply. "My word is bound to yours, then. I'll leave him be."

Realizing the gravity of the pact they had made, Meg stared at the hard, bitter man who had replaced the boy visible in Sean a year earlier. She whispered, almost uncertain, "Is it really you behind those cold eyes, Sean?"

A joyless laugh escaped Sean's lips. "More's the pity, it's truly I."

Chapter 15

David's mount responded to his urging, lengthening his stride until the surrounding hillside blended into a blur of brilliant gold. Leaning low over Max's neck, David pushed the powerful animal beneath him to greater effort as the cool morning air rushed against his skin and the brilliant sun flickered rapidly through the branches of the trees overhead.

Stumbling unexpectedly, Max righted himself a split second before a violent spill, and sanity returned to David's mind. Reining the laboring horse to a more sensible pace, David cursed his own stupidity. He then cursed the frustration which had kept him sleepless through the long night after Meg had left him standing in the darkness of her backyard.

It was Meg's fault—all of it!

Uncle Martin and he were at an impasse, and he had not bothered to dress for the office upon arising. With one glance at his attire when David arrived in the foyer, Uncle Martin's demeanor had darkened, and in the short conversation that followed, nothing more had been communicated than the confirmation of their differences.

It had come as no surprise when Uncle Martin informed him that he had already dispatched someone to Meg's house to tell her that her employment at the manor had come to an end. Neither had it been unanticipated when his uncle informed him that he was continuing with arrangements for David's departure for England in two weeks. It had been at the tip of his tongue to tell his uncle that there was not a chance in the world that he would leave Meg, but chafing under strain created by Meg's stubborn attitude the night before, he merely turned and left the house without response.

Holding Max to a more cautious pace, David ran an impatient hand through his hair. His nerves were as taut as wires and, although he fought acknowledging it, panic had begun making silent inroads into his thoughts.

Damn it all! He still couldn't fully comprehend what had happened. Meg had told him she loved him, and he knew she meant it. He had felt her love when he held her in his arms. He had felt it in the surrender of her lips, in the melting of her body against his, and in her spontaneous response to his own increasing passion. Their love was a golden glow encircling them, drawing them ever closer. It emanated from within them in a way neither could fully understand or restrain, and he knew Meg was as much at its mercy as was he. He had seen the pain in Meg's eyes when she restated the convoluted reasoning that now kept them apart, but even loving her as he did, and admiring her as he must for the integrity so much a part of her, he knew he still did not understand her.

Other priorities . . . What priorities could possibly come before their love? Despite the social barriers between them, the truth was that together they had everything, and apart they had nothing. It was as simple as that, and everything else was secondary. He could see that so clearly. Why couldn't she?

Oh, Meg . . .

His throat choking unexpectedly, David rubbed his hand across his forehead in an unconscious gesture of despair. He was tempted to ride up to Meg's front door right now and thrash the whole thing out. Her uncle, the stingy bastard that he was, would be grateful to have Meg off his hands, but he knew Meg's brother would have another reaction entirely. He wasn't afraid of the surly lout, but he knew a confrontation between them would only complicate the situation.

There was no simple solution to the affair, but he knew he had no chance at all if he didn't find a way to talk to Meg alone. He had already determined that next time he wouldn't let Meg run away from him. He would convince her that their love was worth any sacrifice, because it was a truth he felt deep inside him.

But the how and where of finding Meg alone was a problem that had plagued him the morning long.

A sudden thought striking him, David glanced up at the sun as it approached its zenith in the brilliant, cloudless sky. Cursing himself again for his stupidity, he wasted not a moment more before jamming his heels into Max's sides, startling the powerful animal into an abrupt leap forward.

• • •

"You're not to worry, Meg." His expression reflecting concern as he stood opposite Meg in his small office, Father Matthew realized his attempted consolation did little to relieve the girl's anxieties. "Your employment on the hill served its purpose. It allowed you time to improve your reading skills while earning a sum that temporarily satisfied your uncle. I've no doubt I'll be able to find another position for you quite easily now."

"Do you really think so, Father?"

Father Matthew nodded, dismissing his lie with the excuse that it was necessary.

Meg had arrived at his office a short time earlier. Obviously distressed, she had told him that a groom from the house on the hill arrived at her door that morning with her wages due and the notification that her services were no longer needed. Her brief description of the events that followed led him to believe that Timothy O'Reilly's reaction to the dismissal had driven her to his door in desperation. However, nagging viciously in the back of his mind was Meg's reluctance to discuss the reason for her discharge. She was holding something back.

Breaking the silence, Father Matthew spoke, a frown creasing his youthful brow. "It surprises me that the Langs should dispense with your services so suddenly. You have no idea why you were dismissed?"

Meg's gaze dropped away. She shrugged and Father Matthew felt her growing distress. The silence between them lengthened until she whispered, "Aye, I know the reason. There was talk about David Lang and me."

A knot in Father Matthew's stomach tightened at the mention of David Lang's name. John Law's warning again returned to mind and he struggled to maintain a level tone.

"Was there any truth to the talk, Meg?"

Meg's tormented gaze snapped up to his. "I can't say if there was any truth to the talk, for I was not openly accused."

Pausing, Father Matthew pressed on quietly. "Then I can only ask you, my dear, if anything transpired between you and David Lang that you now regret."

Tears sprung into the eyes firmly holding his as Meg responded. "Nay, Father. Nothing happened between David and me that I regret."

Relieved beyond measure, Father Matthew curved his arm

around Meg's shoulders and pulled her briefly against his side in an awkward attempt at consolation.

"Then find a smile in your heart and put it on your lips, Meg, for your discomfort will be temporary, I promise you. There are few enough in this town who have the natural skill with ciphers you possess. Once that fact is known, there'll be employment for you waiting around the corner. You must have faith."

Father Matthew reached for the knob and drew the door open. "Try to stay out of your uncle's path for a few days, Meg. I'll find you a position. I'll not let you down."

Quickly closing the door behind Meg as she started down the steps, Father Matthew could not resist going to the window to follow her slender figure down the street. He frowned as she drew her shawl tighter against the gusting wind and glanced up at a sky that had turned a leaden gray in sharp contrast to the bright sunshine of earlier in the day. Meg took an unexpected turn, and Father Matthew's frown darkened. If she was not careful she would be caught in the storm before she reached home.

The irony of that thought touched Father Matthew as she turned out of sight. Meg was already caught in a storm that had been brewing long before she was born, and it was up to him to see that she did not suffer permanent injury from it. Aye, the storm that presently darkened the skies over their heads would pass with little damage, but the other that threatened all Meg held dear—where would it lead?

A shiver passed down David's spine as a damp wind gusted through the swaying branches overhead. Unconsciously drawing his jacket closed, he again scanned the uneven rows of the deserted cemetery, then looked up to assess the sky. The dropping temperature was as ominous as the blackening of the swirling clouds. The weather had changed dramatically during the time he had spent waiting, concealed in this particular growth of trees. He was angry, cold, restless, and were he not desperate as well, he knew he would have given up hope hours earlier of seeing Meg.

But he was determined, and he knew Meg. He knew she had loved her mother deeply and that they had exchanged succor freely and with love. In her present dilemma, with a brother past reasoning, an aunt and uncle not in her confidence, and a priest who appeared to have lost her confidence of late, she would come to visit her Ma sooner or later. His only fear was that he might have missed her.

Another chilling gust stirred the dried leaves at his feet, and David shivered again, his gaze returning to the rain clouds overhead. They'd soon release their deluge, eliminating any chance of seeing Meg today, but he'd be damned if he'd leave a minute sooner than he had to. It made little difference to him that he had arrived here, tethered his horse out of sight, and taken up his watch hours earlier. Time and discomfort meant very little with so much at stake.

A sudden flicker of movement on the path caught David's attention, pulling him upright. All thought of physical discomfort fled from his mind as Meg moved into clear sight, her slight figure bowed against the increasing turbulence of the approaching storm. The branches above his head waved wildly as miniature whirlwinds of loose dirt and leaves danced with increasing frenzy between the sagging grave markers, but David was unconscious of all but Meg's steady approach.

Realizing the impending storm aided his purpose by distracting Meg, he watched as she pulled her shawl over her head, hunching against the chill, her direction unfaltering. She came to a halt a short distance away, beside the marker that bore her mother's name.

Allowing her a few moments with her thoughts, David watched with growing impatience as Meg remained motionless beside the mounded ground. Long agitated minutes passed, and unable to wait any longer, he started forward. The chill wind whipped his face and hair wildly, blowing his jacket wide and flattening the fine linen of his shirt against his chest as he advanced to within a few feet of her. Engrossed in her thoughts, the noise of the impending storm muting the sound of his approach, Meg remained unaware of his presence.

"Meg."

Whirling around to face him, her eyes wide, Meg gasped. She swayed and he grasped her arms supportively, startled by her sudden lapse of color.

Blinking, Meg shook her head. "I thought—" She paused, then closed her eyes briefly with a mumbled, "I don't know what I thought."

But Meg knew what she had thought. For a brief moment she had imagined that the intensity of her contemplation and the silent pleas for aid she made to the woman buried beneath the earth at her feet had conjured David up behind her. Childish fantasy, when she must consider only cold reality.

"I frightened you. I'm sorry, Meg."

Frowning, Meg hardened her heart against David's tormented expression. "Why are you here, David?"

"Because I knew you'd come here, and I had to see you alone."

Another fierce gust of wind, and Meg turned her back to the blast, shivering. But she was well aware that the violent shuddering suddenly assailing her was only partially due to the assault of the elements. Unprepared as David gripped her shoulders, turning her against his chest to shield her with his broad frame, she struggled to free herself. Holding her fast against him, David scanned the area, his gaze halting on an overgrown arbor at the rear of the yard before dropping to meet hers.

"Meg, please, I have to talk to you. Let's get out of this wind—over there."

Panic touched Meg's mind. She didn't want to talk to David. Watchful eyes were everywhere, and every moment she spent with him endangered his life.

"We have nothing to talk about, David."

"Meg . . ."

Meg's throat tightened. She saw determination beginning to edge the misery in David's gaze, and she knew what that meant. He would not give up while he thought he still had a chance to change her mind, the stubborn, spoiled fellow that he was. The dear, stubborn, spoiled fellow . . .

Sean's image appeared before her mind in silent threat, his eyes as frighteningly frigid as she had seen them the previous evening, and Meg's throat closed with an almost debilitating fear. She had seen death in Sean's clear eyes last night, and the chill was with her still. More powerful than the physical cold presently assaulting her, it had settled into her heart, eliminating the last remnants of hope during the long, sleepless night.

She remembered lying abed, the promise she had made Sean—to stay away from the Lang house, to forget all about David—echoing over and again in her mind. She was still awake when he finally slipped into their room an hour after midnight. She did not need to ask where he had been. She had felt it in her bones and read it in the brief glimpse of his grim expression before he dropped into his bed. She was somehow certain that her dear brother had joined the ranks of those who surrendered their souls for vengeance. At that moment it became clear that to break her promise to Sean would be to force him to take the first step on the path to damnation.

Ma's voice had echoed faintly in her ears, reminding her of the promise she had made when they spoke that last time. She had known then, as she knew now, what she must do.

Realizing salvation for them all depended on David's leaving the valley, Meg abruptly surrendered her protests and turned at his urging. Encircled by his protective arm, she ran toward the arbor tucked in the rear of the graveyard as the first oversized drops of rain began pelting the ground around them.

Breathless, Meg followed David as he plunged under the structure made thick and impenetrable by the tight latticework of aging gnarled vines and stubborn leaves that covered every inch of its sagging framework. The pungent odors of dampness and mildew accosted her nostrils as she realized their temporary haven from the storm was open only on one end, creating an intimate atmosphere where the chill of the wind and rain was restrained.

David turned her toward him, the anguish in his gaze clearly visible. His gentle touch excruciating, he slid the shawl from her head and brushed curling tendrils back from her forehead and cheek, but Meg recognized the service as an excuse to touch her, which she could not tolerate if she were to maintain her resolve. She drew back and the anguish in his gaze deepened.

"Meg, we were both angry last night, and we both said a lot of things we shouldn't have said. I was awake most of the night, going over everything in my mind, and I realized the most important thing that happened was that you said you loved me. Those are the words I wanted most to hear, and they're the only words that are really important. We can resolve any other differences between us."

"There's nothing to resolve, David." Meg forced all warmth from her tone, freezing the love that surged at the strain in David's voice. "Nothing has changed. You're still the privileged young man you always were, and I'm still the girl from the valley. Can't you see that? Your uncle does. He sent Harry to my house with my wages this morning."

"I know. You expected that, didn't you?"

"Yes. But Uncle Timothy—"

Hot color touched the tense lines of David's face. "He didn't hurt you, did he, Meg? If he did, I'll—"

"What would you do? What *could* you do that would change anything?"

"You know the answer to that as well as I do. I could take you to Philadelphia with me. I *will* take you, Meg."

Her face draining of color, Meg shook her head. "How many times must I tell you that I can't go to Philadelphia with you? I can't go anywhere with you. Open your eyes and accept reality, David."

David's handsome face softened. "My eyes *are* open when I look at you, Meg. What I see is a small, beautiful girl with skin that's velvet under my fingertips, and a body that fits so perfectly against mine that I—"

"Listen to what you're saying, David. You're talking about physical attraction you could feel for any woman."

"I'm not a child, Meg. You can't convince me that what I feel for you is pure lust. I've lusted after and been with many women, but I never loved any one of them."

Startled by the sharp pang of jealousy David's admission evoked, Meg gave a short laugh. "Then shall I tell you what your uncle and everyone else see when they look at me? They see a small, common young woman as compared to the handsome appealing man that you are. They see my poor dress and speech in comparison with your sophisticated tastes and educated ways. They see the simple future that lies ahead of me, and the exciting, fulfilling life that awaits you."

Pausing, Meg then continued. "And if they saw us together, they'd say you carried gratitude and affection too far, and that I allowed it to happen out of sheer shallowness and greed. They'd begin to suspect that you're less than they thought you to be because you were taken in by the likes of me, and they'd turn away from you. Finally, they would pity you, and they would despise me, and in the end we'd fit in nowhere. Are you prepared for that, David? Do you think your love would survive that reality?"

David appeared injured. "Do you really think as poorly of me as that, Meg? Didn't it ever occur to you that those questions are as shallow as you claim others would find you to be? Do you think I would care if everyone else in the world turned away from me because of you, if they pitied me or despised you, or if we were ostracized from any society that would turn its back on us for such superficial reasons? Do you think the most brilliant future in the world would be worthwhile to me if it meant losing you? Oh, Meg, none of those things mean anything to me."

The sincerity in David's handsome face tore at Meg's heart, but she steeled herself against the weakness assailing her. She had little experience with the kind of love she felt for David, the love that was now rending her in two, but the love that had caused her to give her dying Ma a promise was familiar. That love was a whisper of sanity when the heart was overwhelmed. It sacrificed personal gratification and accepted shortcomings, no matter how severe. It was understanding and forgiving, and it gave without expecting return. It was far different from the shattering emotion she felt for David, but it was equally strong.

David was unaware of the threat he incurred in loving her, but Meg was not. He was a stranger to this other face of love, but she saw it clearly. And she knew what she must do, even though David would never truly understand.

The pain she concealed almost more than she could bear, Meg allowed a moment to freeze all trace of emotion from her gaze before she replied.

"You don't care about all those things, David, but did you never think that I might—that I might not be as satisfied as you to give up all I know to be shunned in return? Did it never touch your mind that my pride might mean more to me than you think, that I'd not tolerate having it trampled into the dust? Did it never occur to you that you might be willing to forsake everything because you don't know what it is to do without, while I've had enough uncertainty to last a lifetime?"

David stiffened with incredulity, and the pain in Meg's heart stabbed anew. But the fury that replaced his incredulity, tightening his hands on her shoulders to the point of pain, was unexpected.

"You're lying, Meg! Damn it, you're lying! I know you too well to believe any of the nonsense you just spoke. You don't have a selfish bone in your body. And you're too damned innocent to be so calculating."

Meghan refused to react to the torment in David's voice. Instead, she paused, summoning the strength to speak the words she knew she must say. A gentle smile touched her lips in an attempt to temper her deliberate cruelty.

"Perhaps you're right, David, but the only remaining possibility is that there's another truth as well—that the real barrier between us is that I don't *want* to go to Philadelphia with you."

Waiting a few seconds for her statement to register fully, Meg continued. "Aye, I love you, David. There's no denying it, but in the end the simple truth behind it all is that I don't love you *enough*."

The color drained from David's face and he shook her hard.

"Liar! You love me enough. I know you do, even if you don't.

And you want me as much as I want you. I felt your response, even if you won't admit to it."

David was suddenly pleading. "You're so young, Meg. That's the real problem. You don't have enough experience to realize what you're throwing away. Let me show you how beautiful it can be between us, Meg. Let me love you."

Quaking with emotion, David did not wait for her response as he drew her roughly into his arms. The hunger and yearning she fought so valiantly to suppress rose anew as he kissed her demandingly, his hands moving in bold caress. Her arms ached to move around his neck; her lips burned with the need to separate under his. Her body craved his and the loving that would be unleashed with her simplest encouragement. It took all her strength to remain stiff and unyielding as David tore his mouth from hers.

Meg realized with a start that the hatred that flared in David's eyes as he drew back from her was self-directed. When he spoke, David's shaken question shattered her with its depth of despair.

"What did I do, Meg? What did I do to make you turn against me?"

The last of her reserve tottering as David's eyes suddenly filled, she shared the anguish of his final, fervent plea.

"Meg, please . . . please let me love you."

The rasping break in his voice was more than Meg could withstand. Dear David . . . proud David was pleading with her.

Raising her lips to his with a low sob, Meg felt the tremor that shook David as he took her mouth. The last remnant of restraint slipped away as she clutched him close. Harsh reality fled as David's kisses drew her deeper, as his loving ministrations became more intense, as he schooled her in the fine tenets of desire with each touch of his hand. Surrendering herself to him, she bathed in the beauty, the rapturous colors that inundated her senses. The hard ground against her back was welcome, because it allowed the sweet weight of David's body against hers. The damp odor of the deserted bower became sweeter than perfume because it mingled with the stirring, musky scent of David's skin. Her bared flesh did not feel the chill of the storm with David's love to keep her warm.

David's lips moved against her breasts and Meg gasped with the depth of sensation he aroused. She felt his joyous reaction to the sound, and it was suddenly as clear to her as it was to him that she had been created for this moment. David's passion feeding her own, she reveled in the muscled contours of his body as it moved against hers. She ran her palms against his back, clutching him close, fingers splayed to encompass their full measure of his sinewy flesh. Her soft protest was instinctive as he drew back unexpectedly, his hands sliding past her ribcage and stomach to tangle in the dark, moist curls below. He caressed her intimately, raising a low moan from her lips as he suckled the swollen, roseate crests of her breasts.

David's passion seared her as he raised his head to whisper raggedly, "You see now, don't you, Meg? You know now what I've been trying to tell you. This is only the beginning, darling. There's so much more . . . so much . . ."

The hard shaft of David's passion probed her, and fear edged Meg's hungry anticipation. Torn between equally strong desires to thrust David from her and to draw him closer still, she began shuddering violently.

"Meg, don't be afraid." David's voice throbbed with tenderness. "Just let me inside you."

Long moments of anxious probing and delirious apprehension climaxed with sudden penetration. Joy laced with pain as David came to rest inside her, and Meg closed her eyes, suddenly motionless. Tears slipped from beneath her thick fringe of black lashes in the moment before Meg looked up again. Poised above her, David was unable to tear his eyes from her face. His cheeks were as wet as hers as he whispered in a breaking voice, "I love you, Meg. I'll always love you."

Moving gently, David gradually increased the tempo of his lovemaking, finally shuddering his love into her body as he gasped her name. Loving him, Meghan accepted his body's homage with a swell of emotion that touched her soul.

David's flesh was warm against hers, the perspiration of their mutual passion uniting them. His breath was sweet against her cheek, his strong arms holding her possessively close, as reality slowly returned.

Myriad emotions assailed David as he looked down into Meghan's face. Meg had made the world suddenly beautiful by loving him. The ancient arbor under which they lay, the damp ground from which Meg was shielded only by discarded clothes, even the raindrops seeping through the heavy foliage above them took on a rosy hue in the afterglow of their love.

But Meg was most beautiful of all, more beautiful then he had ever dreamed. Her slender, white body had not yet reached the full bloom of womanhood, but it was flawless to his eye and sweeter than he had imagined it could be. He quelled the guilt that assailed him at the thought of her youth with the knowledge that no matter their age, their time was at hand.

Lowering his head, David pressed a kiss against Meghan's lips. Meg's eyes were closed and she did not respond, but he knew she was as overwhelmed as he by the tumultuous loving they had shared. Filled with the joy of their intimacy, David smoothed sweat-dampened curls from Meg's face, indulging himself as he traced the fine arch of her brow with his fingertip, the thick lashes that shielded her incredible eyes, the line of her cheek. He traced the fullness of her lips, clenching his teeth against the desire to indulge himself more deeply.

"I love you, Meg." A world of feeling emerged with those simple words, and David suffered the thought of how close he had come to losing her. Swallowing tightly, he cupped her cheek with his hand.

Meg looked up at him, her lips working, but no sound emerged. She glanced away, and the first nudge of uncertainty touched his mind. Raising her chin with his finger, David forced her to meet his gaze.

"Did I hurt you, Meg?" She did not answer, and David briefly closed his eyes, his heart pounding with regret. "I'm sorry, Meg. I couldn't hold back any more. But it'll be better next time. We'll—"

"You didn't hurt me, David."

Meg moved uncomfortably under him, and David rolled to his side. He stiffened as she attempted to get up, restraining her with an arm across her breast. "Not yet, Meg."

"I have to get back home."

Meg's unexpected behavior confused him. "What's wrong, Meg?" And then when there was no response, "I thought it was as perfect for you as it was for me." Still no response, and David whispered desperately, "It *will* be better next time, I promise. We'll have our own place in Philadelphia. It'll be warm and clean, and we'll—"

Meg met his gaze unblinkingly. "I'm not going to Philadelphia with you, David."

"You're not go—" David's voice trailed off into incredulity. "What do you mean?"

"I'm telling you that nothing has changed."

"Nothing has changed?" David's incredulity turned to fury. "Are you trying to tell me that everything that just happened between us meant nothing to you? I know better than that, and even if it wasn't as good for you as it was for me, you can't be foolish enough to think—"

Suddenly thrusting his arm aside, Meg stood up and reached for her clothes. On his feet beside her, he turned her forcefully to meet his eyes.

"Meg, tell me what's wrong!"

"Nothing is wrong." Meg's eyes were filled with pain. "Everything's right—the way it should be. We made love, David, and it was right that we should say goodbye that way."

"Goodbye!"

"Aye, goodbye. We haven't changed what we are with the physical act of loving, as beautiful as it was. And it *was* beautiful, David. I'll always remember it."

"Remember it! Don't be a damned fool, Meg! There's nothing standing between us that a little courage can't overcome."

"Perhaps."

"Perhaps?" Grasping her shoulders, David gave her a hard shake. "Perhaps?"

"Let me go."

"I won't let you go. That's the what I've been trying to make you understand."

"And I've been trying to make you understand that the choice isn't yours. I love you, David. I suppose that love will always be a part of me, but the truth is that I don't love you *enough*."

Meg paused to take a deep breath, her eyes brimming. "Go to school, David. Go to England, get your degree, and have a great, glorious future. Forget me, because as surely as I lay in your arms a few minutes ago, and as surely as the loving we shared was more beautiful than I could have dreamed, I tell you now that I *will* forget *you*. I've made myself that promise."

Meg's gaze caressed his face. It moved him as did everything Meg did or felt. She touched him in so many ways that he suddenly realized the part of him that came to life with knowing her would shrivel up and die without her. And he knew that where he had lived contentedly without the joy of Meg before she came into his life, he could not lose her without forever mourning the loss.

"Please, Meg." Drained of anger, David whispered, "Please don't leave me now."

Silence stretched between them before Meg turned and reached for her clothes. Running a hand through her tangled curls, she looked up at him at last, her expression sober.

"Forget me, David. We were born to the pattern of our lives. There's no changing it now."

"Meg . . ."

"Goodbye, David."

Too quick for his startled mind to react, Meg slipped her shawl over her head and dashed out into the rain. David watched her sure-footed steps between the rain-soaked grave markers. He was still staring long minutes after she disappeared from sight.

Breathless from her mad race through the rain-slick streets, Meg rounded the corner of the house and slipped through the kitchen doorway. Gasping, she pulled her shawl from her head as Aunt Fiona turned toward her. Concern deepened the lines on the older woman's face as Meg darted a glance at the clock.

"Is Sean upstairs, Aunt?"

Aunt Fiona swept her with an assessing gaze, and Meg raised her chin against the older woman's appraisal. She was no longer a child. She was now a woman who during the last hour had taken several difficult steps that would change her life forever. She knew the change those steps had effected within her were as visible as the dirt stains on her clothing. She also knew that she appeared disheveled and upset, and that her eyes betrayed far more than she desired. But although she had done what she must and regretted none of it, she needed time. She could not allow Sean even a suspicion of what had passed between David and her, or the result would be catastrophic.

Aunt Fiona did not speak, and Meg prompted again urgently, "Is he upstairs, Aunt?"

Aunt Fiona shook her head, then looked away. "Yer brother was home and left again with the word that he wanted to speak to you after supper."

Suffering her aunt's gaze, Meg walked out of the room without another word. Closing her bedroom door behind her a few moments later, Meg allowed the sanctuary, however temporary, to quell the anxieties besetting her mind. She fought welling tears. There was no time to think of the intimate beauty she had experienced in David's arms, or of the love she had sacrificed forever. There was no time to think of the emptiness inside her and the long years she would spend with David's memory eating at her heart. She had done what she had to do, and it would all be for naught if Sean discovered what had happened under that quiet, protective arbor of vines.

Suddenly snapping into movement, Meg locked the door behind her and pulled off her stained clothing. Pouring water into the wash basin, she scrubbed herself fastidiously from head to toe. Fully dressed a few minutes later, she rolled her soiled garments into a ball and tucked them under her arm.

Halting briefly to look at her reflection in the mirror, she saw that the old Meghan O'Connor had returned—a slender girl with damp, curly hair, light blue eyes, and a mouth that smiled easily.

But Meg knew that, inside, she would never be the same girl again.

Dropping her stained clothing into the kitchen washtub a few minutes later, Meg turned to find her aunt looking at her. She did not smile, for in truth, the new Meg could not find a smile within her.

Chapter 16

David did little to ease the uneasy silence that reigned over the Lang dinner table. He could feel the weight of Uncle Martin's accusing gaze and Aunt Letty's torn sympathies, but he did not look up. Neither did he need to look up to know that Grace, unnaturally silent as well, looked at each of them in turn, waiting for the first to speak.

The unnatural state of affairs between himself and the other members of the family had existed for the past week, since Uncle Martin's ultimatum and his final meeting with Meg under the rainswept arbor. He had exchanged nothing but necessary conversation with his uncle and the other members of his family in the time since, but the tension that knotted his stomach, destroying his appetite for even the most tempting of Cook's dishes, had little to do with his feelings toward them.

Disbelief still filled his mind. Meg had deserted him. He had spent every day since their last meeting alone in the hills, going over his conversation with her word for word in an effort to sort out his thoughts. Tortured by the beauty of the intimacy they had shared, he had been able to think of little else but her.

Through the agonized confusion of his thoughts, one truth had emerged. Meg loved him, but she didn't love him enough to turn her back on everyone and everything for him. The result was the same as if she did not love him at all.

Realizing the futility of attempting to eat, David lowered his fork to the table.

"What's wrong, David? Isn't the roast to your taste?"

David looked up at his aunt. Her brows were knit in a frown and lines of concern marked her cheeks. It occurred to him that she looked pale. Her eyes filled unexpectedly, and guilt touched his mind.

"No, the roast is fine." David attempted a smile. "I'm not hungry, that's all."

"You haven't finished a single meal this week, dear."

"Leave him alone, Letty," Uncle Martin interrupted, turning to David with his expression tight. "If David isn't hungry, he doesn't have to eat. He isn't a child."

"I know, dear, but—"

"Leave him alone, Letty!"

A single tear slipped down Aunt Letty's cheek, and the strained silence that followed was suddenly broken by Grace's gulping sob.

"Everything's gone wrong in this house! Everyone's unhappy and no one cares about anyone else anymore!"

Suddenly jumping to her feet, Grace made it as far as the door before Letty caught her and folded her into her arms. Grace sobbed onto her mother's shoulder, and, turning back to the head of the table, David saw his uncle get up with a discouraged sigh, his expression penitent as he walked toward the two women.

"I'm sorry, Letty. Grace, don't cry. Everything will be all right." And when Grace's sobbing continued, Martin instructed softly, "Take her upstairs, Letty."

The two women left the room and Martin turned back to David. "It appears no one else is hungry either, David. Ring for Mabel and tell her to clear the table. We're finished here for the evening."

The door closed behind Uncle Martin, and David reached for the small silver bell which had always been Aunt Letty's province at the dinner table. He paused, guilt again plaguing him as he touched the carved handle.

The emotional scene he had just witnessed had shaken him from the lethargic stupor into which he had slipped since Meg had turned her back on him. The pain of the moment was with him still, cutting into his vitals, drawing blood and draining him dry. But it suddenly occurred to him that Meg's cruel dismissal had been necessary, since she had been able to convince him that it was over between them no other way. However, his own cruelty to the family that had taken him in when he was orphaned, and still loved him, was motivated by his own self-centered behavior.

David briefly closed his eyes against the realization that Meg knew him better than he knew himself. He was selfish, thoughtless—everything Meg had accused him of being without saying the words. Perhaps that was the reason Meg had been unwilling to take a chance with him. Perhaps she felt his love was as shallow as she saw him to be. Perhaps . . .

The ache within him deepening, David took a deep breath designed to clear his mind and put an end to the misery of his futile thoughts. Whatever the reason, it was too late for Meg and him. He had given her all he had to give but it was not enough, and while he could not halt his agonizing thoughts, it was time to act like the man he claimed to be. He had been neither generous nor fair with the family that loved him, and the time had come to rectify the situation.

Standing up, David shook the silver bell and relayed Uncle Martin's message to Mabel as she appeared in the doorway. He then turned toward the hall.

"I owe you an apology, Uncle Martin."

Martin Lang surveyed his nephew's sober expression where he stood just inside the doorway of his study. He had been surprised to find David at his door only moments after leaving him in the dining room under such tense circumstances. His nephew had alienated himself completely from the family during the past week, and Martin was both angry and surprised that the boy should allow his anger over their bitter disagreement concerning his future to influence his treatment of his aunt and cousin.

His frown darkening, Martin remembered his nephew's frigid departure from the house the morning after their confrontation in the study. David did not return to the house until dinnertime, and then went directly to his room. David's daily routine had not changed in the week following, and he had no idea where his nephew spent the day, except that he appeared dutifully at the dinner table each night, uncommunicative and eating little.

David did not look well. It was obvious that he had lost considerable weight, and dark circles beneath his eyes revealed he had lost considerable sleep as well. Unable to make himself believe that David would agonize over their altercation to the extent that it affected him physically, Martin felt his anger surge anew. There was only one person who could affect David that deeply, and whatever David's mission in coming to see him now, he was determined not to allow Meghan O'Connor back in their lives again.

The direction of Martin's thoughts were reflected in the tight lines of his face as he turned away from his nephew unexpectedly and walked to the window. He stood there, staring outside into the twilight for a few silent moments before turning back to David just as unexpectedly.

"You say you owe me an apology, David? Yes, you do, and you owe your aunt and cousin an apology as well."

"I'm aware of that, sir."

Martin's eyes narrowed. "Since we are agreed there, I suggest you state whatever else is on your mind. Your conduct of the past week has left me short on patience."

David winced visibly at his response, and Martin experienced momentary regret for his harshness. But his nephew's behavior had been abominable, and he had no intention of allowing him to escape unscathed. His gaze fixed on David's face, Martin glimpsed a carefully concealed torment as David started to speak.

"I realize my conduct has been unforgivable this past week, and my only defense is that I didn't truly realize the extent to which it affected the family. I suppose the truth is that I was so involved in my own feelings that I neglected to consider the feelings of others. It's a shortcoming that I've been accused of many times, but I've only just now realized the truth in that criticism." Torment flashed again in David's eyes. "I want to say that I'm sorry for the trouble I've caused you, Uncle Martin. I also want to tell you that I've decided to take advantage of the opportunity you offered me."

Taken by surprise at David's unexpected statement, Martin paused again, carefully examining his nephew's expression. The anguish lurking in David's eyes had deepened.

"You mean by that, that you've decided attending school in England is a wise move?"

"Yes, sir."

"You're certain?"

"Yes, sir."

Martin paused, deciding in the favor of caution. "In that case you must be prepared to leave within a week's time."

"I know that, sir."

Martin released a silent sigh of relief. He had no idea what had happened between that little Irish witch and David, and he didn't care now that everything appeared to be off between them. Martin suppressed a smile. David had obviously made the decision to consign his relationship with the girl to the past, and no matter the depth of the boy's present misery, time would take care of the rest. A year from now David will have forgotten the tawdry little miss even existed.

"All right, then. I'll inform your aunt of your decision. She'll be relieved, to be sure." When David still hesitated, Martin raised his wiry brows questioningly. "Is there anything else?"

Temporarily at a loss for the pain momentarily visible in David's expression, Martin waited uncomfortably through David's uncharacteristic hesitation.

"Yes, I'd like to thank you for your patience, Uncle Martin, and your generosity as well. I've come to realize that I've taken too many things in my life for granted. I appreciate your forbearance."

Martin's throat tightened as David held out his hand, obviously uncertain if his uncle would accept it. Taking a few steps forward, Martin grasped it and shook it firmly.

Standing at the window again after David had left the room, his face averted to disguise the emotion there, Martin Lang was struck with the thought that David's brief fling with the O'Connor girl might have done him more good than he had thought possible. Obviously, the girl revealed her true self to him in some way, and the affair ended. Just as obviously, David still suffered, but it seemed his nephew had learned an important lesson. From now on, he would never question the value of those who truly loved him, *or* the disadvantages of stooping below himself.

That thought providing him considerable comfort, Martin suddenly realized that with all now settled and done, he would miss the boy sorely.

Chapter 17

His traveling case in his hand, David turned for a last sweeping glance of his room, intensely aware of the finality of the moment. He sought to impress the images of the heavy mahogany furniture, the map of the coal fields on the wall, the mementos of the boy he once was, deep into memory with the sudden premonition that on leaving this room now, nothing would ever be the same again.

The sounds of movement in the foyer below drew David from his thoughts, forcing him to close the door behind him and start down the hallway with the realization that the moment was upon him. He was leaving the valley on the late afternoon train, uncertain when, if ever, he would return.

"David, hurry!"

Grace's excited summons drew his gaze to her face as he reached the top of the staircase, and David was grateful that the dear girl had accepted his apology and forgiven his extended neglect of her. He had not deserved her forgiveness.

"We've instructed Harry to put your other cases in the car, dear." Aunt Letty's eyes filled as she spoke. "The train won't arrive for another hour, but Uncle Martin and I thought you might like a leisurely ride to the station since you'll be away for such a long time."

At the bottom of the staircase, David dropped a light kiss on his aunt's cheek. "Four years isn't so long, Aunt Letty."

"Isn't it?" Aunt Letty brushed at a tear. "Perhaps not, to one as young as you. But to me, it will seem a lifetime. I shall miss you, dear."

Meg's image appeared before his mind, and unwilling to admit that four years seemed a lifetime to him, too, David turned toward Uncle Martin where he stood waiting beside the door. He flashed his uncle a smile.

"I'm ready. Shall we go?"

Uncle Martin did not smile in return, and David knew this

parting would not be easy for either his uncle or himself. All differences between them had been settled during the past week, although they carefully avoided any discussion of Meg or the reason for David's abrupt change of mind.

The appearance of the household staff in the doorway delayed their departure. He had gone out of his way to make his peace with everyone before leaving, but his discomfort was still acute in the presence of Cook. Berating himself for not being as forgiving as they when resentment stirred anew at the memory of Cook's harsh treatment of Meg, David forced warmth into his farewells.

"All right. Let's go." Curving his arm around his wife's shoulders, Uncle Martin spoke to all in general. "Dear ladies, David must be on his way."

Stepping up into the carriage a few minutes later, David turned back for a final farewell, realizing that he was indeed "on his way."

Muff Lawler's saloon was filled with its usual crowd, but there were a few men there that Sean had never seen before. Having gotten off his shift a short time earlier, he had hastily bathed the black coal dust from his skin, changed his clothes, and met Lenny for a very important meeting in this place. Reading the question in Sean's eyes as he scanned the unfamiliar faces, Lenny lowered his head to whisper in his ear.

"That fella over there's Alex Campbell, owner of the Columbia House at Tamaqua—an important man. Rumor has it that he's bodymaster and division chief of Molly's boys there."

Sean nodded, his gaze intense as Lawler approached them with the tall raw-boned Campbell at his side. Lawler's, "Shake hands with me friend, Sean O'Connor," brought a brief appraisal, a twist of the fellow's lips, and a weak handshake. As Campbell walked away, Sean had the feeling his hopes for official acceptance as one of Molly's boys that afternoon were doomed.

Still at the bar a short time later, Lenny at his side, Sean was startled when Campbell walked past him with a brief, "Good luck, O'Connor," and a fleeting smile. A broad smile swept Lenny's face and, behind the bar, Lawler smiled with the same satisfaction.

Pretending an interest in his drink that he did not feel, Sean became aware of the subtle shifting of men within the room immediately following Campbell's departure. Mrs. Lawler assumed her husband's position behind the bar as the big man disappeared into the kitchen. Ed Ferguson, Pete Monaghan and Tom Hurley, one by one, slipped into the kitchen as well. A few minutes later, McAndrew sauntered over with a smile and motioned to them to follow him as he walked toward the doorway to the kitchen.

His heart pounding, Sean followed Lenny's lead through the back rooms and up the rear staircase to the second floor, aware that McAndrew remained behind on watch.

The conviviality of the saloon below was absent from the faces of the dozen or so men in Lawler's upstairs sitting room when he arrived, and Sean's throat tightened. He had not seen some of these men enter the saloon, and he realized they had arrived unseen at this secret rendezvous with the aid of long practice.

His gaze darting to Lawler where the fellow stood behind a small table, Sean saw he held a slip of paper in his hand which he appeared to be studying. The men around him shifted into a circle, and Sean's heart pounded as he was ordered to stand in the center. Each Molly made a devout sign of the cross, and instructed to do the same, Sean followed suit.

Lawler broke the silence. "The neophyte will kneel."

On his knees, Sean watched Lawler walk to stand beside him. His expression stern, Lawler read solemnly from the paper in his hand.

"We are joined together to promote friendship, unity, and true Christian charity to our members, raising money for the maintenance of the aged, the sick, and the infirm. The motto of the order is Friendship, Unity, and Christian Charity. It is the desire to promote friendship among Irish Catholics and especially to assist one another in all trials. You are expected to keep all matters accruing within the division room a secret in your own heart. None of the workings of the society are to be recalled to those not known to be members."

Still on his knees, Sean repeated the vow as instructed. "I, Sean O'Connor, having heard the objects of the Order fully explained, do solemnly swear that I will, with the help of God, keep inviolably secret all the acts and things done by this Order and obey the constitution and by-laws in every respect. I will obey my superior officers in everything lawful and not otherwise. All this I do solemnly swear."

Ordered to kiss the written sheet, Sean complied.

On his feet again, Sean watched as the other men filtered out of the room one by one, as they had entered. Not speaking a word until Lenny and he were standing at the bar below once more, Sean turned to his friend with dark sobriety.

"I'll have you know that I've not crossed myself since the day my Da was put under the ground, and were it not for the assemblege present upstairs, I'd have refused to do so there."

Lenny's short laugh was devoid of mirth. "Don't be misled by them simple words in the oath ye just took, me boyo. It's not God's work ye'll be doin' now that yer one of us. But an oath is an oath, and it holds ye fast to the blood. And I'll ask ye, now that it's done, do ye have any regrets at becomin' one of Molly's boys?"

A smile touching his lips for the first time, his brilliant O'Connor eyes cold as ice, Sean shook his head. "Nay, for the truth is, with the words you've just said, a great weight's been lifted from my shoulders, and I feel my life's begun again. And I give you my pledge as well, for the true friend that you've proved to be, Lenny Dunne."

Sean's eyes were suddenly bright with zeal as he continued. "I'll not falter, no matter what's asked of me, and I'll carry through to the death, be it that of another or my own. And I'll bend to no threat or coercion now that I'm assured that behind the weak spoken words of the pledge I just took is the strength of Molly's boys, for hers is the only courage and hope for justice remaining in this sad place. I'm where I want to be, Lenny, and where I shall remain."

Lenny hesitated, then questioned Sean hesitantly. "Ye'll not bend to threat or coercion—even if it should come from within yer own family?"

Knowing Lenny could be referring to no one other than Meg, Sean stiffened. "I'll set your mind to rest on that score, here and now. My sister's heart is pure, and O'Connor blood flows in her veins. She's no threat to me or mine, and never will be. And another thing I'll make clear to you is that Meg is dearer to me than any person alive, and I'll not suffer that question on your lips again, at the expense of the friendship between us that I value so well. Is that understood, friend?"

Challenging his gaze for long moments, Lenny abruptly extended his hand. "Understood—brother."

His handsome O'Connor face relaxing at last, Sean accepted Lenny's hand. "Aye, 'brother' under Molly's smile. And we'll make her happy, the two of us will. We'll make her grin."

Lenny's gaze locked with his in a pledge that went far beyond his simple word of response. "Aye."

David looked out the rail car window as a screeching whistle heralded the train's departure. His eyes moving from the teary-eyed group frantically waving on the platform, he searched the surrounding area for the appearance of the slender figure he unconsciously awaited.

David's eyesight blurred as the platform faded from sight, as a voice in his mind battled final acceptance, insisting—*Meg wouldn't let you leave her.*

The cold voice of reality wrenched his heart in two, responding—*But she did.*

David closed his eyes. *Oh, God, she did . . .*

Tears running down her cheeks, Meg stared out her bedroom window as the screeching whistle of the afternoon train grew faint and slowly died away. David was on that train. Until this moment somehow, she hadn't truly believed it. David wouldn't go off and leave her. He couldn't.

Her mind returned an unyielding reply—*But he did.*

Oh, God, he did.

1875

Chapter 18

Five hundred in number, the striking miners surged down the snow-dotted, early-morning Ashland street toward the mines. Blood rage in their eyes, bludgeons in their hands, they traveled as one angry beast, chanting their hatred of the infamous "black-legs"—the "scabs" imported into the fields to break the strike.

Foxworth Colliery came into view, and the good-looking, dark-haired fellow in the lead whispered to the men beside him. Waiting only until small groups separated from the main body of the strikers to take positions at the perimeter of the area, the stone-faced leader then called with a bold warning shout to the dozen or so armed policemen approaching them.

"Lay down your guns, you damned fools!" Looking directly into the eyes of the uniformed officers one by one as silence fell over the tense tableau, the leader allowed his gaze to settle on the captain, a large man with a dour, unyielding expression standing in the center of the line that stretched out on either side of him. "Tell your men to lay down their guns, Linden, or you'll be signin' their death warrants here and now."

The sober policeman matched daring with calm tenacity as he responded gruffly. "Seems to me you have things a bit mixed up here, Sean O'Connor, for it's my men who have the arms and the advantage over all of you here."

"Is that so?" Spittle wet Sean's lips with his short burst of laughter. "Have you never learned to count, then? You would run out of bullets long before you could down even the smallest portion of the men behind me, and there's not a man amongst us who'd not risk death for his convictions and to save his family from starvation at the hands of the bastards that employ you!"

An angry grumbling swelled from within the miners' ranks as the big policeman's heavy brows furrowed. "So you think to feed your families from the graves, is that it, then?"

"And if we should, you'd not be here to see if we succeed or fail, Linden, for you'll be the first to go!"

An uneasy silence followed Sean's threat as men on both sides tensed for the captain's reply.

"Your Da would turn over in his grave to see you so engaged, O'Connor."

"Don't speak of my Da to me, you bastard!" Sean's eyes blazed. "You were never his friend, except after he was in his grave and unable to deny it!"

Responding to Sean's reply with a short shake of his head, the big policeman looked at the huge sandy-haired man to Sean's rear. "You, too, Donovan?" Not waiting for a reply, Linden then looked at the short, mustached fellow on Sean's left. "As for you, McKenna, you're proof of the saying that trouble attracts trouble, for I doubt you've done more than a month's honest work in your life. You're in your element here, aren't you?"

McKenna did no more than laugh in reply, but Sean did not let the remark go unchallenged.

"It goes against your grain to see men who're not afraid to stand up to you, don't it, Linden? Well, we've only simple words in reply to your threats. You can tell your bosses that not a single blackleg will get past us to take the place of a good hardworkin' man in this mine. And you can tell them—"

"They're comin'! The whole, blasted pack of them dirty thievin' scabs! Let's get 'em!"

Turning at the shout from within the midst of the strikers, Sean halted the men with a sharp command. Pushing his way through their number, he faced the terrified column of strikebreakers where they had paused in their approach. Uniformed guards waved their guns uncertainly at the angry mob held barely in check, and Sean laughed mockingly. His expression threatening, he looked at each scab worker in turn, hatred spilling from his lips.

"You filthy, black-hearted bastards! You think to steal food from the mouths of our families while we battle for a fair wage, but you'll not see a cent of the blood money you come here seekin'!" Dismissing the guns trained on him with a wave of his hand, he continued hotly. "Them puny weapons is nothin' compared with the vengeance you'll know if you set foot in them mines this day, or any other! Take fair warnin'! Get back from this place and never return, or the only thing you'll get here will be the few feet of earth you'll be buried in!"

The replacement workers hesitated, and Sean turned to the men around him, speaking loud and clear. "Did you hear what I said, men? Are you with me?"

A loud chorus of "Aye!" thundered into the stillness as Sean turned back, his eyes gleaming maniacally. "What do you say to that, you dirty scabs?"

No response.

"Eh? Answer me, you bastards!"

Without response, the terrified laborers began scattering, running for their lives as their guards stood helplessly by.

"Stand your ground, you fools!" Captain Linden's voice broke into the panicstricken scene as his men and he edged forward, guns ready. "Stand your ground!"

"You're wastin' your breath on that bunch of cowards!" Sean's laughter bore a victorious note as the last of the blacklegs showed them their backs. He looked up into the big policeman's flushed face, his smile dropping away as he met the Scotsman's silent fury. Challenging him with a fury of his own, Sean continued contemptuously. "Or maybe they wasn't cowards. Maybe they was just smart, seein' that the Coal and Iron Police has no chance against the mob of us who travel with right on our side, and us who won't consent to sellin' our souls to Benjamin Franklin Gowen."

Linden responded flatly, "I'm thinking you flatter yourself in believing you have a soul left to sell, my fine fellow."

Sean took a spontaneous step forward, his face hot with anger, and Captain Linden snarled, "You'll think before you act, if you're wise."

The big man behind Sean gripped his arm, staying him. "He's right, Sean. He's but lookin' for an excuse to shed blood, and we're not goin' to give him one today." A quick look over his shoulder revealed the last of the blacklegs' retreat, and the fellow added, "We've no need. We've won."

"Fool that you are—" Captain Linden spoke low in warning. "You've won the day, but you know well that the battle's lost. It was lost from the day it was declared."

His eyes bearing a fanatical gleam, Sean replied in a low rasp. "If that's so, you can be sure it won't be a bloodless scene, for there's them who've vowed not to surrender."

His zeal just as intense, Captain Linden returned, "And if I've my choice, I'd not have you be one of them that dies for a lost cause, laddie."

"Get out of my way!" Turning, Sean waved the men behind him forward with a shout. "Them scabs won't return to this place. We've won the day, boyos!"

The sudden crush forward swept Captain Linden and his men to the side, but not before Sean O'Connor's clear eyes met his once more in silent promise of that which was to come.

Strike.

The word echoed in Meg's mind, increasing her tension as she stood at the window of her room, peering outside through the snow-dusted pane. Her gaze trailed the deceptively tranquil scene beyond, the skeletal outline of the idle breaker in the distance, the mounds of slag and cinder, the great pools of effluent pumped from hundreds of feet below the earth—all sheathed in a pristine cover of white deposited by an unseasonal snowstorm.

Raising her gaze briefly, Meg saw that snow covered the house on the hill that had once been such an important part of her life. The roof glittered in the afternoon spring sun, but it was already shedding its mantle, as it had shed significance in her mind when the Langs sold their mine to Franklin Gowen two years previously and moved away.

Memory recalled an autumn day five years earlier when the whistle of a departing train closed the door on a part of her life forever, but she forced it from conscious thought with the realization that the turn of the year 1875 had brought a violence to the coal fields from which she suspected it would never recover.

With deepening anguish Meg recalled the sweeping changes that took place at the Lang Colliery, and across the coal fields in general, after Franklin Benjamin Gowen gained control. Wages fell, working hours were reduced, and new waves of immigrants flooded into the Pennsylvania anthracite counties, swelling the already overfull labor pool. Gowen and other employers like him refused any concession to the delegations of miners who appealed to them for relief, and Meg was acutely aware that there were now very few miners in the fields who did not see slow starvation in their futures.

How long had it been? Four months? The strike called by the Mine Workers Benevolent Association in December of the previous year had caused thousands of men to lay down their picks and shovels, but it had seen little success. The union's treasury was exceedingly low, and the workers had neither cash in their pockets nor food in their larders. In every county there were collieries where the call to strike had been ignored, and the result was that enough coal was dug and prepared for market to supply a fair portion of the nation's coal needs, thus weakening the strikers' position. As Christmas gifts to the striking miners and their families, Gowen and other operators had given bobtail checks and a complete stoppage of credit at the "pluck me" stores. Since the shelves of independently-owned grocery stores near Lang's mine had long since been emptied, each day saw bellies growing emptier, and the union growing weaker.

But Meg was well aware that the same could not be said of the Molly Maguires. As a result of Gowen's deliberate planning, the Irish now comprised only a minor percentage of the miners in the fields, and of those, few were Mollies. But Molly's power did not lie in numbers, and the toll taken by her "sons" was terrible. Breakers were burned and men beaten all across the fields, coal cars dumped, scores of scab workers driven away, and Meghan feared the worst was yet to come.

The Mollies and Sean . . . The two had become synonymous in Meg's mind, and the pain of it squeezed her heart. He was openly a member of the Ancient Order of Hibernians and did not admit to membership in the Mollies, but she did not have to hear him speak the words to know that Sean had fervently embraced the organization. The many times he had left the house in the dark of night over the past years without explanation, his satisfaction at each heinous deed the Mollies accomplished, the deep, abiding hatred that had become so strong a part of his personality, all were irrefutable signs of Molly's domain.

But then there was the other side of Sean, the loving, gentle side he showed to her, which had grown along with his darker side. If Sean and she had been close before, they were closer still, and if they had felt responsible for each other before, they now felt an even deeper commitment to each other's welfare as the turmoil around them increased.

Suddenly seeing her tortured reflection in the lightly-frosted glass, Meg forced it away with the aid of long practice and affixed a suitable mask to her expression. The image that then looked back at her was not of an uncertain girl, but of a calm, mature woman.

Carefully controlling the direction of her thoughts, Meghan assessed the vague reflection, wondering what the reaction of some might be to that woman, could they see her now. Her face was the same. Maturity had sculpted a delicate grace to her cheekbones and stubborn chin, where there had been youthful fullness before, accenting the ripe curve of a mouth that did not smile as easily as years earlier. The only truly significant visible change was the absence of innocence in her clear blue O'Connor eyes. She wore her unmanageable curls confined in a tight knot atop her head most of the day now, and she was no longer the shapeless lass she had once been. Somewhere along the path to adulthood she had filled out, her youthful breasts becoming fuller, the curve of her hips more pronounced. Her waist had remained minute, a delicate balance between the two that often turned heads with admiration, but such attention meant little to Meg. Her appearance was merely a matter of heredity, her O'Connor blood proving true. But her achievements were her own, and of them she was justly proud.

A small, satisfied smile touched Meg's lips. The position Father Matthew had found for her almost five years earlier had gradually progressed from that of general clerk to unofficial manager of McCall's apothecary. She supposed James McCall's absence of progeny to assist in the family business was in her favor, but she knew she had diligently earned Mr. McCall's confidence in her. It was that position that now sustained them as the strike stretched on, and it was her fervent hope that matters would settle in the coal fields before establishments like Mr. McCall's were driven into the ground.

But the general problems of the area meant little to Meg at that moment as she looked out the window, waiting. There was trouble in Ashland—scabs being brought in to work at the Foxworth Colliery. The call had come to join ranks and drive them out, and many of the men from Shenandoah had responded. So far, none of them had returned.

Sounds of movement from the kitchen below alerted Meg to someone's arrival there. She heard a familiar, rapid footstep on the staircase. She turned to the door just as it burst open and a big, sandy-haired man entered. The gaze of his warm brown eyes touched hers, and in a running step she met him halfway across the room as his brawny arms crushed her against him, his mouth descending to muffle with his kiss the single word that emerged from her lips.

"Terry!"

David eyed the slender, distinguished gentleman seated opposite him in the large executive office of the Philadelphia and

Reading Coal and Iron Company. His gaze was discerning. He had met Franklin Benjamin Gowen at a party in New York a week earlier, just after his return to the country. Gowen had invited him to his office for "a talk" upon hearing his plans to travel to Philadelphia. Curious, David had come, but the instinctive distrust for Gowen that marked his first meeting with the man years before still remained.

David glanced at the lovely young woman seated beside him, realizing that she was partially responsible for his presence in Gowen's office, and the idea amused him. Having elected to remain in Europe to work with a Swiss engineering firm for a year after graduation, he had already become restless and decided it was time to return to America when he met Elizabeth Marklin a month prior to his planned departure. It had not taken the beautiful, strong-minded debutante long to boldly alter her travel plans to match his.

Elizabeth smiled and David nodded in response. Blond, wealthy, beautiful, and intelligent, Elizabeth Marklin had left no doubt in his mind from the first moment they met that she wanted him. The embers of that desire smoldered in her dark eyes as she met his gaze with a hypocritically innocent stare. "Well, what do you think of Ben's idea, David?"

David turned back to consider Gowen's patrician face, and addressed him directly in response.

"I admit to surprise at my own interest. After Uncle Martin sold the mine, I divorced myself completely from all connection with the coal fields, and I've given little thought to the time I spent there during the past few years." David's expression turned into a frown. "My aunt and uncle's European tour brought them to visit me in Switzerland just after the turn of the year. They told me what was happening, and I became intrigued. I've read everything I could about the strike and its ramifications in the newspapers since I returned."

Gowen appeared pleased at David's interest. "I admit to some surprise of my own when your uncle told me he was putting the mine up for sale two years ago. Prior to that, he seemed opposed to my strategy in the coal fields and determined to carry on as he saw fit at Lang Colliery."

A familiar knot tightened in David's stomach. "Yes . . . well, I think about that time he began seeing little use in continuing the struggle. My cousin Grace is his only child, you know. She married well, and since her husband's family fortune is tied up in other areas, there was little interest in the mine. As for myself, my studies led me in another direction entirely."

"An educational background in engineering could be very useful in a mining operation."

"I made it clear to Uncle Martin at that time that I had no intention of returning to the colliery."

Ben Gowen hesitated, running a finger thoughtfully along his well-trimmed mustache as he appeared to study David's response. "May I ask why you came to that decision?"

David hesitated. His eyes darkened before he responded briefly. "I lost interest in mining after a few years abroad."

Ben Gowen shook his head, darting a quick glance toward Elizabeth. "Elizabeth appeared to believe just the opposite when we met at the governor's party last week. She seemed to think you'd welcome the opportunity to return if it proved financially profitable for you."

A smile played at the corners of David's mouth as he gave his lovely companion a thoughtful glance. "I think it would be more accurate to say that *Elizabeth* would welcome the opportunity if it proved financially profitable for me. You see, I gave up a lucrative position in Europe when I decided to come home. She knows I won't come into my inheritance for almost two years, and that although my assets are presently limited, I have no current prospects for employment. A shortage of funds would embarrass her."

"David! What a terrible thing to say!"

David raised his dark brows, amused at her protest. "*You* know it's true, and *I* know it's true, Elizabeth. And I'm sure Mr. Gowen is aware of my financial situation, or he wouldn't have asked me to come here today."

Not allowing time for discomfort, Gowen nodded. "Inquiries led me to believe that we can both benefit from an association right now."

David paused, uncertain, finally deciding upon candor. "I'll be honest with you, Mr. Gowen. I haven't been in complete sympathy with your activities in the past, and I'm still uncertain if I agree with your methods."

"I can't believe an intelligent man like you can say that, David." His fair face flushing in an uncharacteristically spontaneous display of annoyance, Gowen stood up and walked to the window. He turned back a few moments later, in full control again. "But I'm grateful for your forthright reply. In response, I'm going to explain how I feel about the dangers inherent in the coal field situation, and my intentions. If you feel my actions unjustified when I'm finished, you can simply turn down my offer."

Waiting for David's nod, Gowen seated himself again, leaning forward in an earnest posture as he began.

"You must know that the coal industry has been its own worst enemy in the past, and you must also be aware that having been involved with it most of my life in one way or another, I feel a commitment to it. About six or seven years ago, I sat back and looked at the industry in general. Mines were failing, the market fluctuating. The reason was very clear: lack of control over production and marketing. Middlemen, coal factors, were sitting at the water's edge like leeches, sucking the lifeblood of a healthy trade, and I was determined to do something about it. I began by buying up coal lands, but contrary to the expectations of some who suspected my motives, I encouraged individual enterprise by leasing back much of the acreage to individual prospectors and by making loans to colliers, and by giving advances on mortgages for renovations of old collieries and construction of new ones. However, I was unsuccessful in overcoming the heritage of wastefulness, poorly financed organization, and of lethargy and ultraconservatism. Mines continued to fail."

Gowen paused, his brows knit in an expression of concern. "Finally, in possession of forty thousand acres of coal lands and with my position as President of the Road, I attacked control of the amount sent to market. I was successful to a degree in my attempt and am proud of many things I've achieved that are to the good of the industry. One of my greatest successes has been the upgrading of the country's coal through institution of rigid inspection procedures and penalties against colliers who sought to perpetuate the country's reputation for 'dirty' coal."

Gowen paused again, his expression hardening. "However, there are several impediments to progress that must be overcome. One of them is the control the Molly Maguires has over the coal fields." David's frown darkened, and Gowen nodded. "I see you remember the activities of the Mollies well. The situation hasn't changed, despite the influx of new miners into the fields in recent years. The Irish are now only a small percentage of the work force, but the Mollies' grip has become even stronger. Terrorism is their tool, and I've vowed to destroy the damned organization and all it represents."

The knot in David's stomach tightened. "Not all Irishmen are Mollies, sir."

"I'm of Irish descent myself, David, and I'm well aware of that. The problem lies in determining who the Mollies are and putting them out of business. I have a separate plan underway in that regard, but the most pressing problem is that the Mollies are presently working hand-in-hand with the union during this strike."

David shook his head. "I find that hard to understand. The activities of the Mollies are too abhorrent to most Irish for them to condone the organization for any reason."

"You've been away from the fields for a long time, David. Some things have changed."

"I doubt that the basic values of the people have been affected."

Gowen's gaze silently challenged his remark before he proceeded. "Whether the Mollies are behind the union's position or not, the fact remains that the Mine Workers' Benevolent Association resents me and the necessary steps I've been forced to take. They say I intend to manipulate prices so that wages will go down. They want controls over the labor pool that I cannot guarantee and, in short, their demands are unreasonable. The murders continue, the fires, the destruction . . ."

David stiffened, remembering a particular stable fire years earlier. It still raged occasionally in his nightmares, and although it had never been proven, he knew the Mollies were responsible for it. His voice hardened as he responded. "And how do you suppose I can effect a change in the downward spiral of events?"

His keen eyes searching David's face intently, Gowen suddenly sat back. "The Lang Colliery is presently without a superintendent. Aaron Belcher, whom I placed in that position after your uncle sold out, was recently injured and has had enough. The violence has since abated and more men are returning to work each day, but the colliery operation is in the hands of men unequipped to handle its complex nature. I have fortified the position there with an increased number of Coal and Iron Police, but I need a man who knows the mine and the men there—someone who can step in and take over—someone who is not afraid to look those men in the eye and do what must be done."

"And you think *I* am that man."

"Yes I do. You were uncompromising in upholding your uncle's policies when you worked alongside him, and I ask no more of you than that. And I'm willing to pay you well to do the work."

David gave a short laugh. "I'm not certain whether I should be flattered by your confidence." Pausing to assess Gowen for a few silent moments more, David stood up unexpectedly. Drawing Elizabeth to her feet, he waited until Gowen stood as well before continuing.

"In any case, I'll have to think this over before I give you a definite answer. In all honesty, I must tell you now that my first inclination is to decline."

"David, you can't!" Elizabeth's protest was spontaneous. "This is an opportunity to establish yourself in the industry! Ben is offering you a tremendous opportunity."

"I'm aware of what Mr. Gowen is offering me, Elizabeth." Surprised by the fleeting glimmer of approval in Gowen's gaze as he efficiently quelled Elizabeth's interference, David extended his hand. "I'll give you my answer in a few days, if that meets with your approval."

Gowen shook his hand firmly. "You're the man for the job, David. I trust your good sense, and I know you'll come to see that as clearly as I do."

Turning with a nod, David ushered Elizabeth out beside him, the feeling lingering that much lay unspoken behind Gowen's friendly manner and carefully cultivated facade. Through his uncertainty, one thing remained abundantly clear. He still did not trust the man.

Terry Donovan's arms tightened around Meg, crushing her against the rock-hard strength of his chest as his mouth moved hungrily against hers. The familiar taste of him stilled the gnawing trepidation inside her, and Meg returned the pressure of his lips in a heartfelt kiss. She drew back a moment later with a breathless whisper. "You and Sean were gone so long that I was beginning to worry."

Terry's craggy face was soft with emotion as he paused in response. His dark brown eyes glowed in a way with which she had become as familiar during the past year as she had with the great towering size of the man and the gentleness that was so much a part of his nature. When he spoke, his deep voice bore an affected rasp.

"Ye need not have worried, darlin'. Did I not tell ye I'd be back before suppertime this evenin'?" And then his low, satisfied laugh. "But I forget. Worryin's the province of a wife."

"Nay, not this wife!"

Aware of the untruth in her feisty response, Meg shook her head and hugged the big man tight against her. "But the truth is, I would never have forgiven myself if anything had happened to you. I know you've no true interest in the activities you attend with Sean, and that you only go with him because you're his friend and because you want to keep an eye on him for me."

Easy laughter rumbled in Terry's broad chest. "Yer right about that, Meg, me darlin'. I'd much rather be feelin' yer arms around me than be lookin' down the barrel of a gun."

"A gun!" Meg's heart skipped a beat.

"Now, now . . ." His callused hand caressed her cheek as she pulled back to assess his expression, and Terry shook his head with obvious regret. "That was a fool thing for me to say. Aye, the lot of us faced guns today, but that Captain Linden had a meager force as compared to our five hundred men, in spite of his weapons, and they was the ones to back down, not us."

"Sean—is he all right? I want to see him."

"He's downstairs. The generous fella that he is, is allowin' us newly married folk our reunion in private."

"Newly married?" Meg's brows rose skeptically. "We've been man and wife for over a year!"

"Nay, it can't be!" Terry's eyes were suddenly wide with mock surprise. "It seems just like yesterday! But I suppose I could make certain of it by countin' the nobs on me head from where ye've been landin' that fryin' pan of late . . ."

"Oh, Terry!" Laughter was a part of Terry's nature, and he had made it a part of her own as well. Not for the first time, Meg realized that it was that part of Terry that had drawn her to him when he arrived in Shenandoah from Ireland two years earlier.

From the doorway came another response. "And I'm thinkin' she's not used that fryin' pan as often of late as she should."

Relief filling her throat, Meg disengaged herself from her husband's arms and in a few steps was hugging Sean with all her might. But all sign of merriment disappeared as she questioned simply, "All's well, Sean?"

Directly addressing her unspoken fears and putting them to rest, Sean nodded. "Aye, all's well. We backed them blackhearted scabs down and they fled like the cowardly rats that they are. We beat them one more time, Meg."

Knowing better than to remind her brother that this was but one victory in a long line of defeats since the strike had begun four months previously, Meg attempted a smile. "Terry said—"

"Aye," Terry interrupted. "I told yer sister that we was the bravest of the lot, the two of us, and that we personally overcame a score of gun-carryin' policemen and fought them to the ground."

Sean shook his head with mock disgust. "How the man lies, Meg."

The spontaneous burst of laughter that followed laid to rest the last remaining tensions between them, and Meg was again grateful for Terry's entrance into their lives. And if she did not love him with the passion he exhibited for her, she loved him for his goodness and the gentleness he showed for all his hulking size, and for the healing power of his laughter. And she loved him for being the only person other than herself who had ever been successful in earning Sean's true affection, and for restoring her hope for Sean when it had been at its weakest point.

A small, comradely wink passed between the two men as Sean slipped his arm around her. "And shall we go down to the dinner table now to make sure Uncle Timothy has his daily quota of rage?"

Meg's smile dimmed. Uncle Timothy had never accepted any of them, and she knew he never would, despite the hefty sum she and Sean had repaid him over the years, and the monthly rent they continued to pay. But while Uncle Timothy barely tolerated Terry and her, he hated Sean. She was well aware that the only reason Sean still maintained his residence in the household was to obtain his own version of revenge. As for herself, she had never been able to bring herself to abandon Aunt Fiona.

But she would not harbor dark thoughts now. Sean and Terry were home safe, and they were all together again. They would celebrate, and she knew Aunt Fiona would join in their celebration, even if she did so in silence.

Allowing Terry to sweep her forward as Sean started for the door, Meg ignored the knot in her stomach and the nagging voice in the back of her mind warning her that despite this morning's brief victory, defeat was inevitable. But Sean was an O'Connor, and he would never admit to defeat. Raising her chin, Meg fixed a smile on her lips. Neither would she.

Sharp, potent memories returned to David's mind as he walked the familiar Philadelphia street, and he gave little thought to the attention he drew from two young matrons as they emerged from a small shop nearby. He had always attracted the female eye, and he knew that maturity had added a breadth of shoulder and muscle to his frame that naturally attracted women. He was not aware, however, that the air of a polished European gentleman he had unconsciously attained went deeper than he realized. It added a quality of aloofness to his strong profile and firm chin that often made his smile more caustic than true, and it stilled the gold flecks that formerly animated his unusual eyes. The effect was to erase all trace of the young man who had sailed for England five years earlier; an outward transformation that reflected the changes in the inner man as well.

It was the new David Lang who had put Elizabeth Marklin back on the train to New York the previous night with a cool smile. He knew instinctively that the bold little baggage had been waiting for him to suggest that she remain in Philadelphia with him for the weekend, but he was too wise to step into that trap.

After Elizabeth's train had pulled out of the station, he had taken a room and lain awake most of the night with Gowen's offer dominating his thoughts. He had arisen at the first light of dawn, an inexplicable unrest inside him. Now, several hours later, well-breakfasted and ready for the day, he walked along Walnut Street, refreshing his memory of the sights and sounds of Philadelphia.

He had been gone five years, but it might just as well have been a lifetime. Graduated with an impressive degree, he was no longer the arrogant but unworldly young fellow he once had been. The high opinion he had had of himself those years ago amused him, for he now recognized the immaturity Uncle Martin had seen, and admitted to himself that his uncle had probably saved him from an error in judgment that could have ruined his life.

A pang David thought he had long conquered squeezed at his innards. He had set to rest the difficult circumstances under which he had left Philadelphia when he finally realized that he was the only one, including Meghan O'Connor, who had been unable to see the situation clearly those many years ago.

In retrospect, he supposed it was only natural for him to become involved with Meg. He had been in a particularly vulnerable state after the fire, and he had begun thinking of her as indispensable to his well-being and happiness. Meg was beautiful, warm, and giving, with an uncommon maturity for a girl of her youth. She was different from any person he had ever known, and in his need, he had taken and taken from her until she became a crutch he was unwilling to lose.

A touch of his old bitterness returning, David gave a low grunt of self-approval. He had learned to walk alone again, and he was a better man for it, but he would be the first to admit that it had not been easy. The first two years at the university had been nothing short of hell, with the devil tormenting him wearing the face of Meg O'Connor. His heart had jumped a beat with every curly-haired woman he passed on the street, with each slender female figure that turned a corner ahead of him, and every mail call was an excruciatingly painful disappointment. He wrote dozens of letters, only to tear them up with disgust at his own weakness, and it seemed he was never free of thoughts of Meg. But pride and common sense had finally prevailed, and he was finally able to look back on that time with Meg O'Connor without the pain that had been a necessary part of healing.

His life had changed dramatically after that. His grades improved, and for a short time he gained a just reputation for being a relentless womanizer. He was graduated at the top of his class, and when the opportunity for a lucrative position in Switzerland presented itself, he accepted it.

But he had gotten restless again. Uncle Martin and Aunt Letty's surprise visit before beginning their European tour brought his restlessness to a head, and it was then that he decided to come home.

Home—the term taunted him. He supposed Philadelphia was his home. He had been born here and lived here with his parents until they were killed. After leaving Shenandoah, Uncle Martin and Aunt Letty had made their home here, and his only other living relative lived at the end of this street.

Pausing briefly in front of the house he sought, David suddenly bounded up the steps and rang the bell. Within a few seconds, the door was flung wide and a graceful young matron threw herself into his arms.

Father Matthew's slender fingers tightened on the missive in his hand, and the familiar paragraphs blurred before his vision with his growing rage.

The "white paper" Father McDermott, he, and six other priests has signed the previous year condemning the Molly Maguires had been a farce. Published in the *Catholic Standard*, the official newspaper of the Philadelphia Diocese, it had set forth the most outspoken condemnation of the villainous group to date, with the express intention of influencing the majority of Irish Catholics against the organization. It had caused quite a stir at first, and his colleagues and he had maintained high hopes for a change of affairs, but no such change had come about. Now, this most recent missive from Father McDermott had been delivered this morning, and he was sick to death with the inadequacy of words!

Another Saturday had come around—to Father Matthew's mind the most infamous day of the week. In a few minutes he would go to the confessional and face the line of penitents already forming, and he was sick at the thought. Aye, the Mollies had even managed to make a travesty of that sacred function.

A glance out at the street beyond his window brought a frown to Father Matthew's face and silent confirmation to his thoughts as he viewed a familiar couple approaching the church. Meghan O'Connor Donovan had grown more beautiful with the passing years. His intense gaze moved to the large man at her side who held her arm so possessively, and he frowned. Dear Meg, if she but knew the truth hidden from her by those she loved the most . . .

Father Matthew turned away from the window. He reached for his vestments, the anger inside him exceeding all priestly bounds.

"David, you're home at last!"

Grace clung to David's neck, sobbing happy tears, and a thickness rose in his throat at the warmth of his cousin's reception. Disengaging himself a moment later, David took a step further into the foyer, allowing the door to close behind him as he held her at arm's length. Astounded, he shook his head.

"Grace, when did my little cousin turn into such a beautiful woman?"

Smoothing the dampness from her cheeks, Grace responded without hesitation. "About three years ago, but you weren't here to witness the transformation. It happened the day I wed Freddie."

David could not suppress a smile at his cousin's unembarrassed candor. "Grace, you'll never change."

Seated across from Grace in her tastefully-furnished sitting room a few hours later, David realized he was wrong. An extremely indulgent Freddie Haas III had put in an appearance and left again for an appointment. Grace's healthy two-year-old son had been introduced, cuddled, and then removed by his nanny for a nap. Alone, their conversation had slipped into reminiscence that had somehow stirred the same nagging discomfort with which he had awakened, and Grace's scrutiny had deepened.

"I thought of you often while you were gone, David. Far more often than you thought of me, no doubt, but it was always that way. I did worship you so. In a way, I suppose I still do. And you haven't disappointed me, for you've become a handsome man."

"And you're a beautiful woman, Grace." David smiled. "I suppose we should be grateful for our heredity."

Grace nodded. "Yes, that's true, but even as a child I knew you were something special. I started to think of you as my own personal possession, because I knew I had a special place in your heart that was surpassed by no one else. The day I realized that was no longer true was one of the most difficult days in my life. I'm afraid I handled it very poorly and I regret the discomfort my behavior caused you."

Sensing the direction in which his cousin was heading, David shrugged. "That's all in the past, Grace."

Not to be deterred, Grace pinned him with her surprisingly intuitive gaze. "You said Mr. Gowen offered you an opportunity to run Papa's mine and you're hesitant to accept. Will you be honest with me about the reason, David?"

"I'm not sure I know the reason, Grace." His discomfort increasing, David attempted to avoid Grace's scrutiny. "I don't trust Gowen. I never did."

"But you said you're concerned with the way things have been handled in the coal fields. That would indicate your interest hasn't lagged."

David shrugged. "No, it hasn't, to my surprise. I didn't think I'd ever want anything to do with coal mines again."

Grace hesitated, then offered softly, "Your aversion to the industry wouldn't have anything to do with your personal experience, would it, David? With some unfinished business you might have back in Shenandoah?"

David stiffened, a slow heat climbing into his face as a short, surprised laugh escaped him. "You *have* grown up, Grace, and you've become a romantic. I hate to disillusion you, but I have no unfinished business in Shenandoah."

"I'm sorry." Grace gave a delicate shrug. "I was such an obnoxious child at times, so selfish and self-centered. I've changed, of course, and you have, too, in some ways. I just want you to be as happy as I am."

"I'm not unhappy, Grace—only unsettled."

"I'm glad, David." Leaning forward, Grace kissed his cheek and changed the subject.

Hours later, as he walked back down Walnut Street, David felt a familiar irritation. Grace had not changed as much as he thought. As fond of her as he was, she still managed to annoy him.

David suddenly realized he wasn't being entirely honest. He couldn't blame Grace for her unexpected insight, only her unexpected candor.

With a caustic laugh, David admitted to the truth at last. He simply had not realized that old wounds could still bleed.

Chapter 19

Terry hunched his broad shoulders over the bar, his brow drawn into an uncharacteristic frown. "Fill me glass again, sport. I've a heavy thirst tonight."

"Aye, fill mine as well."

Muff Lawler made another pass with the bottle as Sean pushed his glass forward and watched as the amber liquid splashed expertly to the brim without a drop of spillage.

Terry and he had arrived at their favorite *shebeen* almost an hour earlier. They had wandered around the room, mixing with friends and exchanging conversation, conscious of the prevailing aura of doom that shrouded the room and those in it.

Turning at a snort beside him, Sean met Jim McKenna's almost boyish countenance as the undauntable Irishman retorted, "You're both a step behind me tonight, boyos, and I think you've to do some fancy drinkin' if you expect to catch up."

"I'm not that much a fool, Jim!" Terry's short laugh lifted his heavy features into a smile for the first time that evening, turning heads toward him with curiosity. "Yer a single man. Ye've not a young bride at home waitin' to greet ye with a mean look in her eye if ye come back two sheets to the wind."

"Are you tellin' all these good men here that my sister's a shrew, Terry Donovan?" Sean's question was delivered with a touch of levity that elicited a surprisingly sober response from his brother-in-law.

"Nay, never that. She's a rare one, is me Meg, and I count meself a lucky man to have her. And the truth is that I'll not risk me place in her heart for a bit of whiskey at this bar or any other."

Pausing only a moment at Terry's unexpected earnestness, Sean then lifted his glass to the smaller man beside him. "Then I suppose it's up to us single men to take up the slack, Jim." Sean raised his voice. "So let's hoist our glasses, boyos, and drink to victory over them that would cheat the Irish in these fields from their due."

A round of approval resounded throughout the room as drinks were raised and tossed back with the first enthusiastic response of the night.

"Come on, give us a jig, Jim."

Similar prompting echoed along the bar.

"Aye, you're the only fella from the old sod that's light enough on his feet to bring us a taste of home."

"We're in need of a light touch tonight."

Protesting, Jim McKenna finally succumbed to the chorus of urgings as the fiddle in the corner struck up a jig. Sean was watching his friend's nimble feet with amusement when Terry leaned toward him with a casual smile.

"I'll be driftin' out now, Sean." Pulling his oversized frame to his feet, he tossed down the last of his drink and touched his pinkie finger to his cap. "Tell the fellas that there'll be snow in Tipperary before long, and it'll be a foot if it's an inch."

His expression stiffening, Sean mimicked his gesture with a brief reply. "And the rains'll not wash it away."

Watching as Terry ambled through the crowded room toward the door, Sean moved a few steps down the bar.

The night had deepened and the kitchen candles were snuffed. Coals glowed in the kitchen stove, the only light in the darkened house except for the kerosene lamp that flickered shadows across the parlor where Aunt Fiona sat opposite Meghan in her favorite rocker. The occasional hours of solitude they shared at night while everyone else in the house entertained themselves otherwise had become a ritual between Aunt Fiona and herself. Meghan had not sacrificed it since she married, realizing it allowed Terry time with his friends. In the two years since Terry had come to Shenandoah, she had rested more easily with the knowledge that Sean was included in that group, and that Terry was a steadying influence on her brother.

Meg amended that thought. It was not as if Sean's anger had mellowed. To the contrary, the pressure of the strike had intensified his feelings of bitterness and betrayal. She knew Terry's easy disposition did not lean toward retribution, and she often worried that Terry's friendship for Sean would draw him into trouble along with him. But in the back of her mind the knowledge remained that Terry was levelheaded, not given to acting on impulse and rage like Sean, and she depended upon him to balance her brother's more impetuous ways.

"Yer man will be returnin' soon, won't he, Meg?"

Meg glanced at the clock on the wall and frowned, realizing he was late. "Aye, he should be home soon."

It was later than usual, but the dire circumstances of the strike brought men together nightly in the drinking establishments around town. It would not surprise her if the talk was hot and heavy, for despite the victory at Foxworth's in Ashland the previous week, things were not going well. More men had quietly returned to work at Lang's the following Monday, their empty stomachs defeating them, and Sean had been livid.

Aunt Fiona's weary eyes were intent on her face, and Meg attempted to erase all sign of concern. But it was apparently to no avail.

"Are ye thinkin' somethin' might have happened, then? Would ye like me to walk with ye to see if there's any commotion about town?"

"No, Aunt. Terry will be home soon."

With a reassuring smile, Meg turned back to her mending. Terry would return soon, because he was a man who enjoyed coming home to her. He was dependable, loving, with not a vengeful bone in his body. It had been those facets of Terry's character that had turned her to him when she began to believe that her single status was one of the major impediments in the way of Sean's marriage to her dear friend, Sheila McCrea.

With a small smile, Meg recalled Terry's surprised expression the night she told him she would marry him, and she knew that although their marriage had not inspired Sean to take a similar step, she did not regret it. Terry loved her, and if her love was based less on passionate emotion than was his, if the many nights spent in Terry's arms had not erased the memory of a leafy bower and the blissful loving of another man, her love was nonetheless sincere.

For the past was past, and Terry was the present. And he was a good man, one of their own.

The room was silent, the sociability of the saloon below significantly absent as Sean studied the faces of the men who had soundlessly filtered into Muff Lawler's sitting room at careful intervals. In the five years since he had first entered this room, Sean had come to know these men very well, and their keen anticipation at being summoned to this unexpected meeting of the brotherhood was clearly visible to him. Ed Ferguson, Pete Monaghan, Tom Hurley, Frank McAndrew, Jim McKenna and others stood lining the walls. They were his brothers, born to their kinship with an oath sworn to protect each other as well as the honor of all Irishmen, and baptized in a stream of violence against their oppressors that had sealed their power in blood.

Standing within the informal circle, Sean saw Muff mentally count the dozen or so men present before turning with a nod to the man standing in the shadows just outside the perimeter of the circle. That man was their new bodymaster, fresh from Ireland a few years earlier with credentials so powerful that he had almost immediately been thrust into his present position. Fiercely dedicated to the cause, he had not let his brothers down, and Sean knew the men gathered here would follow him into Hell itself if the fellow so directed.

Acknowledging his feelings to be the same, Sean watched as the big man stepped out of the shadows and strode into the circle of waiting men. His immense size all the more imposing for the air of threat with which he walked, his craggy face appearing to be cut from stone as his brown eyes burned with zeal, Terry Donovan started to speak.

David moved quickly toward the morning train. It occurred to him that he had spent the greater portion of the last week on the train between New York and Philadelphia, only to find himself boarding the train again. But this time he was headed in another direction.

So much had happened during the past week. Gowen's offer of employment and his visit to Grace had freed memories he had thought long ago set to rest. He had left Philadelphia shortly thereafter, and spent the next few days reveling in the splendor of Elizabeth Marklin's many charms. The sheer inventiveness of the woman during the long nights they spent together amazed him still.

For that reason, he had been startled to realize after a few days of Elizabeth's entertaining that he could no longer avoid the reality that his dear, naive, unworldly cousin Grace had been right. He had unfinished business in Shenandoah.

He had returned immediately to Philadelphia. Assured by Gowen that he was free to supervise Lang Colliery at his own discretion, he had then accepted the fellow's offer. Two days later, he was rushing for the train that would deliver him to Shenandoah.

The conductor's call interrupted David's thoughts, alerting him as his train jerked into motion, and David broke into a run. Leaping onto the car, he paused to catch his breath before putting his suitcase down and turning back to view the station as it slipped into the distance. His sense of relief startling, it was suddenly clear to David for the first time that it was this unfinished business in Shenandoah that had brought him home.

The afternoon sun was warm on her head as Meg labored over the washtub behind her aunt's house. Raising a soapy hand, she brushed back a nagging wisp of hair, her bright O'Connor eyes straying to the scarred back door as a worried frown creased her brow. Her work at McCall's had been cut to three days weekly, and she feared it would be cut further if the strike was not settled soon, but that was not the cause for her present uneasiness. Sean and Terry had been home most of the day and had been surprisingly absorbed in a private conversation. Her questions had accomplished no more than to elicit a strong hug and a smile from her husband, along with a response tinged with humor.

"Come now, darlin'. Sean's fair to wear poor Sheila out with the spare time he's had on his hands of late. I'm just makin' an attempt to distract him for a few hours to allow the poor girl some rest."

But Terry's lighthearted attempt at reassurance had stirred concerns of another kind that had given her little rest in the hours since. The shame of Sean's behavior—years of accepting all Sheila had to give without giving the girl his name. And the shame of her own behavior, in keeping silent and allowing him to continue.

Realizing that there would be no better time to discuss the matter with Sean than while her feelings were pitched so high, Meg dried her arms on a nearby cloth and started back to the house.

The buzz of low conversation in familiar tones caught her ear as she entered the empty kitchen. Heading straight for the sound, she walked across the hall toward the sitting room, only to stop abruptly just out of sight of the door as the whispered words became clear.

". . . tonight. The information was sent straight to Muff and it's all arranged, but we've to move fast. The bastard will be arrivin' on the evenin' train. We'll leave the fellow the *surprise* he's deservin' and the men will support the strike again. They need this to realize . . ."

Sean's voice drew to an abrupt halt as Terry loomed unexpectedly in the doorway in front of Meg. Terry's expression was threatening, almost unrecognizable in the moment before he exclaimed with a stiff laugh, "Aha, so 'tis only me wife with her ear to the wall." Reaching out, he wrapped his brawny arm around her and pulled her close to his side as he drew her into the room. "If ye had a need to hear our conversation, Meg, ye need not have listened in secret."

Terry's eyes were warm and true. They lingered momentarily on her face before he surprised her with a kiss on her stiff lips, his voice deep with unexpected fervor. "Yer the love of me life, ye know that, don't ye, Meg? The best thing that ever happened to me, and if yer brother wasn't sittin' here right now, eyein' us both, I'd show you how well I mean what I say."

But the underlying tension of the moment was not allayed by Terry's loving words. Meg remained stiff at his side, her gaze moving directly to her brother with her tight question.

"What's going on here, Sean?"

Terry's voice was low with reproval. "Should ye not have asked yer husband that question, Meg?"

Unwilling to allow Terry to intrude into the truth of the moment, Meg responded quietly. "I asked the question of my brother, and it's from him that I'd like a response."

Sean was suddenly on his feet, his eyes flashing with anger. "Do you really expect an answer about somethin' that's none of your concern? And I tell you now, it'll do you no good to spy. You're of my blood, but that don't give you the right to live my life for me. Back off, Meg! My life's my own, as well as my thoughts, and I'll explain neither of them to you unless I so choose."

Turning abruptly, Sean left the room. The slamming of the front door echoed in the silence as Meg looked up at Terry. Her stomach tightened at his obvious resentment when he spoke.

"So yer forced to turn to me for an answer." Terry's brow furrowed. "It seems this little scene is a bit more tellin' than it appears at first, when a man's wife looks to someone else before him."

"Sean's my brother. He won't lie to me."

"And so yer sayin' I will."

Terry assumed an injured expression, and Meg was suddenly

stunned by the implications of her own statement. What *had* she meant? What had she seen in Terry's eyes in that brief moment in the doorway to make her doubt him?

"Ah, Meg . . ." Unexpectedly reaching out to encompass her in his overwhelming embrace, Terry clutched her close. The familiar heat of him left her strangely cold as he held her in silence for a few long moments.

Abruptly separating himself from her, his brown eyes limpid, he whispered softly, "And the irony of it all is that ye've made a mountain out of a molehill. Sean has his back up because some fellas in the patch have been tryin' to get the men to return to work. He's plannin' to take it out on them one way or another. I've spent half the day tryin' to talk some sense into him, but he's not heard a word I said."

Meg did not respond to his explanation, and Terry shook his head, his expression sad. "Don't burn me with them clear eyes of yours, Meg. If ye choose to disbelieve me, I can do no more for ye."

Meg stared at Terry. Something crumbled painfully inside her and hardly aware of the words she spoke, she whispered, "Why are you lying to me, Terry?"

Color flooded Terry's blunt features as he pulled his muscled bulk to full height. "Believe what ye must then, for I've no more to say."

Turning abruptly, Terry strode from the room, leaving Meg standing in silence as the door slammed emphatically behind him.

The train shuddered along the tracks as David sat slouched in his seat. His jacket and hat flung across the carrier overhead, David tugged absentmindedly at his cravat. Loosening it another notch, he glanced at the man who slept a few seats away, his only fellow passenger, before turning back to the passing landscape.

Strangely, he had forgotten the tortured quality of the terrain through which he traveled, the ugly piles of debris brought from underground, the dead lakes of effluent pumped from below, the fine layer of black dust that dulled the natural color of the seasons. There was little to dispel the aura of wretched misery that clung to the clusters of patch houses he viewed as the train crawled from one stop to the next, but he had not been away long enough to forget the ignorance of the miners, their arrogance, and the stupidity of their unrealistic demands that kept them living under those conditions.

Strike. The damned fools! Don't they see they have no chance for victory?

David paused to consider that thought. No, he supposed they didn't, as short-sighted, stubborn, and proud as they were. He remembered that pride. He had known it firsthand. He had seen it close up, reflected in glorious blue eyes that affected him even now in memory. And he remembered that particular pride had proved stronger than love, and that all he had once had to give had not been enough to overcome it.

Despising his own weak lapse into the torments of the past, David turned back to contemplate the landscape. Daylight was beginning to wane. His heartbeat quickened despite himself, as the terrain became more familiar and his destination neared.

Reaching into his vest, David retrieved his pocket watch and flicked open the cap. He would arrive in Shenandoah shortly. Firmly curbing the unexplained anticipation building inside him, he confirmed in his mind that he had not come back to relive the past, but to face it. Then his unfinished business—the anger, prejudice, resentment, and love stored up inside him—would be truly settled at last.

The sun was sinking toward its nightly rest behind the mountains as Meghan ran along a familiar dirt road and up the hill above the railroad yards, compelled by an inexplicable sense of urgency. The urgency had grown stronger with each moment that had passed after Terry and Sean left the house after supper without a word.

Her mind steeped in the past, Meg remembered a dark night long ago when Sean awakened her from her sleep to drag her up this same hill. She remembered the excitement in his eyes when they crouched in a place of concealment and waited. She remembered the elation on his young face when a departing train below them was blown from the tracks. The sound of groaning metal was still clear in her ears, the bitter taste of fear still fresh in her mouth, as she relived the horror of the moment that was etched forever into her memory.

A short prayer escaping her lips, Meg climbed faster. She did not want to believe that Sean and Terry were no better than those men who had stumbled upon Sean and her as they made their escape from the scene of their heinous crime. She did not want to believe Sean and Terry could have the same coldness of death in their gaze that she had viewed in the eyes of those other men.

Meg reached the crest of the hill and looked down on the tracks below. The words she had overheard Sean whisper a few hours earlier resounded in her mind as the train rounded the curve and came into sight.

He'll be arrivin' on the evenin' train. We'll leave him the surprise he's deservin' . . .

Her mind argued that she was wrong, that the man Sean referred to was not someone who had been declared an enemy, that she would not see her brother and her husband this afternoon become heinous criminals who—

A sudden explosion rocked the air, stealing Meg's breath as the tracks below burst with flame, hurtling the racing locomotive from the tracks! As if in slow motion, Meg watched the train tumble, dragging the cars behind it like a giant wounded snake as it fell with a groan of tearing steel into the embankment below.

Clouds of billowing dust momentarily obscured her vision, but instinct compelled Meg forward the instant she saw motionless bodies lying on the ground where they had been thrown free of the train. Meg was suddenly running full speed toward the wreck. Slipping and sliding on the downward slant of the grassy terrain, she was breathless, crying, struggling to hold herself upright when she was suddenly swept from her feet by a strong arm. Gasping as a wide palm clamped across her mouth stifling her frightened scream, she struggled furiously as she was dragged behind an outcropping rock.

Managing to turn around, Meg met familiar brown eyes filled with unfamiliar fury, and she went suddenly still. She saw a second man crouched beside them the moment before his accusing blue eyes met hers.

"You couldn't stay out of it, could you, Meg? Well, now you know what Terry and I were plannin'! And if there's any luck in it, one of them fellas over there, bleedin' his life's blood into the ground, is the new mine superintendent!"

Terry's hand fell away from her mouth, but Meg emitted no sound. Aghast, she looked at him briefly before turning back to her brother.

"Don't you realize what you've done? You can't really believe you have the right to take a person's life just because he's a company man! Sean, think! If you don't care for the lives of others, then think of your own soul!"

"This is war, woman!" His face a bitter mask, Sean continued hotly. "I'll hear no more talk of my soul, and if you know what's good for you, you'll keep out of this and stay home where you belong!"

Her eyes transfixed on her brother's face, Meg saw his intense gaze shift to Terry. A look passed between them, and an inexplicable tremor shook her as Sean then drew himself to his feet, surveyed the area, and gave the signal to move on.

Silent through the whole exchange, Terry lifted Meg to her feet. Unable to do anything else as her husband gripped her hand firmly, Meg stumbled behind them as they made their escape.

Consciousness faded, then returned again, renewing the stabbing pain in David's head that dimmed his sight. He remembered a flash of light that was simultaneous with an ear-ringing blast, the sound of metal wheels abrading the track, and the groan of tearing steel as the world began tumbling around him. He remembered the pain as he hit the ground with a bone-shattering crack.

And he remembered seeing her.

The slender woman he had seen high on the hill when he first opened his eyes remained stationary at first. Then she burst into movement, stumbling down the mountainside toward him with headlong haste. She stopped as abruptly as she had started, and in that split second, with vision blurred by pain and settling dust, he had seen a mane of curling black hair and great silver-blue eyes staring directly at him.

Meg.

But she was gone again, and he could hear only the ring of male voices nearby and the crunch of footsteps moving cautiously through the grainy mist. He cried out, but there was no sound. With a supreme effort, he raised a hand to his pounding head. His fingers came away sticky with blood, and he groaned against his helplessness. Sound and light again began drifting away, and through the unreality, he was certain of only one thing.

He had seen her.

Taking care not to look directly at Meg, Terry gripped her hand more firmly as they approached the back door of the house. Maintaining his silence, he waited as Sean slipped cautiously into the kitchen, then reappeared to motion them inside.

He walked past Aunt Fiona where she stood in the corner of the room and followed Sean upstairs, pulling Meg behind as her step lagged. The door of the bedroom closed behind them at last, and Sean turned to Meg with obvious anger.

"I've no time to waste on words, except to say you've compromised Terry and me this afternoon with your interference. A job that was clean and free of complications can now rebound on us and on all the men waitin' at Muff Lawler's to give us an alibi."

When Meg averted her gaze, Sean commanded harshly, "Look at me, Meg! Do I have your word that you'll stay here in this room until you've gained enough control of your senses not to give us away?" At Meg's silence, he demanded, "Answer me!"

Terry's heart sank at the pain of Meg's response. "You have my word."

Urging him to follow, Sean turned to the door. Looking directly at Meg for the first time, Terry felt the full weight of her tormented gaze as she whispered, "How could you let him do this, Terry? You were supposed to watch over him for me. I trusted you."

Unable to respond, Terry slipped out into the hall and pulled the door closed behind him.

Minutes later at Lawler's saloon, drink in hand, Terry looked down at Sean where he struck a deceivingly casual stance at the bar beside him. His voice was heavy, his expression tight.

"Do ye despise me, Sean, for the deceit ye must practice on your own sister to keep me presence here secret?"

Raising his glass to his lips, Sean took a sip, pausing to swallow before he responded. "It's for my sake and for the sake of every self-respectin' Irishman as well as your own, and I don't deceive myself that it's anything else. Every man in the Brotherhood knew from the day you set foot in Shenandoah that you were wanted by the police in Ireland, and we knew the only way we could use your experience was to conceal your identity. We knew the torment you faced when you were forced to flee the old sod, and we considered ourselves lucky to have a man like you with us."

His expression flickering, Sean paused. His eyes narrowed as he continued in a softer tone. "But I admit I didn't expect I'd be protecting you from my own sister in the end. And now that you're bringing it all out in the open, I'm tellin' you that although you play the part well, I've spent many a night wonderin' why you condemned yourself to the pretense of bein' a man other than your true self in your own home. For that's what you'll be forced to do all of your life, if you expect to grow old as man and wife with my sister."

"If it makes ye feel any better, I feel less a man for lettin' ye take Meg's abuse when it's I who should be sufferin' her questions."

Sean shrugged, suddenly averting his gaze. "Meg is Meg. She's true to her convictions, and would've spoken the same no matter what part I played in the train wreck today. But the truth is, Meg'll forgive me anything, just as I'll forgive her. And for that reason, and the love she gives me, it stings that I've deceived her."

His spirit aching, Terry whispered, "It's not the way ye think, Sean. I'm thinkin' ye'll find it difficult to understand, but I'll try to explain, because ye have an explanation due ye."

Terry paused, grimacing as he searched for the right words. "Ye see, me heart was turned to stone in the old country. Hatred festered inside me for the landlords and all them that treated me family and our like no better than animals, killin' us with their greed. There was not a drop of pity left in me when I was finished watchin' me Ma and all of me six brothers and sisters taken by slow starvation and sickness while them same landlords raised their rents higher and higher. And all the time, them in power turned a blind eye and a deaf ear to the sufferin'."

Terry's heavy features hardened. "I buried 'em all, Sean. And then when they was gone and I had nobody but meself to worry about, I stood up like a man to make the bastards take notice. They knew me name, Sean. They knew that when I called the Brotherhood together, they couldn't hide behind their money anymore, because someone bearin' me message would find 'em out.

"And so the blood flowed, and I had not a single regret. Had it not been for an informer in the midst of it all, I'd still be there, doin' the work that need be done. I barely escaped the hangman's noose, but the truth is that when I made me way to this place, I carried the hope inside me that it would be different here in this 'land of plenty.'"

Terry's face hardened into familiar lines. "Plenty! Hah! Plenty for some, but precious little for them of us with a pick and shovel in our hands and coal dust on our faces. Aye, Sean, and when I saw the misery and the hunger was the same, and the sufferin' and dyin' of the babes and young ones still goin' on while no one cared, me frustration turned to blood rage."

Pausing, Terry took a deep breath and reached for his glass. He emptied it and turned back to Sean. "And then I met Meg. I didn't think I had it left in me, but make no mistake about it, I love the woman, Sean." Terry hesitated, his voice dropping a notch lower. "And the truth is, me heart's as pure as the driven snow when she's in me arms."

Pausing again, Terry continued. "Ye think I don't know that

Meg would never had married me if it hadn't been for ye, Sean, but I do. Funny, isn't it, that she thought to save ye by marryin' me, when it's I who's leadin' ye in the path she despises?"

Sean's eyes clouded. "Nay, you're wrong. Meg loves you."

"Aye, I believe she does, now. But I'm second to ye. I always will be."

Sean did not bother with denial, and Terry gave a short laugh. "The truth be known, I've slept many a night with yer sister in me arms and jealousy gnawin' at me, knowin' she'll never love me as much as she loves ye. And each time, I pulled her closer, knowin' she belongs to me and knowin' she chose me over all the others, and consolin' meself with the sheer luck of havin' her."

Terry laughed again, but there was little mirth in the sound. "So ye see, I'm two men, Sean. One who's sworn to fight to the death, and another who's sworn to love yer sister all of his life. And if the truth be known, both men are in trouble tonight, boyo. And you and I both have a way to go to redeem ourselves in Meg's eyes. I'm thinkin'—"

Halting abruptly, his head jerking toward a commotion outside the saloon door, Terry felt his warmer feelings drain away as young Chris O'Reilly burst through the doors with a shout.

"There's been a train wreck—an explosion on the tracks! The police are headed this way!"

Affixing a familiar facade, Terry concealed his true reaction to the boy's announcement with the aid of long practice. Dismissing Meg from his mind, he cast Sean a hard glance.

"Drink up, me boyo. We've a few hard hours ahead, but we can console ourselves that it's precious little to pay for the good work we've done today. With any luck, Gowen will be lookin' for a new mine supervisor soon, and if not, we've the consolation of knowin' that no coal will be travelin' on them tracks for a while. Aye, we've done good."

His gaze unblinking, Terry raised his glass to his lips.

Chapter 20

The conversation progressed in conservative tones, but David was having trouble concentrating. He knew that the vague sense of predestination he presently experienced would have been far sharper were his head not throbbing so incessantly. However, seated across from Franklin Gowen and Captain Linden in the study of Lang Manor where Uncle Martin had conducted so much of his mine business, David realized only too painfully that vague sensitivities were the least of his troubles.

Raising his hand to his forehead, David pressed his temple lightly and closed his eyes in an attempt to control the pain pulsing there. He had been delivered to Lang Manor semiconscious after the train wreck, and the progress of events after that was still unclear to him. He remembered awaking this morning in the master suite that Uncle Martin and Aunt Letty had once shared, to find himself surrounded by unfamiliar faces. Every bone in his body had ached—they ached still—but Dr. Hiram Wilson had introduced himself and assured him that, despite his discomfort, his injuries were minimal.

Unwilling to remain in bed to be inundated by fragmented memories of bursting light, tumbling cars, and a shadowed figure whose light blue eyes gave him no peace, he had made his way downstairs to find his present visitors at the door. His agitation controlled, Gowen had expressed his regrets at the infamous reception he had been accorded, and they had been seated in this room ever since.

Suddenly aware that the room had gone quiet around him, David opened his eyes to find himself the focus of attention.

"I apologize, David." Ben Gowen's aristocratic face bore a sincere expression of regret. "In our outrage against this incident, Captain Linden and I have been inconsiderate of your injuries."

Attempting a smile, David shook his head. The effort was a mistake that set his head to pounding with greater intensity as he strove for a coherent response. "My injuries are minor, a few cuts and bruises that are causing me momentary discomfort. I appreciate your concern and the time you took out of your busy schedule to extend your reassurances personally."

Gowen did not smile, and David had the feeling that the man had not a smile left in him. He supposed he couldn't blame him. The train wreck had made a difficult situation even worse in the valley, by tying up shipments at a time when enough miners had deserted the lingering strike to enable coal to be produced with reasonable regularity. He knew the interruption in rail service was a victory for the strikers and the Mollies, whether they were truly one group as Gowen claimed, or separate from each other as the strikers adamantly professed. But he was learning firsthand that Gowen was a fighter who did not flinch at the sight of blood.

"I have several reasons for my visit here today, David. Not the least of them was to pledge to you my continuing support in whatever tactics you plan to use to combat this situation. I find it personally repugnant that an intelligent man like yourself cannot embark on a project of importance in these coal fields without having an attempt made on his life. And I tell you now, I'm pledged to effect a change in the intolerable situation here."

David hesitated, his eyes intense as he considered that thought for the first time. "Do you really believe *I* was the target in the sabotage of the train?"

Gowen's response was unblinking. "Yes, I do. Support for the strike has been waning here. Finances are becoming tight for the miners and a symbolic gesture needed to be struck. I think the bloodthirsty bastards would have been far more satisfied if you were seriously injured or killed, but the interruption in rail service, as well as the personal setback your injuries will accomplish, will have the desired effect of instilling fear in the hearts of any other men who might have been considering returning to work."

David's jaw stiffened. "The setback will be of short duration."

"But I feel I should warn you, sir, that this probably will not be the end of it." Captain Linden's solemn interjection turned David's attention toward the big Scotsman as he continued in his characteristically level tone. "I've no doubt that you'll be closely watched, and your success here will depend on the attitude you display when you formally take over operation of the colliery."

The big policeman's warning stirred heated sparks of gold in David's eyes. "I'm no stranger to violence perpetrated by the

Mollies of this area, as you may recall, Captain, but the difference this time is that I'll be in a position to fight back."

"Aye, that may be a problem." Linden's face was grave. "If the Mollies don't feel they've instilled enough fear in you to make you malleable, they'll try again."

David's expression tightened further and Gowen interrupted their exchange. "The situation isn't as black as it's presently painted, David. We're winning here, you know. The strikers can't hold out much longer, and the days of the Mollies are limited."

Observing the interest his last comment evoked, Gowen added, "That isn't loose talk either, my boy. In view of the pressures under which you will be taking this position, I'm going to confide a secret I've told no one else."

Captain Linden's head jerked toward Gowen in spontaneous protest. "You're making a mistake, sir."

Gowen was obviously annoyed. "This is *my* decision. I trust this man, Captain. Our secret will be safe with him."

"The walls have ears, sir." The big man's reply echoed similar sentiments expressed to Martin Lang long ago, and David did not doubt that the policeman's words bore a note of truth. But Gowen was not dissuaded.

"I realize the staff here is new and will have to be appraised as to its loyalty, but David deserves reassurance." Addressing David directly, Gowen lowered his voice. "We have an operative in the Molly organization. He's a Pinkerton man who has been working effectively within the group for some time. He'll soon have enough evidence to decimate the heinous organization once and for all. Of course, his safety depends on our silence, and I will expect you to maintain this confidence."

"Of course, sir." David's head was throbbing more strongly than before, and he fought to maintain his concentration. His physical discomfort did not go unobserved by Gowen, who then drew himself to his feet.

Waiting until David and Linden stood as well, Gowen extended his hand. "I apologize again for keeping you this long, but I wanted to reassure myself that you were all right, David. It's my belief that your presence here will be the salvation of this mine and this area. We've not had an effective man here since your uncle sold the mine to me, and its future depends upon you, as do the futures of the very miners who will resent you the most. It was my thought that you might be feeling very alone here right now, injured as you are and surrounded by an unfamiliar staff. You've had a poor welcome, and in the hope that you'll continue to call this place your home, at least until you've satisfied yourself that you've beaten the problems here, I've arranged for the transfer of a block of Lang Colliery stock into your name."

Startled, David protested, only to have Gowen continue with a small smile. "It's not a gift, David. The transfer is effective under the condition that you remain in your present position for at least a year. You will earn each and every share."

Not allowing David to reply, Gowen turned toward the door. "Don't bother to see Linden and me out. A carriage is waiting to deliver me to Mahanoy City where I have some additional business to conduct. The captain will remain in Shenandoah to assist you in any way he can. Get some rest. Your first day in Shenandoah hasn't been a good one, but I have confidence that you'll change things to suit you."

Gowen paused, turning back to look directly into David's eyes. "You impressed me from the first day I met you, David, those years ago when you were still a boy. I saw reservations in your observance of me, a keen intelligence, and a determination—an arrogance, if I may use the word without your taking insult—that reminded me of myself at your age. Those attributes have served me well, and I know they'll serve you well, also. If you need me, don't hesitate to get in touch. Otherwise, I leave the rest to you and Captain Linden, with utmost confidence."

Standing in the foyer, David waited until the front door closed behind the two gentlemen before turning toward the staircase to the second floor. Bound for his bed and the powders Dr. Wilson had prescribed, David experienced new uncertainties, not the least of which stemmed from the implications involved with the thought that *he* had been a target in the train wreck.

As for the dubious compliment of being compared to Gowen in his youth, David was too weary to react.

"Tell me true, Sean! I want to know. Did you know all along that it was David Lang who was on that train?"

Catching Sean's arm as he walked through the front door, Meg ignored her husband as he entered behind, her mind intent on her brother's response.

His handsome face tightening with anger, Sean darted a quick look around the hallway as he grasped Meg's arm to pull her up the staircase with a warning glance. Halting only after the bedroom door had closed behind the three of them, Sean released her with a grunt of disgust.

"Has this whole affair addled your brains, Meg? Do you hope to give Terry and me away, after all? Empty bellies make the pay of an informer seem appealin' even to those you'd not suspect. Or did you forget that in your concern for David Lang?"

"Is it true, Sean?" Meg's eyes pleaded for a denial. "I want you to tell me if it's true."

"What difference does it make who was on that train?" Sean felt Terry tense behind him as he pressed on sharply. "A man's life is a man's life. Or do you value David Lang's life more highly than the lives of others? Is that it?" Sean's gaze narrowed. "Would you value his life over mine, Meg?"

Sean waited only until his sober query registered in his sister's eyes, before continuing in a lower tone. "You asked me for the truth, and here it is. It may yet come to a choice between him and me, Meg, and I pray you have the strength to make the right one."

When no response was forthcoming from his sister's still lips, Sean turned back to the door. The sound of it closing behind him reverberated in the silent room as Terry met Meg's empty stare.

Abed but unsleeping, Meg heard the sound of the doorknob turning the moment before the bedroom door swung slowly open. The clock on the dresser was not visible in the darkness of the room, but Meg sensed the lateness of the hour. Moving with a surprisingly light step for a man his size, Terry closed the door behind him, and within minutes slipped into the bed beside her.

Stiff and unmoving, Meg felt Terry's strong arm slip around her. His breath against her cheek was scented with spirits, but she knew it was not drink that had kept him from returning home. No, it was she, herself, who had driven him away with her silence. And her lack of remorse astounded her.

"Meg . . ." Terry spoke into her ear as he drew her back against him. His gentle brawn enveloped her, but the former peace of that haven had deserted her as she remained rigid in his arms. "Meg, I'm sorry, darlin'."

Turning abruptly to face him, Meg strained to read the blunt features of the man she had come to know so well. But did she really know him? Terry had lied to her, denied the plan he and Sean had been formulating laboriously the day long. Had she known that in her heart? Was that the reason she had instinctively questioned Sean instead of him?

"Oh, Terry—" The words escaped her lips in a surge of despair that caused Terry's arms to tighten compulsively around her. A shaft of moonlight illuminated his face as he moved, and she saw that his despair matched her own.

"Aye, Meg, it hurts to feel this strangeness between us. I've suffered for it the evening long and I've just gathered the courage to come home to face ye. I'll not lie to ye, Meg, for yer senses are keen and ye realize that there's much to me that ye did not suspect before. And I tell ye now, despite all the pain it gives us both, that there's much ye'll never know."

The coldness inside Meg grew. She attempted to withdraw from Terry's embrace, but he would not allow it, forcing her to speak the words she had avoided. "If you're not the man I married, Terry, who are you? What have you changed into?" And then in a flash of insight, "Or was all that went before a farce, with your true self now emerging?"

"Ask me no questions, Meg, and I'll tell ye no more lies. I can only tell ye this, me darlin' Meg. The man who loved ye, loves ye still. The man who swore to cherish ye and care for ye all of his life, still swears the same. None of that has changed, and it never will."

"But—"

"There are no buts, Meg, and to show ye that I mean all I say, I'll not ask from ye what I'm not prepared to give in return. I'll not ask what David Lang meant to ye once, or means to ye now. And while I pledge me love to ye, I pledge something else as well." A new fervor entered Terry's rasping tone. "Sean made no excuses for what he did and neither will I, either for me lies or for me part in the train wreck, except to say that this *is* war. I'm a soldier, Meg. When me and mine are threatened, I depend on me instinct to get me through. So, I tell ye now, whatever David Lang was to ye, if he stands in the way, he'll go down."

Meg made no response to Terry's cold, flat statement, experiencing a sense of unreality as Terry's mouth descended to cover hers with a deep, loving kiss. She heard the threat in his voice, as well as the love, as he declared in a whisper, "Yer mine, Meg. I'll never let ye go."

Chapter 21

Meg finished speaking and Sheila averted her face, avoiding the scrutiny of her friend's clear blue eyes. The sound of their footsteps echoed hollowly against the boardwalk, emphasizing the unusual quiet and lack of activity on Main Street as they walked side by side. Sheila knew the town's silence was deceiving. It hid the turmoil seething beneath the surface calm since the train wreck two days earlier. Wary, the residents of Shenandoah had heard one shoe drop. With long experience in matters of violence and retribution, they waited for the other shoe to fall.

But Meg and she were not amusing themselves today, glancing in shop windows and passing the time in casual conversation as they had many times before. The silence between them grew uneasy, and Sheila looked up at the blue sky overhead, allowing herself momentary respite in the graceful wisps of clouds artfully stretched against the endless blue and in the heat of the sun's rays against her strong shoulders. She was barely twenty-one, but her Ma had accusingly pointed out a gray hair amongst the blond strands that morning, and accustomed as she was to all forms of her Ma's nagging at her spinsterhood, she had been unable to dismiss it.

The silence between her and Meg lengthened as Sheila automatically shortened her stride to match her friend's. Glancing toward her, Sheila recalled the many times she had envied Meg's petite stature, her gleaming dark curls and flawless skin. And those shining O'Connor eyes. She loved her friend all the more for them, while suffering from jealousy as well.

But Sheila had long ago come to terms with her heavy straw-colored hair that refused to curl, with skin that freckled with the first touch of the sun, and common features that laid little claim to beauty. She consoled herself that she had grown into a full-bodied woman, ample without being obese in the areas that gave pleasure to a man.

She was healthy and strong, built to bear many children, and she knew it was only her visits to Ita McFee, started early on in her loving affair with Sean, that had saved her. Most said the woman was a witch and would have nothing to do with her, but Sheila knew better. Liberal use of the woman's herb brews and salves had saved her from bearing physical proof of her alliance with Sean, but that knowledge was a bitter victory, indeed. That last thought caused her a familiar pang of despair, and Sheila glanced at Meg once more. It occurred to her, not for the first time, that they loved the same man dearly, if in different ways, and while both were dedicated to his welfare, they could agree on little concerning him.

Growing uncomfortable with the silence between them, Sheila offered Meg a reluctant smile and an admission.

"You're right, Meg. I know you are. And so's my Ma."

Sheila followed behind as Meg turned off Main Street toward the path that would eventually separate them, bringing Meg to her residence and Sheila to the small patch house where she still lived with her parents. Sheila was taken aback by the unexpected intensity in Meg's gaze as she turned toward her abruptly when out of view of the street.

"Aye, I'm right, Sheila. You've known I'm right all along, but for all these long years you've done little more than remain at Sean's beck and call." Unexpected tears turning her eyes to liquid silver, Meg grasped Sheila's arm with a fierce grip. "It's not a lack in you that's at fault, Sheila. If Sean could truly love anyone, I know it would be you. I've always known something happened to Sean when Da and the boys died, that something died inside him as well, but it's more than that now. It's a sickness that affects the way he thinks and the things he does. It won't allow him to love."

"But he loves you, Meg."

"Aye, he loves me." Meg spoke the words, knowing the heavy burden in that truth. "But that love was fixed deep inside him before his heart turned cold. You don't know the things I know, Sheila, the things I can't reveal. If you did—"

"I know more than you think." Her words emerging past the thick lump in her throat, Sheila pushed a strand of hair back from her face, realizing that she was beginning to perspire although the day was only pleasantly warm. Her voice dropped a notch softer. "I know about the meetings Sean attends over at Muff Lawler's saloon. I know he feels a satisfaction far greater than any he can receive in my arms when he does the bidding of the group gathering there. I know he's dedicated his life to the hatred he carries inside him, and should he die tomorrow while getting his revenge, his only regret would be leaving you."

Sheila paused, forcing back the sob rising in her throat as she spoke her next words. "And I also know Sean will never marry me."

"Oh, Sheila—"

"But you mustn't pity me, Meg." Her sudden lack of color belying her stiff smile, Sheila continued. "I knew the direction my love for Sean was taking me from the beginning. Sean was honest with me, you see. He warned me from the first of all that you've said now, and I accepted his terms."

"Why, Sheila?" Meg's tortured expression cut Sheila deeply, and a great swell of compassion rose within her as Meg continued raggedly. "You were made for a full life—to be a wife and a mother. You mustn't spend your youth on Sean with no promise for the future. There're men who would look favorably on you if you'd but give the nod. Charlie McGee, Willie Clancy—good, honest men."

"But none of them are Sean." Sheila shook her head, her anxiety rising. "Ah, Meg, can't you see? I saw that first seed of darkness take root inside Sean. And when it started to grow, my love for him didn't change. Oh, there were times when I thought I'd had enough for sure, and I sought to turn my back on him. But you know as well as I that it didn't work. I only ended up hurting the fellas I encouraged, and then had to swallow my pride even more than in the past when I begged Sean to take me back."

Sheila's eyes filled with the deep sincerity of her words. "He's the only man for me, Meg. One glance from Sean and my heart flutters. One smile and the fluttering takes wing. One kiss, and I know I could never truly turn away from him, no matter what the future holds." Sheila's chin dropped as she hesitated briefly, but she raised it again with determination. "I know the darkness inside him is growing, but when Sean holds me in his arms, he's loving, not hating. I'm thinking it's his only chance against the sickness of his soul."

Pausing again, Sheila glanced away, only to return her gaze to Meg more fervently than before, her voice a whisper. "And I made the decision long ago, Meg, that if Sean's path closes the gates of heaven to him forever, I'd at least have given him joy here, on earth. So it's all up to me, you see."

"What's up to you?"

"To make it good enough for Sean now to last for eternity."

"Sheila . . ."

Meg started to cry, and Sheila rubbed her friend's shoulder comfortingly as she had done when they were children.

"And if you're thinking that I'm making myself a martyr for Sean's sake, believe me when I say it's not so. For, you see, I've taken what I want from life. And what I want is Sean."

"But will you regret this, Sheila? Will there come a day when you'll hate Sean and yourself for—"

"Never."

With her short, unequivocal response, Sheila dropped her hand back to her side. "Don't worry for me, Meg. I've my eyes open and I'm as content as I will ever be. And maybe between the two of us, we'll yet turn that handsome brother of yours around."

"Aye, maybe we will."

The lack of conviction in Meg's brave response more than she could bear, Sheila turned toward the patch, further speech beyond her.

Meg watched Sheila walk away with her head held high, her fair hair swinging against her erect shoulders, but the image blurred as the injustice of it all returned the heat of tears to Meg's eyes. Willing away her weakness, Meg found herself following the road home, when the thought struck her that she was in no condition to face inquiring eyes.

Continuing past the house where Aunt Fiona's silent scrutiny awaited her, where Uncle Timothy's hawklike stare would fasten on her temporary weakness to use it to his advantage, where she ran the risk of encountering Terry and Sean if they had returned from their secretive early-morning trip, Meg unconsciously sought a haven that had once given her comfort in similar times of despair.

The towering breaker and its mountainous dumps of cinder and slag behind her, Meg started up the overgrown path she had used as a child. Sean's part in the train wreck two days earlier had forced her tense conversation with Sheila, but Meg now realized the uselessness of her endeavor. She knew now that Sheila was as wed to Sean in her mind as she was wed to Terry by the church, and that Sheila would stick with Sean to the end, wherever that led him.

A spot of shame stirred inside Meg. She knew the distance that had come between Terry and herself since the train wreck was her fault, but she could not seem to come to terms with his deceit. The thought haunted her that if her husband was not the man she thought him to be, she did not truly know him at all.

And through it all, Meg realized that the turmoil in her life again revolved around the arrival of David Lang.

Briefly closing her eyes, Meg heard the name reverberate in her mind. *David Lang. David* . . . She had not even seen him, and her life had already begun coming apart again.

Word had spread quickly through town that the colliery would be run by a true Lang again, and that although injured in the train wreck, David would be on the job in a few days. Sean had not taken the news lightly and Terry—

The ache inside Meg deepened. True to his word, Terry had not pressed her about David, but she knew rumors had been rife at the time of David's departure five years earlier, and that David's return had stirred speculation that would reach her husband's ears. She knew she had done little to ease the situation, but the truth was that although Terry had shown little change in his loving consideration of her, his warmth left her cold. His resentment of that coldness went unspoken, but she could not help but feel that the arms clutching her close each night had begun to reflect stubborn possession more than love.

The intense rays of the sun soothed the chill of Meg's torment as she climbed the hillside, gradually becoming aware of the sweet scent of new growth that permeated the air, the freshness of the warm breeze, the sense of freedom that had originally drawn her to this hill when similarly disturbed as a child.

A few steps more and Meg found herself in a familiar leafy bower overlooking the valley, and she breathed deeply. Honeysuckle. Her eyes misted as she remembered the young girl who had fearfully scrambled out of sight to hide within those fragrant branches. Dropping to her knees, she saw that over the years the violet bed had made inroads into the carpet of moss beneath the trees; but there was little other visible change. It was still lovely and peaceful, and Meg found herself wishing, as she had once before, that the whole world could be as beautiful as this spot. That the serenity of this place could—

Suddenly freezing into stillness, Meghan attempted to identify an unexpected sound nearby. Footsteps approaching on the trail!

A familiar sense of panic ensuing, Meg stood up, holding her breath as the sound drew closer. Darting a glance at the honeysuckle bush to her rear as the footsteps neared, Meg briefly closed her eyes. Memories overwhelmed her. She had been a child those years ago, and frightened beyond belief that she would be found trespassing. She was frightened again, this time for a reason she could not define.

Stepping unexpectedly into sight, as if materializing out of memory, David Lang suddenly stood before her. Unable to speak, Meghan returned his stare, noting with silent distress that David limped as he took a few steps toward her, and that fresh bruises marked his forehead and cheek. Hard muscle and sinew had replaced the thinness of youth, and strength and character was now etched into the lines of his handsome face, but he had otherwise changed very little from the day she had first met him in this secluded spot. Even the frigidity of his gaze was the same, and the coldness froze her heart.

"So it *was* you that I saw on the hill above the wreck." David broke the silence between them with a harsh statement that was unexpected, sending her an unconscious step backwards as he continued accusingly. "When my mind cleared, I tried to convince myself that I had imagined seeing you running down the hill after the train wreck, because there was no explanation for your being there other than the most obvious one—that you were on that hill waiting for the explosion. Damn you! You were a part of it, weren't you!"

"No, I wasn't!"

"I saw you! You ran toward me, and then you disappeared. You wouldn't have left if you didn't have something to hide."

"I . . . I saw the wreck and wanted to help. Then I thought someone might think it was suspicious that I was there, so I ran away."

His gaze reflecting disbelief, David laughed harshly. "You never did lie very well, Meg."

Suddenly closing the distance between them, David grasped her arms and shook her hard. The years slipped away at his touch, blending old pain with new as David's rage abruptly fled. His expression softened with his agonized question, "What have you turned into, Meg? Are you one of *them* now?"

David's fingers burned into her skin, and Meg could feel herself paling as she whispered, "You never wanted to believe it, but I was always one of *them* from the valley, David."

"And you never wanted to admit that you were different than most of the rabble below."

Meg was assailed by a familiar pain. "The difference you saw was in your mind."

"Was it?" David's face stiffened and his hands dropped from her arms. "Then why do I see regret in your face? Why did you wince when you saw me limp, and why do you look at the bruises on my face as if they pain you?" David's voice dropped a notch lower. "And why do I see tears in your eyes, Meg?"

"Oh, David."

Bridging the years between them with one step forward, Meg slipped her arms around David's waist, a low sob escaping her throat as she lay her head against his chest. David's arms closed around her and his warmth spread to expand within her as he whispered against her hair. "I wondered if it would still feel the same when I held you in my arms." He paused. "I missed you, Meg."

Stiffening, Meg drew back from his embrace. Her withdrawal was more than physical as she wiped the tears from her face.

"I'm sorry, David. I was so relieved to see that you're all right. I didn't know you were on the train that day. I . . . I saw the explosion and ran toward the train without thinking. Then I saw others coming to help and decided it would be best if I didn't get involved. But if I had known you were lying there injured I wouldn't have left."

David's gaze searched her face. Suffering under his scrutiny, Meg attempted a smile. "But that's all in the past now, isn't it? You're here now and you're mending well. And I'm glad to see you, David."

"Are you, Meg?" Agitated flecks of gold stirred to life in David's pensive gaze. Grasping her hand, he clutched it tightly as she sought to withdraw it. "Then come home with me now. You can have dinner with me. We have so much to talk about—years to span."

Meghan forced a smile. "Thank you, David, but I can't. I have to go home. It's almost dinnertime and Aunt Fiona will be expecting me."

"I'll send someone to tell your aunt you have other plans. Your uncle will be glad to have one less at his table."

Forcing herself to hold his gaze without flinching, Meg responded. "It's not my aunt who'll miss my presence there. My husband—"

"Husband!"

Closing her mind to David's shocked dismay, Meg maintained

her smile by sheer strength of will. "Aye, Terry Donovan. He's new to the valley—here just two years. He's a fine man."

Her hand slid from David's grasp, and Meg swallowed tightly. Gathering her courage, she asked, "Have you brought a wife with you to the manor, David? The old place could use a bit of life."

His eyes growing ominously cold, David shook his head. His delayed response was filled with the anger and pain of long, absent years.

"You never forgave me for being a Lang, did you, Meg? No, I haven't brought a wife back with me, because the sad truth is that I was never able to love any woman but you."

Motionless as David turned abruptly and left her, Meg listened to the echo of his retreating footsteps. With a sinking heart she realized that the sound of his step on the path had brought David into her life, and that same sound now signaled their final separation.

Crow's feet marked the outer corners of Jack Kehoe's piercing blue eyes, and there was an occasional gray strand amidst his full head of dark hair, beard, and mustache. He was a big man, athletic and erect, and Sean realized the "King of the Mollies" had changed very little since the day he had first seen him years ago.

Seated around the table in Kehoe's living quarters upstairs from his Girardsville saloon, a full glass provided for all, Sean saw present were Danny Canning, Tom Donohue, Tim Clark, Dan Dougherty, Michael O'Brien, and numerous other division bodymasters and officials with whom he was not well acquainted. At times like this the memory of Lenny Dunne returned full force, and his friend's death two years earlier in a mine accident stung as deeply as if it were yesterday. Terry had arrived in Shenandoah a short time later to fill the void of Lenny's loss, but Sean had not forgotten Lenny. Neither had he avenged his friend's death to his satisfaction—but he knew he would.

Kehoe surveyed the men around him and Sean noted unconsciously that Jack Kehoe was not as tall a man as he had first believed. But although the "King" was dwarfed by Terry's massive size, Sean knew the power of the man had nothing to do with physical proportions. For as he talked, there was death in Kehoe's eyes.

First on the agenda was Bully Boy Thomas.

Kehoe's level tone belied the import of his words as he began. "I'm troubled over the bad state of affairs in Mahanoy City. I was there a couple of days ago and the Modocs are raisin' mischief."

Aware of Kehoe's hatred of the Welsh group that was so active against their own, Sean felt his apprehension growing as Kehoe continued. "At first I thought I'd call a county meetin', give the boys pistols, and challenge the Modocs to a fight. We'd shoot them down in daytime. Then we'd find out who was boss. But on second thought I didn't like that idea."

Jack Kehoe paused again, and Sean knew he was just blowing off steam because he was too smart to show his hand so openly. Everyone knew that Kehoe hated Bully Boy. The big Modoc's personal vendetta to avenge a Molly assassination Brother Dougherty had accomplished held Dougherty's life in jeopardy. Going unspoken was the knowledge that there was a need to keep the Molly organization strong by permanently settling the matter to the Mollies' satisfaction, for anything less would be to show a position of weakness that they could not afford.

A gleam in his eye, Kehoe continued. "I've decided to open the matter to the floor."

A vigorous exchange followed, but Sean kept his silence, satisfied to have Terry speak for their group. A short glance toward Jim McKenna revealed his reaction was the same.

"Shoot the bastard in broad daylight, right on Center Street in Mahanoy City—in front of everybody!"

A derisive snort from O'Brien tabled O'Leary's suggestion as he made one of his own. "There's only one way to do this right. A pair of shooters lyin' in wait for him on the side of the railroad tracks near Bully Boy's home in Shoemaker's Patch, just east of town."

"Aye, that's right. We'll get him fine, then!"

The round of approval that followed saw the suggestion accepted, but Kehoe's expression remained grave as he spoke again.

"There's somethin' else to be made clear here today. The strike's lost." Protests sounded around the table but Kehoe shook his head. "It's plain to see that the men have had enough. They'll last no more than a month more, and then go crawlin' back on their empty bellies, and so we've a chance to make the bastard Modoc's death mean more than it's truly worth. Timing is the thing, me boyos. I want to see Bully Boy hit the dust no more than two weeks after the men have settled back into the shafts. Molly's sons will be renewed then, and we can go from there with full strength."

Waiting only until the silent nods demonstrated general agreement, Kehoe added, "And there's the matter of a rumored informer in the ranks." The threat in his gaze deepening at the mumbles of concern, Kehoe continued. "But the bastard'll not be there long, for we'll find him out like we did every other. And we'll take care of him. Of that ye can be sure."

Straightening his shoulders as the men began showing signs of restlessness, Kehoe continued in a lower tone. "We've one last item of business to conclude." Kehoe looked slowly around the table, halting abruptly on the three from Shenandoah. Sean felt the heat of those small blue eyes burn him as Kehoe stated flatly, "Bully Boy belongs to yer group, me boyos. Get it done, and make a clean job of it."

The momentary silence that followed was broken by Terry's nod and the sound of scraping chairs as the men prepared to slip out of the room as secretly as they had come.

Meeting Terry's gaze, Sean saw silent determination there, and he knew in that instant that the job was as good as done.

Chapter 22

The month of June arrived with a formidable taste of the summer to come, and the people of the valley suffered the early heat wave with little respite. Stripped to the shirtwaist although it was early morning, David looked out the colliery office window. The physical marks of his injuries had faded in the few weeks since the train wreck, but David was keenly aware that in his mind he had not progressed a step beyond that short, unexpected meeting on the hillside shortly afterward.

With disgust, David recalled the excuses that his mind had invented for his decision to accept Gowen's offer to return to Shenandoah. Unfinished business—his need to come to terms with his past in order to face his future. Rot! Now master of Lang Manor, standing at the same window through which he had viewed the colliery countless times with his uncle, he could no longer deny that his true reason for returning was Meg.

His fateful inclination to walk that familiar hillside path despite his physical discomforts had seemed impulse at first. His first glimpse of the mature Meg, more beautiful than he could have imagined, had aroused painfully confusing emotions. Now, a few weeks later, the confusion was gone but the pain remained.

He had not seen Meg since then, although his thoughts never strayed far from her. Days and nights during which he had sought to rationalize his feelings had only convinced him that the effort was futile. The whisper of an old torment that he had heard in Meg's voice during their brief meeting resounded in his dreams, and he ached to assuage it. With great difficulty, he had finally admitted to himself that he was vulnerable to Meg in a way he was to no other woman—that Meg and he shared an intangible bond which transcended the years they had been apart. More difficult to acknowledge had been the realization that he still loved her.

But Meg had married someone else.

That reality inescapable during the long empty nights recently past, he had finally managed to save his sanity with the determination that while he knew he could never be totally happy without Meg, he would be content if Meg had truly found the right man to make her life complete.

If . . .

David ran an anxious hand through his heavy dark hair, aware that he was perspiring more heavily than the heat of the day warranted. Damn, he loved Meg. Why couldn't she have waited? Why couldn't she—

The shrill blast of the colliery whistle interrupted David's thoughts and he frowned unconsciously at the thickening line of miners reporting for the first shift. The second piercing blast had little effect on the miners' pace, and David was aware, as he focused his attention more intently upon them, that for all intents and purposes, it was again business as usual now that the strike had ended.

The dismal failure of the strike and the knowledge that the miners had returned to work on Gowen's terms had given him little satisfaction, despite his disagreement with the tactic. The strike had been a mistake from the first. Ignorant men with hotheaded leaders were too easily duped into thinking their uncomfortable situation was the fault of others rather than themselves. The strike had garnered its just reward, although he did not believe he had seen the last of the hard feelings resulting from it.

The informal line of miners below him swelled as David perused their number intently. In their miner's caps and grayed clothing, appearing to feel little discomfort in their heavy gear despite the heat of the day, they all looked alike, and it was difficult to tell one man from the other.

The whistle shrieked again and David's attention was caught by a large man within the final group making its approach. The fellow's face was indiscernible in the shadow of the cap he wore, but his unusual size easily identified him as Terry Donovan, and David's heart began a slow pounding. A vague satisfaction registered inside him as the man looked up, boldly returning his stare. Walking at his side, Sean O'Connor glanced up as well, but David refused to allow the hatred in those eyes so similar to Meg's to affect him.

Within a few moments both men had turned toward the transportation lifts to the shafts, but the face of Terry Donovan remained in David's mind as he turned back to his desk and the mountains of work awaiting him. There was something in the man's common face that left David uneasy; something in his eyes that did not quite fit the opinion generally held of him.

Aware that his feelings for Meg could easily color his reaction to the man, David forced his mind to the many duties awaiting him. Progress reports, ore evaluations, shipping schedules, reviews of supply contract conditions—work that had fallen behind with the former superintendent's abrupt departure—had kept him working long into the night since he had formally assumed control of operations. David lowered himself into his chair, and picked up the nearest folder. At the sound of a knock on the door, Captain Linden appeared.

Immediately on his feet, David waited only until Linden walked into the room before pushing the door closed behind him. Unconsciously noting that the man's blue uniform was properly buttoned up to the throat despite the uncomfortable weather, he frowned. Linden was a policeman to the core.

Wasting little time on amenities, David viewed the captain's characteristically dour expression with a short, "Well, it's about time."

"I apologize for the delay, sir, but I needed to confirm a few things with Mr. Gowen before responding to your request."

Irritation tightened the lines of strain on David's face. "Mr. Gowen instructed you to assist me in any way I asked. I see no need for you to check back with him on every request I make."

The big policeman did not appear to be affected by David's annoyance. "It's not a question of your authority, sir." Linden's thick features drew into a frown as he continued in a softer tone. "But a man's life is at risk—a good man's life—and I don't take my responsibility to protect it lightly."

"I asked for a simple report."

"There's nothing simple about a report on the men you asked about, sir."

David was beginning to become angry. "Are you saying you suspect my motives?"

"No, sir, not for a minute." A faint smile touched Linden's lips. "If you'll pardon my candor, sir, I was in your uncle's confidence. I'm not ignorant of his worries about your friendship with the O'Connor girl. She's a good girl, a credit to her father, and I've no doubt it's concern for her that's caused your inquiry. It's the depth of that concern that left me wary."

"My personal life is none of your business, Captain!"

Linden's small eyes challenged him directly. "Aye, it is, when it comes to the request you made of me." Captain Linden gave the room a quick assessing glance. "I'm uncomfortable having this conversation here, where too many can wander in to overhear what we say, so I've taken the precaution of stationing two good men outside the door, if you've no objection to that, sir."

"Do you think that's necessary?"

"Aye, I do." The knot in David's stomach tightened as Linden continued after a brief pause. "I've not written a report for fear of its slipping into the wrong hands, so I must deliver it orally."

His patience fast deteriorating, David responded tightly. "Give me the report any way you prefer, Captain. Just get on with it!"

"Aye, sir. I'm thinking that what I've to say about Sean O'Connor is no surprise to you. He's a Molly, all right. We estimate he's been in the organization four or five years, and we know for a fact that he's been involved in every major aggressive move the Mollies have made in this area during the last two or three years. He's generally accepted to be a bitter fellow with a taste for vengeance who does not make friends easily. The death of his closest friend in a cave-in two years ago only seemed to make things worse."

Captain Linden paused, and continued with a tightening frown. "He's one of the men responsible for blowing up the train that brought you here. Word was leaked that the new supervisor was arriving on it and the decision was made that since the strike was going poorly, a gesture was needed to keep the men in line."

A muscle ticked in David's cheek. "Is this all conjecture, or do you have proof?"

"It's not conjecture, sir, but fact. But we have no proof, as yet."

"As yet?"

"We need a bit more time—which brings us to the second report you requested."

The hackles rose on David's spine as the silence lengthened. "Out with it, man! What about Donovan?"

His reluctance obvious, Captain Linden began quietly. "Terry Donovan's real name is Terry McGillis. He was a high official in the Ribbonmen in Ireland—a real bad one, sir. He made the mistake of becoming too well known, and was finally forced to flee. He was able to get bogus papers and he entered the country as Terry Donovan. Shortly after coming to Shenandoah he joined the organization here. He replaced the current bodymaster after the first six months because of the high regard Jack Kehoe holds for him, and he's been at the head of the organization ever since."

"Was he involved in the train wreck?"

"He planned it and helped O'Connor put the plan into effect, sir."

"I knew it!" David's carefully suppressed fury soaring, he turned and walked toward the window in an attempt to avoid Linden's assessing stare.

Captain Linden's next words attained startling impact in the silence of the room. "Well, if you knew it, sir, you're in rare company. Everything I just told you about Donovan is a secret from most—even his wife."

David turned back with a snap to face Linden. "How do you know that? How do you know any of this is really true? Maybe it's all a story concocted by your agent in order to extort money from you."

"Nay, our agent is one of Pinkerton's finest. He's taken his life in his hands to do this work. He's been working in the Shenandoah division long enough to have gained the confidence of the men there, but it's another thing entirely to obtain physical evidence on such a wary group. But we're thinking that it'll only be a few more months before we're able to take most of the men down."

David gave a short laugh. "And during that time you'll allow business as usual—the violence, the murders . . ."

"We foil them whenever we can, sir, but we can't put our agent at risk. We need to be patient—and I'm asking you to be patient a little longer too, sir—and to be careful not to repeat a word of what I've just told you. O'Connor's involvement is common knowledge, and he's done his best work by fronting for Donovan. In truth, Donovan's pleasant enough to speak to, and well-liked in general. It's common opinion that he's a steadying influence on Sean, and I'm thinking that's the most ironic part of Donovan's secret. But it's crucial to our agent's safety that Donovan's identity remain a secret until he's ready to reveal it."

Captain Linden's point was well taken, and David could not fault him. But he *could* resent the man's discerning eye and his unrelenting appraisal. He had had enough.

"Thank you, Captain." Sober, David extended his hand. "You may rest assured I'll keep everything you've said in mind. Your agent is under no threat from me."

David watched the door close behind Captain Linden, feeling little satisfaction at having his suspicions about Terry Donovan confirmed. For Terry Donovan was Meg's husband, and the same "ifs" remained. *If* Meg loved Terry Donovan, *if* she had found the man to make her life complete, and *if* she was truly happy as his wife, he had no choice in what he must do.

Breakfast had been served and eaten, the dishes gathered and washed, and Meg was presently involved in stacking them carefully away for the next meal. Turning a glance toward Aunt Fiona, where she carried the last of the freshly baked bread to the pantry for storage, Meg noted that she was already limping although the day had barely begun. And she knew that while her aunt worked on her swollen, throbbing legs, Uncle Timothy was still upstairs, sleeping off the result of a long evening at Murphy's saloon.

Meg averted her gaze as her aunt turned back toward her, her frustration deepening. Aunt Fiona's life was her own, and Meg knew she need remember that it was not her place to advise her aunt, especially now that her own personal life was in such a turmoil.

Her face flaming, Meg remembered the deliberation with which she had turned away from Terry the previous night when he sought to take her in his arms. The evidence of his passion had been only too obvious, but no matter his tenderness toward her, she was unable to forget the darker side of him she had glimpsed only briefly. The reality was that her dear Terry was two men. That one of those men was a stranger, numbed her.

Unwilling to face her thoughts a moment longer, Meg forced a smile to her lips. "I'll be going outside for a while if you won't be needing me, Aunt."

"Be off with ye, m'dear. The work's done for a few hours, and I'm thinkin' I'll be raisin' me old legs and relaxin' a bit."

Realizing her aunt's statement had been made for the benefit of her peace of mind, Meg allowed it to go unchallenged. Walking through the back doorway into the yard, Meg paused to look up at the brilliant sky overhead as she tucked a straying wisp back into the coil wound atop her head. Not a cloud in the sky or a breath of air to provide relief from the moisture-laden air that had lain against her skin from the moment of awakening. It would be a long, hot day, and although only just into June, her Ma would have labeled it one of the "dog days" of summer.

That thought briefly restored Meg's smile as she remembered her confusion at the term when she had first heard it as a child.

And she remembered the serious expression on Sean's youthful face as he had patiently explained. "Ma means that it's days like this that dogs go mad in the streets, Meg, from the sheer discomfort of it all." And then as her eyes had widened with fear, his hasty, childish reassurance, "But you needn't worry yourself, for we've no dog to be so affected."

Realizing his reassurance had done little to ease her anxiety, Sean had then leaned down with all the confidence of his seven years to whisper, "Come on, buck up, Meg. I'm a match for any dog in the patch that might turn his eye on you. I'll take care of you. You're my sister, after all."

She had slipped her hand into Sean's then, and through the long hot days of that summer, while the fear had remained fresh in her mind, his hand had always been close by.

The smile faded from Meg's lips. Aye, she was Sean's sister, after all.

Meg walked out into the yard to look at the first sprouts emerging from the neat rows she had planted a few weeks earlier. She had started a small garden in an isolated corner of the yard when her time at McCall's had been cut, and she had found a surprising comfort in the chore. Under the clear blue canopy of the sky with the sun beating on her head and her hands working in the warm, moist dirt, she had found herself feeling a bit closer to her Ma. She was certain her Ma could see her more distinctly then, looking down from the heavenly kingdom where she now resided, and she felt her Ma could hear her more clearly when she spoke.

Kneeling now beside the even rows, Meg picked out the sprouting weeds, inevitably stronger than her struggling seedlings. Despair nudged at her mind and she looked up at the sky again. In her mind she saw her Ma's sweet face within the endless blue, and the words her mind spoke came straight from the heart.

I've not been able to deter Sean from the path of vengeance, no matter what I've tried, Ma. My concern's turned him against me of late. He's been closer to Terry than myself for the past few weeks, and I'm uncertain where that'll lead. I need to hear your voice in my ear, Ma. I need you to tell me what to do. Ah, Ma—Meg's throat tightened with emotion—*I need you to send me the answer. I need to hear you speak my name.*

The absolute silence that followed her silent plea was broken with a single word.

"*Meg.*"

Gasping, Meg raised her head in the direction of the sound. Her shocked gaze focused on David's face as he stepped into sight, and she stumbled to her feet, her voice an incredulous whisper.

"Wh . . . what are you doing here, David?"

"I've been asking myself that same question, Meg. The only thing I know is that there's already been too much time spent in anger between us. I want to talk to you and put all the bad feelings to rest. I want there to be peace between us."

Meg glanced around the empty yard, her heart pounding with the knowledge that there was no safety from prying eyes and wagging tongues despite the privacy provided by the fencing surrounding them.

"Please go, David. We have nothing to discuss, and your coming here can only cause trouble."

"Meg . . ." Anxiety was apparent in David's gaze. "Please. I'd like to be your friend."

"No one would understand a friendship between us, David."

"I won't leave until you talk to me, Meg."

"David, please!" Beginning to feel the onset of panic, Meg looked around her again. "It's far too dangerous for you to be here. You must leave now."

David's gaze searched her face as he whispered, "I didn't come here to cause trouble, Meg. There's been enough of that."

"But if Terry or Sean see you—"

"You should have waited, Meg!" Sudden anger flushed David's face. "You should've known I'd come back for you!"

"What difference would it have made if I had, David?" Meg's gaze implored him. "Nothing's changed except the gulf between us has widened with you now in charge of the colliery. You're the enemy now, even more than you were before."

"I'm no one's enemy! I came back here to straighten out the affairs of the colliery for the betterment of all involved."

Meg impaled him with her gaze. "Did you really, David?"

Anguish clearly visible in his handsome face, David broke the prolonged silence that followed with a softly spoken, "No." Still holding her gaze intently, he continued with obvious determination. "But if there's to be complete honesty between us, there are some things I must say. I love you, Meg. I didn't realize it at the time, but I *did* come back to Shenandoah hoping to find you again. You found your way into my heart a long time ago. When you wrenched yourself away from me, you took a part of it with you."

Meg paled. "These are wasted words, David. I'm married now!"

"Wait, Meg, let me finish. Let me at least do this for you. Let me warn you that your brother is in danger."

The shock of his unexpected words reverberated through Meg's body as David continued. "The police have been watching him, Meg. They know he's working with the Molly Maguires. They don't have anything definite on him yet, but it's only a matter of time until they do. If you want to save him, you'll tell him to get out of the coal fields. He can go out West, change his name, and start over."

"He'll never do that."

"If he stays, he'll be caught, Meg."

"No, don't tell me any more, please." Trembling, Meg looked up into David's impassioned face. "I owe you this much truth in return, David, so I'll tell you now that I love you, too. I suppose I always will. I've suffered endless regrets for letting you leave in bitterness those years ago, and I want to do it right this time. So I'll say the only thing I can to you now, and I'll say it with love. Goodbye . . . my dear David."

Her bittersweet smile all the more beautiful for its brevity, Meg suddenly turned and walked back toward the house. She did not see David staring after her, rooted to the spot by the futility of protest. And as her footsteps faded, she did not see reflected in his eyes the end of a dream.

Meg still had not recuperated from her encounter with David earlier in the day. Closing the kitchen door behind her, she walked toward the street, uncertain of her destination. Everything was changing—Sean, Terry, and the life she had so carefully constructed around them.

She was keenly aware that David had taken a chance in warning her about the danger to Sean. His selfless act could so easily rebound on him, for she knew that the blood oath Sean had taken as one of Molly's sons superseded all else in his mind, including the value he placed on his own life.

A sense of deep futility all but overwhelming as she reached the street, Meg paused to look up into a sky that was clear and serene, unsullied by a cloud. She drew new strength from the sudden certainty that beyond it all, her Ma was still with her and her mind whispered in silent reassurances: *No, Ma, you need not fear. I'll not desert Sean. Nor will I give up on him, no matter the path he takes.*

The irony of it all cut anew as David's image returned to mind.

David and she had been separated for five years, and the bond between them was still strong. Yet, in a few short weeks, the man to whom she had pledged her troth only a year earlier had become a stranger.

But she was bound to the Terry she had loved and married, and Meg breathed a sigh of relief that the confidence David had imparted made no mention of Terry's involvement in Molly affairs. Her husband had not been found out. She saw in that a hope for the future.

Maybe David *would* be able to turn it all around. Maybe he *would* get the men in the mine behind him and bring all the violence to a halt. Maybe there *was* a way out of all this, and the first step had been taken today.

Taking courage from her thoughts, Meg looked toward the colliery road as the whistle signaled the end of the first shift. Unconsciously turning toward the sound, she walked faster. She was breathless from the oppressive heat and exertion when she arrived at a point where the first shift began trailing past her. Wiping the perspiration from her brow with the back of her arm, she absentmindedly tucked a stray curl back up into her bound hair, intent on the gradually thickening stream of men.

In the midst of the almost unidentifiable throng, Sean's subdued swagger caught her eye and she became immediately alert. He came abreast of her and she fell into step beside him, realizing Terry was nowhere to be seen.

"Terry's gone another route today, if it's him you're awaitin'."

Realizing the bite of Sean's tone reflected the recent strain between them, Meg responded, "In truth, I came in hopes of walking home with *you* today."

His expression guarded, Sean raised his brow. "Is that so? And what's the occasion?"

"Nothing much." Slipping her hand into his, Meg offered her brother a tentative smile. "It's just my feeling that the dog days of summer have come a bit early this year."

Sean studied her face, and a long moment passed before his hand closed tightly around hers. The smile that touched his lips touched her heart as well as Sean responded softly, "Aye, Meg, so they have."

Night had fallen and the only sound in the room above Lawler's saloon was the echo of voices from below as twelve men sat around a circular table. All eyes were intent on the carefully folded slips of paper in the overturned derby resting in the center as a familiar figure stepped out of the shadows of the kerosene lamp overhead.

His coarse features drawn into an unrevealing mask, Terry Donovan touched the shoulder of the first man, and the fellow drew a slip. Moving around the table to touch the shoulder of each man in turn, Terry waited until the last man had drawn before reaching in to take the remaining piece of paper. The group immediately disbanded, leaving singularly and in small groups, to go their separate ways.

Standing at the bar below a few minutes later, Terry raised his glass to his lips, emptying it before replacing it on the bar and carefully unfolding the slip of paper in his hand.

Blank.

Turning toward Sean, who stood at his side, Terry waited as his brother-in-law slowly opened his hand to reveal that his slip was also blank.

Intense relief flushed Terry's face, and he briefly closed his eyes. He had been spared the final betrayal of Meg's trust for a little while longer. Three men had received slips with the symbolic drawings of a coffin and dagger that appointed them Bully Boy's executioners, but Sean and he were not among them.

Terry signaled the bartender. "Two drinks over here if ye please."

Barely giving the whiskey a chance to settle in the glass, Sean tossed it down. "I'll be leavin' now. I've things to do."

Terry nodded, familiar with his brother-in-law's abrupt changes of mood. "Off to visit Sheila, no doubt."

"My private life's my own, and not up for discussion!"

Terry snorted with a low, "There's truth in that."

The door closed behind Sean, and Terry tossed back his own drink as well. He had known where Sean was going, for he'd had a similar inclination himself many times in the past. Aye, when a man's blood finished pumping hot and strong as it had this night, he sought to put his feelings to rest deep in his woman's body. Sean would have his relief this night, and he was glad, but he had his doubts that his own relief would be forthcoming.

Suddenly fixing his mind to settle it all between Meg and himself before another day passed, Terry turned from the bar, only to hear Muff Lawler mumble at his back.

"Bully Boy will breathe his last before the week's out, there's no doubt, but I'll not be one of them that'll do the job."

Terry glanced up. His expression hardened as he refused Lawler the information he was seeking in return, and he walked away without a word, his mind on matters of a far different kind.

The narrow dirt road of the patch was shrouded in the shadows of evening as Sheila made her way toward the water pump that served her family's section of houses. A muddy trail signaled the well's heavy usage that day, and Sheila frowned. It had been an unusually warm week, and the thought that the people of the valley might be receiving a warning of the summer months to come depressed her. She knew what that meant. She had made this same trip during previous years only to find the well dry as the season wore on, but it was early in the year for such worries, and she had other things on her mind.

Small frown lines deepened between Sheila's eyes as she recalled her mother's most recent harangue.

"You're gettin' older, me girl. Yer flesh is beginnin' to sag and yer face to line, and in a few years there'll be a new crop of fresh-faced colleens in the patch and ye'll have lost yer chance to catch a decent, hard-workin' man of yer own. Forget Sean O'Connor! He's content to take his pleasures on yer body and to spend his remainin' energy on matters that are better left unsaid. Keep up yer foolishness and ye'll never hold a babe of yer own in yer arms, I tell ye! Ye'll die unfulfilled and alone, cursin' the day ye ever heard the name O'Connor!"

It had occurred to Sheila as she took up the bucket to fetch water in an effort to escape, that her Da had long since given up his sermons, and those of her brothers still remaining at home had long since abandoned her to her commitment to Sean. There was only Ma . . .

Forcing the frown from her face, Sheila gave a short laugh. She could handle her Ma with a deaf ear and a strong back, for while she continued to carry the major portion of the workload in the house, she knew her Ma's complaints would remain under reasonable control. But the grains of truth in her mother's lectures had most recently begun abrading her raw.

Within a few feet of the pump, Sheila stopped and turned to look behind her. A smile picked up the corners of her mouth as she saw Sean walking toward her. She had sensed his presence even before she heard his step, and she knew it was because she loved the man with every ounce of life in her. She was his as long as he wanted her. It could be no other way.

Sheila's smile broadened as Sean took her arm, and she saw the warmth of it touch his eyes as well, despite his sober expression.

"I wasn't expecting you tonight, Sean. It was my thought that after the long, hot day that it's been, you'd be cooling your heels at Lawler's."

Sean's hand moved up her arm to clutch her shoulder and his clear eyes met hers directly. "I've been there and gone, because I had a need for you tonight, Sheila."

Sheila's smile dimmed. "Is something wrong, then?"

"Nay, nothin' that your arms around my neck and your body warmin' mine won't cure."

"Ah, a craving of the flesh." Sheila laughed. "So you've missed my loving."

Sober in spite of Sheila's jocular intent, Sean nodded. "Aye, that's so, but you know it's become more than that with us. The truth be known, you're necessary to me."

Her brown eyes misting, Sheila took his hand.

Her hand still in his, Sheila walked through the doorway of the abandoned mill a short time later and placed a lantern on the floor. She had returned to the house to pick up the light, and no questions were asked when those within saw Sean waiting for her outside. It was a familiar pattern to see Sean and her go off together, but for all its familiarity, it had never grown old to her.

Taking a moment to glance around the small room that had become their own through the years, Sheila remembered the loving those sagging walls had seen. She knew there was more loving to come, and she trembled like a virgin as she turned to Sean once more.

"Ah, Sheila . . ." Curling his calloused hand around her neck, Sean drew her mouth to his. His hand trailed to her shoulder and then to the buttons on her shirtwaist with casual informality. He did not speak again until he had exposed her chemise. "Take off your blouse, darlin'. I need to feel your flesh against me. I'm in need of healin', you see."

Sean unbuttoned his shirt as Sheila slipped the narrow straps from her shoulders, baring her breasts. He stayed her hand when she attempted to loosen her skirt as well.

"Nay, Sheila, not yet. Let me look at you for a few moments this way."

Sean's cool blue eyes moved over her rounded breasts, raising an uncommon flush on her cheeks, and Sheila luxuriated in her man's enjoyment of her partial nakedness.

"Your breasts are beautiful, Sheila." Sean's hands curled around their fullness, holding their weight in his palms. His fingertips stroked the distended nipples and a jolt of pleasure shook her. "You've grown into a full-bodied woman, and there's no other I'd have in your place. Come, press yourself against me, darlin', and tell me you love me, for it's the words and the heat of you I need tonight more than anything else."

Sean's need cried out to her and the response within Sheila was deep and abounding. Curling her arms around his neck, she pressed herself flush against him, a low gasp escaping her as their flesh and lips met simultaneously. Sean's arms slipped around her back and she reveled in his possession, even as she opened her mouth to his, inviting an intimate deepening of his kiss. Returning kiss for kiss, caress for caress, Sheila slid her hands into Sean's heavy black hair, luxuriating as the strands slipped through her fingers, gasping, clutching him close as he tore his lips from hers to trail his mouth along her neck, her shoulders, and fastening at last on the burgeoning nipples that awaited him.

Ah, she ached for him as well. The echo of yearning in his voice had ignited a similar cry inside her. Clutching his head to her breasts, she groaned her appreciation as he took each in turn, loving it, devouring it. Surrendering their abundance, Sean returned to ravage her mouth once more and Sheila welcomed his kiss, loving him, wanting him.

Her hand moving freely at Sean's waist, Sheila freed him from his trousers to take the warm rod of his manhood into her palm. She caressed the hard, palpitating flesh, holding it tightly, wanting it deep inside her. His eyes dropping closed for a brief moment as he indulged her caress, Sean reached around her to free the button on her skirt. With a few agile movements he stripped the last of her garments from her.

Breathing heavily from the stress of his raging emotions, his clear eyes holding hers, Sean cupped her rounded buttocks in his hands, and fitting his male organ to her, pushed it into her moistness with a sudden thrust.

"Ah, Sean . . . Sean . . . Sean . . ." Sheila's low litany of his name trailed into silence as Sean's mouth fastened briefly on her neck, her earlobe, to settle hungrily on her mouth. She was drowning in his loving, the exultation in her growing as Sean's heart pounded against hers. Drawing back, Sean resumed a slow, penetrating rhythm, that left her gasping.

High—higher they soared, when Sean suddenly stopped, breathing heavily as he waited for her fluttering eyelids to settle and her gaze to fasten to his.

"Tell me you love me, Sheila."

"I do, Sean."

"Tell me you'll love me always, no matter what comes about."

"I will."

"Ah . . . my darlin' . . ."

His passion erupting with a low groan, Sean shuddered inside her, toppling Sheila from her sustained emotion with a low, ecstatic cry.

Sean was the first to stir from their intimate posture. Pulling back, he drew himself from within her and stripped off the rest of his clothes. He took her hand, tugging her along with him as he lay down on the mat they had used many times before. He kissed her once, twice, and as she waited, a question in her eyes, he whispered, "We drew lots for a man's life tonight, Sheila."

Sheila remained silent, knowing he was searching her face for a sign of revulsion. Finding none, he continued. "Three picked slips with the coffin and dagger drawn upon them, but I wasn't among that number." He halted, waiting for a response. When there was none, he prompted, "Are you glad that my hands will remain clean of this deed?"

Sheila nodded, sensing he awaited that response. She was rewarded with a cold smile as Sean continued. "I thought you would. But you see, the truth is that I was disappointed when I found my slip clear. I *wanted* that bastard's life in my hands, Sheila. I wanted to put him away and to savor it, but it wasn't meant to be."

Sheila was still silent when the hard gleam in Sean's eyes faded, leaving them unexpectedly sad. "I'm no good for you, Sheila. You should have nothin' to do with the likes of me, for you're a good woman. My weakness for you will have you share the sadness approachin', for as Meg would say, I might've taken a step toward losin' my soul this night."

Raising a trembling hand to his cheek, Sheila finally spoke, her voice a shaken whisper. "But you came to me for lovin' instead."

At Sean's soft "Aye," Sheila's smile was tremulous. She drew him close, tucking his head against her breast, knowing that simple response was all she would ever need.

• • •

Meg heard Terry's step at the bedroom door and closed her eyes. He entered and, moments later, the bed sank under his weight as he sat beside her.

"It's no good, darlin'. That won't work anymore. I know yer awake."

Terry's wide palm stroked her hair with a familiar tenderness and the ache inside Meg deepened. His coarse features were illuminated by a shaft of moonlight and she studied them intently.

He looked the same—straight sandy-brown hair cut neatly; brown eyes under light brows; flat features in a broad face; an endearing smile that creased his cheeks with deep lines and displayed small even teeth; and the look of him gentle and shy, for all the power of his massive frame. Terry's hand strayed to her cheek and his touch felt the same, and his eyes reflected the same sense of wonder that they had displayed the first time he had held her in his arms.

"Yer beautiful, Meg." Terry's voice was a raspy whisper. "I've said that to meself many more times than I've said it to ye aloud, but ye've never been more beautiful to me than ye are right now."

"Terry . . ."

"Let me finish, Meg. The rift between us is growin' worse, and we've a need to talk things out."

Meg's eyes searched his face. "Aye, I'd like that, but the trouble is I'm not sure who's speaking to me now. Is it the Terry I married, or is it the 'soldier' that was hiding behind his face?" Meg's eyes suddenly filled. "How could you do that to me, Terry? How could you betray me?"

"I've not betrayed ye, Meg." Terry's denial was emphatic. "Nay, I've turned meself inside out in the past few weeks, lookin' at things, and it's come down to this. Ye thought ye'd married a man who was a true friend to yer brother, and I am. Ye thought ye married a fellow who would keep Sean from makin' some bad mistakes, and I have. He belonged to the Brotherhood before I came here, Meg, and was a man with a reputation for bein' wild. He's not gone off half-cocked as he would have many times without my watchin' over him, and even while we've done some things you haven't approved of, I've still kept him safe."

"But have you tried to make him see the error in his thinking, Terry?"

"Ah, Meg, don't ye see?" Terry's tone implored her understanding. "Sean and I are agreed on most things, and in that way we're brothers."

"Oh, Terry . . ." Meg's desperation was revealed in those two short words. "What hope is there for us now?"

"Don't say that, Meg!" A trace of the stranger was momentarily visible in Terry's gaze, and Meg stiffened only to see regret replace his anger as he leaned over to brush her mouth with his. "I miss ye, Meg. I miss me wife. I want to see her look at me the way she did, and I want to see love light her face again when she sees me enter the room. And I'll tell ye now that I spent the past few hours walkin' and tryin' to get up me courage to ask ye the next question, for the truth is that the answer could break me heart. But I want to know, without breakin' my promise to ye, whether the distance between us now can come to an end while David Lang is still here in Shenandoah."

The question was unexpected and Meg paused, reading Terry's pain as he awaited her response. She hadn't wanted it to be this way. She hadn't wanted Terry to suffer, but somehow things had slipped beyond her control. Compassion raised her hand to his cheek.

"You're my husband, Terry. David Lang is a part of my past. If he's to play a part in my future, it will only be a small part, for my vows to you were spoken before God, and I'll not go against them." Pausing, Meg's voice dropped a note lower. "But I've not had an easy time coming to terms with the deception you practiced."

"I've not deceived ye when ye've been in me arms, Meg, for me love's true."

"I know, Terry. But the rest cuts deep."

"Aye."

Meg hesitated as she sought a solution to the dilemma entrapping them both. "Will you give me time to get to know you better, Terry? You're in need of comfort, but the truth is, if you were to take me in your arms right now, I'd be no good at feigning love."

"Would it come to that, then?"

Meg's response was a softly whispered, "Aye."

The shudder that shook Terry's broad frame shook Meg as well, and her throat constricted with torment as Terry took her hand and raised it to his lips. He drew himself to his feet with a reluctance visible even in the poor light of the room.

"It'll be as ye wish, darlin'. I'd not have the heart to have it any other way." Terry took two steps toward the door before turning back, a trace of a smile on his face. "I'll be a while returnin', darlin'. Yer not to worry, for I've things to think through."

Alone again a few moments later, Meg's heart was aching. The man who had just left her was her husband, and for all his tenderness, she wasn't sure who he was or what he was thinking. It occurred to her in a moment of painful insight that even after all the years apart, the exchange of thoughts between David and herself was as open and free as if they had never parted. She read his heart in his eyes, and he read hers. It would never change.

That realization haunting her, Meg turned her head into her pillow and cried.

The sounds of Meg's muffled sobs reached Terry's ears as he stood outside his bedroom door, and a slow anger transfused him. His hands balled into fists and the inclination to mayhem became almost overwhelming.

His Meg was crying, and he knew instinctively that she was not crying for him. He remembered the look of David Lang as the fellow had stared down on him each morning from the window of his office. He had seen a man who would steal everything he valued most, if he had the chance. For he'd seen Lang's type before, the kind who believed anything he wanted was his due.

But that fellow'd not get his Meg. He'd fix Lang good if it came to that. And if he did, Meg'd never know. He'd earn her love again. Aye, he would.

Chapter 23

David faced Captain Linden across the desk in his study, barely restraining his anger. The moment the sober-faced policeman's arrival was announced, he had suspected something of the sort was coming, and his reaction was intense.

"Don't tell me how to run the colliery, Captain!"

"I'm doing my duty by explaining the dangers of the situation to you, sir."

"There's no need to explain anything to me. You forget, I'm not a novice here. I know what's going on in those shafts. I know why there have been two cave-ins within the last two weeks. I know why load after load has been spilled in the yard—"

"You're coming down on the men too hard, sir."

"Not hard enough, Captain!"

His frustration soaring, David walked around the desk and ran his hand through his hair as he paced unconsciously. It had been a hell of a month. The strike had come to an end in the miners' minds, but not in their hearts, and rebellion continued. Every corrective measure he had taken had been opposed, and it had not taken him long to become aware that it was the intention of some to force him into the position where he would fail.

Stupid fools! Didn't they realize that if he failed, they would suffer, too? The sabotage in the shafts had been the ultimate stupidity. Thirty men had been put out of work for an indeterminate time because of the grievances of a few, and he had not been inclined to let it go. There had never been a shortage of informers below. It hadn't been difficult to discover the name of the troublemakers, and although Terry Donovan's name had been conspicuously absent, Sean O'Connor's had been prominent each time.

Captain Linden cleared his throat, and David turned his attention back to him, glaring. "Did the Mollies really expect me to take all this lying down? Didn't they expect that those responsible would be found out and fired?"

"No, sir, they didn't." Linden surprised him with his response. "You see, there hasn't been direct retribution by management of late. The Mollies have been successful in forcing almost every corrective measure to be rescinded since your uncle sold the mine. They expected the same success with you."

"Well, they were wrong."

Captain Linden paused in response, his thick brows knit, his craggy face drawn into serious lines. "If you'll forgive my saying, sir, now's not the time for the action you're taking."

"The hell it's not!"

"You're stirring the Mollies up at a time when there's already agitation enough. An assassination attempt on Bully Boy Thomas in Mahanoy City failed, and they're in an uproar. They're embarrassed by their ineptitude. They feel it weakens their position at a time when they should be showing strength. They're in the mood for blood. The killing of Patrolman Yost in Tamaqua has put fear back in many minds and silenced protests against them. They're going to have to regain their status in the eyes of the people here, too, and there's only one way to do it."

"Mahanoy City and Tamaqua have nothing to do with Shenandoah."

"The Mollies are a tightly knit organization, sir. They react to situations as a unit."

"So you're telling me that I can't fire the men who everyone knows are responsible for the trouble in the shafts simply because they're Irish? You're telling me that I must modify my policies and bide my time so the arrogant bastards can walk over me as if *they're* running operations."

Linden's frown deepened. "I'm telling you, sir, that you're asking for trouble. You've fired five Irishmen within the last two weeks, and there are grumblings below that your policies are just another version of the old 'Irish Need Not Apply' postings. There's talk that you're trying to drive the Irish out of your mine completely."

"That's nonsense, and you know it. I fired troublemakers— incendiaries, every one of them. That they're Irish has no reflection on my decisions." David gave a short laugh. He leaned over his desk, snatched up a folded slip of paper and placed it in Linden's hand. "I suppose you'd also say I should let them intimidate me with *this*."

Captain Linden unfolded the paper, his head jerking back up at seeing the crudely drawn coffin and the succinct message below it: "Heed Molly's warnings or you're dead."

"When did this arrive?"

"Yesterday morning. The first one arrived last week."

"Last week? I should have been notified immediately, sir."

"I thought your agent would keep you informed of what was happening, Captain, and I wasn't about to let the Mollies think they had put a scare into me by moving about with an armed guard trailing behind. They're bluffing. Gowen's back is up. He'll come down on them with both feet if they try anything against me again, and they know it."

"Our man in the organization knows nothing about these threats, which means the Shenandoah chapter leadership is becoming suspicious enough to take precautions. And I tell you, you're underestimating these men. They're not afraid of Mr. Gowen or anyone else. You're taking your life in your hands, sir."

David shrugged off Linden's warning, only to be struck by his own cavalier attitude. When had he become so casual about his own life?

The answer was blatantly clear, and David went still. His less than admirable conduct toward Captain Linden was also suddenly clear, and his regret was instantaneous.

"I'm sorry, Captain. I shouldn't be taking my frustration out on you. You're a professional—a man of principle—and you're doing a difficult job. Although we disagree, I appreciate your dedication. I'll consider what you've said, but I don't think anything will be gained by prolonging this discussion. Thank you for coming tonight."

Linden frowned at the abrupt dismissal. "You don't seem to understand the seriousness of your situation, sir. You received this 'coffin notice' yesterday, and fired another Irishman this morning. Whether you realize it or not, you're deliberately provoking them. They won't let this pass. You need protection. I can station additional guards with you within the hour."

"Your men are already guarding the colliery and manor house grounds."

"You should have a personal guard, sir."

"No."

"But—"

"I said, no."

Speaking quietly into the silence that followed, David extended his hand. "I appreciate your concern, Captain. Thank you."

The door closed behind Linden a few moments later and David was alone in the paneled room once more.

Alone—it all came down to that.

Meg's image invaded his thoughts, and David unconsciously resumed his pacing. It had been a month since he had talked to Meg, but he now realized his efforts to evade thoughts of her were driving him to a fanaticism that nearly equaled that of the Mollies. He had ignored Elizabeth's letters and invitations to return to Philadelphia, and he had been deliberately remiss in extending an invitation for her to visit him. But the truth was that he wanted no woman but Meg, and a solely physical satiation of the aching need building inside him held little appeal.

He needed to see Meg. He needed the comfort of her presence, her reason, her friendship—if, indeed, he could have her no other way.

Terry leaned against the bar, his brawny frame hunched over his drink as the conversation progressed around him. The heat of the day had settled in Lawler's saloon without allowing a breath of evening air to cool it. Stripped down to his shirtsleeves, as were most of the saloon patrons that night, he was still uncomfortable to the point of distraction.

A bead of perspiration ran down the side of his face and Terry pushed back his cap and wiped his forehead with the back of his arm. He surveyed the room circumspectly. The scraping tones of Tom Donnigan's fiddle were getting on his nerves, and he cast the fellow a veiled glance of annoyance. Had he his choice, he would stride over there and dispense with Donnigan and his creaking instrument with one swipe of his hand. But he did not have his choice, and Donnigan fiddled on. Aye, it had come to appear that he had little choice in many areas of his life of late, and he was growing impatient.

Another look at the clock on the wall, and Terry shifted. It had been a hell of a month in many ways, but he was only too aware that his private hell was filled with the beautiful face of his darlin' Meg. His eyes closed briefly with the thought that he had lost her, but his next thought was sharp denial as he reminded himself that he had had little time during the past month to devote to closing the distance between Meg and himself, with the work he had been pressed to do for the Brotherhood.

Terry's face drew into an unconscious frown. David Lang was the cause of his problems on both fronts, and it gave him little comfort to know that he had been right about the fellow from the first. Arrogant, heavy-handed, Lang had taken over the colliery with an unyielding stance that had immediately started the men grumbling. Reduced pay—reduced hours—he had used every manner of underhanded tool to bring the men to heel, while refusing to hear the complaints of the union with the excuse that his changes were needed for the solvency of the mine.

Solvency. Hah! All but a fool would not realize that Lang waged a personal vendetta against those who sought to oppose him in his all-powerful position. He had forced the Mollies to acts of retribution, and had then worked hand-in-hand with Linden to fire the men most strongly suspected of being guilty. There had been no need for proof, just a claim of drunkenness on the job, or accusations of making threats of violence.

Complicating the matter further, Lang had made certain to spare Sean and him even the slightest harassment, and the reason was clear in the minds of all. Aye, had Lang posted signs around town, the bastard could not have done a better job of reminding Shenandoah of Meg's former association with him. Wagging tongues were having a time of it, and with each whispered word Terry's hatred of the man grew.

As if the turmoil in his own personal life was not enough, the attempt on Bully Boy's life had proved a disaster, and the Shenandoah Division had not heard the last of it. Kehoe had been incensed, claiming the organization's reputation had suffered an enormous blow. The assassination of Patrolman Yost in Tamaqua had followed seven days later, but it was an act of retribution long overdue, and Kehoe was not satisfied that the Shenandoah chapter had restored its credibility.

The final straw was Lang's display of contempt for the Brotherhood by answering the delivery of a second coffin notice yesterday with the firing of Michael O'Malley in the morning. The thought of it tied his stomach into knots. He was not ready to move against Lang, with affairs between Meg and him still unsettled, but the matter had been taken out of his hands. The rumor of an informer in their midst had prompted Kehoe to handle the matter personally, with the knowledge of a chosen few, but the hour was fast approaching when it would be brought to the general membership in a most decisive way.

Another glance at the clock and Terry straightened up. A quick assessment of the room revealed it was time to make his move. Casually downing his drink, he turned to Sean who was still deep in conversation with McKenna.

"It's time for me to leave ye, friends, for the snow's deep in Tipperary."

"And the rains'll not wash it away."

Noting the correct response given to his signal, Terry sauntered toward the door and out onto the street. A short time later, Terry's circuitous route through the back streets of town returned him to Lawler's back door. Upstairs within minutes, he took a deep, fortifying breath before walking into the familiar sitting room.

The kerosene light hanging over the circular table reflected a golden circle of light on the twelve men seated below. A mumble moved among the men at his appearance, and Terry's eyes caught Sean's as he mentally counted. All were present. Turning to the man standing in the shadows, Terry nodded and Kehoe stepped forward to toss a derby onto the table, his small blue eyes pinning each man in turn.

"Dig deep, me brothers, for we've a hard score to settle here."

Moving around the table to signal the draw, Terry waited until all had drawn before reaching in to again take the last slip. The sound of scraping chairs broke the silence as the men prepared to leave in the prescribed manner. It was not long before the door had closed behind the last of them and Terry was alone with Kehoe.

Kehoe laughed unexpectedly and slapped his shoulder, and Terry frowned. As Kehoe moved closer, Terry saw that the laughter had not reached the man's eyes—that the bright blue was surprisingly void of life as he grated, "That farce is over, so buck up, me boyo. By this time tomorrow David Lang will have breathed his last."

Ill at ease with his thoughts, David walked toward the mount awaiting him outside the colliery office. He snatched up his horse's reins and mounted, turning the animal automatically onto the trail that led to the top of the hill.

The late-day sun burned against his back and perspiration trailed past his temples as he spurred his horse to a faster pace. At the top of the trail at last, he drew his horse to a halt, aware for the first time of the strain he had placed on his laboring animal. He cursed under his breath.

Pausing, he looked down on the colliery, aware that the huge, sprawling monster that consumed the earth on which it stood was so much a part of his problem that it could hardly be separated from it. He had tried to take Meg out of its reach and failed before finally making his own escape years earlier. Then, despite all efforts to the contrary, he had allowed its writhing tentacles to entangle him again and draw him back.

But things had not worked out as he had unconsciously hoped. What was the answer? What could he do to salve the aching emptiness inside him?

A sound nearby interrupted his thoughts, setting his mount to snorting, and David turned. He saw movement in the bushes and became immediately alert. His hands tightening on the reins, he was about to call out when the bark of a gun sounded simultaneously with the burst of pain that slammed into his chest.

Knocked to the ground with the impact of the bullet that struck him, David clutched his chest, feeling the sticky wetness of blood, groaning with an agonizing effort to draw breath into his lungs. He heard a second shot, and a third, and the blue sky over his head wavered in and out of vision as he strained to breathe. His labored rasps echoed in his ears and the pain grew more intense until sound abruptly began fading. In a moment of complete lucidity before darkness overwhelmed him, David realized that he was fading as well.

Meg entered her room, stripped off her dress with a low sigh, and tossed it on the bed. She had arrived home late from McCall's Apothecary because of Mr. McCall's request that she deliver a prescription to an ailing family. That errand had brought her too close to the colliery for full comfort, and the realization that she ran the risk of meeting David leaving his office at that time of day had shaken her badly.

Taking the soap from the dish nearby, Meg worked up a lather between her palms and spread it on her face. Relief was instantaneous as she spread the fragrant bubbles onto her neck and shoulders. With little regard for the trickles that ran down her chest and between her breasts to spot her chemise, she rinsed herself clean and dried the moisture from her skin, feeling fresh for the first time that day.

A sudden shouting from the street below interrupted Meg's thoughts, and an inexplicable premonition sent chills moving down her spine. Running to the window, she leaned out, straining to see the street, her fears escalating at the agitation of the pedestrians below. Her heart pounding, she was about to call out when the sound of rushing footsteps in the hallway turned her toward the door the second before it burst open. Terry and Sean paused in the doorway for a fraction of a moment before stepping inside to close the door behind them.

They were breathing heavily, their faces damp with perspiration and Meg swallowed her escalating fear. "What happened? Why is everyone in the street shouting?"

Terry's small eyes pinned her, but it was Sean who responded, his eyes cold.

"We wanted to make sure you were all right. Someone said they saw you near the colliery a little earlier."

"Aye, I had to deliver some medicine for Mr. McCall."

No response.

"Sean?" Meg's heart was hammering and a creeping terror was beginning to overwhelm her. "Sean, tell me what's wrong!"

"Lang's been shot."

Gasping, Meg swayed. Both men stepped forward, but she held them back with an outraged "No!" Shuddering as a portion of her mind registered the growing commotion on the street below them, she rasped, "Is he dead?"

"We're not certain."

Terry's low response turned her toward him, only to have the eyes of a stranger return her gaze. But she was not intimidated by the coldness there. "Did you do it?" Turning to include Sean, she continued with growing rage. "Did you have anything to do with it at all? Did you?"

No response. Meg grabbed her dress and slipped it over her head.

"What're ye doin'?"

Terry's question was a low growl that she answered with a biting snap. "I'm going to him."

"No, ye won't!"

"Oh, yes, I will!" Her quaking increasing, Meg hissed, "You wouldn't be satisfied with anything less than his death, would you? Well, I hope God can forgive you both for whatever part you played in this evil, because I know *I* never can!"

Grasping her arm, Terry shook her hard. "Ye'll not go anywhere. Ye'll stay here, in this house, where you belong!"

"I belong wherever I want to be, and right now I want to be with David." A low sob escaped Meg's throat and she paused momentarily to regain control. "And I tell you now, if David Lang dies, I'll leave this valley forever, and neither of you will ever see me again!"

Meghan attempted to pull herself free, only to feel Terry's grip tighten to the point of pain as he glared at her with barely controlled fury. "Yer *my* woman, and ye'll stay where I tell ye!"

Sean took a step toward them only to have Terry snap, "Stay back, ye fool! Would ye have her out on the street now, to have the whole world hear what she has to say?"

"Let me go!"

"Ye'll stay here, woman!" And at her struggling protest, Terry muttered a low curse the moment before he picked her up bodily and threw her onto the bed. She was still disoriented when Terry signaled Sean and started toward the door. Holding her gaze for only a moment, Sean followed Terry out the door and pulled it closed behind him.

Jumping to her feet, Meg was almost across the room when the click of the lock sounded in the silence, and she stopped still.

Shaking uncontrollably, she was still pounding on the door minutes later, her hands battered and bruised, when reality registered with full impact for the first time. David had been shot and it was her fault! He would never have returned to Shenandoah if not for her, and now—

Desperate, Meg resumed pounding.

An indeterminate time later, breathless and frantic, her face wet with tears, Meg heard footsteps outside the door. The sound of a scuffle reached her ears and then Uncle Timothy's drunken raving, "I tell ye, woman, I'll beat ye to within an inch of yer life if ye go near that door!"

She heard Aunt Fiona's grating response. "Leave me be, I say!"

Again a scuffle and Aunt Fiona's voice sounded with a grunt. Silence.

Meg caught her breath as the key turned in the lock. The door opened to Aunt Fiona's flushed face, and a gasp of relief escaped Meg as she looked past her aunt to see Uncle Timothy sprawled on the hallway floor behind her, his expression incredulous.

"The drunken sot had not the strength of a flea."

Aunt Fiona's low explanation touched an unexpected chord inside her, and had not the occasion been so grave, Meg was certain she would have laughed. Instead, she threw her arms around the woman with a gasping word of thanks, and, still buttoning her dress, fled down the staircase without a backward look.

Labored breathing, sharp and rasping, filled the room, and Captain Linden looked again toward the bed where David Lang lay. His craggy face tightened with concern at Lang's pale countenance; the veil of perspiration that covered his twitching features as he thrashed in the throes of tortured unconsciousness.

Linden silently cursed. Had they arrived a few seconds earlier, his men would have been able to thwart this foul deed. Instead, the guard he had assigned to David Lang despite his protests reached the top of the hill only in time to fire a few shots at the assassins before they escaped.

His men had wasted little time after that, although the damage had already been done. Within minutes David Lang had been rushed to his home and the doctor summoned, while he accompanied another group into Lawler's. In truth, he had not been surprised to find that all were accounted for with alibis sworn by a score or more.

Linden had realized then that the draw conducted the night before in Lawler's upstairs room, as reported by their Pinkerton agent within the organization, and the plan to kill David Lang slated for a week hence, had been a blind to cover this action by assassins brought in from out of town.

The labored breathing from the bed stopped, and Linden's heart leapt in the second before Lang coughed raggedly. Despite Dr. Wilson's pessimistic prognosis, he knew that while David Lang still breathed there was a chance for survival from his serious wound, for the fellow was a man not given to surrender of any kind.

Linden nodded. Aye, young Lang had demonstrated that plainly enough with his management of the colliery. His visit to the O'Connor girl revealed that his strategy was the same in his private life as well, and he had the feeling that if the Mollies had not tried to kill him for one believed crime against them, they would have for another.

Lang was mumbling again, his breathing becoming more labored, and Dr. Wilson turned a frustrated glance toward Linden. "He's started the bleeding again with his thrashing about, Captain. If we can't get him to settle down, he'll do himself in. Did you send that wire to his family?"

"There's only his cousin in Philadelphia, sir, and I've no doubt she'll come as soon as she can. His aunt and uncle are out of the country, and I know of no one else."

"Did you stipulate in the wire that if she doesn't hurry it may be too late?"

"Aye, I did."

A sudden commotion in the foyer below drew Dr. Wilson's attention from the policeman with an impatient frown. "Tell your men to settle whatever problem they have down there. Mr. Lang doesn't need any more agitation."

Turning without reply, Captain Linden slipped from the room, spotting the reason for the disturbance as he pulled the door shut behind him. Moving with surprising speed for a man of his size, Linden reached the bottom of the staircase and snapped a short command.

"Leave the girl be." And then, with a look of concern directed into frantic blue eyes, "What are you doing here, Mrs. Donovan?"

"I have to see Mr. Lang."

Captain Linden assessed the girl's breathless response. Satisfied at what he saw, he instructed, "Follow me."

David groaned. Each breath fanned anew the burning pain in his chest and the heat of it threatened to devour him. But he fought the searing flames, for within them flickered fragmented images he would not surrender to be consumed.

Meg, seated in front of him on the saddle as they galloped across the sunlit hilltop—Meg in his arms in the secluded glade, learning the myriad facets of love—Meg lying beneath him as the rain beat against the leafy arbor over their heads—Meg clutching him close, returning his love. Then the sober word, "Goodbye."

Pain seared again as David fought the finality of that word, and he called out as he had so many times without receiving a response. Suddenly stilling, David saw a glimmer of light in the darkness surrounding him. He concentrated on the glow, and it grew larger, gaining a voice that he strained to hear with the last of his remaining strength. Uncertain of the sound, he fought to lift his heavy eyelids. His eyes slowly opened.

Glittering pools of brilliant blue met his gaze. They were so close that he could see the shimmering dampness that clung to the thick dark lashes bordering them, and he gasped with relief. He felt an unexpected touch on his cheek, and heard Meg's voice as her lips moved with a whisper. "You're not alone, David. I'm here with you."

Her small hand slipped into his, and David gripped it tightly, reveling at the temporary possession. He tried to speak, but was not up to the effort. He felt Meg's lips move briefly against his cheek as she whispered into his ear, "Don't slip away from me, David, for I could not bear the loss."

David fought to focus on the beautiful face so close to his. Meg's warm breath bathed his lips, and he drank it in. Fear deserted him, and he knew it was because Meg had breathed life back into him, with her breath, with her touch, and with her love.

David went suddenly still, and Dr. Wilson moved quickly to David's bedside. Meg glanced up to see relief sweep tension from the doctor's face as he mumbled, "He's resting. For a minute I thought—"

Addressing Meg directly for the first time since she entered the room, Dr. Wilson spoke softly, his tone grave.

"If you value this man's life at all, I suggest you send word to your home that you'll be detained for an indefinite period, for it's my belief that if you were to leave right now, it would finish him."

Uncaring of the manner in which it might be misconstrued, Meg looked back at David's pale face as she responded, "Nay, I'll not leave him—not while he's needing me."

That commitment spoken aloud became fixed in Meg's heart more firmly than a sacred vow.

Chapter 24

The crunch of rubber boots against the dusty road grew louder as the line of miners reporting for the first shift at Lang Colliery thickened. The heat and moisture-laden air of the previous day had not abated, but Sean was unconscious of the beads of perspiration that dotted his forehead and upper lip as he sought to ignore whispered discussions of the previous day's shooting of David Lang that continued around him.

Sean had slept little after the events of the previous evening and darting a glance toward Terry, where his brother-in-law walked at his side, Sean felt his resentment grow. Cold as ice the bastard was, and while he had often admired that quality in Terry in the past, he felt little regard for it now. As for himself, his fury was barely restrained. The attempt on Lang's life had sent everything wrong.

"I know what yer thinkin', Sean, and yer wrong."

Terry's unexpected statement turned Sean toward the bigger man with resentment. "So you know what I'm thinkin' now, too."

"Aye, I do. Yer thinkin' that we're reportin' to work like two fools while everythin's comin' down around us." Terry's face lost some of its hardness. "While yer sister and my wife is up on that hill tryin' to save the man whose life we drew lots for."

Sean's handsome face drew into a sneer. "That drawing was a farce and you knew it all along."

"It was a necessary deception, Sean. Kehoe was worried—"

"Kehoe . . . Kehoe! It's not *that* man I'm thinkin' about now! Nor am I thinkin' about David Lang, for I've not a care in my head whether he lives or dies. It's my sister I'm worryin' about. I want her home, where she belongs, where I can care for her and know that she's safe from that arrogant lecher who'd use her and then throw her away."

Terry stiffened. "Lang's past usin' anybody right now. Ye heard

363

the report. He's hangin' on to life by a thread, and once he's gone, Meg'll come home. She has nowhere else to go."

Sean directed a pointed look into Terry's eyes. "Aye, I suppose that's true, but I'll make myself clear to you right now. Meg was my sister before she was your wife, and when it comes down to it, the bond of blood is stronger. So whatever happens between you both, I'll not stand for a hair of her head to be touched."

Terry's coarse features tightened. "I'd never hurt Meg."

Skepticism touched Sean's face. "Would you not?"

Terry was obviously angered. "Did I not tell ye that I love the woman?"

"Many a blow's been struck in the name of love."

"Nay, not by me."

Sean unconsciously glanced up. The window where Lang had looked down on them every morning was conspicuously empty, and Sean laughed. Terry made no comment, waiting until they drew near the lift that would soon take them underground before he drew Sean back to a point of partial seclusion. "I'll say this once and not say it again. Yer sister gave me her trust and, because of circumstances, it was somewhat undeserving. But she knows the truth now, Sean, and that truth binds her closer to me than lies ever could. We'll be together again, yer sister and me, and I'll make it good for her somehow. Ye can trust in me word."

Terry's face was open, and Sean could read his friend's pain. Aye, the man loved his Meg, but that was not enough. "If it comes to a choice between the two of you, you know who'll be the one I'll choose."

"Aye. I know."

Sean nodded. "Just so's we understand each other."

Terry's unexpected smile was rife with unspoken warning. "It's a strange reaction yer sister has on her men. They'd rather lose their lives than lose her."

Sean's response bore a warning in return. "So they would."

The bedroom door clicked closed behind Dr. Wilson as he left the room, but Meg did not look up. She stroked David's cheek gently, swallowing against the rush of emotions that filled her. *David . . . David . . .*

Beads of perspiration lined his brow and upper lip and, taking a cloth from the bedside table, she blotted his face dry. Morning had come but his waxy pallor remained, and although less agitated, his breathing was still uneven. A lock of hair had fallen on his forehead, and Meg gently stroked it back, studying him more closely than before.

She had never known a man more handsome than David Lang. His strong, masculine features had become even more appealing with the passage of years. His wide shoulders seemed all the more broad for the bloodstained bandage that covered his chest, and when closely scrutinized, the full length of him from head to toe, David's powerful presence had not abated even in his helpless state. But through it all came a touching vulnerability that was not solely the result of his weakened state, and Meghan realized that it was a vulnerability that was visible to her alone. Because David loved her.

With deepening anguish, Meg knew that she saw this side of David simply because she loved him in return, and a sense of utter futility overwhelmed her. David was fighting for his life while she knew in her heart that the two men closest to her had somehow been involved in the plot to kill him.

The bedroom door opened, and Meg stiffened as Dr. Wilson came back into the room. Walking to her side, he whispered, "There's someone downstairs to see you."

Meg's heart began an anxious pounding. Slipping her hand from David's lax grip, she left the bedroom and started down the staircase, only to halt abruptly midway when she saw her aunt standing just outside the open front door. Her heart thudding against her ribs, she burst into motion again, her feet fairly flying over the steps the rest of the way down.

Gripping the woman's shoulder, she gasped, "Aunt Fiona, what happened?"

"Nothin', me dear. Ye need not fear." Hastening to reassure her, her aunt continued. "I've not come with bad news, for everythin's quiet at home."

Meg scrutinized her aunt's round, lined face. There was something different about her as she spoke again. "I heard the young master here is gravely injured, and it was me thought that ye'd made yer decision to remain until the fellow is out of danger." Aunt Fiona hesitated. "I knew ye'd have difficulty if ye stopped back at the house for fresh clothes, so I brought ye a few things."

Meg's surprise was clearly reflected on her face. "You did that for me, Aunt?"

Aunt Fiona raised her chin. "Aye, I did. Me only regret is that

I was so long in lendin' ye the support ye was deservin' all these years."

"But Uncle Timothy—"

"Ye need not worry about him." Aunt Fiona's chin rose a notch higher. "We've come to an understandin' that was long overdue, and I'll not cower again to his bluster."

Speechless, Meg saw the first trace of uncertainty accompany a new sadness in her aunt's expression as the woman added, "But if I'm to be truthful, I must say ye've not heard the last of it from yer two men, there's that much tension between them at home."

Meg was incredulous at her aunt's unexpected display of courage. "And you risked their displeasure by coming here now? I don't know what to say."

Aunt Fiona's unexpected smile kindled a glow in eyes that too often had only reflected anxiety. "Aye, Meg, and I do it gladly, for ye've been more than a daughter to me all of these years, and I'm able to look meself in the face for the first time. And I tell ye now so I may make things clear. Ye may call on me whenever yer in need, and I'll not let ye down again. I'll not judge ye right or wrong in comin' to this house, for I know all ye do is in the name of love, and not many can say the same."

Tears brightened her small brown eyes as Aunt Fiona kissed Meg's cheek unexpectedly. "Ye've but to send me word, Meg."

Still standing in the doorway moments later as Aunt Fiona disappeared from sight around the corner of the house, Meg clutched the package of clothing the dear woman had brought her against her chest. It was more than her clothing. It was a symbol that was long overdue, and it was all the more precious because of it.

Suddenly aware of her extended absence from David's room, Meg glanced up at the second floor. Her steps following her thoughts, Meg pushed open the door a few moments later and paused at the sight of David's renewed thrashing.

From the dark deed that had been done, a spark of good had emerged. But the evil and pain remained.

The heat of the day showed no abatement, and Terry had felt little inclination to obey the summons from Kehoe awaiting him at the conclusion of his shift. The dim hope that Meg had returned home was dashed at the first sight of Fiona O'Reilly's stiff countenance as he walked through the kitchen doorway, and it occurred to him in passing that he'd never seen the woman present such a strong mien before.

But the old woman meant little to him in comparison with the dire state of present affairs, and he had quickly bathed, changed, and, barely avoiding an argument with Sean, had caught the next train to Girardsville.

Arriving at Kehoe's back door, he had found security to be especially tight. Pressed to repeat the sign and password for admittance despite recognition of his face, his temper had flared, and he had reached Kehoe's upstairs room in a black mood. But his own short temper was eclipsed by Kehoe's rage as the meeting of division bodymasters began.

"Fools that ye are, it seems I can depend on none of ye to do a job well!" Turning to the Tamaqua bodymaster whose men had been pressed to return the "favor" of Patrolman Yost's assassination with the attempted assassination of David Lang, he hissed, "Ye and yer men've brought the Brotherhood down another notch with yer fumbling! Lang still lives!"

"It was not the fault of me men, Jack." Defending himself, McClelland gestured wildly. "There's not a man here who could've done better! Linden was warned of what was comin', I tell ye! There could be no other reason for the personal guard bein' put on Lang that mornin', and it was lucky me men was able to make their escape."

"I'll not tolerate yer excuses!" His high color deepening, Kehoe continued hotly. "Lang's off limits for the time being, with half the Coal and Iron Police force outside his door, but I have me thoughts as to who the informer would be. And so I tell ye now, we'll wash this blot from our luster with blood, and more blood. The first will be accomplished before a month is gone, and we'll have put Squire Thomas Gwyer six feet under, where he belongs."

Low grunts echoed around the table as the name of the Welsh Justice of the Peace, a long-established foe of the Mollies, was introduced, but Kehoe had not yet finished.

"And we'll not be satisfied until Gomer James follows him down."

The mumbling grew louder, and Terry was aware that most were in vehement agreement that the hated Welshman who had gunned down Edward Cosgrove, a member of the Brotherhood in high standing, on the streets of Shenandoah a year earlier was only getting his due.

As for himself, Terry felt little satisfaction as the plans were affirmed, for he had seen Kehoe's eye rest on him with special significance, and he knew what was in store.

The heat of the meeting far exceeding the increasing temperature of the room, Terry listened in silence as it drew to an end. Rising from his chair with the others, he made his way toward the door, only to feel Kehoe's hand on his arm.

Meeting the man's eyes with a level gaze, Terry did not flinch as Kehoe stated flatly, "We've things to discuss, Terry."

Nodding, Terry allowed the others to file out the door, and as he turned to face Kehoe once more, it occurred to him that the bloody pattern of his life was set—that Meg had done well to work her way free of him. And he realized with a sudden sadness, that even in knowing that, he was still unwilling to let her go.

David slowly opened his eyes. His sense of disorientation complicated by the pain in his chest, he glanced instinctively to the bed beside him. He groaned softly, his pain increasing. It had been a dream. Meg wasn't there.

David closed his eyes, submitting to the wave of weakness overwhelming him as memory returned. He had left the colliery and had ridden his horse wildly to the top of the hill. He had been looking down on the valley when he heard the shot.

Total recall returned the crushing pain that slammed into his chest, the helplessness as he had awakened briefly and found himself looking up at the blue sky above him, unable to move. The rest was a blur of shouting voices, breathless torment, and embattled dreams. Then he had heard Meg's voice. It had seemed so real, so right to open his eyes and see Meg beside him. He had felt her breath against his lips, had felt her hand caress his cheek. He had looked deeply into her eyes and gained strength. And each time he had awakened after that, he had seen her there.

Glancing toward the window, noting the setting sun was sending shafts of gold across the darkening sky, he realized he was truly awake at last, and he was alone.

A sound at the door caught his attention the moment before it opened to admit Dr. Wilson, and he saw the man halt, surprised to see him totally lucid.

"Well, conscious at last." A smile briefly picked up the corners of Dr. Wilson's mouth and his full mustache twitched. "There'll be hell to pay when it becomes known that after three days of constant attendance, you finally awakened in the few seconds when you were left alone."

"Three days . . ."

"That's right." Dr. Wilson examined him briefly as he continued talking. "And I don't mind telling you that I had my doubts that you'd pull through for a little while there." Stepping back, a pleased smile on his face, the doctor continued. "But barring unforeseen incidents, you should be as good as new in a month or so."

The door opened and Grace's joyful exclamation turned David to his cousin's flushed face as she rushed toward him. Halting abruptly beside the bed, Grace wiped a tear from her eye as she leaned toward him and gently kissed his cheek.

"Oh, David, you've tortured me so."

David would have laughed had he possessed the strength. Instead, he managed, "I'm sorry, Grace. I didn't do it purposely."

"I suppose you didn't, but—"

But David was no longer listening. His gaze riveted on the doorway, he was unable to take his eyes from the image of Meg he saw there. Unwilling to test the truth of the apparition, he did not speak as she approached the bed. At the first touch of her hand on his, David closed his eyes.

"David?" Meg's voice, sweeter than any sound he had ever heard, was close beside him. "Are you feeling badly? David . . ."

Turning his hand to hold hers fast, he looked up into Meg's eyes. "I'm fine, now."

Unnoticed, Dr. Wilson and Grace withdrew to the hallway and closed the door behind them as David attempted to speak again. His voice failed, the weakness accomplishing his wish more adroitly than he could have consciously maneuvered as Meg drew closer.

"Meg, I want . . ."

Her clear eyes became intense as his voice faltered again and she urged, "Aye, what do you want, David?"

"I want you to kiss me, Meg."

A watery glaze momentarily diluted the brilliant silver-blue of the eyes so close to his. David saw Meg's lips tremble as she emitted a small, shaken laugh.

"Ah, David. You're ever the one to press your advantage."

Beginning to succumb to the darkness hovering around him, David attempted a response, only to find it cut off by the warmth of Meg's mouth against his. The taste of her a joy unsurpassed, David raised his hand to her hair, tightening his fingers in her stubborn curls to hold her lips against his for as long as his strength remained.

Content, the scent of Meg's nearness warming him, her breath bathing his lips, David drifted off into peaceful sleep.

Chapter 25

Meg walked swiftly along the hallway, carefully balancing the loaded tray in her hands. A familiar annoyance creased her brow. Three weeks had passed since the attempt on David's life, and in recent days her life had begun bearing a disturbing resemblance to a period long ago.

Meg recalled the scramble to make up David's tray that she had just witnessed in the kitchen, and the care with which David's special meal was prepared. How had he done it? How had he managed to wind the household help, those three world-weary spinsters in the kitchen who could have been nothing more than strangers to him a short time ago, so efficiently around his finger?

"Oh, Mr. David likes his toast buttered . . ."

"Oh, Mr. David likes his roast *very* well done . . ."

"Oh, Mr. David has a weakness for berry pie . . ."

Meghan groaned. If they were not such truly dear women, she would probably strangle them!

The thought suddenly occurred to Meg that she was being unfair. Actually, the three below were a tremendous improvement on the staff that had formerly served Lang Manor. They evidenced none of the resentment that had been the bane of her existence when she was employed here, although she supposed every one of them in the kitchen had a perfect right to protest her supervision of household affairs after Grace Lang Haas had returned to her home in Philadelphia two weeks earlier.

In the time since, following Dr. Wilson's recommendations for David's care to the letter, she had begun having daily consultations with the staff and everything had run exceedingly smoothly. David's recovery was going well, and for the most part he had almost returned to his former self, except for bouts of weakness. She suspected the reason he still insisted on having supper in his room was because she had begun taking supper with him after

Grace left, and he did not want to relinquish the private world that enveloped them there.

Sadness touched Meg. In David's and her private world there was no hatred. There was no prejudice, and no one swore blood oaths of retribution. They were able to talk reasonably to each other and discuss the differences that had come between them, and for the first time she believed she occasionally saw understanding in his eyes. But as they had drawn closer in so many ways, Meg had made certain to put distance between them in others in an attempt to avoid the obvious danger.

The outside world intruded with visits from Captain Linden, however, and the aura remained for hours after he left. David encouraged her to stay while the sober policeman made his reports, but she refused. Despite her private feelings, she wanted no knowledge of anything that might eventually bring down some of her own.

She had had little contact with the valley with the exception of Aunt Fiona, who returned several times to bring her things from home. She had not asked questions about Sean or Terry, because she could not bear to know.

Father Matthew had visited her briefly, but had been strangely formal. His eyes assessing the situation, he had gauged the tenor of affairs between David and herself, and satisfied that David was still recuperating, had left without much to say. Strangely, he had not advised her to go home.

Reaching David's door, Meg balanced the tray carefully as she tapped on the door with her foot. A brief reply from within brought her into the room to see David's frown. His voice bore a note of frustrated sarcasm.

"I suppose you think you have me at a disadvantage, and that's the reason you've become so stubborn of late."

"Of late?" Meg carefully placed the tray on the table that had been set up in the room, and watched as David drew himself to his feet. He had insisted on dressing each day as soon as he had been able to stand. In his trousers and slippers, his unbuttoned shirt exposing the bandages that still covered his chest, he appeared almost cavalier, and she could not resist some lighthearted teasing. "Didn't you always tell me that I was difficult?"

His expression deadly serious as he sat at the table, David clamped his hand over hers as she attempted to remove the plates from the tray. "I don't want you working like a servant in this house, Meg. Let Myrtle carry the tray and serve us."

"Release my hand, David." David frowned, reluctantly complying, and Meg continued. "I'll not have the women serve me, for I have no true place in this house."

"You have a place, dammit!" Anger flushed David's face red. "You're here because I want you here. You're my guest." David's voice suddenly softened, as did the anger in his eyes. "A very cherished guest. Oh, Meg—"

Grasping her around the waist with unexpected strength, David pulled her onto his lap, holding her prisoner in his arms as he hushed her struggling protests with a soft admonition. "Be still, Meg. You wouldn't want to reopen my wound."

David's lips were only inches from hers and Meg's heart began a heady pounding as she mumbled, "This is unfair, David."

Their mouths touched for the first time since those critical hours when he hovered near death, and David's soft groan echoed deep inside her as he pulled her closer. His kiss deepened, drawing from her with a passionate thirst. His long fingers slipped into her hair, tightening in the stubborn curls, refusing to relinquish them even as he drew back, his mouth a hairsbreadth from hers.

He was trembling, and Meg warned breathlessly, "You're still weak, David. You shouldn't strain yourself."

"It isn't weakness that's quaking through me, Meg. God, no." Sipping from her lips with short, nipping kisses, he halted her attempt to pull away. "No, Meg, don't. You know what a stubborn sort I am, and I'm not going to let you go until we've talked some things out."

"No, David."

"Yes. Look at me, Meg."

Drawn to his gaze by the tone of plea in his command, Meg was instantly mesmerized by the heated sparks of gold that had come to life in his eyes. She remembered that look and the passion that evoked it, and a familiar longing stirred inside her. She was trembling as much as he when David whispered, "We belong together, Meg."

She attempted to shake herself free but his grip tightened. "No, please, Meg."

When her protests again stilled, he pressed his mouth lightly to hers, trailing his loving attentions across her cheek to her temple, her brow, and the lashes that fluttered under his lips. "I love you, Meg. I want you with me. Neither of us is complete when we're apart. You know that as well as I."

"David—"

"No, let me finish. You've never truly been out of my mind since the day I pulled a disheveled little girl out from under that bush on the hillside, her face scratched and dirty, her hair covered with webs and leaves. That little girl's blue eyes burned me, and I somehow knew I'd never be able to forget her.

"I loved you all those years ago, Meg, and I love you now, but my stubborn pride got in the way. It wouldn't accept your placing duty before our love. As it turned out, we were both wrong, Meg. You dedicated your life to a deathbed promise and a bond of blood that's only resulted in blood being spilled. And I've proved to myself that pride is a poor substitute for love."

David caressed her, his hands following the contours of her body as he adjusted her more intimately against him, but there was no sense of violation in his touch, only a sense of fulfillment long denied. The truth of David's words knotted deep inside her and she attempted to avoid his gaze, but he refused to allow her escape. Curving his arm around her back, he raised her chin until their eyes again met.

"Meg, we've wasted too much time already, and we've come so close to losing it all. If these last weeks have proved anything to me, it's proved the importance of our love." David's voice dropped a notch lower. "You know as well as I that it was your love that breathed life back into me when it almost slipped away."

Her control fading under David's heady coercion, Meg whispered, "I've said my vows to Terry, David."

"That was a farce, Meg! You didn't really know the man you married. You thought he was a good, gentle person, a man who could give you the things you were lacking in your life, but he isn't what he seemed."

A creeping realization turned Meghan cold. "You know—"

"Yes, I know. Did you really think it would remain a secret long—that your husband was part of the plot to kill me?"

Meg's shuddering increased, and she felt David wince as he pulled her closer still. Her low confession was her first actual concession to the reality she could no longer deny.

"I didn't want to believe that either Terry or Sean were capable of such horrible acts. I told myself that they would realize where their bloody vows were taking them before it was too late."

"I tried to get Captain Linden to work around them for your sake, but it's gone too far, Meg."

"I know."

"There's no way out for them, but there is for us. Look at me,

Meg." Forcing a distance between them so he might view her face, David whispered earnestly. "I'll soon be good as new. When I am, I'll give Gowen my notice."

"You made a commitment to him."

"Listen to me, Meg! The only commitment that's irreversible is the one I made to you years ago. I'll take you away from here—far away. We'll forget this place and everything in it, and we'll start a new life. I'll come into my inheritance soon, and there's nothing we can't do then."

"Except marry."

"You'll get an annulment."

"No."

"We'll find a way."

"No!"

Twisting unexpectedly from his grip, Meg jumped to her feet. Her eyes great glaring saucers of pain, she shook her head, incredulous. "Do you know what you're asking? You're asking me to throw away everything I believe in, every tenet of thought my Ma ever taught me. You're asking me to discard the things that make me what I am. What will I be then, David? What will I have left?"

"You'll have me, Meg." David stood uncertainly and took a step toward her, but she waved him back.

"No, stay where you are! I don't want you to touch me!"

"Why, Meg?" David's eyes held hers. "Is it because if I do you won't be able to walk away from me?" And when she did not respond, he took another step toward her. "Then *let* me touch you. Let me hold you in my arms and make love to you until you can think of nothing and no one but me, because that's the only place you'll ever be truly happy, Meg—in my arms. And that's the only way either of us will ever be complete."

David took another step toward her, and Meg's eyes widened with panic. "Stay back, I say!"

"Meg, please—"

"No, I must think." Retreating to the door with backward steps, Meg pulled it open, her gaze still pinned to David's face. "I need some time alone to think. Please, David."

Turning, Meg stepped quickly into the hall and drew the door closed behind her, realizing full well that she was doing exactly what she had accused David of several minutes earlier. She was taking advantage of him—of his weakened state—but she felt no remorse. The scales were all tipped in his favor, because everything he had said was true.

A sudden need to escape propelled Meg down the hallway and to the foot of the staircase without conscious intent. Twilight beckoned through the glass panels beside the front door, and Meg obeyed its summons. Responding to the inquiring glance of the armed guard on the doorstep, Meg replied, "I'm going for a walk."

"Take care not to walk too far, ma'am."

Hardly conscious of his response, Meg walked off onto the shadowed trail beyond.

Terry walked briskly along the darkening street, his shoulders held carefully erect. His cap sat low on his forehead, emphasizing the frown that was more common to his face of late than a smile. He turned toward the train station. His heavy features tightened as he sought to keep his gaze from straying to the manor house on the hill, but even as a screeching whistle heralded the train's approach, he knew the effort was doomed to failure.

The puffing engine rounded the turn in the track, and Terry watched its approach with a carefully controlled expression. It had been three weeks since Meg had left him for the house on the hill, and the desolation was deadening to his soul. He missed Meg. He missed her during the long hours underground, when he knew he would not see her smile of welcome when he emerged into the light of day again. He missed her during the silent hours of night in their empty bed. He missed her then, and now, and in every waking moment of tormented fear when he realized she might never return to him.

But Terry knew he was not alone in his tribulation, for he saw that Sean suffered deeply as well. Strangely, Meg's leaving had caused a rift between Sean and himself, and he suspected Sean somehow blamed him. The secrecy newly imposed upon him by Kehoe had caused the rift to widen, and Terry had often looked at Sean of late to see in his face the coldness of a stranger.

The engine hissed to a stop and Terry gave the station a last cursory glance before boarding. Finding the car empty except for two dozing passengers, he took a seat by the window and stared out into the darkening twilight. The car jerked into motion, and he thought of the meeting to come.

He had spent more time than he felt comfortable with in Girardsville these past weeks. With the suspicion of an informer in the Shenandoah division, Kehoe had demanded utmost secrecy for the plans underway. Swift justice would be dealt to Thomas Gwyer in Girardsville and Gomer James in Shenandoah within a week's time. An exchange of favors had already been arranged within the organization, with men coming from divisions in opposite ends of the coal fields to do the jobs. Past experience had proved that identification of the men was more difficult that way, and the final plans would be made tonight. Once that was accomplished, he would be free to go on to devote his time to more personal areas of his life.

Settling himself down further into his seat for the familiar trip, Terry relaxed into the swaying rhythm of the car and closed his eyes. Sleep would be impossible with his mind so heavily involved, but he would use the time to allow images of Meg free access to his thoughts. Somehow Meg had known he was involved in the attempt on David's life, and he consoled himself that he had allowed her to stay up on the hill for a limited time to assuage her conscience. If he was to believe the rumors that came from the manor house, Meg had tenderly nursed David Lang back to health, and the fellow was not content to let her out of his sight.

Terry suffered again the cutting edge of jealousy, but he reined it carefully under control. Meg was his wife. He knew she would not violate her vows. He also knew that at the conclusion of these Brotherhood matters one week hence, he would put a quick end to the situation. He would get Meg back then, one way or another.

The shadows of twilight deepened as Meg walked through the overgrown garden of the Lang estate. Her step driven, she followed the stone path, noting unconsciously that the rose beds were badly in need of weeding and that the hedges had grown wild and shapeless. The birdbath that had welcomed so many songbirds in the past was dry, and the imported Roman sundial no longer saw the sun, shaded as it was by overgrown shrubs. Once so carefully tended and loved, the garden had gone to seed.

As had her life.

Halted by the despair overwhelming her, Meg took a deep, shuddering breath. It had all gone wrong somehow. She was so sure she was doing the right thing. After David left Shenandoah and his uncle sold the colliery, she was certain David would never return. She was sure that after spending years among wealthy, educated, sophisticated people, David would not even be recognizable as the person he once was. She was equally convinced that time would erase from David's mind all memory of a simple coal-town lass. Then she met Terry and saw in him the answer to her prayers, the person who would help her put Sean back on the right path.

She had been so certain—and she was so wrong.

David still wanted her. He loved her and needed her, and if she were to be honest, she needed—

"Meg."

Jumping with a start at the sound of her name, Meg stared incredulously as Sean stepped out of the nearby shadows. Quickly scanning the area for watchful eyes, Meg turned back to her brother with a shocked hiss.

"What are you doing here, Sean!"

"I came to talk to you, Meg."

"Are you mad?" Unable to believe Sean's disregard for his own safety, Meg continued in a hushed tone. "The police are patrolling the grounds. You could've been shot!"

"There's not a policeman alive who can keep me from goin' where I want to go."

The animosity in Sean's tone was achingly familiar, and Meg's despair deepened. "You must leave here, Sean."

"I want you to come back with me."

"No."

"I won't let you stay with that Protestant bastard, Meg! I won't let him change you into something that you aren't."

"Is that why you tried to kill him?"

"I didn't have anything to do with it, Meg, I swear." Sean's gaze flickered. "I might have, if things were different . . . but I didn't even know it was bein' planned for that day."

A spark of the Sean of old suddenly returning to his eyes, Sean gripped her shoulders. "Ah, Meg, you're my sister. You're blood of my blood, and dearer to me than anyone else in the world. I want you back, where you belong."

Meg steeled herself against his plea, responding tightly, "*Terry* knew, didn't he." Sean's silence was clearer than a spoken response, and the pain of it was almost more than she could bear as she spoke in a rasping whisper. "You betrayed me, Sean. You put me second to your bloody vengeance."

"I didn't."

"Aye, you did, or you wouldn't have allowed Terry to deceive me."

"That was a mistake, Meg. I know that now, but I didn't see it that way then. The man loved you—he loves you still."

"His hands are stained with blood, Sean! Or did you not think of that? Did you not think I'd resent being touched by hands that did murder? Or were you inured to the thought because your hands are bloody as well?"

Sean's eyes held hers intently as his hands dropped from her shoulders. "I swear on Ma's grave that I knew nothin' about the attempt on Lang's life until after it was done." He hesitated. "I've given it a lot of thought, and I'm thinkin' I was saved from any part in the affair by Ma's guidin' hand. She can see into your heart, Meg, wherever she is, and she knew the pain it would cause you. She didn't want that between us."

"Don't speak to me of Ma, Sean! You're only speaking words! If you really cared what Ma wanted, you would've given up your vengeance long ago."

"It does no good to look back, Meg. We can only look forward, and I'm tellin' you now, all's lost if you don't come back." Sean's strong body quaked as his voice dropped a notch lower. "The hatred eats at me without end when you're not near, Meg."

"Don't put the burden of your hatred on my shoulders, Sean, for I'll not allow it. You've done what you've done despite anything I've said."

Sean paused in response. His voice became a rasping whisper. "I've not yet killed a man, Meg."

Sean's low confession sent a chill crawling up Meg's spine. "Not *yet*, you say! How can you bear to utter words that could send you to hell?"

"I say them because they're true. The bitterness will not abate. I've known for longer than I care to say that you're all the goodness that's left inside me, Meg. Without it, I've gone all bad."

"Sean . . ."

"Come back with me, Meg. If you stay here, it'll be the end of Lang one way or another." At Meg's look of horror, he nodded. "Aye, it's true. My feeling's aside, Terry won't wait much longer."

"I won't go back to him."

"You need not. I know Terry well. He'll be content just to have you near until things are settled, and I'll see that he knows you're to be left alone. Things will be right again, Meg. I can feel it. We'll work things out between us the way we always did."

Meg shook her head, confused. "How can things ever be right again?"

"If you come home there's at least a chance. If you don't, there's none." Allowing a few moments for that thought to register fully in Meg's mind, Sean continued. "You must make a decision, Meg, and the hard truth of it is that the future of us all depends on what you do."

Sean held her gaze, and Meg looked deeply into the silvery blue eyes so alike her own. She saw many things. She saw Da and the boys. She saw the good times and the bad—the dreams they shared. She saw six lonely graves and remembered the pain. She saw Ma's face, her eyes silently beseeching. She saw anguish and uncertainty, hatred and fear. She saw love and despair, and in seeing all that in Sean's eyes, Meg knew she saw her own soul mirrored there.

And she knew. To give up on Sean would be to give up on herself. To abandon him would be to lose herself as well. There would be nothing left to give another.

That painful truth the only certainty she knew, Meg whispered, "All right, Sean. I'll come home."

Sean did not respond other than to grasp her hand. He made an attempt to draw her behind him as he stepped into the shadows, but she held back and he turned with a frown.

To his unspoken question she responded, "I have to tell David first."

"Nay, he'll try to stop you! Come with me now."

"I'll be home within the hour. I give you my word."

Taking a long moment to consider, Sean nodded, and within moments he disappeared into the darkness. And Meg knew the hardest was yet to come.

Meg stood stiffly just inside the bedroom doorway as David stared at her incredulously.

"Meg, think what you're saying!"

"I know what I'm saying, David. Aye, I know." A brief flicker of pain passed over her beautiful face, but David's sense of unreality remained as she continued. "All you said is true, for you know I love you more than I've ever loved another man, but I can't stay with you."

"This is all nonsense, Meg!"

David took a step toward her and Meg cautioned tightly, "Stay where you are, David. I've taken all I can bear tonight."

Realizing Meg was poised for flight, David halted abruptly. Despising the physical pain in his chest that grew with his agitated breaths, he continued tightly. "Meg, you've denied what we feel for each other before, and look where it's taken us. We need each other, Meg. We need to be together. You feel that truth inside you, but you still deny it. Why? What happened since you left this room to affect you so desperately? Who—"

"Nothing happened, except that I've had some help with my thinking, and I realize that I have no choice to make. I made it long ago, David, long before tonight, and the only thing left for me to do is to follow it through to the end." A single tear slipped from Meg's brimming eyes, and she brushed it away. "Forget me, David. Do as you said. Give your notice here, walk away, and don't look back. There's naught but heartache in these hills. There's no escaping it for me, but you've your way clear."

"Meg—"

"Do it for me, David. Keep yourself safe and be happy, for I'll take consolation in that. As for myself, the die is cast, you see, and there's no turning back. Goodbye, my love."

David stood stock still, disbelieving as Meg quickly turned and slipped out of the room she had entered only moments before. The click of the door closing behind her echoed with exaggerated finality in the emptiness that followed.

Still staring at the closed door, uncertain how long he had remained in that frozen posture, David slowly walked to the window. Silent, his anguish almost more than he could bear, he stared into the darkness, listening to the sounds of the night.

Chapter 26

The bold music of a brass band broke the silence of morning and the day of celebration began! Marching proudly in their gaudy red shirts and burnished helmets, the Shenandoah Rescue Hook & Ladder Company followed the high-stepping band down Main Street to the cheers of an appreciative crowd.

Meg walked amid the throng following the parade to the pleasure grounds for the annual picnic, grateful for the diversion. The smiling faces and laughter all around her were a welcome change from the tension in the household since she had come back from the house on the hill earlier that week.

Glancing to her left, Meg saw Aunt Fiona's lined face creased in an uncommon smile, and she knew the excitement of the moment was not totally responsible for the dear woman's pleasure. Uncle Timothy had announced unexpectedly that morning that he would accompany his wife to the picnic, and he then surprised them all by picking up and carrying the heavy hamper she and her aunt had prepared without complaint. Although she doubted Uncle Timothy would finish the day as sober as he began, Meg's throat tightened at the joy these few moments brought her dear aunt. It was such a small thing, but it was an uncommon show of consideration from Uncle Timothy that she noticed was becoming a bit more common each day.

Glancing to her right, Meg met Sean's gaze and his smile tugged at her heart. In the week since she had returned, he had carefully subdued the bitterness that had become so much a part of his personality. There had been little brooding of late, or displays of anger and frustration. She glimpsed the Sean of old more often now—watchful, protective, and loving. He was making a conscious effort especially for her, and she was touched beyond measure.

Terry walked beside Sean, and as he caught her eye, the frivolity of the day momentarily dimmed. Her husband and she

383

now treated each other as polite acquaintances, and she knew there was bitter truth in the term.

Forcing warmth back into her smile, Meg side-stepped an anxious group of youngsters coming up from behind and grasped Sean's arm to steady herself, laughing. "The Scanlon children will run us down if we're not careful, they're that excited."

"I'm thinkin' you'll not be run down by anyone." Sean winked. "Not my Meg."

Her gaze slipping to Terry where he walked at Sean's side, Meg saw his unrevealing expression flicker, and discomfort surged anew. True to his word, her brother had played the buffer between Terry and herself, allowing them little time alone after their meeting the first night of her return. The hard lines that had set in Terry's face when she told him she would no longer share his bed were burned into her memory.

Diverting her attention to the bright banners flying briskly in the breeze, Meg attempted to concentrate on the joy that abounded around them. She didn't want to think about the small, lonely room she had taken behind Aunt Fiona's kitchen where visions of David, never far from her mind, were especially strong during the long hours of night. The sound of his husky voice returned then to haunt her, and the glitter of gold in his eyes and its unspoken promise would not leave her mind. Her guilt was strongest then, and the complication of strained relations between Terry and Sean, a result of Sean's careful guarding of her privacy, added to her sleeplessness.

Uncertain where this all would lead, Meg only knew that even if David had not returned, she would have been unable to remain a true wife to a man whose hands were stained with another man's blood.

Suddenly realizing that Sean was watching her, Meg forced a laugh as she looked down at a second food hamper he carried. "Are you hungry, Sean? I'm thinking Aunt Fiona insisted upon taking enough food to feed an army, and you must do it justice or she'll never forgive you."

"You needn't worry, Meg. Sheila will be joinin' us at the grounds, and I've no doubt one or two of her hungry brothers will be willin' to eat up anything left over."

"Nay . . . nay . . ." His small eyes pinning Sean with their birdlike stare, Uncle Timothy huffed, "I'll be carryin' any leftovers home. No need to waste what we can eat on the morrow."

Aunt Fiona's low grunt of disapproval turned her husband toward her with an uncomfortable glance, and Sean's unexpected amusement lifted Meg's heart. The strain between Uncle Timothy and Sean had lessened with Aunt Fiona's newly established assertiveness, and Meg now occasionally glimpsed a spark of affection in Sean's gaze when he spoke to his aunt. It gave her hope. Perhaps the hatred was on the wane. Perhaps they could all one day look forward to a normal life where—

"Come on, Meg! Hurry up!" Suddenly grabbing her hand, Sean pulled her ahead of the throng as the picnic grounds came into view. "There's a table over there in the shade that's close enough to the bar to make us all happy, and far enough from where the band will set up to save our ears some wear."

Hampers firmly ensconced on the wooden table of Sean's choice a few minutes later, Meg turned to survey the quickly filling grove, the laughing children, and the exhausted musicians as they made their final approach to the grounds. Aunt Fiona was already unpacking the food, and Uncle Timothy was concerned with tasting the jam tarts. Sean was scouting the area, no doubt looking for Sheila's fair head among the crowd, and Terry . . .

Meg paused at the frown that creased Terry's brow. She followed his gaze as he looked from the long wooden bar set up nearby, to the table, and then back again. His eyes narrowed with antipathy as he looked at the tall Welsh bartender who stood, arms crossed, awaiting the first thirsty rush. Appearing suddenly to realize that she watched him, Terry looked directly into her eyes, finally breaking contact with her gaze as Chester Flanagan grasped his arm with a welcoming shout. Drawn into a nearby group of men, Terry then left Meg to puzzle at the strange sense of discomfiture that remained.

The band struck up another tune from its location in the shade of a large oak, and determined to dismiss all nagging concern, Meg affixed a smile on her face that said, "Let the festivities begin!"

The bright, sunlit day progressed into afternoon, the heavy August heat having no effect on appetites as Aunt Fiona's delicious feast was consumed with gusto. Content, the woman was seated with a group of matrons nearby as Uncle Timothy led a heated discussion at the crowded bar. The aroma of coffee freshly brewed over an open fire filled the air, and the shouts of children happily swimming in the dammed creek at the other end of the grove punctuated the occasional silence between tunes from the tireless band. The squeal of a pig recently greased for the chase added to the din of sack and three-legged races being run nearby, and amidst the joyful confusion, the throbbing in Meg's aching head assumed the thunder of cannon.

Glancing up at the brilliant blue of the cloudless sky, Meg heaved a silent sigh. It was no good. Pretending to be happy just did not work.

Movement within the grove of trees a small distance behind the table caught Meg's eye, and she saw Sheila's fair head, and then a flash of Sean's darker one. Their figures blended, and the heat of tears warmed her eyelids. She looked away and took a deep breath. Sheila and Sean seemed closer than they had ever been. She wanted to see them happy, to see their lives take shape together. She wanted to believe that the longing inside her that began the moment she closed the door of David's room behind her would cease. She wanted to think that the future was not as black as it looked to her right now as she stood in the glaring sunshine, listening to the sounds of other people's happiness all around her. She wanted to believe she would be able to go on, when at this moment it seemed hopeless even to try.

Each successive shout of laughter becoming a blade that cut her more deeply than the one previous, Meg made her way with rapidly quickening steps into the thick grove to her right, inwardly bleeding from the pain of despair. She did not stop running until she was out of sight and sound of the crowd. Alone at last, her own laboring breath the only sound that broke the stillness, she walked to the edge of the narrow creek that wound its way between the trees.

Sunlight filtered through the leafy canopy over her head, sparkling on the rippling water, and Meg was grateful that someone had seen fit to dam the stream for the children a distance away, so she might enjoy the solitude without threat of interruption.

Succumbing to impulse, Meg sat on the shallow bank, stripped off her shoes and stockings, and dipped her feet into the sparkling water. She gasped. It was colder than she had expected and her breath caught in her throat. She started to laugh, but a sob emerged, and Meg raised her hand to her lips to block the sound.

"Meg."

Jumping with a start, Meg turned to see Terry behind her. She attempted to stand, only to have his hand on her shoulder press her back down as he sat beside her. Her heart thumping against her ribs, she saw lines of pain and stress tighten his sober face, and she drew back from him instinctively.

"Don't be afraid of me, Meg. I'll do ye no harm."

"I . . . I'm not afraid of you, Terry."

"Aye, ye are. Ye don't know what to expect from me anymore, and I can't blame ye."

In the brief silence that followed, Meg examined Terry's appearance closely. He hadn't changed physically. The great size of him was the same; his straight, short-cropped, sandy-brown hair and comfortingly plain features were the same; the gentleness in his eyes and in his voice was the same. But he was *not* the same, and a chill slipped down Meg's spine at the thought of what lay behind the harmless facade she had believed so real.

Without conscious intent, the question on Meg's mind slipped out in a whisper. "Why did you do it, Terry? Why did you hide your true self from me?"

"Aw, Meg." Terry shook his head, sadness visibly overwhelming him. "I had no choice, for I loved ye, ye see. I didn't tell ye about the violence that ruled me life before I met ye, for I knew ye'd have nothing to do with me if I did. And the truth was that the man who did all those things was a stranger to me when I held ye in me arms. Ye brought out the good in me like no one else ever did, and with ye I saw a light at the end of the dark tunnel that was me life."

"But," Meg shook her head, incredulous that this quiet, gentle man could be guilty of such heinous acts, "but didn't you think I'd find out someday?"

"I thought by then ye'd love me too much to ever leave me."

Meg swallowed against the knot in her throat, determined to continue. "You thought I would stay with you even after you plotted to kill David?"

A heated, unidentifiable emotion flashed in Terry's small eyes. "It was a blow for a cause I've devoted me life to, Meg. It wasn't me own choice. Can't ye see that?"

"No, I can't! No man should be committed to murder, no matter how just he believes his cause to be!"

"This is war—"

"Don't speak to me of war, for if it's war, it's one of your own choosing. The decent Irish in the valley claim no part of it. They're as anxious as the others to see the end of bloodthirsty ways. You bring shame on us all, and resentment grows greater each day because of it. You must know that you can't win."

Terry's whispered reply was gentle, but unyielding. "Aye, we will."

Meg slowly shook her head, incredulous. "So it's not come to an end yet." She swallowed. "Will you try to kill David again?" And when silence was Terry's response, she demanded, "Will you?"

"Nay. Not again."

Meg released a relieved sigh, only to stiffen as Terry took her hand in his. She attempted to snatch it back, but he would not allow it. Instead, he raised her palm to his lips and kissed it tenderly before looking back into her eyes.

"I love ye, Meg. I don't blame ye for goin' to Lang, for I know it was the shock of learnin' about meself that drove ye there. But ye came back, and we'll take it from there. Ye said I deceived ye, so I've been truthful with ye today. I'm bein' truthful with ye now when I tell ye that I think the end of all our trouble's in sight. Gowen won't take much more before cavin' in."

Astounded at his misconception, Meg shook her head. "You're wrong! Neither Gowen nor David will be *frightened* into quitting." She did not choose to say that the only way David would walk away from it all would be if she walked away with him. She tried again to withdraw her hand, but Terry held it captive within his as he spoke more earnestly than before.

"I tell ye, it's soon to be over. And I'm also tellin' ye that when it is and we've received our just due, I'll never return to these ways again. I'll be the husband ye want, Meg. And I'll be a good father to our babes."

Meg shook her head, stiffening with aversion. "There'll be no babes. I'm your wife by law, but not in my heart. I've no love for the man I've found you out to be, and I'll not let you use my body as if I did."

"You'll love me again, Meg. You'll see." Reaching out unexpectedly, Terry cupped Meg's neck with his broad palm and drew her toward him. Her struggling was to no avail against his superior strength as he clutched her tight against him, smothering her in his hungry embrace. "I've missed ye so much, Meg. Me life's been empty as it's never been before, and I've come to know that if I gain all there is to gain in this world, I've nothin' without you. I want ye back, darlin'."

Terry's lips descended toward hers, capturing her mouth

warmly despite her struggle, and Meg fought the seeking intimacy of his kiss with all her strength. She was crying, sobbing, but the sound did not emerge. She was frantic to escape him, even as his kiss surged deeper, separating her lips. She was filled with revulsion—a raging nausea assuming control—when she was suddenly jerked from his embrace.

Stunned as Sean flung Terry backwards on the ground with a loud thud, Meg jumped to her feet. Pushing her behind him protectively, her brother, seething, faced the bigger man as he drew himself to his feet.

"So this is how you keep your word! You promised you'd leave my sister to make up her own mind about you!"

"This is none of yer affair!" Rage distorted Terry's face. His shoulders hunched threateningly and his hands balled into fists. "Now step away from me wife."

"Not while there's a breath in my body."

There was a short silence and then Terry's cold laugh. "So be it then."

"No!"

Her voice reverberating in the wooded glade, Meg took a fearless step toward Terry. "So you'd try to gain my love by murdering my brother! Aye, that's the act of a loving husband."

"If I can have ye no other way—"

"You'll not get me back by shedding blood!" Meg's eyes flashed and her lips tightened into a straight, determined line. "Aye, you're a big man. Were you to get past my brother, you could beat me into submission and use my body, no doubt, but don't you see? You could never *make* me love you."

Halting in his tracks, the anger draining visibly from his body, Terry stared at Meg in silence. He took a short step forward only to halt again.

His chest heaving, utter desolation clear in the lines of his face, Terry rasped, "Aye, I know that as well as ye do, Meg, and I swore to meself that I'd earn back yer love. But it seems I misjudged me control. It'll not happen again." Pausing, the strain of his effort evident, Terry attempted a smile. "I'm not the monster ye think me to be, Meg, although I played the role well this day. I promise ye now, I can be all ye thought me to be when ye spoke yer vows. I'll wait till ye realize that, till ye can see it for yerself."

"No, Terry. It's too late. It won't work."

"Aye, it will."

Meg's mouth twitched with the hopelessness of further speech. She took Sean's arm. "I want to go back now, Sean." Snatching up her shoes and stockings, she looked back at Terry.

Her lips parted, but words failed her. It was no use.

The revelry of the day increased as the afternoon wore on, but Meg was strangely numb. Dismissing her brother with a smile upon reaching the pleasure grounds, she assumed a seat by Aunt Fiona where the older folks talked and looked back through the years in lively reminiscence. Her eyes followed the dancing couples across the uneven ground as they moved inexhaustibly to the music of the quadrille band, but she felt little of their joy.

Working beside her aunt, she later placed the evening meal on the table. Aware of the unnatural silence between Terry and Sean, she carefully avoided the eyes of both, and was greatly relieved when Terry retired to the bar once more and Sheila swept Sean away to dance.

When darkness fell, fireworks lit the sky, and Meg was intensely relieved that the time had come when tradition demanded that women and children return home so the serious drinking might begin.

Glancing at the bar nearby, Meg saw that the big Welshman behind it was stripped to the waist in deference to the heat. She watched as he deftly slapped open another spigot of barreled lager, filled a seidel of beer with practiced speed, and almost in one motion, slid the foaming brew down the wet counter to where eager hands awaited it. The thought occurred to her that there would be many an aching head tomorrow, but glancing toward Terry with some surprise, she realized from his sober expression that he would not be among that number.

"Are you ready, Meg?"

Turning to Sheila's flushed face, Meg could not help but smile. Sean had been openly attentive, and she knew her dear friend's hopes ran high.

Meg replied jokingly in return. "Are you sure you want to leave that brother of mine with these fellows at the bar? He has the look of a man who's about to cast all care to the wind."

"Nay, not tonight, Meg." Sheila's gaze was knowing. "Sean's promised to walk me home."

Meg nodded, envying her friend for the first time with the realization that she had taken the man she wanted at the expense of all else. How she wished she had been able to do the same.

A last glance toward the bar revealed Uncle Timothy was well into his cups, but Aunt Fiona did not appear to mind as she turned to Meg with a smile.

"Are ye ready, m'dear? It's been a glorious day."

Picking up an emptied basket, Meg walked silently beside her aunt as Sean and Sheila followed behind. Terry unexpectedly took up step beside her, and as she stiffened, he smiled, sadness in his eyes.

"I'm thinkin' I'll make an early night of it. I'm not in much of a mood to celebrate tonight."

Meg had no response.

Grateful to be in Aunt Fiona's kitchen at last and spared another moment of the strained silence of the walk home, Meg turned to the others, forcing a smile. Sean lingered, his hand on Sheila's arm, and it was obvious that he would not leave until she was safely locked away from any amorous intent that might remain in Terry's mind.

Sean's intentions obviously clear to Terry also, he gave a tight laugh. "Well, I guess it's up to me to make the first move, so I'll be sayin' good night to ye all." Taking an unexpected step forward, Terry grasped her shoulders unexpectedly and kissed her mouth. Meg felt the blood drain from her face.

Terry's face flushed. " 'Twas not the kiss of death, darlin'. Merely an expression of me love."

Unable to do more than nod as Terry turned and walked out of the room, Meg did not realize she had heaved a deep sigh of relief until Sean's hand touched her shoulder.

"It'll be all right, Meg. It just takes time."

"Aye." Turning back to her aunt, Meg kissed her wrinkled cheek and spoke with an attempt at levity. "I'm thinkin' we'll have our choice of seats at early mass tomorrow, Aunt. I'll see you then."

A smile for Sheila, and Meg stepped into her room and locked the door behind her. Aunt Fiona was still bustling around the kitchen when the last echo of Sean and Sheila's departing footsteps faded away.

Wearily sliding her fingers into her hair, Meg began removing the pins. She had taken up the brush for a few short strokes when the sound of Aunt Fiona's gasp stopped her short. Frantic movement from outside the door and the scraping of kitchen chairs freed her from immobility, and she quickly unlocked the door.

Aunt Fiona turned at her anxious question, "What's wrong, Aunt?"

Her aunt's stubby hand moved seekingly to her neck and she swallowed tightly. "It's me necklace—me cross. I've lost it. It's nowhere to be found in the kitchen." Her obvious panic increased. "It was yer uncle's present to me on our weddin' day. He'll not forgive me for me carelessness."

"You've seldom had it from your neck in thirty-six years, Aunt. I doubt Uncle Timothy would believe you're careless." Seeing her words were of little comfort, Meg attempted a smile of reassurance as she patted her aunt's trembling hand. "But we'll find it, you'll see. When was the last time you remember feeling it around your neck?"

Her aunt's tear-filled eyes became thoughtful. "I don't know . . ." Her eyes suddenly widening, Fiona gasped. "It was when I was holdin' Betty McCloud's young babe. He was playin' with the chain and—"

Not taking the time to finish speaking, Aunt Fiona started toward the door. Her intent was obvious and Meg stopped her with a cautioning hand. "No, Aunt, I'll go. I'll take the lantern and go back to check around the table where we were sitting."

"I'll go with ye."

Meg glanced down at her aunt's swollen legs, remembering her laboring step on the return home. "No, I can make it faster without you." At her aunt's protest, she insisted. "My eyes are better than yours, and my step quicker. Don't worry, I'll find it."

Snatching up the lantern, Meg was out the door before another word could be spoken.

Pacing tensely in his upstairs room, Terry heard Sheila's low laughter and the sound of Sean's and her footsteps leaving the yard, and a jealous torment increased his frustration. Sean would soon be holding Sheila in his arms, while his own wife, the woman he loved more deeply than he had ever loved another, was downstairs, locked away from him in a solitary bed. If it were not safer to be far away from the pleasure grounds right now, he would have stayed and drowned his sorrows, but—

That sound . . . Terry hesitated, his strong jaw hardening with concentration. It had sounded like the slam of the kitchen door, and he was puzzled. Timothy O'Reilly was not likely to stagger home until the wee hours, as were any of the other boarders, and Sean was doubtless otherwise involved. He paused again, hearing the clatter of unusual activity in the kitchen below.

A chill of foreboding crawled up his spine, and Terry sprang into motion. From the kitchen doorway he saw Fiona moving chairs with a frantic hand, searching. She turned, her anxiety apparent.

"What happened?" Meg's bedroom door hung open a crack and he demanded, "Where's Meg?"

A tear slipped from Fiona's red-rimmed eyes. "It's me cross—I've lost it somewhere. Meg's gone back to the pleasure grounds to see if she can find it for me."

His expression freezing, Terry gasped, "Meg went back to the—"

With a few running steps, Terry was out through the kitchen doorway and into the yard. And then he was running full tilt, stumbling in the dark and running again, as fast as his feet would carry him.

Breathless from her rapid pace, Meg walked up the final approach to the grove, battling the belief that she was on a fool's errand. Even if Aunt Fiona's cross and chain had not already been found and stashed in an empty pocket, the night was darker than she had realized, and she knew the chances of finding it were all but nil.

The familiar notes of an Irish jig sounded as she arrived at the grounds, and Meg could not help but smile at the sight that met her eyes. Pat Scanlan, his thirteen-year-old feet faultlessly executing the difficult steps of the Irish folk dance, performed in the center of a swaying group of Irishmen. The music came to a sudden conclusion, and the boy's eyes popped wide as the appreciative fellows, feeling no pain, tossed coins at his feet. Meg reached the table where she had spent most of the day just as the boy dropped to his knees to scoop up the change.

Pausing, Meg glanced at the bar a few feet away, unconsciously amazed by the stamina of the Welsh bartender, Gomer James. Seidels of beer continued leaving his hand to slide down the bar without interruption as they had most of the day. The fellow was a giant of a man with a face like granite, and even if he was vigorously disliked by many, he was nonetheless—

A gunshot, and the joyous tableau froze! A second shot sent revelers scattering and dropping to the ground even as Meg spotted a stranger at the edge of the clearing, his gun pointed at the big Welsh bartender. Paralyzed with terror, unable to move, Meg watched as the gunman fired again—once, twice! Her breath caught in her throat as Gomer James's body jerked spasmodically with the impact of the bullets that struck him.

The big Welshman's eyes bulged as blood spurted in gushing streams from the holes in his chest, and a scream that would not leave Meg's lips echoed over and again in her mind. Gomer James was so close. She felt the deadening thud as his body hit the ground; she heard his breath rattle in his chest. She watched in breathless terror as the stranger leveled his gun again—

A strong arm unexpectedly jerking her to the ground, Meg felt a heavy male body pin her protectively even as she struggled to escape its crushing weight.

"Don't move, Meg. It isn't safe, yet."

Terry's low rasp halted her struggle just as shots sounded again, and the sound of escaping footsteps left behind a shocked, unnatural silence.

Shouts of panic and outrage suddenly erupted within the grove, filling the air, and Terry drew his bulk off her, obviously shaken. His fingers bit into her arms as he pulled her to her feet. "Fiona told me you were on your way back here. I was afraid you might be—"

Cutting himself short, Terry swallowed and glanced around nervously as Meg's gaze drifted to the crowd encircling the prostrate Welshman a few feet away. The circle separated momentarily, and Meg saw James lying motionless, his chest splattered with blood. She knew he was dead, and she suddenly realized—

Turning to stare at Terry, Meg gasped, "You knew, didn't you? You knew this was going to happen! Oh, God, you knew . . ."

The truth of it all was in Terry's eyes—her husband's eyes—a murderer's eyes, and in that moment Meg also saw the end of everything between them.

Chapter 27

The colliery whistle shrieked the start of a new week, drowning out the sound of Captain Linden's vehement protests, but David knew he had not heard the last of them. Waiting until the last dying echo faded, the stiff-faced policeman gave the office another guarded glance before continuing in a low tone.

"Two men were killed this weekend, sir—within nine hours of each other. Thomas Gwyer in Girardsville, and Gomer James right here in Shenandoah. Both were declared enemies of the Mollies, and it's plain to see the warning intended. You've barely escaped death yourself—"

"You're wasting your breath, Captain." David's voice was determined. "I'm going down into the shafts today, and I'm going to walk this operation from one end to the other until I get a clearer understanding of what's going on down there."

"Your intentions are good, sir, I've no doubt, but the timing is wrong." Linden continued speaking, his eyes searching David's face, and David knew what the concerned officer saw. He saw a man who had not fully recuperated from a grievous wound—a man who had insisted upon returning to work despite his doctor's warnings. He saw a man who was still weak and pale, but David knew all that was merely on the surface, for the man inside him was thinking clearly for the first time.

David briefly closed his eyes. He had read the warning in these latest killings. He knew what they meant. There would be no lessening of Molly activity now, for the tide was turning and the leadership was becoming desperate. The labor pool had changed and the Irish were a lesser minority than before. Condemnation of the organization was at a new height with the murder of Gomer James; and under the new, fearless editorship of Tom Foster, the *Shenandoah Herald* was waging a relentless attack against it. The church's unceasing denunciation of the organization had begun being felt at the last bastions of its support, and public outrage against the endless violence was at such a height that the Mollies now had their backs to the wall. The Mollies were not ignorant of their dire circumstances, and they knew they need maintain the level of fear that had protected them in the past or they were lost. They were going to push until something snapped, one way or another.

David opened his eyes to Linden's concerned gaze. Well, he would not be the one to snap. Nor would he run, or give up, especially now when he had already lost so much.

"Are you all right, sir?"

David attempted a smile at the man's concern. "I'm better than I look, and my thinking is more lucid that it's been for a long time, Captain. I suppose that's because I've done little else but think for the past week."

"Well, if you're thinking as clearly as you say, sir, you know that the miners are upset over these latest atrocities."

"Precisely the reason to show them I'm as upset as they are, that I intend to do all I can to work out their problems with fair concessions on both sides."

"They won't be fooled, Mr. Lang."

David returned the policeman's level gaze. "I have no intention of fooling them, Captain."

Linden's doubts obviously remained, and David sighed. "Let me try to explain. It's like this. Force and threat have been tried on both sides without true success. The mine owners as well as the miners are suffering for the lack of understanding shown for each other's points of view, and it's time to take a step beyond mutual prejudice.

"You see, during the past week I've had the chance to go over in my mind thoughts that I dismissed too easily before. Someone I care very much about once asked me if I knew what it was like down in those mines, and I said yes, but I've only just realized the hypocrisy of that response. I've studied the operation of this colliery—the production figures, the profit and loss, the future potential of this mine as well as the potential of the Pennsylvania fields in general. I've gone below to observe firsthand the techniques being used to mine the coal. I've gone over the safety problems and the measures we took to correct them. I've studied it all until I was too tired to think, but it occurred to me only recently that I'd never actually taken the time to *really* talk to the miners themselves."

David gave a short laugh at Linden's raised brow. "That's right.

I walked past them as they labored at the breasts, stepped around them as they loaded coal, and did no more than nod in response when they looked me straight in the eye. And when the union representatives came to my office all steamed up, I answered them with anger without giving their grievances true consideration. I've held the past disturbances of a few against the lot of them in general. I've been so sure that I, and all the mine owners and supervisors like me, were right and they were wrong. But the truth is, I'm not so sure anymore."

"Mr. Lang—"

"I'm going to sort this thing out, Captain, or make a damned good attempt at trying."

Captain Linden nodded, his frown deepening. "Everything you've said is very commendable, sir, and I'd agree that you're doing the right thing, except that the timing is wrong."

"The timing?"

"Aye." Linden looked uncomfortable. "It's dangerous for me to speak of this, but . . ."

"Yes?"

"But it's soon to come down, sir. All of it."

David shook his head, confused. "What are you talking about?"

"We have a witness to the murder of Gomer James who thinks he recognized the fellow who did the shooting and is willing to testify against him."

"Who?"

"John Williams, a friend of James. It's the first time anyone has had the courage to testify against a Molly. This, in combination with the case our man inside the organization has prepared, should be the beginning of the end."

David frowned, hesitating at the first concern that touched his mind. "How closely are Terry Donovan and Sean O'Connor tied up in all this?"

Linden paused, appearing to realize that David would not be satisfied with less than the full truth. "Donovan's in deep. O'Connor's been behaving strangely of late and it's uncertain which way he'll go."

David knew that if anyone could have worked a change in O'Connor, it was Meg. Over the long week since she had left him, he had come to realize that there was no one else but her brother—Terry Donovan included—who could have made her leave him. He was now sure that Sean O'Connor had somehow gotten to Meg that last night.

But that realization changed nothing, and David knew even more certainly than ever that the gulf between Meg and him, the irreconcilable differences that would always keep them apart, could only be narrowed by himself and the dissolution of the prejudices he had so stubbornly maintained.

He wondered why it had taken him so long to realize it.

"Where is this witness now?"

"He's on the job. He'll stay there until we're ready to move."

"No one knows he intends to testify?"

"No."

"Good." David picked up his jacket. In light of the warmth of the day, it was mute indication of his intention to go below-ground.

"I'll send a few of my men with you, Mr. Lang."

"I'll go alone. The foreman in each shaft will show me around."

"Mr. Lang—"

But David had already started toward the door.

Kehoe's piercing gaze burned into Terry's face. Seated across the table from him in Lawler's upstairs room, Terry felt the heat of the man's fury. His own was no less. In the last few days since Gomer James's death, he had seen one part of his world come to an end, and he was not anxious to see the rest of it fall down around him.

"They have a witness who's willing to testify, ye say?" Terry was incredulous. "What man would be fool enough to speak out against us?"

"A damned Welshman close to James, that's who!" Kehoe's full lips pulled into a sneer. "Ah, if I only had the luxury of takin' care of the man meself. Them damned Modocs are behind much of our problems here with their jealousies. They're gettin' too bold and it's up to ye this time, Donovan. This is yer town and yer responsible for straightenin' this mess out. Ye can do it in only one way."

"Ye need not spell it out to me." Terry was incensed. "I know what me duties are! I've done as much and done it well many times before. Ye've but to give me the name of the informer."

"That's the easiest part. John Williams."

"I know the greasy rodent."

"Aye, and ye've to keep in mind he'll be as slippery as a rodent, too."

"I'll get him. Everyone'll think it's an accident."

"Nay. That won't do." And at Terry's raised brow, "Ye must teach all them braggin' Welsh what to expect if they try to finger one of us again. Ye can only do that by makin' it obvious that it was one of us who did it, even if ye must take care not to be identified. And I want it done right. There's been too much gone amiss here already."

"I'll do the job meself."

"Ye'll take two men with ye."

"I'll do it alone."

Kehoe's eyes sparked fire. "I said *take two men with ye!* Ye'll need one at yer back and one at yer front to do the job right." Kehoe paused. "Are ye tryin' to tell me that ye've not two men ye can trust until we're clear who the informer in our organization is?"

Terry's small eyes narrowed. "Nay. I have two I can trust, all right."

Kehoe assessed Terry's tight expression for a long moment before drawing himself slowly to his feet. He gave a caustic laugh as he cast a quick glance around the room. "I think of the many times the membership's been gathered around this table to listen to our plans with full confidence, and it makes me stomach turn to know there's an informer that's one of our own. But we'll find him out soon, and when we do, we'll fix him good. In the meantime, it's up to ye, Donovan."

"Aye, and it'll be done right. I give ye me word. Williams will breathe his last before the week is out."

"It can't be soon enough."

Exchanging a last glance, the two men parted, Kehoe to the staircase to the street and Terry back to the bar below.

Raising his glass to his lips a few minutes later, Terry glanced into the corner where Sean sat quietly conversing with Jim McKenna.

He knew he need not fear losing Meg any longer if he pressed Sean, and his stomach twisted painfully. Meg had turned her back on him for good. So much did she despise him that he didn't know that to implicate him would be to implicate her own brother as well. Memory of the loathing in those great eyes where love had once shone twisted the knife of pain inside him anew. She would loathe him even more before this week was done.

The anguish in Terry's expression slowly turned to stone. But he had determined another thing as well. If he would never again hold Meg in his arms, neither would David Lang. It was only a matter of time.

A strange sense of unreality filled Sean's mind as he stared at the pistol Terry placed in his hand. It was heavy and cold despite the heat of his upstairs bedroom. The alien feel of it brought a frown to his face as he looked up into Terry's close scrutiny.

"The job must be done." Terry's voice was a low monotone. "There're few I can now trust with the job. Yer one of them, despite our personal differences of late. Are ye up to it?"

Sean hesitated. His eyes narrowed as he wondered at the reason for his delay in responding. He had known this time would eventually come. He had once anticipated it with an eagerness that now seemed unreal, but he had not anticipated the feel of this weapon in his hand. It was as cold as the death it could evoke. His hesitation became prolonged.

"Have ye lost the heart for it, then?" Terry's tone became an angry growl. At the further narrowing of Sean's gaze, Terry's face flushed with suppressed fury. "I didn't take ye for such a fool! What will ye do now, me boyo? Will ye take yer buxom little Sheila to wife and settle in a house in the patch? And then will ye produce yer progeny year after year until yer house is full and yer table is lean? Will ye then wait for yer oldest to reach the age of seven so he might help out with the expenses by workin' in the breaker, and then in the mine alongside ye at the age of twelve so he might pull a fuller wage?"

Terry paused and straightened his broad shoulders. "But I warn ye, while ye are doin' that ye'll see the faces around ye changin'. There'll be less and less Irish in the mines, and only the last and the dirtiest jobs will be left to them that remain. But ye'll have missed yer chance to change all that, so ye'll have no choice but to be thankful to take yer meager wage while they spit on ye for bein' what ye are. Ye'll keep yer mouth shut, but it'll all start festerin' inside ye then. The sore will get bigger and bigger every day until ye curse the day ye were born 'cause there'll be no way out, save the one ye threw away."

When Sean still did not respond, Terry's face contorted with rage. "What's happened to ye! Have ye forgotten that yer less a man in the eyes of them in charge just because of the Irish blood that flows in yer veins? Have ye thrown yer vows to the Brotherhood aside and yer vow to avenge yer Da and brothers as well? Will ye sacrifice yer manhood for the sake of a woman— even if that woman be yer own sister? Fie on ye, Sean O'Connor, for the weaklin' yer sister has made of ye!"

"Don't speak of my sister to me!"

"I will, for yer sister's me wife as well! I love her as do ye, but I'd not have her turn me into what that bastard on the hill, and all them like him, would have me be. I made me choice, and ye know I did it well when ye heard of Gomer James's fall."

His rage slowly subsiding, Terry stared at Sean with great sobriety. "Think carefully of what ye do now, me friend, for ye'll live with it the rest of yer life. Think of the years past, then look to the future and see if ye can live with what ye see, for there'll be no change unless we make it happen now. Then look at the gun in yer hand and judge if it be a small price to pay for all that might be achieved with it."

Sean was staring at the gun as Terry posed one last whispered question. "Tell me, will ye be content to live yer life knowin' ye sacrificed yer honor in this hour?"

The silence of the room was long and pronounced as Sean's hand slowly closed around the handle of the gun. He looked up to meet Terry's keen stare. "I knew my time was soon to come when Gomer James fell to the dirt in that grove. In the time since, I've searched my heart for what I would do when it did. And it's come down to this. I've no choice in what I must do, you see. My life's been forfeit the many years since my Da and the boys died, for I knew then, as I know now, that fate kept me from the shaft that day for a purpose. That purpose wasn't so I might eke out a livin' to the end of my days in that dank hole where my Da and the boys met their end. I was to make a difference, you see. I've not told this to anyone else, for I've known none would understand, but I'm thinkin' you do." His eyes holding Terry's, Sean continued tightly. "You're right that I faltered because of Meg, for she's dearer to me than any other on this earth, and I've no desire to hurt her. She loves me, and knowin' what I've to do with this—"

Sean's hand tightened spasmodically around the handle of the gun and his eyes dropped briefly closed. "But all that's come to pass has been for naught if I turn my back on it now, and if I fail to do what I must, there'll be no use in my havin' survived at all."

Sean took a steadying breath. The smile he forced to his lips was as cold as the smile Terry returned. "Aye, you can count on me to get the job done. When's it to be?"

"Before the day is out."

Sean's heart began a heavy hammering. "It's to be the two of us?"

"Nay, three. McKenna will be included."

Sean's jaw tightened. The gun still in his hand, he was unprepared as the door suddenly opened.

A cold hand of panic closed around Meg's throat. A gun in Sean's hand . . .

Unexpectedly snatched out of the doorway as the door slammed closed behind her, Meg pushed herself free of Terry before addressing Sean in a ragged whisper.

"What are you doing with that gun?" She whitened. "Not David . . . ?"

Sean's gaze was chillingly cold. "Lang's as safe as he'll ever be, and what I've to do with this is none of your affair."

Meg's relief was fleeting. "Is it not my affair that my brother is about to lose his soul?"

"Don't speak to me of souls, Meg!" Sean's eyes suddenly spit fire. "You'd not accept that I've no soul to lose, but it's true, for if it ever existed inside me, it's been long lost these many years."

"Nay, Sean. You've not used one of those before." Meg looked at the pistol in his hand with a barely suppressed shudder. "You told me you haven't."

"Then that was my mistake."

Uncertain how to take her brother's cryptic remark, Meg glanced at Terry to see he observed all with an unfeeling expression. She turned hot with rage.

"The devil in disguise is what you are, Terry Donovan! Does it give you pleasure to drag my brother down with you?"

"Nay, don't lay the blame to Terry. He—"

"Ye needn't stand up for me, Sean. I can speak for meself." Terry looked at Meg and she felt the full weight of his intense scrutiny as his eyes suddenly softened, resembling those of the Terry she had once believed true.

"Ye see me as a devil, Meg, and that's strange because ye took on the look of an angel to me from the first time me eyes touched on yer beautiful face. I wanted ye then, and I want ye now—but not to bring ye or yer brother down—nay, not that. I cherished the hope inside me that ye'd bring me up to match the beauty I saw within and without ye. But there just wasn't enough time, and it wasn't to be. I know that now. It's too late for us, but if ye understand nothin' else about me, I want ye to understand that I never meant ye any harm. Ye must know that I do what I do because me convictions are as strong as yer own, and I can no sooner deny them than ye can deny yers. We're driven by a need, Sean and me. We're the same inside—"

"You're not the same! Sean has no blood on his hands."

The silence that followed made its own emphatic statement, and Meg gasped. Uncertain what she meant to do, Meg turned suddenly and made for the door, only to be snatched from her feet by Terry's strong arm as his other hand clamped across her mouth.

She was fighting Terry's relentless grip when Sean barked, "Let her go!"

Sean gripped Terry's arm in an attempt to free her as Terry hissed, "Desist, I say! Would you have yer sister turn the whole bunch of us in to the police in a misguided attempt to save ye?"

Sean's hand stilled. "Meg wouldn't—" Halting midsentence to stare down into Meg's face, Sean read the truth in her eyes before he allowed his to drift briefly closed.

"Over there—get yer spare hose."

Terry's curt order raised Sean's eyes to his face with unspoken protest.

"Do as I say! Her hands and ankles tied and a gag around her mouth will keep her here long enough for us to get our work done. Once it's over we'll have nothin' to fear, for she'd not turn ye in then."

Her heart pounding, Meg watched Sean slowly turn to retrieve his hose, and her struggling increased. No, she couldn't let Sean do this! She had to stop him!

Securely bound moments later, Meg lay on Sean's bed. Her eyes were filled with incredulous terror as the two men walked to the door. Pausing there, Sean suddenly turned and walked back to her side. He crouched beside the bed and she fought to speak through the heavy gag but it was no use. The pain in Sean's eyes grew as he stroked a strand of hair back from her damp cheek.

"Hush, Meg. I'm doin' what must be done, and whatever the sacrifice, I have no true regrets. If you fear the devil may eventually take my heart and soul, you may console yourself that he'll take all but the parts where you reside. Those parts are pure and clean, Meg, and they'll ever belong to you."

The weight of her tears too heavy to bear, Meg closed her eyes, and when she opened them again the door was closing behind them.

• • •

The pain in her knees was steady as Fiona turned the corner and her home came into view. Breathing another grateful prayer, she clutched the cross around her neck with a shaking hand. With all the horror of that night in the pleasure grounds and the tension in her own home in the time since, her cross had been forgotten.

She had never expected to see it again, and she had been overwhelmed with gratitude when little James McNulty brought it to her door that morning. Walking around to the rear door of the house, Fiona entered the kitchen and stopped short at the silence there. It was empty, just as she had left it, and a sudden apprehension crawled up the back of her spine. A quick look revealed Meg was not in her room. Where could she be?

A dull thumping from the second floor intruded into Fiona's thoughts, raising her eyes unconsciously to the ceiling. Swallowing tightly, she followed the sound up the staircase to Sean's room. The thumping grew louder as she called inside. Carefully unlocking the door with her spare key, she pushed it open, a shocked gasp escaping her lips.

Within moments she was at the bedside, her hands clumsy with haste as she unfastened her niece's bonds.

"Meg, me darlin' girl—"

Her gaze frantic, Meg jumped to her feet the moment her bonds were freed. She stumbled on her benumbed limbs and Fiona pressed, "Tell me who did this to ye!"

Meg shook her head. "I have to go! Oh, Aunt, I must try—"

Snapping her lips closed, Meg turned abruptly and was out through the doorway and running down the front stairs. Fiona's heart became a deadening weight within her. Suddenly shuddering, a dreadful premonition crawling up her spine, Fiona covered her eyes.

Meg ran through the late-afternoon streets, unconscious of the curious looks she drew as she turned another corner, gasping. How long had it been before Aunt Fiona came home? An hour? More? A sob tore at her throat.

Guided by instinct, Meg turned onto a familiar path, stumbling, falling, and pulling herself to her feet again.

The guards at the manor's front door made no attempt to stop her as Meg rushed into the foyer. Her frantic step came to an abrupt halt when she saw David in the doorway of the study, and a sharp, hysterical laugh escaped her throat. David was safe.

Within moments his arms were tight around her as he questioned anxiously, "Meg, what's wrong?"

"David, I thought . . ."

Meg was momentarily unable to continue, causing David's concerned demand, "Meg, tell me what's wrong."

Meg shook her head, her panic increasing. "No, I must go. They didn't come here, but I must find them!"

"Find whom? Meg, look at me!"

A sob escaped Meg's throat as she met David's eyes. "Terry and Sean. It may be too late already."

Frantic, Meg attempted to free herself from David, only to have him hold her more firmly than before.

"Please, Meg. I can help you if you'll only tell me what happened."

"A gun . . ." Meg's voice emerged in a whisper. "Sean had a gun, and he left with Terry. They're going to kill someone. I was afraid it was you, but—"

Meg halted in midsentence as David's face whitened and his hands fell to his sides. Realization dawning, she rasped incredulously, "You know who they're going after, don't you . . . ? You must tell me so I can stop them!"

"When did they leave?"

"Awhile ago. I'm not sure how long."

David reached for the doorknob. "Stay here, Meg. You'll be safe. I'll take care of this."

"No!" Meg clutched his arm as he shouted for the guard. "I'm going with you!"

David's expression hardened as he turned to the policeman suddenly at his side. "Keep Mrs. Donovan here, Sergeant." And then to the men at the door. "Wilkins—McGregor, come with me!"

The two policemen fell in behind David and Meg went abruptly still. "David, I trusted you . . ."

Holding her gaze for a long, silent moment, David turned and walked quickly out the door.

Sean wiped the perspiration from his brow with the back of his arm, aware that the heat of the sunny, late August day was not the sole cause of his discomfort. Surveying the street from the position of concealment he and his companions had occupied for the past hour, he glanced at the men beside him, aware that their faces bore a similar sheen. There was not a trace of nervousness in Terry's careful scrutiny of the street, or on Jim McKenna's smooth, boyish face, and he wondered if they were shaking inside as much as he.

Sean tightened his hand around the pistol in his pocket, aware that his companions carried similar weapons. He looked down the nearly deserted street again. The lateness of the hour had lengthened the shadows of the uneven row of frame buildings against the dusty street, and a small dog wandering aimlessly near the corner was the only sign of movement.

Impatience ticked Sean's cheek as his clear eyes squinted tighter. The supper hour was already in progress, accounting for the lack of traffic on the street, and for the past hour and a half they had watched the patrons of Burton's Welsh saloon emerge one by one while John Williams still remained inside. Terry's whispered reassurance had confirmed that Williams was well known to be the last to leave on most days, but Sean still could not dismiss the uneasiness that had grown inside him as the long minutes had continued to pass.

Tensing as the door of the saloon opened again and the sound of mumbled conversation echoed in the silence, Sean held his breath. Two men emerged, squinting into the sun, and his frustration mounted. Damn the man! Where was he?

Sean was watching the two men's progress up the street when a sound snapped his attention back toward the saloon. He froze. John Williams, his homely face unmistakable, stood in the doorway. The fellow turned back to someone inside with a low comment and then stepped out onto the street.

Beside Sean, Terry and McKenna tensed, and, as if on a prearranged signal, the three of them drew their pistols.

Aware that Linden, running beside him, was laboring as much as he, David turned down the familiar street, his heart pounding. The image of Meg's white face remained in his mind as the footsteps of policemen running at their rear echoed in the semi-deserted street. But he hadn't had time to explain to her that he had realized almost immediately who Donovan and O'Connor were after. Nor had he had the time to convince her that he would try to protect all involved, but that the most important thing was that she remain safe at any cost.

To his everlasting credit, Captain Linden had mobilized his men on a moment's notice, knowing exactly where Williams was most likely to be. The corner of Main and Oak came into view. Only a little farther and—

A gunshot rang out in the silence, and a ragged breath caught in David's throat. Charging forward, David saw out of the corner of his eye that Linden had drawn his gun, that the men behind had done the same. They turned the corner to the sound of another gunshot, and another, and David's step faltered as a man in the doorway of the saloon at the opposite end of the street slumped to the ground.

Captain Linden called out in warning as three men stepped out of the shadows opposite the fallen man. Standing boldly a moment longer, two of the three aimed their guns at point blank range and fired at the inert figure again.

Turning on a run, two men started for the wooded area beyond as Captain Linden shouted a command to halt. The command went ignored and gunshots rang in the deserted street, a heavy barrage that jerked the taller man upright for the space of a moment before he stumbled onward. Another shot knocked him to the ground as the man beside him turned to glance over his shoulder.

Those unmistakable eyes so similar to Meg's . . .

Gunshots rang out again and the second man's running step jerked to a halt as he pitched forward onto his face.

"Cease your firing!"

His command bringing the shooting to an abrupt halt, Linden raced toward the two fallen assassins as the third man disappeared from sight. Signaling a few of his men to follow, Linden kneeled, examining each man in turn.

"Williams is dead, sir!"

Linden nodded in silent response to the report shouted from across the street. He turned to look up at David, his expression grave. "As are these two."

Blood pooled beneath the fallen men and David closed his eyes, snapping them wide again at the sound of a gasp behind him.

He turned as Meg rushed past him to stand rigidly between the bodies of the two fallen men. He stepped toward her as she swayed, then sank silently to the ground.

Chapter 28

A crisp autumn breeze ruffled Meg's hair as she walked the dusty, deserted road from town. She looked up at the partially denuded branches of the trees around her and paused to follow a swirl of brightly colored leaves to the ground. The breeze whipped harder, flaying her face with curling strands of hair, but she brushed them back, resuming her step. A glance toward the position of the sun in the afternoon sky told her it would soon be time to start back home.

Home. There had been little comfort in the word in the two months since all feeling came to a shattering halt on a dirt street stained with blood.

Gunshots echoed again in Meg's mind. It was a sound that haunted her both awake and sleeping. She would never forget it. Nor would she forget three bodies sprawled in the dust, their life's blood draining into the ground.

Meg glanced up at the swiftly moving clouds over her head. She was strangely without tears the day Terry and Sean were lowered into the ground, but she had grieved. She mourned the lapse of love inside Sean that left him only bitterness. She lamented her failure. She sorrowed with a pain that would not abate for the profanity of his last act, for his violent death, and for the aching void within her that grew more agonized each day.

Filled with regrets, she had mourned Terry, too. But she did not grieve for the "soldier" whose cold eyes had made him a stranger, or for the man who had guided her brother the last few steps to his violent death. She lamented the loss of the loving man she glimpsed so briefly, the gentle man inside Terry who did not have a chance to grow.

Meg shuddered, her sudden chill unrelated to the nip in the air or the lengthening shadows that had begun to block the warmth of the sun. She had walked for several hours, as she had every day since she left Sheila at Sean's freshly covered grave. The image of

Sheila's pale, strained face as she looked up from Sean's last resting place was burned as clearly into her memory as her words:

"Aye, it's over, Meg, and it's not ended the way we hoped, but the way we feared." And then at Meg's attempt at consolation, "Don't grieve for me, Meg, for I've no regrets, you see. I told myself long ago that Sean's time with me would be short, and it was only briefly that I allowed myself to believe otherwise. But I'd not have had it any other way, for I loved him, Meg, and I can console myself that I gave him all I had to give. In his way, Sean returned the same in kind, and the memory of that will live with me all of my life."

Fighting the return of another memory, Meg walked faster, but the image of David, waiting just beyond the small circle of mourners at graveside, would not fade. She had walked past him then, without a word, but she had come to realize in the time since that no amount of walking or mourning or regrets could alleviate the torment of turning her back on him forever.

Meg shivered. She was tired, but she didn't want to return home yet.

Yielding to impulse, Meg turned into a small grove of trees and continued walking. Suddenly realizing she had walked a circuitous route back toward town, she continued on, knowing full well where that particular road would lead.

Drawn to the abandoned mill despite herself, Meg approached the stone structure, her heart beginning a slow pounding. She paused briefly in the doorway, then walked inside, the constriction in her throat expanding to the point of pain.

Closing her eyes, Meg felt the aura that remained, the heady presence of Sean and the tenderness that had transpired there. Gratitude swelled inside her for the munificence of Sheila's love even while her dear friend knew that her loving would never be enough for Sean.

Meg heaved a heavy, shuddering sigh. Love, sorrow, regrets, no matter how profound, would change nothing. It had all gone bad. And in the midst of it all, Meg knew that she was lost and could not find her way back.

A sound, and Meg stiffened. She opened her eyes as a masculine shadow appeared in the doorway. It grew gradually larger and Meg held her breath, her eyes widening.

"Meg."

"No!" Pressing her hand against her mouth, Meg shook her

head as if to deny the violation of David's entrance into this place. "Don't come in here! Get out!"

"Meg—"

"I said get out! Get out!"

Suddenly charging, Meg threw herself against David, knocking him back through the doorway with the strength of her attack. Her fists flailing, she pounded and scratched, her frenzied assault growing more intensely frantic despite David's attempts to calm her.

Suddenly grasping Meg's wrists, David twisted her arms behind her. His voice was filled with pain as he muttered hoarsely, "Stop this, Meg. Please."

The strength drained from Meg's limbs at his low plea, and she went suddenly still. David's face was so close to hers. She could smell the scent of his skin, feel his breath against her lips. The dark pupils of his eyes were dilated, narrowing a ring of green in which golden sparks revealed the emotion he suppressed with his rasping whisper. "Let me talk to you, Meg. Let me explain."

"Let me go."

David's chin hardened into stubborn lines. "I won't let you walk away from me again. I've tried to be patient, Meg."

"I said, let me go!"

His gaze narrowing, David slowly released her.

Unconsciously rubbing her sore wrists, Meg returned his stare with growing intensity. "I've made many mistakes, David, but I'll not make the same ones again. Sean told me I'd regret believing in you someday, and he was right." Her breathing grew more ragged. "When Sean left the house with a gun that last day, I was terrified. But it wasn't Sean I was afraid for. Fool that I was, I was afraid for *you*! I ran straight to you as soon as I could, and it was only after I saw you were safe that my thoughts returned to Sean."

David reached for her once more, halting at Meg's low hiss. "Don't touch me! I trusted you! I believed you when you said you would help me. I put my brother's life in your hands, and you betrayed me. You threw my brother's life away!"

"No, Meg, it wasn't that way! I had to try to stop him."

"By going to the police? You knew what they would do!"

"They did the only thing they could. Donovan and your brother were out to kill a man."

"No!" Meg shook her head. "I don't want to hear any of this!"

"You must!" Grasping her arms, David held her firmly despite her struggle. "You mustn't blame yourself or me for what happened. Things had gone too far."

"I could've found Sean and talked to him."

"Just as you talked to him before he left? He didn't listen then, and he wouldn't have listened if you had followed him to that street and begged. Don't you see? I couldn't let you get in the middle of it all and risk your life. I had to keep you safe."

"Safe—at the expense of my brother's life?"

"Meg, you can't change what happened by denying everything that led up to it. You knew where your brother was heading a long time ago. What happened wasn't your fault, and it wasn't mine."

"It was!"

"You have to try to forget."

"Forget?" A harsh laugh escaped Meg's lips with the slow, pained admission of the guilt that consumed her. "Do you really expect me to forget that I allowed you to make me an instrument in the death of my own brother?"

"Meg . . ." His arms slipping around her, David pulled her close against him, but Meg remained rigid against the consolation of his embrace. She could feel his strong body trembling, and she fought her growing response to the torment in his voice as he whispered against her hair, "I made no conscious choice in what I did that day. I did what I had to do, just as you did what you had to do when you came to me to stop the deliberate taking of a life. Don't punish me . . . don't punish us both for behaving instinctively."

"It should have been instinctive for me to save Sean and Terry instead of a person I didn't even know. I should not have sacrificed their lives for my own conscience."

"You wanted to save them, not sacrifice them! And I wanted—"

"No! I'll listen to no more of this!"

"You must! Meg, please, I've tried to be patient. I wanted to give you more time to come to terms with your grief, but I can't wait any longer to say the things that must be said. I love you, Meg. You've never been truly out of my mind since that first day I dragged you out of that bush and you challenged me with your anger, and I've spent too many years of my life trying to forget you to fool myself into thinking that I ever can. I don't want to forget you, Meg. I want to love you. I want to take care of you. I want you to be with me all of my life. Meg . . ." David's voice broke with the intensity of his plea, "Please let me love you."

A gradual desperation began overtaking Meg. David's eyes shone with an anguish that lived inside her as well, but she closed her eyes against his pain. His body trembled with the same aching need as her own, but she resisted the sweet solace it promised. His mouth met hers and she fought the surge of warmth that touched the frozen core of her heart. She sought to resist the mesmerizing beauty that assailed her, even as she cleaved to him, as she—

"No!" Suddenly tearing herself from David's arms, Meg took a step backwards, her eyes wide, appalled. She raised a clenched fist to her lips, shaking her head. How could she have forgotten, even for a moment?

Turning, Meg ran for the trees, bolting from her own weakness. David's footsteps pounded behind her and she ran faster, rasping for breath even as David's hands clamped on her shoulders from behind. Stumbling under the weight of his grip, Meg fell to the ground, gasping as David's weight fell partially upon her.

Momentarily stunned, she felt David's hands on her face, saw the anxiety in his eyes, those beautiful eyes that drew closer still until the golden sparks numbed her will. She was lost to their wonder, aglow with their flame. Their heat consumed her. She became a part of him, wanting as she was desired, giving as she received, loving as she was loved. She felt the bite of the cool air against her flesh, but David warmed it with his lips. She felt David's hunger and her own soared anew. Myriad emotions assailed her, each of them potent and demanding, each of them raising her need until she called his name, pleading.

She gasped at their joining. She raised her body to meet his with each passionate thrust, loving his loving—loving him.

David's body was motionless atop hers, replete, when reality made the first inroads into her mind. And Meg closed her eyes, her heart breaking at what she had done.

David stood at the window of his study. The afternoon shadows continued to lengthen as the sun made its descent toward evening, touching the foliage outside the window with a fading amber. The colors of autumn were in brilliant display, but a faint smile curved his lips with the thought that its splendor paled in comparison with the beauty Meg and he had rediscovered in each other's arms only a short time earlier. He had not wanted to part from her, even briefly.

His expression sobering, David turned away from the window and walked toward his desk. He halted, looking at the pile of papers there, knowing instinctively it was senseless even to attempt to work. He was too filled with the glory of Meg to do else but remember.

Elation reverberated inside him. She was so beautiful, his Meg. She was his bliss, his future, his love. And she was finally his alone, never to be lost again.

Suddenly impatient with this enforced separation, David questioned the wisdom of allowing Meg to return home, even for a short time. But he had been unable to deny the distance that had come between them when the heat of their mutual passion had passed. He had sensed her withdrawal, and when she did not respond to his inquiry, he had decided against pressing her. He did not fool himself that he had totally erased the pain of the past months from Meg's mind. That would take time, and he was determined that he would give it to her, as difficult as it would be.

His heated trend of thought interrupted by an unexpected knock on the door, David turned with an impatient response. He froze into stillness at the peculiar light in Captain Linden's eyes as he entered the room and closed the door behind himself.

Tightly clutching her traveling case, Meg stood in the deserted train station. A whistle echoed in the distance, heralding the approach of the late-afternoon train, and she squinted at the dark puffs of smoke rising into the brilliant blue of the horizon. Sadness, panic, desperation moved over her in succeeding waves, increasing her trepidation as she glanced nervously over her shoulder.

Releasing a quivering breath, Meg straightened her shoulders, her eyes on the train rounding the curve into sight. She did not remember making a conscious decision to leave. Even now her presence on this deserted platform seemed unreal—almost as unreal as her shattering response to David's lovemaking. But the soul-shaking realization that had followed as she lay in David's arms, the knowledge that despite herself, she had returned David's love with all the power of her aching heart, had been too much to bear.

Meg trembled anew. How many times must she fall before she admitted to herself that David's loving gaze manipulated her will, that she was presently defenseless against it? How many times could she betray Sean before she was unable to live with her regrets?

Those thoughts had been foremost in her mind even as David

and she had parted, his words of love resounding in her ears. Driven by shame, and deaf to Aunt Fiona's protests, she had thrown her meager belongings into a bag, taking the time only for a brief note to Father Matthew before she left, so desperate had she been to bring the turmoil inside herself to an end.

The train made its final, hissing approach, and Meg's heart raced as she reached into the pocket of her coat to touch the ticket there. Glancing around again as the train shuddered to a halt in front of her, she quickly climbed the narrow metal steps and walked into the car without looking back.

Drawing back behind the grilled protection of the counter, the startled ticket clerk eyed David's white face warily as David demanded again, "Are you sure? Damn it, man, are you?"

His face flushing, the young fellow stammered nervously. "Of course, I'm sure. I saw the lady leave. Real pretty she was with them big eyes and . . ." The clerk's words trailed off as David's threatening expression darkened, and he paused to swallow nervously before continuing. "She bought a ticket for Philadelphia and she jumped on that train as soon as it stopped, like the devil was after her." Flushing more darkly, the fellow finished in a rush. "The train left about five minutes ago and I didn't see nothin' else."

Outside the station, David searched the empty platform with a desperate gaze. A train whistle echoed in the distance and David stared in the direction of the sound, disbelieving. It couldn't be true. Meg couldn't have left him!

He cursed, the desperation inside him growing. If only he hadn't doubted Linden's report that Meg had been seen at the train station with a suitcase in her hand. If only he hadn't stopped at her house first to check if she was there, he might have arrived in time to stop her.

His throat suddenly tight, David ran a shaking hand through his hair. She was gone. How many times did Meg have to turn away from him before he realized that she had had enough? How many times did he—

Another thought suddenly striking him, David stood stock still. Springing into movement a moment later, he ran the few steps to his horse, mounted, and spurred the animal into motion.

Reaching his destination a short time later, David leaped to the ground and hastily tied his mount's reins to the nearest branch. Following the familiar trail the rest of the way on foot, he felt the knot of tension inside him tighten with each step. Halting briefly as he approached the familiar bower, he gathered his courage and stepped between the overgrown honeysuckle bushes that surrounded it.

He saw Meg then. A suitcase at her feet, she turned to meet his gaze, and relief pounded through him. She searched his face intently as he closed the distance between them with a few rapid steps. He crushed her against him, hungry for the feel of her as he whispered, his voice breaking, "Meg . . . I thought you had left me."

He kissed her once, twice, but she drew back from him, determined to speak.

Meeting his gaze squarely, she whispered, "I *meant* to leave you, David. I bought my ticket and climbed on the train, but at the last second, I couldn't do it. I was confused. I needed to think, so I came up here to be alone and sort things out."

Meg's voice faltered, and she took a deep breath before proceeding with quiet intensity. "I felt so lost. All I could think about was the ways that I had failed—in maintaining my promise to my Ma—in saving Sean from himself—in keeping the gentle Terry, the man to whom I'd said my vows, from being overwhelmed by the side of him that was too despicable to bear. I felt I had betrayed those who loved me, those I loved in return, and I felt by loving you I was betraying them even more. I hated myself, David. And I hated you, for loving me. I was filled with grief and close to despair."

Meg paused again, her expression slowly changing as a smile touched the sober line of her lips for the first time. "It was then that my Ma's voice came to my mind. It was sweet and clear in saying as she had that last day, 'Be true to yourself, Meg.'

"I put aside my grief then, David, so I might honestly search my heart. And in the searching, deep inside, I realized that my heart's been torn in two all these many years, and that in all that I had done, there was only one person I had truly failed." Tears filled Meg's eyes as she raised her hand to David's cheek. "That person is you."

Pressing closer, her voice breaking, Meg whispered, "Damaged and sore as it is, my heart's whole at last, David, and it's yours. If I'm to be true to myself, I know now that I must love you. I must stay with you all of our lives, for in truth, my love is such that I have no choice at all."

A sobering elation robbed David of speech. Trembling as Meg

trembled, loving her at that moment more than he had ever loved her before, he drew her close. He held her almost reverently as the full significance of the moment sank into his mind. Meg loved him as he loved her.

Crushing her close against him, David cherished that thought. He savored it in his mind, his mouth covering Meg's in silent promise as a gentle breeze caressed them, raising the scent of honeysuckle, although the blossoms were long gone.

AUTHOR'S NOTE

The Molly Maguires controlled the coal fields for twenty-seven years. The organization's reign of terror came to an end in 1877, largely through the efforts of Pinkerton agent James McParlan, who worked effectively within the Shenandoah Division for three years under the name James McKenna. Through McParlan's testimony, seventy members of the secret society were brought to trial and convicted. Twenty were executed. One of the last to reach the gallows was "Black Jack" Kehoe, father of six, and "King of the Mollies."

Franklin Benjamin Gowen, President of the Philadelphia and Reading Coal and Iron Company, personally participated in the trials of the Mollies as representative for the prosecution. Hailed the savior of the coal fields, he was elated at the success of his endeavors. Ironically, he was found some years later in his room at a luxury hotel, dead at his own hand.

The Pennsylvania coal fields fared no better than Gowen, for the anthracite industry in Pennsylvania never fully recuperated from the strike of 1875. Where once flourishing coal mines prevailed, the coal yards now lie abandoned and only rotting skeletons of the towering breakers remain. The mountainous dumps of waste generated by the labor underground have become permanent parts of a landscape still bearing grotesque scars of a defunct industry.

The only true victories after years of conflict were in the cessation of violence, and in the individual, personal triumphs of the spirit prevailing for those such as Meghan O'Connor and David Lang, whatever names they bore.

Dear Friends,

I hope you enjoyed *Wishes on the Wind*. It was my intention to bring the tragedy and courage of this period in history to life for you through my characters. I hope I've made you understand them, and I hope you see Meg and David's love as a light in the darkness and a wish on the wind of change.

I have enjoyed your letters in the past, along with your enthusiasm. It is always a pleasure hearing from you.

Sincerely,

Elaine Barbieri
P.O. Box 536
W. Milford, NJ 07480

Elaine Barbieri

Wings of a Dove

Allie and Delaney met on a harrowing train ride, along with hundreds of other orphans. Travelling from the rough tenements of nineteenth-century New York City, to the vast farmlands of the Midwest, their friendship soon blossomed into starry-eyed romance. And as they grew into adulthood, so did their passion...

Tarnished Angel

Devina Dale—beautiful, defiant. An adventurous pioneer who dares to face the wild West. She will allow nothing to stand in the way of her dreams. Not even the handsome outlaw who kidnaps her for revenge—the enemy she cannot help but love.

__WINGS OF A DOVE 0-515-10205-9/$4.50
__TARNISHED ANGEL 0-515-09748-9/$4.50

From the *New York Times* bestselling author
of <u>Morning Glory</u> and <u>Bitter Sweet</u>

LaVyrle Spencer

One of today's best-loved authors of bittersweet
human drama and captivating romance.